MEMPHIS BLUFF

ALSO BY GERALD DUFF

Fiction

Memphis Ribs
Memphis Luck
Blue Sabine
That's All Right, Mama: The Unauthorized Life of Elvis's Twin
Dirty Rice: A Season in the Evangeline League
Coasters
Snake Song
Graveyard Working
Indian Giver
Playing Custer
Nashville Burning
A Crop of Circles
Fire Ants and Other Stories
Decoration Day and Other Stories

Poetry

Calling Collect
A Ceremony of Light

Nonfiction

Fugitive Days: Trailing Warren, Ransom, Tate, and Lytle
Home Truths: A Deep East Texas Memory
Letters of William Cobbett
William Cobbett and the Politics of Earth

MEMPHIS BLUFF

a novel

GERALD DUFF

FORT WORTH, TEXAS

Library of Congress Cataloging-in-Publication Data

Names: Duff, Gerald, author.
Title: Memphis bluff : a novel / Gerald Duff.
Description: Fort Worth, Texas : TCU Press, [2020] | Summary: "Memphis, the Bluff City, is at the heart of Gerald Duff's hilariously violent story about lies, crimes, and those who must dig down to the ugly truths hiding beneath false claims made by movers, shakers, and criminals high and low. Memphis cops J. W. Ragsdale and Tyrone Walker spend their days and long into their nights peeling back the counterfeit claims of old wealth, gang lords, and the brutal truths of thievery, murder, and deceit. J. W., a one-time cotton farmer, now chops away in the weeds, brambles, and lies of Memphis, high and low. His African American partner, Tyrone Walker, steers a straight path whenever he's able. He believes little of what he sees, and he trusts only part of what he senses. Together in Duff's third book about the partners, J. W. and Tyrone tackle the Ku Klux Klan, crooked aristocrats, black gangs, and the many bluffs, real and imagined, proclaimed in Memphis on the Mississippi. It gets darker each day in that great and gritty town on the river called the Old Man. Ragsdale and Walker are again seeking a beam of light and a glimpse of truth. And they're not bluffing"-- Publisher information.
Identifiers: LCCN 2020001741 (print) | LCCN 2020001742 (ebook) | ISBN 9780875657455 (paperback) | ISBN 9780875657547 (ebook)
Subjects: LCSH: Police--Tennessee--Memphis--Fiction. | Murder--Fiction. | Deception--Fiction. | Counterfeits and counterfeiting--Fiction. | Memphis (Tenn.)--Fiction. | LCGFT: Detective and mystery fiction. | Novels.
Classification: LCC PS3554.U3177 M455 2020 (print) | LCC PS3554.U3177 (ebook) | DDC 813/.54--dc23
LC record available at https://lccn.loc.gov/2020001741
LC ebook record available at https://lccn.loc.gov/2020001742

TCU Box 298300
Fort Worth, Texas 76129
817.257.7822
www.prs.tcu.edu
To order books: 1.800.826.8911

Text Design by Preston Thomas

for Brenda and Jim Lanier

Memphis in the heat of one more summer, a little after midnight, where Peach Street dead-ends into a street with no name, and all streetlights on all sides shot out as usual. This time the maintenance department hadn't seen fit to try replacement until a new mayor was elected, or maybe when all shooters had run out of ammunition. Lack of artificial light did make it possible, though, for a squad from the Bones Family to hem up two claimers of Latin Lords on a dead-end street, and the Dodge Charger the Latin Lords were occupying had ended up stopped against a curb with two blown tires, a racing engine about to seize up, and no way to turn, no place to go.

The black Charger was what had caught the attention of the Bones claimers as four of them sat parked minutes earlier in the gravel lot of Mama's Hot and Ready Chicken, eating double orders of wings and swigging from Bud tall boys. It was the rumble and throaty roar of the pipes as the Dodge drifted by Mama's that they all noticed. It was impossible not to.

"Listen to that motherfucker grumble," Sonny Johnson, a.k.a. Jump Steady, said as the last real American muscle car floated by. "Sound like it wants to tear the heart out of something, don't she?"

"She sound like she looking to fuck somebody up," Baby Shanks said. "She wanting to feed, that baby is. Bitch is hungry."

"Let's go rescue that bitch," Jump Steady said. "Don't you drop them goddamn wing bones on my carpet, though. Them beer cans, neither."

They caught up to the black Dodge Charger just as it turned off Madison, and its driver, Juan Castro, a.k.a. Two Teeth, seemed to have seen the hell coming up behind him, but couldn't figure out how to use a stick shift smoothly enough to pull away, almost killing the engine by flooring the accelerator in a weak high gear. The two Lords claimers had hijacked the Charger from a white man coming out of a downtown bar two nights ago, and now it was loaded with a delivery they were supposed to be taking down into Mississippi. Learning to shift all those forward gears while depressing and releasing the clutch took time and study, goddamn it.

"Get this Charger going," the passenger, Fado Moody, yelled. "Stomp on this motherfucker. Them's Bones behind us. You seen that gold skull sitting up there in the back window when we went by the chicken place, didn't you?"

"Yeah, I saw it, Dog. But I can't get the fucking stick to do right. Too many gears."

"I told you we wasn't supposed to be showing this bitch off before going down to Mississippi. The man told us that."

By the time they'd turned the corner onto Peach Street, run squalling into the curb and busted out the front tires, killed the engine and put their hands to their foreheads to feel where the momentum of the crash had pushed them into the windshield hard enough to crack it, the Bones bunch was right up there behind them, the bumper of the Cadillac Deville tight against the rear of the Dodge.

"Get out the car, motherfuckers," Jump Steady was saying, showing a piece in his right hand. Two of the three Bones claimers behind him had nines, and another one was showing a blade, a long, thin one.

"We going to take this beast, *putas*, if you ain't ruined it for good. What y'all carrying? And who you be claiming?"

"We ain't carrying nothing," the driver of the Dodge said. "And we ain't claiming nothing or nobody."

"He's lying," Bootsie said. "Look at his pinky on that left hand. He done been broke."

"I know he lying. His mouth's moving, ain't it? What's in them boxes in the back floorboard, boy?"

"Nothing. Baby formula for my twins. I'm a working man. Just going home from the night shift."

"Shit, you ain't never hit a lick of work in your life. See what's in one of them boxes, Bootsie. Hold it up in front of the headlights."

Bootsie did that, tore off the taped-down top of one of the boxes, and looking inside, began to speak in a rush. "Holy shit," he said. "What the fuck?!"

"What is it? Smack? Weed? What?"

"Shit, no, it's money, bro'. It's so much fucking money you can't count it. Man, it is Franklins, Franklins, Franklins. And some other bills. Who is this fucker?" He held up a neatly bound-together sheaf of bills as rare in appearance in that part of Memphis as a college graduation diploma.

"Look," Bootsie said. "It say numbers five hundred on it, and it's got a picture of a fat white man."

"Look, you fucking nigger," the driver of the Dodge said. "We don't know anything about that except to say it ain't real. They told us it ain't. Them gringos. All we're supposed to be doing is taking it to a rich man down in Mississippi."

"Don't call me a nigger, spic," Jump Steady said. "You tell me them bills ain't real, and I know you're lying. Who you taking it to, boy?"

"I don't know him. I don't know his name. But you let me get out of here, and I'll find out."

"I'm going to find out right now, spic. Get this fucker spread out on the ground, Bootsie. Baby, take that other one off over yonder in them bushes. Lay him down."

"We got some work to do," Baby Shanks said with a yodel. "We fixing to make a long night of it."

"Ain't real, my ass," Jump Steady said, fingering a sheaf of the Franklins. "Only way you can tell if money's good or not is if you can buy something with it. It looks damn good to me. And your ass is going to buy everything, Lords boy."

"I ain't Lords, I ain't Lords, I ain't been broke," the man riding shotgun cried out. "Look at my fingers. See?"

"Well, I'm Lords through and through, you chitlin'-eating bastard," said the driver of the Dodge to Jump Steady. "I'm Juan Castro Two Teeth. You're going to get your share of some bad shit when the time comes."

"Says you, motherfucker," said Jump Steady. "Let's get down to business. Get ready to say something. Tell me a story right now."

The street lights stayed knocked out all night, and it wasn't until full daylight that what had happened in the dark on Peach and Montgomery could be seen. A third-grader named Precious Love waiting for a school bus was the first witness the next morning in Memphis. A good girl, she ran back home and told her mama, and that made her miss the bus. A Memphis police lady gave her a ride to school, and since Precious Love was late, the police lady went inside and told the teacher why. Precious Love would not be called absent, and that was one of the best things that happened to her that morning. That, and getting to ride to school with the white lady in the police car.

2

"Tell the truth now," Willis Sutcliff said, laying his hand on Tommy Beechum's arm and leaning toward him as he spoke. They were seated at a prime table in the lobby bar of the Peabody Hotel in Downtown Memphis, two Early Times bourbons to the good. "Don't you think that something big is ruining what used to be a main interest of the people we're trying to reach?"

The time was well after the noon rush hour of businessmen, politicians, and good-looking women, the females all much younger than their employers who'd reprieved them from secretarial offices and administrative assistant desks to the Peabody for lunch and a further exploration of possibilities, and Sutcliff and Beechum were seated well apart from late drinkers. Time for real talk now, circling the point and touching the topic and seeing what head might stick up.

Tommy Beechum leaned toward Sutcliff, both fists clenched in agreement. "You're right as rain, Willis," he said. "I hadn't made that particular connection, but as soon as you said it, I could see the bald-headed truth of it. Let me put it this way. There's not a hell of a lot of money in the pocket of any one of these people, but if you could get focused on something that got them fired up and crazy to lay their dollars down, they would do it. It takes blood or the promise of it."

"And be glad to hazard that cash," Willis said, patting the arm beneath the blue seersucker summer jacket he'd been clutching. "They used to just thank you for taking their money, no matter how hard they had to work to make it. Remember how it was in the old wrestling venues, how nutty that bunch of rednecks would get when Barry Tee would come down that aisle and hop up on the edge of the squared circle? Grinning like a jackass eating briars."

"The old ladies would go all goggle-eyed, pop them mouths open so wide you could see to their tonsils and him perched there sweating like a hog."

"If you could stand to look close at those women," Willis Sutcliff said, causing both men to laugh loud enough for a couple two tables over to turn to see what was going on. "And them old boys and the young freaks would get so pumped up they couldn't stay in their seats."

"It was beautiful," Tommy Beechum said, "watching all that loosening up take place. They had all laid money down to get in and they'd pay to get out in the lobby and buy all that souvenir crap. And they wouldn't think twice about what it cost them. You could raise the price at every damn event, and they'd still come like pigs to the slop trough. And the concession stands. Don't even talk to me about it."

"Yeah," Willis said, shaking his head mournfully, "true, true, but Lord God these days. It has all gone away now. A whole demographic has shifted in a new direction, and how you get it back I do not know."

"One thing I do know. Whatever you do, it will not involve the old hero, Barry Tee, the Battler. Not now, not ever again."

"Where is Barry these days?" Willis said. "I hadn't seen hide nor hair of him, and he sure ain't in the *Memphis Commercial Appeal* no more. Not to be found. He is officially missing in action."

"Aw, the last time he got any real play is when he about killed that old comedian from New York that came down here to wrestle women and then made the mistake of taking on Barry Tee. Thought he'd just poke some more fun at Southerners and make money doing it."

"It wasn't no mistake, the way that match was set up," Willis said. "That got national attention and made everybody money. True believers in wrestling, feminists, gays, rednecks, soul brothers, the perennially unemployed. You name it. They all wanted to see Barry Tee make that Lenny Spritzer squall and holler and carry on while he's getting his ass whipped."

"True enough, but that was early in the game. Nobody gives a good goddamn about fake wrestling any more. Much less seeing some skinny Yankee Jew get his ass kicked by a fat old redneck boy. He's dead now anyway, that comedian. Cancer or some wasting shit like that. Barry Tee about broke that sissy's neck, but that wasn't what led to Mr. New York City dying pretty quick after."

"You hadn't answered the question, though. What do you hear about the Strongboy now, Barry Tee of Memphis, Tennessee? Is he still making money for somebody or at least himself?"

"He's fat as a pen-fed Poland China hog these days. He is through and finished for good. I saw him not two months, eating in that barbecue place on Union Avenue close to the hospital. He's got so big, fat, and out of shape now he has to take every breath with his mouth open."

"Even while he's eating barbecue?"

"Especially while he's eating barbecue. He don't even look up from his plate these days except to reach for another rib."

"You're saying Barry Tee is past making anybody any money. Is that what I'm hearing from you, Tommy?"

"That is what you're hearing. Yessir. All he ever was and the enterprise in which he moved and profited is gone, son. Gone with the wind. I don't know what Barry's living on now. It sure ain't residuals."

"Shit. That's kind of sad. Well, what did you get me down here in the Peabody lobby for to tell me something I already knew, then? Was it just to mourn the old days or do you have something in mind that might turn up a dollar or two for us?"

"No, I didn't get you here just for us to cry together over wasted days and wasted nights. There might be something working, though, that would interest you enough to open that damned old sealed money bag you got hid somewhere. Just listen to me."

"You not talking about about freaks in the ring, are you?" said Willis. "Midget rassling or women throwing each other down, is it? That horse has done left the stable. And it died once it got outside."

"No, it is not something wore out and cast aside because folks got tired of it," Tommy Beechum said. "It's something hot right now, and it's going to get hotter before it burns out and something else takes over. You ever heard of MMA or seen it on the tube?"

"MMA. Mamas messing around?" Willis said, pausing to let Tommy chuckle if he wanted to. "I know that ain't it, of course."

"You know what I'm talking about," Tommy said, slowing down his rate of speech so as to announce fully each word as though it was sharp enough to cut the lips carressing it. "Mixed martial arts. That is the current craze right now, mixed martial arts, and it has not yet come to Memphis. But if we jump quick, we liable to be able to milk that sucker while the cream is still rising."

"Well, yeah, I've seen some of that on the tube late at night or right around the time Judge Judy comes on in the afternoon. A bunch of muscled-up little old Brazilians and Japs kicking and hitting at each other. You mean that, huh? I don't know, though. It hasn't got the color real wrestling used to have. And the ones doing it all look just like each other, and they act like they think they're athletes, you know. Hell, you'd think they were playing in the NFL the way they conduct themselves."

"Yep, you are right about that," Tommy said. "The current staging of the MMA just pure-dee sucks. Who give a damn, really, about who wins, or who gets busted up and bleeds, or passes out, or gets an arm broke, or whatever if all them so-called athletes look just alike and act the same way and shake hands and hug each other when the bell rings to stop the fight?"

"That ain't no fun," Willis said, nodding his head so hard the flesh around his throat area jiggled. "That's what I'm trying to say."

"But what if we took on that concept, and put a Memphis spin on it? One that'd appeal to our people," Tommy said, hunching forward in his chair and putting both hands on the table as though he was about to crawl up on it. "That's what I want to talk to you about."

"A Memphis spin?"

"You bet your ass. Now think about this. Can you imagine a crowd of Memphians at a public event where there's the possibility of blood flowing and folks foaming at the mouth to get at each other, can you imagine that Memphis crowd cheering together and chanting some kind of slogans as they watch what's going on in the ring?"

"Together? Hell, no. Hollering and bellowing and cussing, yes buddy. But doing something organized like a bunch of cheerleaders, nuh-uh. No thank you. Not in the Bluff City."

"Well, that's what it's like at these mixed martial arts bouts. You'd think the crowd was all from Argentina or somewhere like that. England, you know, or France. Ignorant pissant countries. The crowd hollers out together slogans that they got memorized. They act like what's going on down where the fists are flying and the blood's popping up is some kind of a game."

"Aw, no kidding?" Willis said. "I really hadn't watched any of it close because it's so boring to me, but now I think about it, I believe you're right."

"Okay, listen to this," Tommy said, his voice picking up rhythm and his hands pumping like an auctioneer's nearing a close. "Here's what I figured out what might work here, and it's all a part of logic and ideas and what makes sense in Memphis. Now just listen and don't argue about little things until I get delivered what I've been thinking about and working on for a good long while."

"I'm listening. Lay it on me."

"Why did the Barry Tee thing work as good as it did back in the day? Why did the Lenny Spritzer bout get so much notice and airtime? Why did people give a damn about what everybody knew was coming, and that was a good ass-kicking for that New York weakling, and why was everybody tuned into it for weeks before and after? I'll tell you why. It was symbolic. It wasn't just some wrestling match. It was the Memphis good old boy redneck life taking on the prissy holier-than-thou lifestyle of New York where nobody believes nothing."

"Except to laugh at us," Willis said. "That's what they love to do. That and come to Beale Street and listen to bad music and eat sorry barbecue."

"Tell me about it. But when you got symbols fighting each other, you got something a lot bigger than two men trying to knock each other's brains out for folks just to watch the blood fly up. You got the clash of ideas. You got different concepts of meaning at work against each other."

"Let me ask you where you got that idea, especially the way you put it. That doesn't sound like the real you exactly. Concepts of meaning. What's that mean?"

"The idea is mine," Tommy said. "Meaning is meaning, and I can claim saying it, but I got to admit where I got some of the language is from a professor at Rhodes College. He give me the words for it."

"Did you take a class at Rhodes? Night school or something? Community outreach? Don't try to tell me that."

"Hell, no. I ran into this guy, this Rhodes professor, at Bad Nickel one night late. He was drunk as a lord, and he was babbling to anybody that'd listen. The rednecks would let him buy them drinks, but they wouldn't pay attention to what he was saying. Wouldn't, hell. They couldn't. I listened, though, and I took notes on a napkin. It was like going to college, and it gave me the words to say to fit what I'd already been thinking. He was a professor of culture, he said, whatever that means, and he knew everything. He wrote books. His name was Dr. Lanier."

Tommy looked around, caught the eye of one of the good-looking Peabody bar girls, and gave the high sign, twirling his forefinger in a tight circle. She nodded, showed her teeth, and took off.

"Now, let me put some flesh on those bones, and show you what I've figured out might well put us in reach of a good chunk of that Memphis money. Here it is, then. Put this in your mind. You got an eight-sided ring, they call it the octagon, all fenced in, and into it comes two women ready to do battle. It's a grudge match which we've advertised and built up to. The first one in the octagon is a overweight, ugly, tattooed bitch, resentment just writ all over her. She's never had nothing, and she realized that early and it festered in her like an infected boil. She's wearing clothes way too tight for her body, and they're bright and dull at the same time. Cheap looking as hell, with the fashion taste of an orangutan monkey. She's barefooted, maybe, but I hadn't decided about that yet. She might be wearing some busted-out old work boots or maybe men's oxfords. She might have a tooth or two missing. She's got a lip full of snuff. She carries a coffee can to spit it into. Her hair looks like shit. Sticking up with stiffener, cut all ugly on one side and left long on the other. When the referee looks in her mouth to check for hardware, he has to jump back to show how it stinks inside that head."

"Hell, I saw her last night on Union Avenue walking along with a fellow that looked worse than she did," Willis said and laughed. "They were holding hands, for Christ's sake. Looked like two shit-birds in love. She outweighed him by sixty pounds, at least. Had a few more teeth, too."

"See, see? You're already showing signs that what I'm thinking about is going to be on the money. But back to the grudge match. I might call it The Clash of Cultures, but that'd probably be over the heads of the people I'm looking to lay their dollars down to see it. We'd get a better name than that. Something with sweat and blood and yet a touch of magnolia in it. Here, though, imagine this. After this redneck, low-class, uneducated, never-had-nothing-and-not-going-to woman comes waddling into the octagon, behind her up the aisle from the dressing room comes her opponent in a full procession, surrounding her back and front and side to side."

"Let me guess," Willis said. "She's dressed real nice."

"Don't get ahead of the story, but what you're saying shows it's working. First of all there's nice music playing over the loudspeakers, see. I don't know what yet, but it sure ain't country nor rock nor rap. It'd be something old and sweet. Maybe like 'Isn't She Lovely.'"

"Never heard of that one. What about a lively one like a old ZZ Top tune? 'She Got Legs.' That one."

"Naw," Tommy said, shaking his head. "She's classy, see. This woman is. Not some kind of a redneck's wet dream. The men in the crowd would like to get in her pants, sure, but they know they never could. She's too damn high dollar for somebody like them. And they know that, see, just by looking at her."

"Where are you going with this, then? Ain't she supposed to be just the opposite of the fat, ugly, mean bitch in the bad clothes, the one just dying to kick her ass once they get going?"

"Sure, that's the point," Tommy said. "But see, a society queen like that is way out of reach for folks that make up that crowd. So, that's the beauty of it. They'd give their left nut to get her in bed with her legs all spread and propped up, all right, but they know they never would. She's money. She's a picture of investments in stocks and bonds. She's a condo in town and a big house on a lake. She's gone to Vanderbilt or at least Ole Miss. Her daddy is somebody, and her mama's drunk on cocktails every day and great looking old as she is. Our princess comes from a family, Willis, not a bit like where the crowd comes from. They got born, all right, but it was a damn accident, and nobody really gave a shit when they hit the air. And if somebody asked them who their people were, they wouldn't have one speck of knowing what they're talking about. They'd start jabbering about Maw Maw and Paw Paw."

"I'm reading you. The women in the crowd hate her, but they'd like to be like her, and they know they're really like that fat, ugly bitch. And goddamn, does it drive them crazy."

"You're reading it. And I hadn't even thought yet about what all the money girl would do to drive the crowd even nuttier, but there's plenty of possibilities."

"She could talk into the microphone and tell the gentlemen in the crowd to take their hats off, please. She could spray some deodorant around to make it bearable for her to be around all that trash that's laid their money down to get into the Pyramid. She could smile all the time whether she was happy or not. You know, like these rich bitches do."

"Yeah," Tommy said. "There's a lot we can do with that. She could ask over the mic all the women who'd been in sororities in college to stand up, and the fraternity men to do the same."

"Oh, Lord, I love it. That would burn their asses. They'd holler like they'd been stuck with pins."

"But, listen, I got a whole lot more cultural ideas to add to the arsenal. I mean we can't have the beauty queen from East Memphis in every match. We got to have more clashes of culture coming up, and that's what I want to work on us thinking about. Because when we pitch this thing to Simmons and D'Arcy and Wilde, we got to be able to tell them about other possibilities. Get what I'm saying?"

"I do, I do," Willis said. "But I'd like to think a little bit more about that old redneck fat tattooed bitch tearing into the beauty queen. What a sight to imagine. The money girl with background getting knocked down and drug around by her pretty hairdo, and it getting all messed up, and she'd be squalling and crying and begging for that trash to let her go."

"That's the conventional view to take," Tommy said, "and that's what we want to play off of. See, we are working two or three angles at once in all these clashes of culture I been talking about. The man in the street or the woman washing the supper dishes and slapping at the kids, they'd all think like what you just expressed. And we can play with those concepts. Don't get me wrong. We do that to set things up, see, for the surprises that bring the crowds back with greenbacks to lay down for admission and concessions and T-shirts and all that crap. But what I envision is this. The real bitch, the genuine dirty fighter who gouges and scratches and carries concealed weapons into the octagon is not going to be the fat, ugly, underprivileged tub in the bad outfits. No, it's the money girl, the sorority sister, the one with the great teeth and wonderful background in society. She's the one that cheats like hell and does everything she can come up with to win. She is the queen of mayhem."

"God a'mighty, you have thought about this setup a lot. Turning things upside down, that's what will keep the dummies interested."

"Tell me about it. Money knows all kinds of ways to win, and it's not interested in playing by some set of rules. It does what it has to do, and it learned that from its background, from its people. Money is smart. Get me? How do you think money got to be money in the first place? By being nice? By playing fair? Hell, no. It did all it could to prosper and lay up cash in the till, and it didn't second-guess itself. It is and was cutthroat. It does not give a good goddamn about how to be. All it cares about is what it looks like to the ones that ain't got it, not how it really is."

"I'm getting all wet-thighed and wide-eyed just thinking about it," Willis said. "When do we go see Simmons, D'Arcy, and Wilde? We need money backing to get money, and we need it now."

"Just as soon as we come up with at least two more scenarios for culture clash, I say we go in there with all guns blazing."

"I'm so glad you run into that damn drunk professor from Rhodes College in that shitty bar," Willis said. "Who said they don't live in the real world, them PhDs? They know how to go after money."

"Willis, no they don't. But they do squeeze out a nugget of truth or two now and then, something somebody that lives in the real world can use to make some dough. They say all kinds of stuff that smart folks can use, but they don't know they're saying it."

"Why don't they learn how to do themselves some good with that shit they come up with? Clash of cultures, imminent domain, grain futures, all that word stuff like that. What you call concepts."

"They're too slow witted, Willis," Tommy said. "That's the best I can figure. Just not able to think right, these PhDs. I reckon all the real sense has been flushed and burned out of them."

"God bless them anyway."

"They don't believe in God, Willis, so your blessing is wasted. Let's just take what they drop off the table as crumbs and make us some fucking money with it."

"Yes, Jesus. Grow them crumbs into a full cake. Put them dollars on me."

3

Sunbeams fell strongly upon the dense foliage of the plantings of native trees and ornamental shrubs and flowering arbors that shielded the main building of the University Club in Central Gardens, but the full force of summer light could not reach the windows of the dining area facing south. The architects and builders had known well what in Memphis needed protection from the natural elements of heat, cold, and storm that worked ceaselessly to discomfort all who might dwell in the delta area of the big river through the heart of America. Whether Native Americans or French or Spanish or Scotch-Irish, those who had sought to live and prosper there learned the means to survive or they perished. Yellow fever might take them, unhealthy diets might wither and claim, gunshots and blades might lay them low, but those who stayed strong in will and cunning might prosper. Or they might not. In Memphis it had always been a crap shoot.

Again and as always on a typical summer midday, a gathering of representatives of those able and willing and fit to belong and succeed in the Bluff City sat at exquisitely set tables to dine. The din of conversation, laughter, silverware, the tinkling of water, wine, and liquor glasses, the shuffling of black waiters and busboys all combined in a melody of sound. Loud, to a degree, but controlled, expected, ordinary, and comforting to the ears of those who noticed. Not many did.

At a prime table, near a set of windows forming a bay removed from the paths of servers and the proximity of other diners, sat three men. Two were dressed in the Memphis summer uniform for movers and shakers and those wanting to join that group. That was the seersucker suit, supposedly cooler than dark costumes, and grown over the years to be not clothing but acknowledgment of adherence to tradition. The other diner seated between the seersuckers wore a blue blazer and lighter trousers, acceptable though a bit daring.

"Word is she is nearing the end," said Mason Wilde, pushing a bit of lettuce around on the plate before him. "But that's been thought before, as we all remember."

"Many times, I'd say," Dallas Simmons said. "A consummation devoutly to be wished. I declare."

"One of these times it will come to pass," Walker D'Arcy said, not looking up from the bit of veal cutlet before him not yet vanished. "All of us are living under a death sentence, acknowledged or not."

"Unless you happen to be May Margaret Howell-Reed," Mason said. "Then you have a dispensation, it appears. A lifetime guarantee with a no-terminal clause."

"You couldn't kill that old woman with a yard tool," Simmons said.

"Not if you hit her in the head, you couldn't," Walker said. "That noggin is as hard as diamond."

"It's made of diamond, I'd say."

"Remember, Dallas, eight or nine years back, when she turned pale, dramatically lost weight, and appeared to be in the last stages of the browning of the magnolia blossom?"

"I do, Walker, remember her turning sere and brown," Dallas Simmons said. "We all thought James had been dosing her with rat poison. Or antifreeze. Isn't that what people are often fed by their loved ones in their iced tea?"

"If it was, May Margaret Howell-Reed rallied. She probably uses antifreeze as a sweetener."

"Sweets for the sweet," said Mason, and they all chuckled together.

"Really, though," Dallas said, after his laugh ended and they all returned to their eating duties, "the event will occur sooner rather than later, and unless she makes another amendment or so, that will and its settlement will still be tying up a third of Shelby County after she's gone. And the most lucrative part of it, let me add. James certainly will not want a change to that, and he'll be even more difficult to deal with. He is more stubborn and recalcitrant and hard-headed than his mother."

"He is hard-headed because he has no brain," Walker D'Arcy said. "He has the wit of a snapping turtle."

"And the jaws, unfortunately," Dallas said.

"So whose turn is it to be received into the presence of May Margaret Howell-Reed of Fallen Timbers Plantation?" Walker said. "Not me. Remember I tried to reason with her last fall, and you two claimed prior appointments of some sort. Do you realize she had two great hulking servants physically put hands on me and hustle me not only out of the Great Room, as she calls her office, but also down the halls out of one of the side entrances, down the steps helter-skelter into the parking area. And as I left, that bigger one, the one that played linebacker for the Oakland Raiders, said to me in rude and profane terms not ever to return."

"What was it that Rufus Minden, he of Central High School and Ole Miss and Raider fame, said exactly, Walker?" Dallas said, looking over his glasses not at Walker but at Mason. "Do you recall?"

"You always want to hear that, don't you?" Walker said. "You think I was so stung that I won't repeat his words. One is silent only when one accepts the insults made him. That is not me."

"Oh, tell us again, and get it over with," Dallas said. "We know it's not accurate."

"Rufus Minden, and I don't like repeating it, since it has no merit, told me in these words. 'Look, motherfucker, I'm tired of hauling you and your fat belly out of Miss May Margaret's big old mansion. You come back again, and I'll put a clothesline tackle on your sorry honky ass.'"

"Do you think of that at night when you can't sleep?" Dallas said.

"Wait a minute," Mason said. "Let's get this matter settled for good. I know for certain that at least part of what Rufus called you is utterly inaccurate. You are not fat-assed."

At that, everyone laughed, even Walker, and Mason said he'd call May Margaret Howell-Reed for what he called an informal meeting for an ongoing assessment of where she was. They all agreed that they knew where she was already, but that something had to be done before she checked out of Fallen Timbers for good. Both Mason and Dallas assured Walker that they didn't consider him a literal motherfucker. They left the University Club not cheered nor optimistic, but at least two Maker's Marks each to the good.

"What would those twisted little bastards know about counterfeit bills?" J. W. Ragsdale asked his partner Tyrone Walker. They were sitting in an unmarked Memphis police car parked two blocks down Manassas Street beside a knocked-out street light which had been in that condition since before Elvis Presley died sitting on a golden commode in Graceland. They were glad there was no illumination around them, since it gave some cover to conceal them from the nightclub called Big Ron's Electric Slide a block and a half away.

"Hell, they can't even spell their own names, much less make twenties and fifties that'd fool somebody. They'd probably draw the wrong president's face on every one of them. They'd all look like the Smith Brothers on the cough drop boxes. These dummies would misspell Federal Reserve."

"First of all, J. W.," Tyrone Walker said, "I'd like to know your true age, since the bearded Smith brothers stopped making cough drops forty years ago, I expect. And second, the Bones claimers are not making the money themselves. Give the boys some credit. They've farmed that part of the enterprise out to an expert, the Major says. A first-class engraver from St. Louis, who's served his time in a couple of federal pens, graduated, and perfected his product. Mr. Harold Gene LaRosa."

"All right, I'll buy that, but I want to ask you two things. The main one is this: Didn't you and your schoolmates in them fine grammar schools of Memphis take Smith Brothers cough drops with you to class so you could eat them like candy? They tasted good enough for use in an academic setting, though they weren't worth a damn out on the schoolyard. Thing is, see, the teachers couldn't make you not eat them in the classroom if you coughed enough first. Them nasty cough drops got me through the first six grades in Batesville, Mississippi, and I salute those beard-wearing brothers. I still owe them boys."

"You are so country, J. W., that I wouldn't be surprised if you didn't break into a hoedown any minute now and start talking about cornbread. No, I didn't eat that particular cough drop. What's the other question you got to put to me?"

"Yeah, and that's the main one, all right. What the hell are we doing chasing around after punks trying to pass fake money? What does Homicide have to do with that kind of low-level jacking around?"

J. W. Ragsdale already knew why Major Dalbey had sent him and Tyrone out to South Memphis on a hunting expedition, but it was always entertaining to listen to his partner explain the mindset of supervisors. It made the long hours of sitting in a worn-out Ford sedan in the dark waiting for something to happen pass a little quicker. At least not to have to sit alone listening to distant gunfire and tires of stolen cars squalling as perpetrators sped away from some Memphis street scene was some comfort. Tyrone Walker began to explain, and J. W. listened as though what he was hearing was news.

Nothing new or surprising would pop up to a man who'd been working the ways of crime in Memphis for almost twenty years now. J. W. felt at times that he'd seen the same things happen over and over so often that what he was observing was reruns of a black and white movie from the last century. It was still entertaining, but the elements of surprise and revelation had long drained away.

"If you'd listened real close to the Major, you'd have heard. It's Bones business, J. W., this new enterprise for our budding entrepreneurs is, and they have already started knocking off Latin Lords claimers who think the counterfeit money deal belongs to them and them alone. It's a trade war, see, about a new way to make Memphis money, and these shooters don't worry about what real citizens of this great city might suffer in the crossfire."

"Well, of course," J. W. Ragsdale said, "they've never let anybody interfere with their successful conducting of business, our little Bones boys, but damned if I like to sit around waiting for them to start killing each other. Why don't they just line each other up and start blasting? Get it over with. Cut to the chase."

"Yeah, I got you, though nobody younger than fifty says cut to the chase these days. But a while ago, while you were over in the bushes doing something natural, I got some more info. It was texted to me just as quiet as a mouse."

"Jesus, texting," J. W. said. "I don't do that shit, and I don't want to be texted to. What else new do I have to worry about now?"

"Everything. You got to learn to get up and stay up with the information times. Workshop's coming next week. Got a teacher I've already met, and she's not only IT savvy, J. W., with a degree in that stuff from Tennessee Tech, she is so good looking it makes me have to look off when I see her coming."

"Oh, you think she might be a possible for me?"

"Yeah, if she's looking for a father figure."

"More likely a grandpa figure," J. W. said, leaning forward and pointing through the windshield at movement ahead as a clump of people were working their way through the door to the outside. "Look up yonder. There's a whole bunch of them coming out of the Electric Slide. I hope the big dog's in that crowd. I'm tired of waiting."

"If he is, we'll recognize him. He makes Big Ron look little, and that's hard to do. And what I got texted from our little friend is that Deangelo is in there, but he's not alone. He's got Tuck Bunny and Toleen with him, and I expect there's one or two more we don't know about."

"Oh, hell, it's an army. And Tuck Bunny is as crazy as a shithouse rat. I don't know nobody called Toleen. Do you?"

"I've heard of him, but the one we're after is Deangelo Dixon. Toleen has not fully made his mark yet. Give him a little time. I think we ought to tail them for a while and see if we can pick off Deangelo without having to worry about the other two. If it's just two."

"Not that they don't need taking in, but we ain't got nothing on them, and we hadn't been told to take anybody but the fat man. I don't want to stick my head in a hornet's nest right now. I ain't wearing the right clothes for it. We ought to be allowed to let them do somebody else first to get eligible for you and me. Let Homicide be Homicide."

"That's a hell of a way to have to look at it," Tyrone said, starting the engine. "That sounds like a motto for Memphis. I got the same jitters as you, though, J. W. It's like just before that kicker puts the boot to the ball. Who am I going to hit first, and who's going to hit me when I'm looking off? Right now, though, I want to be able to go home tonight after this is over, what there is left of this night."

"Yeah, shit, fuck it," J. W. said. "Let's go see what happens."

"It's four of them," Tyrone said. "More than the text message said. A full component, with Deangelo taking the shotgun seat. Let's fall in behind and see if the odds get better. Maybe they'll let somebody off at his hidey hole."

"Texting will lie to you," J. W. said. "Electrons don't know shit. Only thing you can trust is your eyeballs."

"If they're working, and if you haven't confused them by an overdose of something."

"Drugs are what will give you an overdose," said J. W. "Whiskey soothes and sharpens the wits."

"Alcohol's a drug. You still haven't signed up at AA, have you," Tyrone said, not really paying attention to his partner but throwing him enough words back to let him know his mind was where it ought to be. Looking at what needed doing, while staying cool and detached enough not to lose his head.

"Here we go," he said, starting the Ford and beginning to ease forward. "I see there's no license plate on that Charger."

"Well, there's a paper permit in that back window, I do believe," J. W. said, beginning to pat his chest and the right pocket of his pants.

"Got an itch?"

"In a manner of speaking, I sure do. And I'm making sure my medicine is in good supply if I need it."

Tyrone Walker kept a good distance from the Dodge ahead of him, headlights on dim, and by the time they'd gone six or seven blocks, one of the still functioning street stoplights in that part of Memphis showed red. "I've got to run on through this one," he said. "You see any vehicle on your side? I can't let these Bones boys get too far ahead."

"No, I don't," J. W. said, "but it does sadden me to see an officer of the law violate regulations he should be defending."

Tyrone grunted at that, shot through the intersection with a horn tap, and all ways were empty. By the time they had gotten no more than a quarter of a mile farther, the Charger ahead turned right on Dennis, hooked a left on the next street up, and J. W. was able to see the car slowing as Tyrone allowed the unmarked police sedan to drift slowly to a stop.

"I think this nest of Bones claimers has reached its den," J. W. said, popping the door handle. "My considered opinion is that we ought not follow them in there on wheels. Let's take a little stroll instead."

"I do believe you're right, Sergeant Ragsdale. Let's stick to the shadows of all this undergrowth in what used to be yards, and see if we can get there unannounced. Then we'll say hello."

"We got to hurry a little, though," J. W. said. "They might be just tumping one or two out and we could miss our appointment with Deangelo. We'd be on foot, and he'd be hauling ass in that Charger."

"He's not doing the wheeling. He don't haul. Deangelo be hauled. You suppose Deangelo do be staying here?"

"I love it when you try to talk like a brother, Tyrone," J. W. said. "Did you study that lingo at Memphis State? But before you 'fess up, I think that the D man be cribbing somewhere better than this. It looks like a fucking jungle all through here. Streetlights all busted out, trash trees growing everywhere. Vines and stumps. Not a garbage can in sight, but plenty of garbage, though. If Deangelo be staying here, he won't be doing it long."

"I love when you try to talk like a white man, J. W.," Tyrone said. "You ought to have gone to a better school to learn English than the one you did sit through."

"There ain't no school better than what's publicly available in Batesville, Mississippi, son. Look up there, though, the lights are off in the Dodge. You suppose they're all getting out?"

"Let's get there before they do. Damn if I want four of them mobile."

"Mobile, hell, they'll be hostile," J. W. said, breaking into a trot. "Don't trip over this vine and stump crap in the way, Tyrone. I'm going to need every man able to do his duty."

Two figures were standing near what used to be a paved driveway, now a relatively open space of what looked to J. W. like rubble left from a bad job of demolition. Dark as it was, it was clear that one of the two men towered over the other by more than a foot, and his bulk side to side eclipsed the smaller man. That there is Deangelo Dixon, J. W. told himself, it couldn't be anybody else, all that weight in one place. J. W. felt Tyrone's hand on his shoulder and leaned back to listen to what his partner might say.

"You go straight at him," Tyrone said. "Talking as you go, and I'll slip off to the side next to the car. Let him know you're coming."

"Check who's still there if you can see inside," J. W. whispered. "But be ready to help me with that big son of a bitch. I don't want to have to shoot him. But I will if I have to. Right between the eyes. I ain't letting him knock me around."

"We need him alive, so take a lick or two for the team if you have to. Don't go all crazy. Now's not the time for that."

"Shit," J. W. said. "Okay, but goddamn, he'll pack a punch. And listen, if you see a move by Tuck Bunny, kill that crazy fucker for me."

"I won't have to do more than just wing him. I'll hit him where the sun won't shine."

"Now you're talking," J. W. said, then stepped lively toward the two men in the shadows ahead.

"Why if it ain't Deangelo Dixon and his little boy. How y'all doing this fine evening?" he announced himself.

Both men turned to look toward the source of the voice, the huge man moving his head slowly and the small one jumping like he'd been stung by an insect he hadn't noticed. He even slapped at his side, as though that was where the bug had bit him.

"Who you, motherfucker?" Tuck Bunny said. "Middle of the night here where a man's trying to get some rest."

"Don't go jumping around, son," J. W. said, stepping left to stay in the deeper shadows of the overgrown trash trees beside him. "You might make me nervous. Let me tell you who I am. That being Sergeant J. W. Ragsdale, Memphis Police, Homicide Division. And let me tell what I ain't. And that's what you just called me. Motherfucker. I ain't that and never have been, and if my mama down in Mississippi, bless her heart, heard you call me that, she'd first of all put her hands up to her ears, and then she'd grab your ass and wash out your mouth with that old bad-tasting lye soap my granny taught her to use to get out bad stains. And man, if you ain't a bad stain, grits ain't groceries."

By that point, Tyrone had worked his way to within five or six feet of Deangelo Dixon, still unmoving but observing the exchange between

Tuck Bunny and the Memphis police officer. He chuckled when J. W. had finished admonishing Tuck Bunny about his insult to his Mississippi mother long dead, though he didn't see any need to share that fact.

"Lye soap," Deangelo said, his voice surprisingly high-pitched for a man well over six feet tall and three hundred pounds heavy. "I hadn't thought about that shit in a long time. It burns you up. I'm from Mississippi, too, but I don't remember living down yonder much."

"I can't forget it, Deangelo," J. W. said. "Much as I try to sometime. It does get in your bones, the Magnolia state, and it's damn hard to shake it."

"What you here for, officer?" Deangelo said, "This time of night, way down here in South Memphis talking about being in Homicide? Onliest thing we killed is a quart of white whiskey and a case of beer. Looking to lie down for a rest now, before I have to get up in the morning and go to work. Ain't killed nobody not ever. Don't know a thing about homicide."

"To tell the truth," J. W. said, "I'm not here in my capacity as a homicide detective. Naw. Nuh-uh. It's that work of yours you talking about getting some rest for before you get up in the morning and hit the bricks again. That what draws me down here into the jungle."

It was at that point that Tyrone Walker announced his presence by greeting Tuck Bunny by name. "Tuck, would you oblige me by putting your hands behind your back? I see your hands are nervous and keep twitching and reaching around and patting and scratching and rubbing at different places all over your impressive body. Those paws need a rest, and I'm giving them a chance to slow down and stay in one place and not be bothering you while you stand there thinking about motherfuckers and what have you."

"You ain't going to cuff me, motherfucker," Tuck Bunny said, beginning to spin around toward Tyrone, reaching down to his waist as he did.

"Oh, yes I am," Tyrone said, using the spinning motion of Tuck Bunny to force him to tumble to the broken-up concrete slab of the driveway and then twisting the wrist of the small man's left hand up behind his back while jamming his knee beside the spot on his back where the first cuff was already circled and snapped together. He had the other hand of Tuck Bunny attached so quickly that Tuck Bunny hardly had time to cry out.

"See, you are upset," Tyrone said, "Hollering and carrying on and saying motherfucker. Now you can rest."

"That was pretty work," J. W. said to Deangelo Dixon as both men studied the scene as though they were algebra students looking at a solved problem on a blackboard. "Wham, bam, there it is. Done and done."

"Yeah," Deangelo said. "It was well done, for sure. He sure knows how to handle a little fellow."

"We not going to have to lay you down, too, are we?" J. W. said. "On this nasty old driveway. I see you got on nice clothes and necklaces and bracelets and big old nice shoes and shit."

"Naw, you ain't got to put a hand on me," Deangelo said. "I ain't afraid to talk to the police. I hate to miss my rest, but I'll follow directions and do what y'all say. I just hope you'll let me lie down and get me a nap wherever you finally do take me."

"We will sure do that. We just want to talk to you. Or I should say some folks back in the office want to discuss things with you. We just kind of like an Uber, you know. Pick folks up, take them where they're going and drive there in a nice car."

"I never use Uber," Deangelo said. "I get folks to drive me around, but that's cause I don't like to have to watch the road, you understand. It's full of nuts. Driving like retards."

"It is. You take your life in your hands every time you slam that car door. Let me ask you something, though. These other two boys I saw in the backseat of your car. Are they going to be a problem for us? Because if they are, we going to have to take back our promises of nice treatment for you and a place to lie down for a nap."

"If you look at that car, Mr. Officer," Deangelo said, "you can see it's empty. Soon as that big strong brother slam poor little Tuck Bunny down on the ground, them boys just opened the door and slipped away. They gone. I saw them leave into them bushes."

"Could you or would you tell me their names?"

"I don't know them. We just giving them a ride home after a nice night out. They kind of what you might call a hitchhiker, see."

"They're not Bones claimers, that's what you're saying."

"What does that mean, Bones claimer? That's a new way of talking far as I know."

"Aw, and we were getting along so well," J. W. said. "I hate to see you sull up and lie like that. Let's go to the Midtown Central Station. I'll help you into our top-of-the-line Ford sedan. It might smell a little strong, though."

J. W. turned and looked at Tyrone, who was standing beside the cuffed Tuck Bunny, who was cursing now in a steady stream of motherfuckers and threats on various people's lives. "Do you need some help with that mean Bunny, Sergeant Walker?"

"Tuck Bunny doesn't weigh more than a sack of sugar," Tyrone said. "I'll just tuck Tuck under one arm and fit the little cute thing into whatever space Deangelo leaves for him in that back seat."

"Not only is the Bunny comparable in size to a sack of sugar," J. W. said. "He's just as sweet as one, too. Cute little motherfucker."

"Let's go put everybody to bed back in Midtown soon as we can," Tyrone said. "Especially me."

"Now, now," J. W. said. "We're on our way, married man."

By the time J. W. and Tyrone had gotten Deangelo Dixon and Tuck Bunny delivered and processed for questioning about the violent deaths of five Latin Lord claimers over a period of almost two months and the business reasons for the infighting, it was well after 2 a.m. and Tyrone was eager to get home to Marvelle and his sleeping children in their renovated bungalow just off Jackson Avenue. J. W. had checked in the Ford Fairlane they had used for the night's work in South Memphis, and he got into his Chevrolet, which fired right up this time, and drove directly to his place on Tutwiler.

The house was dark, as always, and J. W. announced that to the empty air of his front porch as though answering someone's question about where he lived and what his habits were. "I know it's dark. I know. I don't leave any lights on inside when I go out at night on purpose, see. I don't want anybody thinking I'm leaving lights because I ain't home. I want them to wonder," he said to the door key he was fitting into the lock, "if maybe I'm not gone but laying in there, a piece of ordnance right by the bed just hoping to be able to use it on any intruder wanting to get into my house and mess it all up looking for valuables."

After he'd successfully gotten the door open and worked his way to the kitchen, still in the dark and feeling his way, he spoke for one last time before taking a hit from a bottle of Heaven Hill waiting on the counter. He had no trouble finding it in the dark. "No, I'm not drinking Early Times or Jack Daniels or even J. W. Dant. It's Heaven fucking Hill. I'm an ill-paid servant of the public, and I haven't got more than two quarters to rub together this time of the month. Whatever time of the month it is, I mean, early or late. I'm not paid what I'm worth, but I do get to drive a free car now and then. I get to hang around bars and low places, and if I'm feeling mean, I can rough up miscreants. What's wrong with that satisfaction, I ask you. Most folks can't hit back at all, no matter what's being done to them. And I do tell you one big advantage I got since I moved north from home. The things I do here in Memphis for a living ain't near as bad as being out in a cotton field in the hot sun in Panola County, Mississippi. Hell, I feel good. Right now and most of the time."

J. W. ventured an unexpressed and unspoken thought at that point, just before crawling into bed and pulling a sheet up over him. I have got to stop talking out loud like there's somebody around to hear, he considered. There is not that person here to listen or give a shit and hasn't been for a good long time. And what if somebody heard me talking into the air like that? They might think I'm crazy. That made him chuckle out loud, and doing that let him go to sleep.

"So, J. W.," Major Dalbey said, sitting in his office where he was briefing and debriefing Sergeants Ragsdale and Walker midmorning, "can you tell me any more than you say you told folks last night when y'all hauled in that big bastard and the little'un with him? Did the two of you learn anything I can report and not be embarrassed by?"

"I wish you'd start with Tyrone, Major," J. W. Ragsdale said. "While he talks to you all educated-sounding in his report mode, that'd give me time to think something up that might hold you. It takes a spell to come up with a story that'll help satisfy Bitchhead."

"Naw, naw, don't start with that, Sergeant. You are not going to get me off track and cussing about what the chairwoman of the city council might say and what she might not say when I report progress to her about some of the killings going and what they're coming from."

"You can expect killings, can't you?" Tyrone Walker said. "This is Memphis, after all, and just last week the newspaper said we'd moved up another notch or two in the standings of what cities are doing the best job of murders and violent deaths and what have you in the violence category."

"You think I didn't see that?" Major Dalbey said. "That's what's got Councilwoman Ovetta Birchard all exercised this time. All I can say about them stats is thank God for St. Louis. Wasn't for them and Baltimore we'd break into the open and open up a lead on the pack."

"Don't you worry none," J. W. said. "We're going to catch them two urban centers. Don't go getting down on our crop of killers here in the Bluff City. There's no quit to them. They will rally in the fourth quarter."

Tyrone held up his right hand, offered it to J. W. for a bonding slap, and said, "That's what I'm talking about." His nails were newly manicured and polished and they glowed against the dark brown of his fingers as though from an inner light. His digital half-moons were perfect.

"Damn, you got a good woman doing your nails, Tyrone," J. W. said.

"She is that. She's Vietnamese. She's wonderful. Name is Kay Phong. Her son is a nerve doctor in Chicago. Vanderbilt med school grad. Neurology, partner. That's what I'm talking about."

"The American dream," J. W. said.

"Stop talking about shit like that, you two," the Major said. "Give me something to work with now. What's behind all this uptick in the war between the Bones Family and Latin Lords with the Beale Street Boppers throwed in, and don't just say new ways of doing. That stuff about getting into counterfeiting US money. Where's that coming from? Why here in Memphis? How can they make money in Tennessee counterfeiting? I need material to share with the bosses, some things to get a little relief from all this heavy-duty crap falling on my head."

"I don't understand the counterfeit thing myself," J. W. said. "I don't believe Tyrone does, and he's an educated man. Do you understand it, partner?"

"Well, not just to be making fake money to pass it around in Memphis," Tyrone answered. "They're not doing it for that. No, I don't understand this sudden interest in counterfeit money. How much can a gangbanger make paying for tall-boy beers and American-made vodka and passing a fake fifty and getting real money in change? It doesn't make sense to me. I know our typical miscreant in Memphis is dumber than a doorknob, but he's not going to be satisfied with having to work to pass counterfeit dollars. It doesn't pay enough."

"It takes effort," J. W. said. "It does sound like work to me. Handling money."

“Another thing,” Major Dalbey said, “that people been telling me is that the Memphis bunch got them that damn expert who’s served his time on his current count and was supposed to be considered one of the best in the business before he had to take that long vacation. The one from St. Louis.”

“Isn’t that federal business anyway?” J. W. said. “The Secret Service is the one that defends our country’s beautiful money, I know. So why do we have to worry about people in Memphis making that bad cash?”

“I can answer that one,” the Major said. “The ones from the Secret Service that talked to the chief, he tells me, say they ain’t interested in us being involved in solving pissant mysteries about counterfeiting. They say all we got to do is identify which ones of our local gang assholes is mixed up in this.”

“So we don’t arrest them?”

“Sure, you arrest them, but you don’t have to worry about the details of how they’re doing what they’re doing. Just haul the shitheads in. Let the Secret Service take over then.”

“They’re selling that money,” Tyrone said. “That’s what they’re doing, and what happens to it after it’s sold is nobody’s business but the ones buying it. Nobody knows where they’re located. The gang claimers don’t know, and they don’t care, and all they want is their fair share of Memphis money. They are not a curious breed, our own fine collection of lawbreakers right here at home. Their minds are untroubled by thought.”

“I told you that education Sergeant Tyrone Walker got at Memphis State was going to kick in here finally,” J. W. said. “The people of the Volunteer State made a damn good investment in paying them professors out there to educate Tyrone Walker. I do believe he’s got it figured.”

“Shucks,” Tyrone said. “You’ll make me blush, y’all.”

“Well, like you two, I don’t give a damn what the Secret Service and the feds do to untangle all this mess and find out why something’s going on with fake money and real gangs in Memphis. All I want to do is throw enough of them in jail to slow the part of the deal they’re playing down enough so as to get the feds off our backs.”

“Let me ask you one more time, then, Major,” J. W. said. “Why are me and Tyrone in Homicide having to worry about counterfeiting and the reasons for it? Can you straighten me out on that? Folks killing each other’s our game. We got advanced degrees in that subject.”

"Listen, Sergeant Ragsdale, and you too, Tyrone. Do you think that this whole enterprise that's just eating me up and getting Bitchhead and the mayor all over my ass day and night is not going to inspire more killings in Memphis? Do you think nobody's going to get shot, strangled, stabbed, blowed up, throwed in the Mississippi River, and whatever new ways of killing these fuckers can come up with as people make money, or try to, counterfeit or real, right here at home? Won't there be some brains splattered during all this?"

"Oh," J. W. said.

"Let me second what Sergeant Ragsdale just said," Tyrone volunteered. "Oh."

"Yeah," Major said. "That ought to satisfy, but one more thing before you leave here and get to work. There has been a request come down the chain of command to me, and I'm about to unload it on you."

"Uh oh, what?" J. W. asked. "Tell me it will get us out of the building at least."

"It will do that. It's not only an issue that's got to be addressed, but it involves some of the most well-placed folks around here. It's not a homicide, understand, but it's a request from a member of one of Memphis's most distinguished families. At least one of them, that is. And when this lady crooks her finger, we all got to go running."

"Put it on me. Who and what?"

"I'll tell you who and what, but don't you even mention why. These people don't have to explain why. They never have to beg and they don't have to apologize or explain. All they got to do is not ask, but tell. It's May Margaret Howell-Reed of Fallen Timbers Plantation. And the family foundation and security bank and investments and Lord knows whatall. It all rhymes with money."

"I have never seen her up close," Tyrone said. "But I used to see her picture enough in the *Commercial Appeal*. All those festivals and donor recognitions and endowments and what have you. Until she got too old to let folks see her in public. What do us folks in Homicide have to do with her?"

"Yeah," J. W. said. "She ain't been killed, has she? We'd have heard if it wasn't just fifteen minutes ago."

"No, but she's expressed concern, as the mayor told Bitchhead and as she told me, about her safety. Miss May Margaret Howell-Reed thinks somebody or something is getting ready to kill her. Or at least, as she put it, make her unbearably uncomfortable. And she wants to talk to somebody in the department. You're it, gentlemen."

"Two questions," J. W. said. "First one is what does 'unbearably uncomfortable' mean? And the next one is we going to get to go inside that big old mansion?" J. W. said. "The one looks like Tara before Sherman burned it all up?"

"The two of you are going out there this afternoon at three o'clock, a time Miss May Margaret has designated for the visit. You will gather info, and you'll be respectful and polite, and you take all that she says seriously. That's the mayor talking there, boys. Not me, but I'm as determined as he is not to offend."

"I'll shine my shoes," J. W. said. "And shave, even."

"I'm looking forward to it," Tyrone said. "And I always stay appropriately dressed for such visits."

"Oh, shut up, Dapper Dan," J. W. said.

After tending to a morning of report writing, phone call returning, and bullshitting with Abner Crowley, J. W.'s nearest desk mate in the Central Station, Sergeant Ragsdale asked Flozene Tanner if she knew where Tyrone Walker had got off to. It was part of her job to keep tabs as best she could on the physical location of the police personnel at any given moment. She liked parts of and despised other features of that obligation. She hated to lie, Christian lady that she was. The way Flozene Tanner put it to J. W. one time when he ventured to complain that he didn't know how to get hold of some younger cop of lesser rank whose report was to him, was a message he never forgot.

"Sergeant Ragsdale," she declared, as she looked over her glasses to get him well told not ever to take the chance of criticizing her ability to keep the physical location of each soul and body in the Central Station on instant recall, "you been married, I know. How many times is it now?"

"Well, I'm not married right now," he said in a tone which he hoped would mollify Flozene, "so I don't see what that has to do with my asking where Andre Roberts is. I just got business with him now and then. What?"

"It's two wives last time I noticed," Flozene said, "that you were legally hooked up to before y'all split the sheets and went your separate ways."

"Yeah, happy as a pig in slop, all three of us at that point. Me and the two former Mrs. Ragsdales. All glad and gratified."

"I don't care about that, or the sins you committed, except that I want you to think of that whole experience in both cases. Now wasn't there plenty of times you didn't want either one of them happy wives to know your physical location? Tell the truth now. You can, because I know you're not married now. You've got no reason to lie and shuck and jive now to some lady."

J. W. confessed that was true, but everything worked out in the end to the satisfaction of all parties concerned. Why worry about it now?

"Here's what my answer is. Apart from the wrongs you've done. Put this in your head. Suppose you were married now. When you're out sport-fucking or getting drunk in the daytime or laying up asleep when you should be working, you ain't going to inform the woman you report to what you're doing. Get me? See why I can't be sure of anything people here tell me?"

From that point forward, shocked as he'd been to hear a stoutly Christian woman say the F-word, J. W. tried always to be polite and restrained when questioning Flozene about where some man was, not wanting her to repeat any part of what she'd told him before about the impossibility of nailing down where everything and everybody was located at any given moment. When J. W. told Tyrone about the interchange with Flozene, Tyrone had informed J. W. that the phenomena had a scientific name and explanation. "It's the uncertainty principle. I read and studied about it in a physics class at the university. When you try to locate any particle, the mere act of observing it causes it to shift position. Maybe. Maybe not. You can't truly tell where it is. Observing it changes its location."

"Goddamn, Tyrone," J. W. said. "Don't tell me shit like that. It makes my skin crawl. Keep that to yourself."

So when Flozene informed J. W. early in the day he and Tyrone were to visit the Fallen Timbers Plantation of Miss May Margaret Howell-Reed that she didn't know where his partner was, he did not question her further. He did say one thing to her, though. "The uncertainty principle is kicking in, eh?"

"What you mean uncertain?" Flozene Tanner said. "I am fully certain I don't know where Sergeant Walker is or when he's getting back."

"That's what I just said," J. W. and turned back to a stack of small scraps of paper scribbled with phone numbers lying on his desk. Satisfied he had gotten one by Flozene, though if she didn't know it, would it really be true? Damn the uncertainty principle, he told himself, stop thinking like Tyrone and figure out which barbecue joint you're going to eat lunch in before heading to the rich woman's mansion in the middle of all that property behind those stone walls.

The location of lunch once Tyrone showed up back at Central Station ready to join J. W. was Corky's on Union Avenue again. Close, convenient, and a lot cheaper than barbecue places in Memphis that considered themselves more upscale than chain establishments. The two homicide sergeants arrived a little too late to miss the full crowd, but they did find a table where they could wait until the hubbub of rush died down.

"So where were you this morning?" J. W. asked. "I myself did paperwork for almost three hours."

"I bet you did a bang-up job, too. Shuffling and writing and returning calls. Umm-hum."

"You're not guilty of lying up with some woman, were you?"

"Are you kidding? Are you crazy? I haven't thought about anything strange for years, and if I did, Marvelle would read my mind and slap the living hell out of me. I am a broken man, J. W., and damn glad of it. I can't run with the fast mounts anymore."

"You're lucky then. I can't run with them, either, but I have to keep trying. All I get is mud kicked up in my face and covering up my goggles."

"You ought to get you a hobby, J. W. Collecting stamps or building bird houses or doing good deeds for the homeless. You know, getting joy from small, selfless acts."

"Fuck you, married man. All that kind of advice does is make me want to stick my Glock in my mouth and see if Jesus is really like the preachers claim he is. Let's go put our order in, and cheer my ass up."

In a few minutes' time, after they'd eaten enough to slow down, the homicide detectives turned their attention to the visit they'd be doing to the holdings of Miss May Margaret Howell-Reed in the afternoon. "What do you think's going on out among the idle rich?" Tyrone said. "What would be disturbing enough to that old lady among all that stuff she owns and controls and keeps adding to that'd make her look outside her own staff for help? At least reassurance of attention, anyway."

"All I know about folks of her kind is that they got small armies around them day and night. Don't they? Miss May Margaret must be like one of them. All dug in and well defended around the entire perimeter. Flares ready to set off at the first sign of enemy infiltration."

"You not fixing to have a combat flashback on me, are you?" Tyrone said. "Don't start trembling and jerking around now and calling for your mama. But that aside, I know what you're talking about. I've never been to Fallen Timbers before, but Arleigh Walker has two or three times."

"What was Arleigh there for? He hasn't made an arrest that stuck in the last eight years, has he?"

"Oh, neighbors' watch dogs getting onto Miss May Margaret's property, chasing those sheep she's got wandering around parts of it."

"She called Homicide for that? And why would she have sheep loose on that place? Any animal's trouble to have to worry about. You got to feed them. They get sick and die. They get out. Nobody wants to take them off your hands. Her place is not really a farm, is it?"

"Naw, it's not. She's got sheep loose to feed in the meadows to make it look like England, I expect. Not to eat or shear. They're to look at. Rich folks live on movie sets, J. W. Not like you and me in these little old mortgage shacks where we have to exist. And that kind of living is as real as death to us. The rich live an imaginary life. If you can afford to pretend, you don't have to live all the time in the real world. Dreams become true."

"But doesn't she have a good-size squad protecting her? Hasn't she got that son, what's his name? The one used to be drunk and roaring around downtown every night and twice on the weekends. Wrecking big and little cars on a weekly basis."

"His name is James, as I remember," Tyrone said. "James Howell-Reed. Oh, you know what his middle name is. I just remembered."

"No, hell no."

"It's Forrest, named for that slave-trading, KKK-founding general on horseback. There's some kind of blood connection to that family, thus the name of the plantation."

"You say that word *thus*, huh? I love it when you drop terms like that one on me. Makes me glad I'm running with a fancy crowd."

"You're welcome, J. W.," Tyrone said. "And no, James Forrest Howell-Reed couldn't be relied on to protect anything or anybody, much less his old mother. He is not reliable, I do believe, and she would know that down to her aristocratic bones. I think Miss May Margaret Howell-Reed might be having some of the same night terrors that the officers commanding you grunts had. She probably fears a form of fragging, you understand. Somebody working for her is making her afraid there's liable to be a grenade rolled under her tent flap one of these days. You know, a disgruntled private getting back at her."

"Tyrone, you are a suspicious man. All of us in the military loved and respected the officers telling us to stick our heads up for folks to shoot at us. Hell, we were American soldiers. We loved discipline and the way the officers showed us how to get killed."

"That's what I'm talking about," said Tyrone. "I believe you. Let's go check in at Midtown and then head for Fallen Timbers Plantation. We don't want to be late."

"Okay. Maybe on the way, you can explain why the Howell-Reed spread is named Fallen Timbers. That doesn't sound right for a place that costs that much and looks like a wet dream."

"I'll be glad to give you a much-needed history lesson on the way. I'm encouraged by your sudden thirst for knowledge, J. W. Let's wipe the barbecue sauce off our mouths and go."

After checking email and phone mail and scribbles on torn-off pieces of paper back at the Midtown station, the two homicide detectives piled into the best available car in the compound, a brown Chevrolet with over a hundred thousand miles showing on the instrument panel and in every other aspect and facet of the physical automobile itself, and headed northeast out of the city. As J. W. drove, he listened to Tyrone explain about the origin of the name attached to the Howell-Reed holdings, only infrequently asking for additional details. He knew that Tyrone enjoyed imparting information to the ignorant and ill-informed about as much as he had liked plunging through defensive lines on behalf of Central High School back in the day. Tyrone Walker did both well. His work product had always been entertaining to admire and appreciate. J. W. had learned that when he first met Tyrone Walker in the North Mississippi-West Tennessee high school bowl all those years ago. There was no malice or bragging detectable in what Tyrone could and would do to anyone who tried to stop his progress. He was just running over people, not trying to be mean.

You might as well sit back and enjoy it, J. W. mused as Tyrone talked about Nathan Bedford Forrest at the battle of Fallen Timbers or when he ran through your tackle and disappeared down the field as you lay on the ground and spit out bits of turf. Walker wasn't showing you up for spite. It's just what he did. He didn't mean any insult.

By the time Tyrone had explained the upside and downside of Nathan Bedford Forrest, slave trader in Memphis, cofounder of the Ku Klux Klan, and one of the best cavalry generals, South and North, ever, they had gotten within sight of the stone walls surrounding the holdings of Fallen Timbers. Within just over a mile on the road running alongside the plantation, a glimpse of turrets could be seen through the oaks lining the approach to the mansion.

"There she blows," J. W. said. "Looks like we're getting into Europe. Now all we got to do is find the way through those gates."

"There's a telephone or walkie-talkie or something electronic we'll have to announce ourselves on," Tyrone said. "Miss May Margaret informed the mayor, who informed Ms. Burchard, who informed Major Dalbey of the Central Station, who informed me, now informing you, Detective Sergeant Ragsdale."

"Would you run that by me one more time? I fell asleep during the middle part of all that informing."

J. W. asked Tyrone to engage the electronic connection fixed in the stone wall ready for visitors to speak into, knowing full well that he could do that himself from the advantage of the driver's seat, but also figuring that his partner could get the job done in half the time it would take him to manage it. Let the man who's comfortable with the job take over. No reason to get down on yourself just because somebody else can do something better than you can. Be proud. Be grateful you're sitting in the car.

In less than a minute, a series of electronic buzzes and metallic clicks sounded, the steel gates opened inward, and J. W. eased the high-mileage official police sedan through and into the grounds proper of Fallen Timbers Plantation.

"I hope somebody's home," he said. "And I hope it won't take long to do our business."

"Likely all it'll take is a little reassuring and hand-holding, and Miss May Margaret will be able go back to counting her money and clipping her coupons with a clear mind," Tyrone Walker said. "And we can leave knowing we've done our job and saved the Memphis Police Department from blame and accusation."

"Don't get your hopes up too high. We ain't miracle workers. Oh, look at all them sheep on both sides of this long driveway, not a one of them looking up at us."

"They got nothing to be afraid of, and they don't have to worry. Nobody's going to shear them or shoot them in the head or cut their throats and eat up all the soft parts."

"So unlike our fair city," J. W. said. "Everything and everybody edible in Memphis walks around swiveling their heads back and forth to make certain nothing's gaining on them. We all fixing to run at any given time."

A tall black man in a dark gray suit was standing at a point ahead where the finely graveled driveway divided in two, one lane headed toward the right side of the mansion and the other leading to a parking area in the other direction. He lifted his right hand, gestured toward the space where at least seven or eight vehicles were parked, and held his left hand with palm facing toward the entering car, a classic stop signal the result of his gesture.

"I know how to park a fucking car," J. W. said. "I don't need to be told."

"Sergeant Ragsdale," Tyrone said. "Let that be your last utterance of that crude word or any form of it while we're on the holdings of Fallen Timbers. We are no longer in Mississippi."

"We not been in Mississippi at any time today," J. W. said. "Don't go badmouthing my home country."

"Most times in Memphis wherever you are in the city, you're in Mississippi, at least in that state of mind," Tyrone said. "That's what I'm talking about."

"Here we are," J. W. said, shoving the shift all the way forward and killing the engine. "Parked in Tennessee. Stuck in Mississippi. Let's see what's shaking in the big house."

"Gentlemen," the tall parking director said after J. W. and Tyrone had left the car and walked in his direction. "Miss May Margaret's told me to show you in and take you to where she's waiting. That's going to be in the Great Room where she conducts her business affairs."

J. W. was impressed by the way their greeter spoke, his accent the same one used by TV announcers on news shows and by speakers on the National Geographic channel. Clear, resonant, and impossible to misunderstand, though it did make you want to flip to another channel and see if something more real was going on. J. W. spoke up.

"We're from the Memphis Police Department, me and Sergeant Walker. She said she needed to talk to somebody, your boss did."

"I assumed as much. Miss May Margaret keeps us all meticulously informed about her schedule."

Maybe I ought to just go back and sit in the car while Tyrone does some chatting with this dude, J. W. told himself. They'd get a lot more done a lot quicker than I can handle it, trying to take part in the negotiations and talk thoughtful-like. Meticulously, he repeated to himself, careful not to move his mouth while he considered the word. I have seen that before printed somewhere, but damn if I ever heard anybody say it out loud. I do know what it means, at least. I could just go sit in that Chevrolet and look out the window and watch the sheep eat grass. I could handle that without having to think about how I'd like to do something to get that educated man to forget himself and talk like a regular brother in Shelby County.

Inside the Fallen Timbers mansion, after a series of necessary steps to get through a side door practically hidden from view of anybody approaching the building, J. W. and Tyrone were shown the way down a long hall, through other doors, and up to a portal that had a keypad next to an ornate silver-colored handle. It took the servant a few seconds to punch in numbers, but no sound of locks clicking came from his operations. Instead, a muffled sound of matching electronic signals could be detected on the other side of the door. When these ceased, the door swung open soundlessly, and the way inside was revealed.

J. W. looked at Tyrone to check his response to the operation, but not a sign of recognition of his partner's quizzical look could be seen. You would have thought he had the same setup at that little house of his and Marvelle's, J. W. considered as he fell in behind Tyrone, and that he was used to punching numbers and listening for all the electrical goings-on to take place before he could get through a door inside the bungalow. Damn, I do wish I was watching sheep graze right now.

"Miss Howell-Reed," the attendant said, "these gentlemen from the Memphis Police department have arrived."

"And right on time," a woman's voice called from deeper inside the space that had been identified as the Great Room. It sounded old but strong. "I would say I'm impressed, but I am not ever surprised by efficiency. Addison, would you let Violet know she might bring in the tea?"

"Yes, ma'am," the attendant said, and vanished back into the hall, his steps as quiet as a mouse, J. W. considered, pissing on a Kleenex. Addison, that's his name. Street handle, I reckon.

"Miss Howell-Reed," Tyrone was saying to the woman that J. W. had not yet gotten a full view of, "I'm Police Sergeant Walker, and my partner here is J. W. Ragsdale, also a sergeant of the Memphis Police."

"Ragsdale," the woman said, now stepping fully into view, light from a leaded window falling on her. "Ragsdale. Are you by any chance related to the Ragsdale family in North Mississippi? I remember my father had cotton dealings with a Ragsdale at one point. A very fine grower and gentleman."

"Yes, ma'am," J. W. said, thinking that no one of his Panola County tribe would have had occasion to speak to a Howell-Reed, much less had dealings with him. Maybe a Ragsdale had taken off a hat and said howdy to the old man, somewhere along the way in Mississippi. And my bunch didn't know what the word dealings meant, unless it was a poker hand or two. "That whole bunch is dead and gone now. Only a cousin or two left, I imagine."

"It happens to all of us, doesn't it? All we can do is make our exit as well as we can and leave some positive feelings for others to acknowledge."

"I do imagine so," J. W. said, hoping the old lady would get off of him and jump on Tyrone for a while. Maybe some of Tyrone Walker's family had actually belonged to the Howell-Reeds back in the day. The Ragsdales had never belonged to anybody, J. W. told himself. Nobody wanted them enough to pay money for them.

"Miss Howell-Reed," Tyrone said. "What you're talking about, the fact of mortality, is what gave rise to your wanting to see us, I've heard. We understand you're concerned about some matters which you'd like to discuss."

"Yes. If you call my suspicion that someone is plotting to end my life or drive me insane a concern about mortality, you've nailed it, Sergeant."

Now that is a different tone of voice, J. W. considered. There's some steel in that one, not just magnolias and her thinking about stuff her old daddy used to do messing around in cotton. She's got more than one way of talking, this old lady does. This is the way she talks when she wants somebody that works for her to do their job, pronto and right up to snuff. Here we go.

"Ma'am," he said. "That's why we're here all right, and maybe you can be more specific with me and Sergeant Walker. What are you actually talking about? "

"Sergeant Ragsdale is speaking for both of us, Miss Howell-Reed. The more details you can give us, the more likely we might be able to help."

"Okay, officers," she said. "I'll try to do just that. And call me May Margaret, if you will. I get tired of hearing hyphens sounded. Let me begin by saying I'm not typically a nervous old lady who sees things. I'm old, all right, and I can be nervous. But I don't imagine things that aren't real. I got over that stuff when I was in my twenties, and that's been a long time ago."

"I got you," J. W. said. "Let's just talk like we're in Panola County, Mississippi, trying to figure out what's been bothering the livestock."

At that, Tyrone Walker cleared his throat and cast a look in his partner's direction, but J. W. refused to look back, keeping his gaze on Miss May Margaret instead.

"I hear you, Sergeant Ragsdale," she said. "Look, I know it's early in the day, but would y'all like a real drink instead of tea?"

"No, ma'am," Tyrone said. "We appreciate that offer, but we're on duty now, and any enjoyment of that sort we have to forego."

This time, J. W. was the one who cleared his throat, and Tyrone was the one who refused to meet his gaze. She said y'all, J. W. considered, just like a human being.

"Of course," the old lady said. "I just felt, you know, for an instant, that I'd like a little brandy to help me get through what I have to say."

"Or bourbon," J. W. said and all three of them chuckled a little at that, and the owner of Fallen Timbers Plantation began to tell her tale.

"First, let me provide a little context for you. Please stop me if I'm telling you things you already know. But to begin, this place where my family has lived since late in the nineteenth century is named Fallen Timbers Plantation, as you know. Do I need to explain that name itself to you? I'd be glad to, if it would help advance our discussion."

"No, ma'am," Tyrone said. "Sergeant Ragsdale and I discussed the name of the battle and Nathan Bedford Forrest's part in that, so we do know something about the name of your holdings."

“Well, good,” Miss May Margaret said. “Did you also know that Forrest owned a large part of this acreage, and that at his death a battle in the courts took place as to who would inherit it?”

“I did not know that,” Tyrone said. “And I don’t believe Sergeant Ragsdale knows a great deal about that, either.”

“Not a lot,” J. W. said, thinking that Tyrone is again giving him a dig in the ribs. I’m going to tell him what a bully of the ignorant he is, soon as I get the chance.

“Just before his death, General Forrest lost control of that property, and by all accounts he died cursing the day it was stolen from him. His was not a death of peaceful acceptance. My family ended up with the property, the Howell branch did at least, and ever since this house was built, there have been stories about ghostly possession of it by the unquiet spirit of Forrest himself.”

“That’d be a nice thing to have said about a place if you were ever trying to sell it, huh?” J. W. said. “Or use it for a haunted house at Halloween. Charge admission for folks to go through it and get scared, you know.”

Neither Miss May Margaret nor Tyrone acknowledged what J. W. had offered, and he knew he’d been broadcasting when he should have been tuning in. Again. You try to take part in a conversation, and as soon as you do, folks realize they’re dealing with an unarmed man. And they turn their eyes away in pity.

“I don’t believe in ghosts,” Miss May Margaret said, “not at my advanced age, but I will tell you that someone or something has been attempting to frighten me by apparitions and impossible manifestations and threats of impending death. And they have been successful.”

“This place is well-protected, though,” J. W. offered, knowing that should be a safe thing to say, even for somebody who hadn’t gone to college until his tongue hung out from studying. “So how is this happening? Telephone calls or loud noises outside the house? Lights flashing at night? What is it that’s going on?”

“None of that precisely. It’s more detailed and studied. I would say. Let me call in my son, James Forrest Howell-Reed. He’s waiting to aid me in the room attached to this one. I’d like for you to have another voice to consider. I don’t want you to think I’m just an age-addled old woman. And I must add that James’s middle name is borrowed from N. B. Forrest, as you might think. There is a blood connection.”

"We'd never think you're addled, ma'am," Tyrone said. "But please let us hear what your son has to say. Maybe that would be helpful for us to know."

Lord God and Jesus Christ on crutches, J. W. said to himself. Why didn't I make the connection before? James Forrest Howell-Reed used to do everything in Memphis but paw up dust and bellow like a bull elephant. He went by the handle of Jimmy Reed then. Whores, dope, car wrecks, misdemeanors, girls from good families and bad in Central Gardens getting knocked around and knocked up and aborted, fathers suing, lawyers making money hand over fists from folks going after James Forrest Howell-Reed in court, people getting paid off and laid on, and finding themselves moved out of the city and county and this part of Tennessee. His pictures all over the society pages at country clubs and cotton carnival dances and coming-out parties and tennis games and on the front page drunk and addled and beat all to shit from fists and nightsticks. And all of them showing him grinning like a jackass eating briars. Liking it all, eating it up, showing his ass whenever he got the chance. Lookie here at me.

Then he underwent that famous religious conversion at the All God's Tennessee Apostolic Soul Revival right there on television. Screaming out he was a new body and soul in Christ. Then he tried to preach and quit that after a while. He set up an orphanage and quit that because it kept getting too high a percentage of black kids over whites. Whining about reverse racism. Threatening to paint himself black. Wrote all those articles in the *Commercial Appeal* about how to save Memphis financially and spiritually and how to diet your way to purity and good health. Tried to sell that damn program of some kind of South American overdoses of special kinds of grains. This message being sent to the Memphis barbecue and soul-food eating capital of the world. Just the folks that need to be told to eat your vegetables.

And then all of a sudden just went quiet and crawled into a dark place somewhere and hadn't been really seen nor heard of, or gotten into trouble or advised cures for what ails people of the Mid-South physically and spiritually, or stuck his head up in any way for years now. James Forrest Howell-Reed, the incredible invisible man.

"Do either of you know my son or know of him?" Miss May Margaret said. "I must say there was a time in Memphis and Shelby County and surrounds when any Memphis police officer would have known that name instantly. But I do believe and do know that time is past. He has devoted himself to personal rehabilitation. I am proud of my son now, and so had his father become right up to the time he departed this world."

"I have heard of your son," Tyrone said. "I will say. But, of course, except for a few years right after college, I've spent my entire life in this area. So I had much more chance to be aware of events and people here. My partner, as you understand, didn't move to Memphis until after he left cotton farming in Mississippi some time back. In Memphis terms, he's a newcomer."

"James Forrest has gone through the fire, been seared by the flames, but in that process, he has been burned clean of the old life. He has found and is living a new one." Thus sayeth the mother, J. W. thought, also thinking me a newcomer, my ass.

"Bless his heart," J. W. spoke up, using the phrase he'd heard countless times growing up and falling short of the expectations of others himself. He means well, his Mississippi grandma would say about him. No he don't, his old man would say. Tyrone cut his eyes at his partner, and J. W. considered how gratifying it would be if he were able to send a telepathic message to Tyrone. "So fucking what?" he would project into the brain pan of his partner. "I said it, and I'd say it again. Praise Jesus. Let me at them little crackers and that communion grape juice."

Miss May Margaret Howell-Reed touched a button on the underside of a small table, and in a few seconds, a knock came at a side door of the Great Room in which they were all gathered. It opened slowly, the way expensively weighty and well-installed doors were intended to do, and J. W. considered briefly how the doors of every house and apartment he'd ever lived in would spring open with a rattle and bang as though an explosion had set things off when you pushed on them.

The man who entered the room was a long way different looking from the young hellion and entrepreneur J. W. had encountered in photographs and a few times in person back in the day. He had gained weight and lost hair, but J. W. was not surprised by that. As the fuel-burning function of the digestion system of the young wears down, inefficiency sets up shop in the decaying organism where it lives. Here's what you're supposed to do: Push away from the table still hungry. Drink only one beer with the barbecue. Never look a pie or cake in the face again, much less fried snacks that the afternoon whisky hour screams for. All this conspires to fatten a man up, and the days of unthinking enjoyment fade away like a dream of life that never happened.

James Forrest Howell-Reed was well named by that handle now, J. W. considered. He'd never be drunk or high Jimmy Reed looking for a little action in the Bluff City again. No, he's a good boy now, asking his mama if she called.

"Hello, gentleman," the son with the borrowed middle name of N. B. Forrest said, looking first at Tyrone and then J. W. "I know Mother has been expecting you, and I'm eager to hear what you have to say about her concerns. She's been upset for some time. And rightfully so."

"More than upset, James," Miss May Margaret said. "I'd say at times I've felt beleaguered and fearful. Why don't you let these sergeants from the Homicide Division know what you've witnessed."

"Certainly, Mother," James Forrest said, letting himself sink into an overstuffed chair facing the visitors to Fallen Timbers Plantation. "But I don't understand why the police department has sent staff from Homicide. There's nothing here of that sort to be concerned about."

"I can provide some help with that," Tyrone said. "It's simply the function of an overcommitted personnel in the department. Major Dalbey wanted to respond as soon as he could, and Sergeant Ragsdale and I happened to be available. That's what the choice of officers from Homicide amounts to."

"You're too modest," Miss May Margaret said. "The Major told me you two were the best."

"Shucks," J. W. said and everyone chuckled. Jimmy Forrest knows he's seen me before, J. W. thought. He just then looked at me like a bull looking at an orphan calf. What are you doing here? Huh? Did you take a wrong turn in the corn patch?

"Please let these officers know what you've witnessed, James," Miss May Margaret said. "And I'll fill in what I've been concerned about during this whole business."

James Forrest began to speak about strange noises, flashes of light from no visible sources, conversations between unseen persons, voices raised in anger as though an argument was taking place, sudden appearances of animals inside the mansion itself, animals that vanished when approached, the clinking of glasses as if a party was in progress, laughter and excited voices from distant rooms, car doors slamming and engines starting, and all this within the mansion itself where no possible source for such goings-on could be possible.

"Let me speak about the dietary apparitions," Miss May Margaret said when her son's listing of impossible events slowed a bit.

"Dietary?" Tyrone said. "Do you mean you've discovered something strange in what you've been eating?"

"Not exactly," she said. "I'll give you an example, one from two days ago, just before I decided I had to contact the Memphis police. I told James about it when it happened. I was eating a light dinner alone, as I customarily do these days. My son typically foregoes an evening meal, don't you, James."

"I won't go deeply into the reasons for what I eat and when I eat," James said. "It's part of a strict regimen I hold to, making up for lost time, I suppose."

He's probably holed up in his bedroom, J. W. imagined, eating with a big old spoon straight out of a half-gallon carton of triple chocolate ice cream, the high-powered kind, and chasing it down with a pack of double Oreos. That's a damn strict regimen, all right.

"That night I had Bernicia, our cook for ages, fix me a small breast of a young pullet and a light salad," Miss May Margaret began. "She had served me that herself and left me alone in the dining room. Not the formal room, of course, but in what some might call a family dining area. She had set the dish before me, and I had remarked on how good it looked, and she had told me about the farm the pullet had come from and then left, as I said. I looked up to call after her. I don't know what I wanted to say. Nothing of consequence. Then I looked down at the plate, and there was not the breast of pullet I'd seen, but something utterly different. It was an entire dead rat, battered and fried."

"My word," Tyrone Walker said. "Shocking. What did you do at that point? Did you call out to the cook?"

Did she cut into that booster and see what it tasted like, J. W. told himself, biting his lower lip to keep from laughing. I got to tell Tyrone what come into my head when I thought about that battered rat. Tyrone thought the same thing, I bet, but he didn't crack a smile. He just stored it up to think about later. Then he'll laugh until he might near fall down.

"No, I'm sure I must have screamed out at the sight," Miss May Margaret said. "To this very moment, I can't get that vision out of my head."

"I immediately came in haste at Mother's scream," James Forrest said. "Thinking some health crisis had arisen. And when I arrived at her side, she was standing beside the chair at her dining place in a terrible state of distress. When I asked her what was wrong, she pointed to the plate, and I remember distinctly, she did so without looking down herself at what she was wanting me to see."

"That battered rat, huh?" J. W. said, cutting his eye at Tyrone, who was refusing to look back at him, instead staring down at the notepad in his hand like he was making sure not to drop it.

"That's what she said she'd seen," James Forrest said, "later when she was able to look back at what had disgusted her."

"But?" Tyrone said. "It was there, right?"

"No, it was not. Here's what I saw. All that was there, aside from the salad plate, was the breast of a pullet, looking delicious and ready to eat. Browned to perfection."

"The rat was gone, that's what you're saying," J. W. said, carefully controlling the delivery of that statement, an action which later Tyrone remarked about when they were on the road in the car well out of the domain of Fallen Timbers.

"It was quite an ordinary dish," James Forrest said. "No different from those Mother has always enjoyed. That's what I observed before her place at the table."

"I agree," Miss May Margaret said. "I must admit my son is right. That's all I saw when he convinced me to look down at my plate. It was that breast of pullet. And I thought, well, my eyes have deceived me, and that I must get my glasses prescription changed. I was not seeing correctly, I immediately admitted to James. I was wrong."

"Did you go ahead and eat that chicken?" J. W. said. "Now that it looked right."

"I did not, of course," Miss May Margaret Howell-Reed said, letting a little tinkle of lightness come into her voice. "I just couldn't, you understand."

"No harm done in this case, then," Tyrone said, cutting off J. W., who wanted to say he would have tucked into that tender bird, if it'd been him, and not thought rat at all.

"There's more," Miss May Margaret said, her tone becoming darker and subdued. "Because when I sat down to my salad and took my fork, something from under the edge of the plate brushed against my hand."

Probably a thousand-dollar bill, thought J. W., one somebody had dropped and didn't bother to pick up until they'd eat supper and got full. At the thought, he cautioned himself to keep a straight face.

"When I picked it up, I dropped it immediately when I recognized what it truly was. It was this. The detached, slick tail of a rodent. Hairless. Disgusting."

"That rat again," J. W. said. "Done left his tail behind this time?"

"I will give myself credit for what I did next," Miss May Margaret said. "For though I shrieked for my son to return, I did not drop that hideous tail or throw it from me. No, I kept it in hand to show him and when James burst through the door again I was able to show him what I had found."

"My mother is correct," James Forrest said. "It was the tail from a rodent, it appeared to me, and it had a spot of blood on the larger end. It was truly rat-like."

"Did you find the rest of him lying around somewhere?" J. W. said, but got no answer but a quick sideways look from Tyrone.

"Strange indeed," Tyrone said aloud. "Did you ever figure out what it all amounted to?"

"No," James Forrest said. "I did preserve the tail, though, if you'd like to see it."

"Naw, that's all right," J. W. said. "I seen hundreds of rat tails and the rat they were growed onto when I was raised in North Mississippi."

"What Sergeant Ragsdale means," Tyrone said, "is there's no evidentiary value attached to that matter, so no reason to keep it further."

"I never want to see it again," Miss May Margaret said. "I can assure you of that. Now my question is what can the Memphis Police Department do to help solve these strange occurrences at Fallen Timbers, and when can we expect a response? I imagine you will report to Major Dalbey, and I would appreciate an expedited attempt to put things back in their proper place."

"Hear, hear," James Forrest said, his voice and tone falling into an encouraging rumble.

"We will certainly report what you've told us about your concerns and these strange events," Tyrone Walker said, "and I know Major Dalbey will be in communication with you."

"I hope the Memphis Police can help put all this to an end and do that soon," Miss May Margaret said and left the room, informing all that her son would now see the police officers out of Fallen Timbers and off the plantation. She would be in touch as need arose.

She sure talks different when that sorry son of hers is in the room, J. W. said to himself, not a bit as friendly and down to earth like she was with me and Tyrone before Junior showed up. I wonder why that is. If it was me, I'd talk a lot rougher when I had to look at him staring at me like he was putting the eye on Mama.

On the way down the series of halls toward the entrance to the house proper, James Forrest Howell-Reed kept up a steady stream of comments about what he referred to several times as "the pressing matter at hand."

"You officers can see what I'm being forced to deal with now that my mother's in this time in her life. She's showing indications of some memory loss and dislocation in reality. Don't you agree? I expect you've seen many cases of this kind in your work with older persons who've called on you."

"Well, we're not medical professionals," Tyrone said. "Though we've encountered our fair share of persons in fear and depression and stress. Haven't we, Sergeant Ragsdale."

"Yeah, that's the case all right," J. W. said. "We have sure seen our fair share of every kind of nut in the Greater Memphis area."

"I wager you have," James Forrest said. "The mind begins to play tricks in the declining years, such as those my mother is suffering now."

"We'll be in contact, as need be," Tyrone said. "I know Major Dalbey will be particularly concerned. He's asked us to reassure you and Miss Howell-Reed of that. He'll stay on target. And he'll be in touch."

"As much as possible, I'd prefer you deal directly with me. Mother will want to reach out, but I think in her current state, she's a bit shaky about sharing accurate information. She's always been in control, you understand."

By that point, the way to the air outside was well within reach, and it was all that J. W. could do not to break into a trot to reach it as soon as possible. When he and Tyrone got to that goal of the outdoors, James Forrest stopped and insisted on shaking hands with each of them, his grip on J. W.'s palm the strength and duration appropriate for Delta farewells among gentlemen, and by the time breakaway had been achieved the black man they'd first met in greeting was ready to show them to where the police car was parked.

"Rufus Minden," Tyrone said as the three of them walked across the fine gravel of the parking area. "I haven't seen you close up in a long time."

"Tell me about it, Tyrone Walker," Minden said. "The last time I remember seeing you close up was when we were playing Memphis State at home back when God was a little boy."

"It's the University of Memphis now, Rufus," Tyrone said. "We gone uptown now, don't you see."

"Do y'all still hit a man like a Mack truck when he's trying to get you out of the way of the Ole Miss running back? Just denying a man space to move around on a ball field. You know, messing up his assignments."

"I couldn't deny a fifteen year old kid the right of way these days. He'd put me on my back. Just like you did on that last drive y'all made in pouring rain that afternoon in Oxford."

"As soon as y'all get through all this male-bonding stuff," J. W. said, "I'd like to ask you a question about your boss, Mr. Minden, if you don't mind."

"I'm not at liberty to discuss my employer with anyone," Rufus Minden said. "Much less with somebody showing interest that I can't and won't recognize."

"Oh, now, you're talking real different both in vocabulary and tone," J. W. said. "I didn't intend to mess up the joshing back and forth here between old ballplayers."

"There's joshing, and there's work," Rufus Minden said. "A time to talk and a time to keep my mouth shut. I learned that a long time ago."

"So did your old opponent here, Tyrone Walker," J. W. said. "Or as folks now call him at work, Sergeant in the Homicide Division. Oh, well. It was fun listening to you old buddies talk for a while there. And then it got a little boring."

All three laughed at that, and Rufus Minden watched the homicide detectives load up and drive away. In the car on the way back down the long approach to Fallen Timbers proper, J. W. looked long and hard at Tyrone from the passenger's seat until his partner finally spoke.

"What," he said, "do you think's going on here in the historical seat of Nathan Bedford Forrest's old hangout? Is it all just senile dementia or is there more here than that?"

"I'll tell you my take on it, but you got to wait until I quit talking before you start refining my thoughts. Okay. Here it is, and let me put it in the form of a question. Is the old lady just getting nuttier or is her one and only once-a-black-sheep son trying to get her locked up at Central State? That's my question, and my answer to it I'll tell you when I hear what you're about to come up with."

"You've nailed it in a kind of rough and ready fashion, J. W. But I think it's more nuanced than that."

"Hit me with the nuance then. I can stand hearing another one, and I can prove it wrong."

"All right," Tyrone said, by that time the only evidence of Fallen Timbers the long stretch of head-high fence along the road they traveled. The mansion was now fully hidden by distance and groves of trees. "Here's what I think," he went on. "James Forrest Howell-Reed, as he now calls himself after coming out of his misspent youth all rehabilitated and cleaned up spiritually, is casting about for ways to get Mama to loosen those purse strings and let Junior get inside her pouch. Just like a baby kangaroo."

"You are so poetic," J. W. said. "I'd put it this way, nuance-free. Junior wants Mama to let go of the purse strings all right, but he can't tell if it's best to make her think she's nuts or getting that way or if it's best for him to go a little further than just sticking her in the nuthouse over yonder in Nashville."

"What I'd like to see, and of course never would be ever close to being allowed to lay eyes on it, is the final will and testament. See, I tell myself, Miss May Margaret has real good sense about one thing in particular and it's not whether a pullet is really itself or just a dead rat fried up to look nice."

"Money," J. W. said.

"The shortest and truest thing you ever said as a police investigator," Tyrone said. "Here's what I'm saying. That lady knows money. That will is so designed, I will bet you my next paycheck, so that no matter whatever happens to the current owner of Fallen Timbers and all its resources, the inheritor won't get all of what's there. There will be provisions that take that money out of Junior's pocket."

"She might leave it all to the American Pullet Society," J. W. said. "Or to them two nice homicide detectives in Memphis."

"I'm betting on the pullets. But what it means for the inheritor is that he's got to find a way to shake all that money loose so it can get to him before the mean old mama dies and spoofs it all away to good causes."

"So what he has to do is not just off Mama but make it so that what she may want to do with the goods don't make a damn bit of difference."

"You got it, Sergeant,"Tyrone said."It is a problem for the prodigal son."

"Poor thing," J.W said. "As far as I'm concerned I hope the kill is a clean enough one for you and me to put Junior where he belongs."

"Clean kills, dirty money, fried and battered rats, strange voices in empty rooms,"Tyrone said. "It is going to be a puzzle."

"It's going to be a son of a bitch," J. W. said. "Please get me on home to the house before Major Dalbey dreams up something for me to do tonight."

"Why, got a date?"Tyrone said."Is it with a live woman this time?"

"Leave me alone, married man. Move this vehicle on down the road, and don't poke fun at an old whipped-down survivor of the love wars."

7

Deangelo Dixon lifted the bottle of Crown Royal out of its gold-and-blue velvet bag and just opened not a minute ago from the case beside him, and made a gesture toward Tuck Bunny. "Want you a hit of something decent for a change?" Deangelo said. "Or you going to stick with that white-colored shit?"

"Vodka ain't white," Tuck Bunny said, "it's clear. You can see right through it, on through to the other side where it's taking you. But naw, I don't want no alcohol right now. I need me a snort or two of that sweet-ass powder we got. That stuff gets me on up off the ground a foot or two but still let me think."

"What the fuck you want to think about, Tuck? You ain't never before wanted to let anything get inside your head to make you worry about stuff. Besides, you ain't got the training to think about nothing but the next hit or the next big-assed old girl you want to throw down and put dick to."

The two had just been bailed out on bond by Mr. Irwin Henkel, he of Henkel, Steinmetz, Sharpenski, with law offices in Downtown Memphis, Tennessee, and Uptown West Memphis, Arkansas. Irwin had not been given that name at birth—he had been labeled as Gareth when he hit the open air—but he had learned after his time at Memphis State University School of Law that the kind of jurisprudence he planned to make a living practicing would be one serving those attracted to stronger sounding handles, names like Abraham, Jacob, and Paul. So it was Irwin, not Gareth he chose. And he had made his nut defending the rights of such clients as claimers to the Bones Family, the Beale Street Boppers, the Blue Walkers, and lately a new and powerful organization calling itself the Latin Lords.

"After we had to spend almost twenty-four hours in that cage downtown before Mr. Henkel got us out, I feel like I need something to calm me down, but still leave me room to think about shit," Tuck Bunny said. "That why I'm laying off the Crown Royal. Besides, that stuff makes me want to come up beside somebody's head real hard. Anybody's head. I don't mean you, though."

"What you got to think about, son?" Deangelo said. "You know I do all that kind of cogitating for you and the rest of the Bones Family. That's part of my job, see. Thinking for those who can't think for themselves."

"I know that, I know that, I ain't quarreling. Don't get me wrong, D. I just don't know what we supposed to do with all this fake money they making for us to take care of. Now if I was supposed to take some of them fifties to the store and buy a little bit and get real money come back to me in change, I could go with that right down the line. But . . ."

"Wait a minute, Tuck," Deangelo said. "You ain't been trying to pass none of them bills, have you? You do that, and it'll get what brains you got shot out of your fucking head."

"No, no," Tuck Bunny said. "I know better than that. I just look at them stacks of money that keep on growing. It make me itch, that's all. But why's that white man from St. Louis making all that spending cash and then us told not to do nothing with it. He might as well be making up Bibles and baby books and shit if all we going to do is stack it and get it ready. See what I mean?"

"That's why you worried, then," Deangelo said. "You want to know the end result of this enterprise."

"That sound real smart, the way you said that. Yeah, that's what I want to know. End result, I like the way that sounds to me. Enterprise. That got a sound to it, too. End result."

"First of all, I'm going to tell only what you need to know, and maybe a little more since we been hanging together all the way back yonder to the middle school."

"Yeah, tell me. Put my mind at ease, and you know I'll do what you tell me, D. That's me. I'm as sound as a key of the best powder ever made."

"Okay, here's what I'm going to tell you, then. That product is not money, see, as far as Memphis or this whole motherfucking country we live in is concerned. It's just a fake currency made up for someplace else, somewhere they ain't got enough sense to know counterfeit when they see it. All they see is them pictures of Grant and Franklin, now and then even some of the bigger ones, not even talking about pictures of Jackson."

"Where is that place? Arkansas?"

"Naw, hell," Deangelo said, beginning to laugh a little. "They ain't that dumb for long enough to do us any good, not even in Arkansas. Here's a little more I'm going to tell you. This fake shit money is bound for Colombia, Mexico, Guatemala, all them places like that, where they don't even speak English, most of them. Or read it. Shit. Don't ask me about that. See, though, dumb as them fools are about knowing or not knowing real money when they see it, they got the product we need. And we been buying it, and now we going to buy as much as we can before them dumbass Spics know what hit them. All with them stacks of fake money."

"So we getting real snow and coke and weed and they getting shit money," Tuck Bunny said, his eyes shining and his face lit up with every tooth in his head open to view.

"For as long as they keep believing and as long as it lasts, yeah. Besides, they can pass a lot of that shit to straight folks down yonder, you understand. Them fuckers are dumber than the people we be dealing with. See, stupid works its way down from the top."

"That's what they call beautiful, idn't it?" Tuck Bunny said. "Like on TV and in the movies."

"Yep, that's right, Tuck," Deangelo said. "And the Memphis white boys funding all this need to stay clean, and they are going to. They going to make sure of that. They will not be convictable of passing counterfeit money. Not that they going to get caught anyway."

"How do we talk to them foreign fuckers down yonder, though?" Tuck Bunny said. "They jabber that Spic talk, don't they?"

"They do, yeah. But we can always hire folks that can talk that crap. The schools are full of them. But on this end right here in Memphis on the river, who do you think we going to be dealing with, I mean the ones who can jabber that Casa Casa Taco Amigo shit?"

"The Latin Lords," Tuck Bunny said. "Alphonso and Chuco and that bunch of greasers."

"You got it, Tuck. See, you are thinking a little bit now. You can do that, to some small degree. Now come on, suck down some of this Crown Royal. That powder shit will just make you crazy and stupider than a Mexican."

Tuck Bunny reached for the bottle of Crown Royal, but Deangelo told him to find a glass to pour some into, not wanting to have a dummy like Tuck Bunny putting his mouth on a bottle of perfectly clean liquor. It's going to be a shame, he thought to himself as he poured a generous slug into the glass Tuck held toward him in both hands, when I have to off this dumbass old boy I've been knowing since Beauregard Elementary School in Memphis. But he's starting to try to think about stuff so he can know why he's doing what he's been told to do. That's where he's going wrong. Trying to think. For Tuck Bunny, doing that is like letting a two-year-old kid play with a butcher knife. Like the white man always says, a little learning is a dangerous thing. It can and will get you killed.

"The best thing you can tell me," Major Dalbey was saying to two of his Homicide officers, "is this here. And listen up and pay attention to what I got to say."

It was a little after eight o'clock in the morning, early for both J. W. Ragsdale and Tyrone Walker, each with his own reasons for sucking down mugs of the bad coffee made by whoever in the Central Station first felt most need to get caffeine perking for blood transfusion. Today, unfortunately, it had not been one of the office staff, Lurleen or LaWanda or Benita, all longtime veterans of life in the Central Station of the Memphis Police Department and able through long experience of success and failure to make pots of brew drinkable enough to pass muster. Instead a newly hired patrol officer right out of the academy had tackled the job. It was a game effort, but it not only failed the taste test but also the caffeine strength requirement.

"Maiden piss," J. W. had remarked after his first sip from his favorite mug, one inscribed with the cheerful reminder that Jesus loves all the children of the world. The Total Faith and Full Salvation Church of Total Immersion, South Memphis Cathedral, had donated a case of the ceramic cups to the Central Station some time back, hoping to curry favor. All but two mugs had been broken since then through accidents, droppages, and purposeful smash and discard. J. W. had saved one for his own perpetual use, feeling comforted by the promise about Jesus's love for children, though he had never let any one of his fellow officers know just why he kept his own mug safe in a desk drawer. If he had, he knew somebody would make a joke of it, remind him of his ignorant upbringing in North Mississippi, and he would feel one of two ways about how he should respond. Both were wrongheaded, of course. One way, the one he'd prefer, would be to slap the shit out of the scoffer, and the other would be to laugh along with the joke, thus making fun of Jesus loving children.

Maybe there wasn't a Jesus, and never had been, and all J. W. had been taught to respect and appreciate as a child was ignorant and pitifully laughable, but damned if he'd shit on yet another thing from dear dead old Mississippi days in the Delta. Most everything in his upbringing had been wrong and simple-minded and pitiful all right. J. W. Ragsdale had come to know that truth, but still. Goddamn it.

"Maiden piss," he said again to Tyrone Walker after his first sip. Tyrone had his own past days as a kid in the Mid-South to have to live with, J. W. knew, but he seemed to have more emotional resources than J. W. ever did. That should not have been a puzzle hard to understand, of course, Tyrone growing up a black child in Memphis, Tennessee, and all the bullshit connected with that, but he still seemed to have made a better peace with himself and how he got to be that way than J. W. had.

Too much to think about this morning, J. W. told himself. Let me go out and find somebody doing something wrong and fucked up, and see if I can't get some satisfaction cleaning that up. I feel the need to correct somebody or something. And do it hard as I have to.

Tyrone did nod in agreement to J. W.'s comment about the coffee, and both looked attentively at Major Dalbey, who had announced he was about to tell them what the best thing was he could hear from them this early morning in Memphis. That was always his way of beginning a boss-employee communication. Or an officer-enlisted man duty assignment. "The best thing first this morning is this," Dalbey said. "After y'all had the chance to listen to Miss May Margaret Howell-Reed, please tell me she's just a crazy old lady, rich as she might be, still nothing but a damn good example of what they call dementia or Alzheimer's or something along those lines. Don't tell me nothing else harder to understand than that."

"She is nutty," J. W. said. "I ain't going to quarrel with that. But I hate to say this, but you got me backed into a corner. I think something else might be going on, too."

"Oh, shit," the Major said. "Tyrone, tell me something different. Tell me J. W. is just being an alarmist. Tell me he's just hungover this morning, and feeling grumpy."

"Like Meatloaf said a long time ago," Tyrone said. "Two out of three ain't bad."

"Meatloaf, what are you talking about, Sergeant Walker? Huh? Run that by me at a slower rate of speed."

"I mean J. W. Ragsdale is well known for being grumpy and from suffering at times from overindulgence in mind-altering substances," Tyrone said. "That's two descriptors. The other one, the conclusion he's reached, I have to tell you I agree with. Something else is going on at Fallen Timbers Plantation."

"Thank you for that character reference, partner," J. W. said. "I guess."

"Let me put it to you simply, officers," the Major said. "I have got to report up the line of authority here, and I've to be accurate as I can. But I also got to cover my ass. How much do you think we ought to look further into this bullshit, and how much can we get away with not doing?"

"Can't we just wait a little bit and see what else might happen?" J. W. said. "You know, let things play themselves out a little. Not rush in without some good reconnaissance first?"

"Sergeant Ragsdale," Major Dalbey said. "This is not Vietnam or Afghanistan or Gettysburg. It ain't about being reasonable. It's about money. It is about the good American dollar. It's about millions and maybe a billion of the goddamn greenbacks. What might happen at Fallen Timbers has to do with Memphis, the Delta, the Mid-South, and hell, maybe it might touch up somewhere in the North. It's got a long reach."

"The North?" J. W. said. "Everything is real up yonder. It ain't like living here inside of how it's like a picture show. You know how playing parts in film is. Everybody knows what he ought to be doing and how to do it right. And how the director is nuts."

"You ought to read more, J. W. Not just watch old movies," Tyrone said, and then instantly added, "No offense, partner."

"None taken, Tyrone," J. W. said. "I did try reading once and didn't get much out of it. I still don't in my studies of life in the Mid-South."

"Y'all hush up that joking back and forth," Major Dalbey said. "I got to report to some people that won't listen to reason but about a third of the time. So give me something to work with. What can we do to tamp things down out yonder where all that money is feeling like shifting around some? When that cash money trembles, everybody gets a case of nerves. And when it moves, it makes shit happen, and folks get in a fix. Inquiring minds want to know."

"I know exactly what you mean about having to report to folks that won't listen to reason all the time," J. W. said. Then turning in his chair toward Tyrone, "And what should I have been reading, Sergeant Walker?"

"Older stuff and newer stuff about the South. Some folks I would have advised to read Faulkner or Richard Wright. Others I'd say Erskine Caldwell. Some I'd say Li'l Abner."

"I have heard of that last one," J. W. said. "I'll look into that."

"The mind of the South," Tyrone said. "A contradiction in terms."

"Shut up that going back and forth and tell me something I can report to Bitchhead," the Major said. "I'm meeting City Manager Ovetta Birchard later this morning, and she'll be hot about Miss May Margaret Howell-Reed. Work with me. Give me a hand. We're talking about money now."

"All right," Tyrone said, and launched into a description of what he and J.W. had concluded after their visit to Fallen Timbers.

Damn, I wish this coffee was stronger, J. W. told himself. He looked down at his mug and read again the words about Jesus and his love for children. Don't think about stuff, he said to himself, just love the children and hate damn weak coffee.

Back at his desk, thinking about how to dummy up that couple of paragraphs about the visit to Fallen Timbers so the Major could have a piece of paper to look at as he made his report to Ovetta Birchard, J. W. reared back in his chair and thought once again about Pall Mall cigarettes, the ones in the original pack. "Where particular people congregate," it said in fancy script on each package of twenty. There had been the day when he could suck down great clouds of Pall Mall tobacco smoke and feel it roil out of his nose and mouth after it had done its appointed task of mollifying and comforting. No more, though, he reminded himself. Even if he'd tried to light up again, he wouldn't be able to do it inside the confines of the Central Police Station, now designated officially what was called "smoke-free." And that rule had teeth. Teeth made of fines of money. There was even gossip about one cop in the big headquarters downtown being fired for repeated violations of the smoking ban. And his pension plan cancelled. Oh, well. Chew some damn gum and think about a way to put words to paper for Major Dalbey to mouth at Bitchhead.

"Sergeant Ragsdale," LaWanda Boleen said, looking over her glasses at him from her work station, "it's a call for you for a homicide scene on Cowden, just off of Longmire. It's your turn at bat, the captain says."

"All right, LaWanda," J. W. said. "But I got to finish writing up this report for the Major for when he meets with Ovetta B. It might take me a while."

"Tyrone Walker didn't already tell you he done wrote up that report and give it to Major Dalbey?"

"Naw, he didn't," J. W. said. "I'm both mad and glad about that, though. And don't get me wrong, LaWanda. I do want Tyrone to do as much writing up for me as he's willing to do, but Lord I hate to get in that hot car and drive over there to Cowden and Longmire."

"You don't have to tell me none of that. I know it already, and I'll inform the officer at the scene that you on your way. And happy about it."

"I hope it's a fresh kill at least," J. W. said. "Damn if I want to look at a ripe one."

"I don't know nothing about it, and I don't want to hear about such doings. One of my lines is ringing off the hook. Have fun."

"I'd tell you to go to hell, LaWanda, but it's hot enough in Memphis this morning to satisfy."

In the unmarked police car, not J. W.'s own personal vehicle, a nine-year-old Buick the air conditioner of which had quit some months ago, the windows had not been left cracked open by the most recent driver. A good sign, J. W. considered as he hit the ignition, maybe meaning the cooling function was alive again. It was, and he spoke aloud, "Finally something that works right this morning. I'll drink weak coffee every morning if the trade-off's I can get an air conditioner working on me in Memphis."

The drive to the location of the crime was not that far, and before the air conditioner had time to bring the temperature down to a decent level, J. W. could see two blue and whites parked on the right side of the street, an ambulance across from that location, and an unmarked sedan behind that. He knew that the ambulance kept its motor running at all times, stopped or not, so it was always cool inside. Why did the corpses get all the cold air, and the cops, still alive, walking around working in hot uniforms, got no relief from the heat at all? Still, though, better that than the last long lie-down the corpse was enjoying. Stiffs don't know whether they're cold or hot, J. W. thought, so it all evens out in the long run.

Patrolman Tony Overstreet was standing by the curb where Cowden intersected Longmire, head cover pushed back to give him some relief, not looking at all professional in his stance, and if Tony had been ten years younger, J. W. would have called him out for that dereliction from uniform protocol, but hell, why do it now? He's just marking time for the pension to kick in.

"Officer Overstreet," J. W. called out after he'd parked, "hot enough for you this early in the morning?"

"It's shank of the night for these two," Overstreet said. "It ain't never going to be morning for them again. This 'un's it. Looks like they been here since right before first light. That's when it went down."

"That's what the coroner team says?"

"Yeah, ain't but one here, and she says some of it went down about then. Did something with a thermometer she stuck in them, and then she said that. I guess it spoke to her."

"Where'd she stick it? Which orifice received the instrument?" J. W. said, keeping his gaze on Officer Overstreet and knowing the answer he'd give. Just asking for what humor might be in the query. Might as well find a way to handle this scene before having to dig into it.

"Here she comes," Overstreet said. "You can ask her yourself, if you want to, Sergeant."

Oh, God, J. W. said to himself, hoping he wasn't showing any sign of surprise as the woman dressed in the green scrubs walked toward him and Overstreet, carrying a clipboard in one hand and a cloth bag in the other.

"Hello, J. W.," Nova Hebert said. "I didn't know you'd be on call for this one."

"Not me, neither," he said. "They kind of surprised me with this one. There I was at my desk in Central Station, having a hell of a good time writing up a report, and next thing I know I get torn away from that to come look at some dead folks."

"I'll bet you were having a good time doing that report writing," the assistant coroner said, chuckling a bit. "I've always known you had the heart of a clerk beneath that tough cop exterior."

She's not really laughing, J. W. Ragsdale told himself. She's just not letting a thing show, and I'll see if I can match her in doing that. "They got you out on the street looking at a kill these days?" J. W. said. "I wouldn't have thought they'd had a woman at your rank out taking body temperatures here in the hot sun."

"Oh, we all take turns doing that," Nova Hebert said. "It keeps us grounded, Dr. Ryan says. He even goes out himself on a run now and then."

"Uh huh," J. W. said, not knowing how he ought to respond to mention of the man he'd felt like killing at one point. He'd got over that, but he still couldn't let himself forget the smooth-talking PhD, MD motherfucker getting in between him and Nova. Be honest, though, he said to himself as he looked at the woman in green scrubs who he'd told he loved not more than two years ago, I was the one that made the whole thing turn to shit. I just couldn't pull the trigger again, and that ain't the fault of the target I had in my sights.

"How fresh is this one?" he said. "Patrolman here says it went down a day or so ago."

"Well, looks like a couple of days. One did take place first, the African American one, give or take a while. The other one was some time well after that."

"Two kills. I thought they both got shot dead."

"One was shot dead. That's the one that checked out second. The other one wasn't just shot, though, the one that went down earlier. He was killed at least three different ways."

"Damn. Three ways? How can that be?" J. W. said, looking not directly at Nova's face as he talked, but off to one side a bit. At a lock of hair that was sticking out of the plastic head cover she was wearing. Looking at that was bad enough for him, too, he discovered, so J. W. shifted his gaze to an empty spot just over Nova's head. Some relief there, but his eyes kept wanting to focus on the woman herself. God-damn a memory, he told himself. To hell and back.

"What do you mean by three ways to die?" Get serious, think about blood and brain matter and bone chips, and flies trying to get at something dead. Cheer up, and focus on evildoing in the Bluff City.

"Well," Nova Hebert said, "I mean that what killed the interesting one here had more than one activity going for it. This other one, I'm saying, took two slugs to the head, .44s it looks like, and boom it was lights out for good. I don't mean he enjoyed it, but it was quick at least. The other one had been worked on by a blade first, it appears, not deep enough or directed to vital parts enough to kill quick. Then there's signs of blunt force to the face, to the fingers, to the knees and where all else I haven't determined yet. None of these injuries were fatal, and I'll bet they weren't intended to be that. Whoever did this one was playing around with it some, doing some entertainment before finally pulling trigger on the niner to sew things all up."

"Suppose the one that took two to the head before flying away home was the one who had all that fun with the other one here?" J. W. said, pointing down at the corpse flat on the ground, its face directly nosed into the earth as though the dead man was trying to see into a thing directly interesting to him and had been surprised by having his head go all to pieces all of a sudden. "Look how you can't even see his face good."

"He looks like he couldn't care less what was coming up behind him. The other one, the one all messed up, he couldn't help but take notice of what all was happening to him. Let me put it this way. He was involved. Totally dedicated to dying and getting away from here as soon as they'd let him."

"I'll look around some more at these two corpses, one African American and the other one mixed Hispanic, maybe, where they're positioned and anything I can see that needs to be recorded about the scene, then you and your crew can haul them off to do what you do once you get stiffs inside your torture chamber."

"Torture's over with for these fellows, J. W.," Nova said. "It's easy from here on out."

"You got me there," J. W. said, thinking everything Nova had ever said to him seemed to say at least two things at once. Sometimes more. He never felt like he had her all figured out, even in a small way. Why did she cut her veal cutlets up the way she did, for example? Little bitty bites all laid out before she put the first one in her mouth. What did it mean when she had called him some cute name, like the label for somebody from the Bible? Was she saying he was like Paul or Judas or Peter? Was she being serious when she'd grab him by his shirt collar at times and say "Listen here, boy, I run you and don't you forget it" and then laugh like she was just having fun? When was she serious and when had she been just jerking him around the way you'd play with a dog until it growled at you?

Too much to figure out, he said inside, and then out loud, "I'm looking for signs of gang tats, and broken bones in the pinky fingers, and hair arrangements, and some more of that shit they do to identify who they be."

"You mean who they be running with," Nova said, lowering her voice as close to a growl as she could make it.

"I be meaning what kind of claimer they is," J. W. said back at her, and then looked off at the front door of the house set back from the murder scene in its yard. Lord, let her get these stiffs loaded up and out of here. I've had about all I can stand of seeing her, this hot morning in Memphis. I got to have some relief, and I won't be able to take a drink until I'm off-duty and sitting in the Owl Bar on Central Avenue a good long time from now.

It was just after nine o'clock about twelve hours later and removed from the crime scene at Cowden and Longmire before J. W. got the chance to see if the Owl Bar, some cop talk, and some measured help from alcohol beverages could help him get his mind cleared up before Tyrone Walker arrived to go with him for an official, unofficial visit to the home of a Bones claimer on Baby Street. If his mind wouldn't be totally cleared up, at least past dwelling on the time he'd spent with Nova Hebert before things all went to shit. Thing of it was, he told himself, as he sipped at his first beer and waited to see if somebody he could stand to talk with would appear, if you keep picking at a sore that damn thing will never heal up. Leave that scab alone, and just because something keeps on hurting doesn't mean you have to think about it or stick something in it to see if it's still there. Rise above it.

That's a crazy way to act, and he knew it, but Lord God it was hard not to see if things that bother and ache are still there. Is it good to know that "Yeah, still hurts when I poke at it" or "Hmm, not so bad now, is it something wrong with me?" Goddamn my head, he was telling himself, not able to count the times in that one day alone he'd picked at that sore spot.

"Shut up, shithead," he said out loud, slapping at his shirt pocket for the package of Pall Malls that no longer rested there.

"Damn, J. W.," a voice said. "Are you so far sunk and drunk you're talking to yourself out loud in the Owl? Don't you know you liable to get locked up in the charity nut ward for that kind of behavior?"

It was Ron Spurgeon, a beat cop J. W. had known since academy days when his particular class had undergone instructions about how to enforce the law right in Memphis and get away with doing that. Ron had never been able to achieve professional escape velocity on a permanent basis since then, at least not without always faltering somehow and being busted back to patrolman. His path had not been that of J. W.'s, which despite some clogging and blockages along the way, had landed him promotions and detective status. But not enough salary to stay ahead of inflation, he could always testify.

But Ron Spurgeon had not been convinced to drop out of the ranks because of his many starts and faults and hesitations, arguing always that in no field of endeavor he might try would he be able to gain instant fear and respect of a sort from the public at large just by putting on his uniform in the morning and strapping a side arm and cuffs and a taser to his belt. "Lookie here," he'd told inquiring minds that needed explanation for his becoming the oldest rookie patrolman in the history of the Memphis Central Station, "when I walk out into the public, people look at me like they're afraid I've learned about something wrong they've done, and they shy away from me. And everybody in the world has done some kind of shit, big or little. Stole something, cheated somehow, come up beside some significant other's head, messed with an underage female or male. You name it. And they're afraid that I know or will find out about it and come down on them like the wrath of God. Tell me that's not a sweet feeling, and you'll be uttering a lie through your teeth."

"Yeah, but the low pay," somebody might offer in response. "Ain't you sick of that?"

"Fuck the low pay," Ron Spurgeon would say. "As a law officer, I got power. And that is as sweet as tupelo honey."

"Oh, hey, Ron," J. W. said in the Owl. "You caught me. Yeah, I talk to myself more and more these days. When there ain't nobody else around who'll listen to me bitch, I got to handle that job all by myself."

"You know, J. W.," Ron Spurgeon said, pulling up one of the worn-out kitchen chairs popular at the Owl up to the table, "you don't have to do that no more. I have found out a way to make it easy on myself when I get to feeling lonesome."

"I don't feel lonesome. Never. I feel just fine wherever I am and whatever time of day it is. I always feel tip-top."

"Bullshit," Ron said, chortling as he leaned in toward J. W. "Time was I used that same argument. Said the same damn thing you just mouthed at me. And you know what? I was lying to myself until I felt sick at my stomach listening to the excuses I'd make up. And the justifications."

"Justifications? What does that mean, Ron? You sound like some kind of a damn lawyer."

"I'm not going to argue with you, but I will tell what I run across that ended up saving me from having to find reasons not to put a gun in my mouth and take the patrolman's guaranteed way out of misery."

"I ain't miserable," J. W. said, "but do tell me what you're talking about. Maybe it'll help pass the time until my partner gets here for us to go do a little business."

"Okay, then. Listen to this and learn. Have you ever heard of the label We 2? I don't mean that two to be spelled out like the number or like T O O, now. Let me write it down for you."

"You don't need to do that. I know what you're saying. The word We and the numeral 2. Right?"

"You ain't as dumb as you look, J. W. Some of that elementary school learning rubbed off on you, for sure. Saying the word *numeral* like that."

"Not enough rubbed off. Go ahead."

His eyes shining as he leaned across the table and put his face as close to J. W.'s as seemed normal and not gay-acting, Ron Spurgeon began to speak, more animated than J. W. had ever seen him, drunk or sober. "It's kind of a dating service, see. Only it's high class, and it's local, not no "send your money to Dallas or Kansas City" bullshit. See, you pay a good chunk of cash to get into We 2, and so do the women you're going to be meeting. That keeps the cheapskates and the broke sons of bitches out of the mix, see, and it makes everybody in We 2 serious and there for the right reason."

"How much does it cost, then? How much is that good chunk of money you're talking about?"

"Three thousand American dollars," Ron said, lifting his head up so there could be no mistake about what he'd said. And repeated it.

"Shit," J. W. said. "You could buy a pretty decent used car for that. One that'd get you to work in the morning for a year or two, at least. Where'd you get three thousand bucks lying around loose?"

"Savings and borrowings, J. W., savings and borrowings," Ron said. "But let me tell you it's the best investment I ever made. See, you get pictures and bios of the women you can couple with, and you can meet them for lunch or drinks or maybe at a musical event or something, and y'all can size each other up."

"And you've met some you could stand? And what do you mean by couple with?"

"Stand, hell," Ron said. "I met some prime women at We 2 with real class, let me tell you. The first time I went out for an introductory encounter—see, that's what they call it when the dance of flirtation begins—I met not only a dynamite lady, but her mother, too. That primary twosome, like they call such double encounters, means you don't meet nobody that's just operating solo like in a lone fighter's stance. That's what they call somebody flying solo."

"All these labels, like encounter and dance of flirtation and what's that other one? The fighter pilot? All that's in the brochures I reckon they send you for that three thousand dollars? Is that right?"

"Well, yeah, J. W. I know you're trying to make it sound like it's cheap or low class or something. A rip-off or scam or something like that. I can tell you it ain't. It has changed my life for the good."

"It's local? Here in Memphis?"

"Yes, anything wrong with that? Memphis and the Mid-South is full of some of the best snatch in the country."

"Do they call it snatch on that brochure, Ron? Looks like that might scare off a nice girl, much less her mother. Talking about her snatch. Or her pussy or something else worse."

"No, that's just me speaking the language you'd understand, J. W. All is aboveboard and nice at We 2. And I'll tell you what. I ended up liking the mom more than I did the daughter. She was more at ease with a man of my experience."

"Did you do them both at the same time?" J. W. asked. "Or did you date one and then the other?"

"I'm not going to talk to you about We 2 any more right now,

J. W. You just trying to nasty it up. But let me give you a brochure. I got a bunch of them. And in case you're wondering, everybody in Memphis is got to make enough money to get by. There ain't a damn thing wrong with trying to make a profit. It's hard to do, and you got to hustle. I don't hold that fee against them. And that's three thousand bucks I'll never regret spending on coupling up."

"Well, for me, I guess I'll just keep on dating Old Lady Thumb and her four daughters for a while, Ron," J. W. said. "But let me have that brochure. I always like to know who's making money in Memphis and where they're located."

"Sure, take this one," Ron said. "I got to go. I've got an evening introductory encounter I've got to make in about thirty minutes."

"Be sure you take your nightstick with you," J. W. said. "Show her what a big one you got."

When Tyrone Walker arrived at J. W.'s table in the Owl a beer and a half later, J. W. had read through the We 2 brochure, noted that there was no physical office location listed beside the website and the telephone number, and told himself he'd check with one of the young IT freaks at Central Station about how he could find out where communications with We 2 actually went. Maybe it'd be worth knowing where that money-making enterprise was roosted in the Bluff City. It wasn't literal homicide, We 2, but shit. Dating can always lead to homicide. It happens all the time.

"Sergeant Walker," he said as Tyrone pulled up a chair and joined him at his table. "It's just about midnight, and I figured you'd be wandering the streets lonely and depressed. Let me tell you how to get out from underneath all that burden."

"How many beers have you drunk, Sergeant Ragsdale?" Tyrone asked. "Not so many you can't carry out your duties of making night calls in the city, I hope."

"Have I ever failed to get off the line at the snap of the ball?"

"I have seen you get run over at the snap of the ball, but never run off the field, J. W. No. But that talk about me wandering the streets lonely and depressed has put me in a quandary. I'm forced to ask what the fuck you talking about. To be technical about it."

"I'm just looking into another announcement about some enterprising group trying to make money in Memphis, Tyrone. That's all. Take a look at this brochure and tell me who you think might be the target for this venture? It ain't Homicide's business to look into such stuff, but maybe it'd work out to be if we're lucky."

"Unlucky. We don't need any more business, Lord knows. Let's don't look for stiffs. But let me see what you got there."

After reading through the We 2 materials, Tyrone looked up at J. W. and reached out to lay his hand on J. W.'s free arm, the one not attached to the beer bottle. "Partner," he said. "I hate to see you having to come up with three thousand dollars just to get a date. Tell you what, I can arrange for a We 2 moment for you a lot cheaper than this. It'll take me about fifteen minutes to do it, since the drive downtown could be delayed by roadwork, but I promise you it won't cost you more than ten bucks and a double shot of penicillin. And you won't have to say you love her."

"I can get We 2 satisfaction for even less than that, and it won't require no drug injections, either. I can keep my money to myself, the one I really love. And I won't have to talk and whine about my childhood and what's my favorite song and shit like that at first, neither."

"Let's go," Tyrone said, after laughing a little. "I think our ace informant might be home by now. While we drive over there to Baby Street, you can tell me who you think might be running this little love connection deal you've found out about."

J. W. had been allowed to take one of the police vehicle fleet cars home with him at the end of the day, since he and Tyrone would be on official business for a couple of hours that night and wouldn't be off-duty until late. J. W. lost the coin flip, and so had to drive and Tyrone settled into the passenger seat as well as his long legs would let him. They left the Owl Bar and headed north toward a section of Memphis which had blossomed after the end of WWII into a complex of VA homes for returning men who'd served their country at hazard of life and limb. For that service they could purchase a home a little above the quality and design of comparable-sized manufactured housing up on blocks, and if things broke right for them in the postwar economy the veterans and their families could work their way up the ladder to better and bigger and more individualized living units later.

As many did that, the economy went into the usual doldrums, and age withered the inhabitants of the homes and the homes themselves, so by the time J. W. Ragsdale and Tyrone Walker drove deep into the one-time bounty granted to Memphis vets of the Big One, the houses and neighborhoods they passed on their way to Baby Street looked like scenes from a Mid-Eastern war zone. Rutted and unmaintained streets and what once were yards, scraps of garbage, permanently parked vehicles which had lost the ability and will to move, downed fences, chained pit bull dogs, starved cats, broken-down bicycles and discarded parts from unidentifiable manufactured objects, prospering weeds, dead and dying trees and bushes and eroded yards, with here and there random excavations which seemed never to have been successful in revealing what the searchers sought. No water was to be found, no tomatoes or collard greens or squash or okra grew in the dry scratchings made in mother earth.

"Home, sweet home," Tyrone said. "Brings a lump to my throat."

"You never had to live like this," J. W. said. "You showed me the house you grew up in over yonder close to the zoo. Nice neighborhood, too. It wasn't anything like any of this bombed-out looking shit."

"Not literally, no," Tyrone said. "But a man can dream, can't he? He can imagine what it might have been like for him if just a small thing or two might or might not have happened. I coulda been raised rough and deprived and discontent. I coulda been as needy as the next man."

"Well, yeah, if you wanted to invent shit inside your own head. But why do that? Ain't things bad enough without having to imagine they could have been worse? Ain't you discontent enough as it is?"

"Yes, J. W. That's true enough, but I'm telling you all that to prepare you for what's happened to Lo Lo Tedrick. I don't want you to be shocked at what you'll find."

"Lo Lo has had a change take place?" J. W. said. "Last time I saw him he was as crazy and sorry as he ever was. Living day to day like a hog in slop, and driving a big car and cramming his head full of crank, staying with two big old fat girls who never pick a damn thing up off the floor, much less cook nothing. Everything just staying where it falls in Lo Lo Tedrick's dream palace. All that trash looked just like what it must be like inside the boy's head."

"All that's true or it was true, I should say. Lo Lo has undergone a conversion experience, J. W., and you're going to be knocked over by what you see."

"Lo Lo found Jesus?" J. W. said, swerving the police car to avoid a hole in the road big enough to swallow a yearling calf. "I can't believe that."

"I thought you would ask if he found Mohammed, J.W, and reveal your prejudice about all things Islamic, but I was wrong about that snap judgment. Lo Lo has found Jesus. Or at least the Son of God writ contemporary. Imagine if you can Jesus in a modern suit, a nice tie, and shined shoes. Close shave, too, and sporting a fresh haircut."

"Don't tell me that Lo Lo Tedrick has gone straight now. If he has, he ain't going to know shit about what's going on with the Bones Family and the Latin Lords and the Beale Street Boppers and you name it. Why are we even going to see him? If he's all morally cleaned up and straight and all that, what kind of informant is he going to be now? Last thing we need's a reformed gangbanger."

"He's working both sides against the middle, J. W." Tyrone said. "Think back to your Bible-reading days. Remember Sunday school? What about vacation Bible school? Didn't you ever pay attention to the kind of people Jesus ran with? I can tell you this. It wasn't nice folks. No, it was thieves and murderers and whores and people full of evil spirits. Even the literal hogs he ran into had devils and demons in them. They ran off cliffs just eat up with bad spirits inside."

"You know you're sort of right, Tyrone. Why, if that old man that taught us Sunday school, his name was Collins, I remember, if he'd told us what you just preached I could have paid attention. It would have been interesting. Whores, murderers, evil spirits, hogs possessed by demons. It sounds just like Memphis today, if you put it that way. Stuff going on."

"That's what I'm saying about Lo Lo. He is burrowing into goodness from within evil itself, J. W. Getting into evil so as to get over it. Finding good where nobody would ordinarily look. Finding the good pecan inside the rotten hull. Then biting into it. Lo Lo is our man now, and he'll heave his guts about all he knows, and if we can cut through some of the sanctimony, we can still learn stuff from that Bones claimer."

"Damn, let's do it," J. W. said. "And look, it's like magic. Cut to the next scene and the new location. Yonder's his crib where he be staying. Let's go talk to that apostle. See will he preach it on out about what he may know about this counterfeit money deal. And Tyrone, let me admit something to you."

"What might that be, my son?"

"If you ever get tired of studying homicide in the city, you can always preach."

"Who says I don't already do that?" Tyrone said. "Don't you feel conviction rising in you like a big gust of swamp gas? Ain't I bringing light to you in darkness?"

"Yes, Lord, yes. I feel it. Praise him. Now let's see what we get out of the new Jesus here on Baby Street."

The first thing J. W. noticed about the little house on Baby Street, which he and Tyrone had visited several times over the last few years, was a difference in the front yard. When he drove up and parked the car directly across the street from Lo Lo Tedrick's place, he could see that there was now open space that could be realistically called a yard. Not that there was a mowed area of planted grass and ornamental bushes or flower beds, but at least anybody looking at where Lo Lo stayed would be able to see some absences. No plastic bags stuck to bushes and tree limbs, no discarded car parts or tumped-over bags of garbage, no signs of abandoned lumber and assorted other items not subject to decay and now rusting away at home.

"Don't tell me Lo Lo has done hired himself a lawn service," J. W. said. "For sure he hasn't started paying folks to pick up castoffs out of the yard and to cut the grass and trim the poison ivy on what's left of them trees."

"Look at the house itself, J.W," Tyrone said. "What do you see different from the last time you laid eyes on 15 Baby Street? Look hard now and don't let past memory deceive you."

"Well, let me think. There's a porch light on. Not busted out like all the rest of them around this area of prime real estate. And lookie there, there's metal numbers up there by the door. Am I just seeing things?"

"Come on up here with me, and see what happens when I punch that button by the door. Don't be afraid, J. W. Lo Lo Tedrick hasn't set a trap for cops here on Baby Street. He does not think that far ahead."

What happened when J. W. pressed the doorbell was the sound of ringing inside the house, and in less than a minute, the door opened and a clear-eyed young man in pajamas invited the Memphis detectives from Homicide to come inside.

There was furniture and curtains on the windows, there was a reproduction painting of Jesus Christ at the center of the main wall of the living room, his eyes luminous and as loving as the original artist could make them, and there was a general sense of order everywhere evident.

"Lo Lo, what the hell?" J. W. said. "Have you had yourself a brain transplant or something? This place looks like a human being lives here instead of a Bones Family claimer."

"Praise Jesus," Lo Lo said. "I am a Bones claimer still, but I'm a Jesus Christ claimer first. I aim to exalt the lord and bring his word and work to my brothers."

"Lo Lo," J. W. said. "Them murdering little bastards will kill you for talking like that. You better watch your ass."

"What Sergeant Ragsdale means," Tyrone said in the comforting tone of a preacher near the end of his sermon, the scary part over and the sweet invitational portion now to be used in closing the deal, "is that he's joyful, though surprised, at your presence in a new life. His language is rough, but it is intended to be supportive. Am I not correct, Sergeant Ragsdale?"

"You are, Sergeant Walker. All I want to say is praise Jesus and his works, and welcome to the righteous community of the Lord, Lo Lo."

"Thank you, Sergeant. I am a new man in Christ, and I say goodbye to my sinful past. Can I get you gentlemen a cup of coffee?"

"No, thank you. Caffeine disagrees with me. Let me ask you something, though. What can you tell us about what you been hearing about Bones getting involved somehow in fake money?"

"We've been told by some liquor-store and convenience-store owners that a good number more than usual of fake money's been showing up. And it seems to be coming from claimers out of more than one family, Lo Lo," Tyrone Walker said. "Turning up in Memphis, Midtown, and even Downtown some, too. That's what Sergeant Ragsdale's talking about. Not a lot, but it's big bills. You know, hundreds with good old Benjamin Franklin's picture on them."

"I done heard that name before, all right," Lo Lo Tedrick said, "But I ain't never seen but a few bills like that. I do hear things, though, I got to say."

"What do you hear?"

"Something about some Latin Lords flashing some money around, you know, like the kind you're talking about. But that's all. I don't know nothing else. I been trying to put all that business behind me."

"You do know what Jesus did to the money changers in the temple, don't you?" J. W. said, cutting his eye toward his partner. "I expect you read your Bible these days, Lo Lo."

"I do read it, and I'm trying to read it all from the very beginning. I done finished the Old Testament, but I ain't all the way through the New Testament yet. I'm ashamed of myself for that, but it's hard going, some of it. I love it, though. Praise the Lord."

"That's a big bite to take, son," J. W. said. "The whole word of the Lord. Just keep going, though, and you'll get there. Let me tell you about Jesus and what he did to the money changers. Here it is. He saw what they were doing, how they were cheating. He turned over their table just full of bad money, you know, and he chased them from the temple. That's what we want to do with these counterfeiters and their bad money. Bad money leads to death of the spirit and death of the body, too. We got to turn them tables over. Cleanse the market place. Turn it toward the good."

"Jesus was a mighty warrior for good," Lo Lo said, reaching out his hand toward the homicide detective. "I promise you I will keep my ears and eyes ready to see what I can tell you about these money changers in Memphis. I want to be a soldier in the army of the Lord."

"Praise him," J. W. said. "The Lord God of Hosts."

Later, about to get behind the wheel of the police car parked on Baby Street, J. W. was stopped by Tyrone. "Let me drive, J. W.," he said. "You done enough tonight to earn the right to doze off on the way back to Midtown. Lord have mercy, I almost had to leave Lo Lo's little cleaned-up house when you started talking about Jesus and the money changers in the temple. I had to bite inside my mouth not to start cackling like a school girl. Where'd you get all that stuff?"

"Fool," J. W. said. "I was raised up as a Southern Baptist in the Blue Water community of North Mississippi. They just pounded that shit into us twice every Sabbath at Sunday school and training union and then at prayer meeting on Wednesday. And in vacation Bible school every fucking summer. All I got to do is put my mind to sleep and that mess will come bubbling up on its own."

"Here I've been going along thinking you weren't formally educated, and I apologize for that," Tyrone said, laughing as he pulled the car away and headed back toward Midtown. "And here you are using the Bible to get a Bones claimer to try to squeal on his kind. Talking about the temple and the money changers. Lord. Lord. Lord."

"Praise him," J. W. said. "And damn Satan and all his works. What you can do for me now is this, Tyrone. Get me to a liquor store. I know a place where you can buy a pint out of the back door at any hour of the day or night."

"It's called Joe's Gins," Tyrone said. "I know it and let's go get you settled in with another spirit."

"It used to be Joe's Gins. You're part right, like usual. Now it's gone upscale. It's called Joe's Wines these days."

"I will not quarrel with a man like you, a man who knows spirits of all description. I know when I'm in debt."

"I'm looking right now for a temple to cleanse," J. W. said, "and I need the right agent for the job. The body itself is a temple, you know. Let's go serve it."

Willis Sutcliff and Tommy Beechum were paying close attention to the construction work being done on what the official Mixed Martial Arts organization always called the octagon.

Early in the evolution of the enterprise, involving two men or two women meeting toe to toe, no holds barred, including the choke hold, to slam away at each other until one fell unable to defend the body any longer, the lightly padded platform on which they met had been called the ring or the arena or the squared circle

That label would do no longer; it would not suggest the crucial differences between boxing and wrestling as opposed to mixed martial arts action, and it would smack much too strongly of rules and referees and coddling and a sissy concern for measures of safety. No, that would never do, and thus the cage with eight sides and no way out would be called the octagon, and that's where the mayhem would be confined, allowed, and encouraged.

"So what do you think, Willis?" Tommy said. "Does it look right to you? Does it look like the promise of serious bloodletting and possibilities of pain and concussions and kicks in the head?"

"I like the way you put it," Willis Sutcliff said, "and I got to agree it looks like it ought to stir up the lust for blood flying and bodies falling in the folks we trying to appeal to. I like it."

"Of course it's a small venue now, just starting out," Tommy said. "But if enough of that bunch of bloodthirsty bastards start showing up, we can move it to a bigger and better place."

"Let's hope so, and I don't see why it wouldn't work. When we can get enough exposure with the right kind of people fighting each other in this little old gym, it ought to start drawing big enough crowds to let us start making some real money."

"Yeah, that is the thing," Beechum said in a pensive tone, "and we got to start off with a bang, I do believe."

"Too bad that we can't get a headliner from the MMA outfit, at least to get it lifted off with a surprise or two."

"Those MMA fuckers are going to hold their thing close to the vest, and they've got every fighter signed to a contract that a Philadelphia lawyer couldn't break. Of course, I don't blame them for that. I'd do the same damn thing if I was the first hog to have my head in the trough. Why not? Shit, it's dog-eat-dog in this world."

"That's truer than death in Memphis especially," Willis said. "There ain't nobody holds on tighter to what he's got than a citizen of the Bluff City. When it comes to money, he is a worked-up snapping turtle. He will take your hand off, up to the elbow."

"And he will not let go until it thunders," Tommy said. "And he ain't listening hard to see if any rumbling's coming. But look at it this way, I do believe our first featured match here in Memphis Martial Arts and Mayhem Maniacs is going to get some damn good attention."

"Newspapers ain't what they used to be, though. So that's a consideration."

"Naw, it's all this online shit that rules now, but we are working that ourselves, and there ain't never been the kind of cultural match-up done before in this game to compare to what we're doing. Hell, you've seen her, Willis. Am I lying? Tell the truth."

"I admit I have seen her, and I ain't never going to forget that first time. And it does not get old, partner. She's the real reason we were able to persuade Simmons, D'Arcy, and Wilde to put up that cash advance for us. She looks like money."

"Yeah, her, she's the reason we got financing so far, but don't forget what a good presentation we'll always make. It wouldn't alone have made Amazon dot com reach for its back pocket, but still."

"I know, I know, but Lord God when she came into that office, not saying a word but just looking at us like we was nothing but a bunch of high school boys with hard-ons, that sealed the deal for that loan. Remember how she sat down. So goddamn cool the temperature felt like it dropped ten degrees. She don't have to show nothing."

"True enough, and I think I have figured a way to get around the fact that she won't be able to speak enough English to convince anybody she's American, much less a beautiful Southern debutant from a real family with connections going back to when the USA got founded," Tommy said.

"And don't forget, we're selling her as a Kappa Kappa Gamma graduate of Vanderbilt and a woman who refused to let them put her up for the Miss Tennessee and Miss America pageants. She just wasn't interested in that low-class display. She's from money, see, big money and class, and she's doing mixed martial arts for cultural and political reasons. Not for money. That's how you called it, wasn't it?"

"It was, it was, and anybody that sees her will believe that shit just as soon as she comes into view."

"But she can't talk English worth a damn, though. And that is the hard sell for us. She could memorize some things we give her to say in English, but it'd sound funny, and that ain't going to persuade a soul that she's what we're selling her as. And the Lord knows it's her story that matters."

"I know that," Tommy said. "All this shit is stories first and foremost. And I know when she steps onto that octagon, we got to be able to seal the deal. She'll be battling that fat redneck gal who never had nothing but bad luck and rickets and tapeworms her whole damn life. Knocked up at age fifteen by her uncle. Didn't get past the eighth grade. We are setting up a cultural war, and we'll be selling Miss Maureen Langlois as representative of all that's classy, and right, and good, and admirable in the South, especially in Memphis, and finally in the good old USA itself. Her blood is pure, her past and her upbringing's been perfect, she's beautiful and she represents all these saps in the auditorium hold to be worthy. She's got something they all want, and they can't even name what that is. But they feel it in their guts, and their uteruses, and their balls, and they both hate it and love it. She makes them feel all excited and trashy at the same time. If that ain't Memphis temperature, I don't know what it is."

"And up against her is a representative of what they are," said Willis, "that fat, ugly, tattooed, snuff-dipping, meth-sucking bitch in bad cheap clothes. She's what they hate in themselves and they are torn to pieces about what they see happening in front of them in that octagon. They hate it and despise it, and they lust for it and they need it like they need water to drink."

"Son," Tommy Beechum said, "you said it better than anybody else in the world could. Or at least in Memphis. Yes, Lord, let this symbolic battle of values go down to the bloody end."

"One question, and it's the big one," Willis said. "What's going to happen when Olga says something?"

"First, don't call her by that name Olga ever again, and second she ain't never going to say nothing in public to a soul."

"Huh? What?"

"Here's what's happened. This is our story. Learn to tell it. Maureen Langlois has gone silent to make a political statement. She will not speak again until peace and harmony prevails in Memphis and through the South. Even the whole damn country if we can sell that notion. At any rate, she ain't saying a word. She will holler out now at the end of every victory she stacks up against these symbols of ugly and hopelessness and bad origins, the ones she kicks in the ass in the octagon. But she ain't saying a thing in English or in no other language."

"Here's an idea," Willis said in an excited voice, "we sell folks a chance to talk to her on her cell phone when she ain't fighting, see. Have contests and shit to do that. We hire some good old Memphis girl with a great sexy voice to play like she's Maureen on the phone. She'll take every call that's prepaid and not longer than a minute, minute and a half. How does that strike you?"

"Like an ax in the middle of my forehead, Willis. That's a wonderful idea. It works in terms of PR, and it makes money doing it. Hot fucking damn. Where'd you get that from? It's so damn good it makes my pecker hurt."

"Great," Willis said, and then, "Where is she from anyway, Olga? What language does she talk in? Just curious. I really don't give a shit."

"I think it's Prague, over there in the Czech Republic or something like that. What do they talk? Praguish language?"

"She sounds like Trump's wife, that young good-looking one. That's why I asked," Willis said.

“They all sound about the same, these foreign women, except for the ones from China and Japan and like that. The yellow ones all jabber stuff that goes ‘yang, yang,’ something like that. But you know what we got to do?”

“What’s that? Tell me, partner.”

“We got our Kappa Kappa Gamma beauty who ain’t going to say a word, but now we got to find us a fat, ugly, tattooed bitch for her to beat on. One that jabbers all the damn time. Of course, that one does get to beat on Maureen Langlois some, too, but never in the face.”

“Or on her tits, not there where the money lives,” Willis said, causing both men to laugh and look back toward the octagon where work was continuing and things were coming along nicely. God, it felt good to be involved in a start-up venture that had in it the promise of money so close and fresh-printed you could smell it.

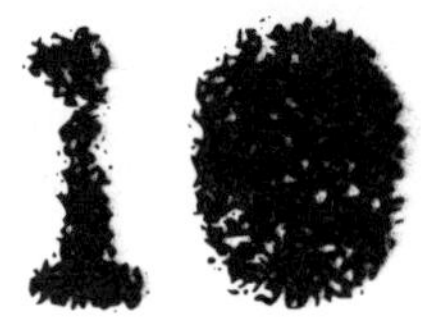

Debriefing time with Major Dalbey, nine the next morning after the late-night visit to Lo Lo Tedrick's, the new Man in Christ on Baby Street. J. W. had arrived at the Midtown station a few minutes before Tyrone Walker had got there, a fact that J. W. noticed as soon as he heard his partner passing the time of day with one of the clerks, maybe Valene. Keeping his head down as though fascinated by some paperwork on the desk before him, he didn't look up at Tyrone until he was spoken to.

"You beat me here, J. W.," Tyrone said. "Even after your late-night date with that half-pint of Heaven Hill. Had trouble sleeping, did you?"

"Good morning, Detective Walker," J. W. said. "I slept soundly enough. Just up bright and early this morning and rearing to get to my data logs, so I raced on in to get that paper done before we report to the Major. I figured you might be delayed a bit. Family responsibilities. Workouts at the gym. You know. Morning prayers, shit like that."

"Don't make me laugh this early in the day, J. W. I want to be grumpy for as long as I can manage, and I know we both got to put on a show for the boss. I'm saving up my smiles and friendly greetings for that. Don't want to waste them on you, sleepy as you got to be."

“Okay, Tyrone, but cutting to the chase now as the young folks say, what do you think we ought to be saying to the Major about our visit to Lo Lo? Think we ought to get into all that Jesus jumping the boy is onto now? Or just say the usual stuff. You know, him saying Bones Family ain’t in this shit. I ain’t Bones anyway. I don’t know nothing about nothing. I’m scared that Sergeant Walker is going to brutalize my poor little self. Yadda yadda yadda.”

“I’ll follow your lead, J. W. When it comes to reporting on new relationships with the Savior and all that kind of thing, you know the language better than I do.”

“I think we ought to soft-pedal that whole business,” J. W. said. “For two reasons I can think of right now, and maybe you’ll come up with some, too. Here’s my first one. If we start talking about making a breakthrough of a new and major kind, it’s going to make Dalbey start to expect more than we going to be able to deliver on short notice.”

“You are touching a nerve, all right. He wants so bad to make promises to Ovetta Birchard that he’ll jump on any news he thinks can help him. Then when nothing happens or takes a long time to start bearing fruit, he’ll blame us for it. Say we didn’t deliver on a pledge.”

“Do not encourage the boss too much,” J. W. said. “I learned that a long time ago when I was nothing but a yearling boy picking cotton for Old Man Dolph Collins in Panola County. I knew I could pick over a hundred pounds a day in high cotton, and I told him that, bragging you know, and the old bastard always rode my ass from then on not only to do a hundred pounds but more. You could not satisfy the old miser, and it was never no relief from expectations from then on. I wrote a check I had to cash with my blood and sweat.”

“Speak softly, but carry a big stick,” Tyrone said. “That’s what you’re saying.”

“Naw, I’m saying don’t never let any boss know what you can really do. He’ll expect you to do just that. That’s in the boss’s blood. He’ll always see it as the bottom line, not the top goal. Don’t promise something with your mouth you have to fulfill with your ass.”

“That sounds like a principle you could live by in a marriage,” Tyrone said. “I’m going to remember that adage.”

“I wouldn’t try that on Marvelle if I was you. She’s a hell of a lot smarter than you.”

“You think I don’t know that? Huh. But what you’re saying about our visit with Lo Lo Tedrick is to downplay it. Tell the Major what Lo Lo gave up about the Bones Family, which wasn't shit, come to think about it, and then go from there."

"You got it, partner," J. W. said. "Let's say we can pick no more than seventy-five pounds of cotton a day and then surprise him when the nut cutting starts."

That's what the two of them did when they huddled with Major Dalbey, and he was ready to listen and not to carp about progress for a change, which surprised both J. W. and Tyrone enough that they took a quick look at each other to see if they were hearing right. Then the Major spoke in a tone they didn't often hear from him.

"Gentlemen," he said, "I've got something to tell you about that double homicide on Cowden the other night. Remember you reported that the Bones claimer was all cut up like he'd been worked on for a while before they took him out. And the Hispanic male was a lot more of just a direct killing?"

"Yeah," J. W. said. "Nova said. I mean the crime scene lab personnel, the ME, she said it was two nines to the back of the head of the Latin Lords claimer and that was what put the lights out for him."

Neither Tyrone nor Major Dalbey made a sign of recognition when J. W. had made the slip and mentioned Nova's name instead of her job title, and he knew by that omission that they knew all about him and her and the breakup and therefore it was general knowledge. Goddamn a gossiping bunch of cops to hell. Did they have to know everything about personal lives? Couldn't they display some of their usual brute ignorance and lack of interest about crime and criminals in Memphis when they start showing what they knew about who was doing who or had done who or couldn't do who no more? Why be all hot to know the personal lives of their fellow professionals? Oh, hell, J. W. thought. Who cares? Who gives a damn? Then admitting to himself: I'm the one. I do.

"Yeah, that's the deal. But what the ME found out when she was breaking them corpses down was a rolled-up wad of hundred-dollar bills in the rectum of the Lords claimer, one Roberto Rivera, street name of Chuco."

"He was keeping his money in his ass?" J. W. said, glad to change the subject his mind had been forced to fasten on by the mention of Nova's name. "So, what's the deal?"

"It wasn't your real United States currency, I bet you," Tyrone said. "It was counterfeit, some of that stuff we've been hearing about."

"It was not the real deal, Sergeant," Major Dalbey said. "You got it. It's been looked at by some technician from the Secret Service, and he says it's a damn fine job that's been done making them hundreds, but it wasn't by the US government."

"What does that tell us, though?" J. W. said. "We suspected the Lords claimers had their nasty little hands in on this counterfeit deal, but any idea where we go with it from here?"

"I know one thing," Tyrone said. "It was nasty all right, from where it'd been put away for safe keeping."

All three snickered a little at that, and then Major Dalbey spoke up. "The idea of where we go from here, J. W., that's the business of you and your partner. That's where we go from here, since you asked the question. Consider yourself assigned to that job, along with the killing part of it."

"I'll start up the first step, then," Tyrone said. "The Lords claimer, Chuco, had put aside this roll of hundreds for his own benefit. He thought it was real, too, or he wouldn't have been keeping it where he did."

"There was more of it than that one roll of fake bills, too," J. W. said. "See, this dead Lords boy had access to more of it, but somebody else had given him and the Bones boy a bigger chunk of it than that one little bit. They were supposed to do something with it, see."

"Otherwise, he'd have had no reason to squirrel some away. He was taking from a lot bigger source," Tyrone said. "That big supply didn't belong to him. He was entrusted with it, and he was sneaking some of those counterfeit hundreds for his own use."

"He thought the whole damn shooting match was real," J. W. said. "Else why take just some of it."

"I purely love to see you two homicide detectives working together to try to figure something out like this," Major Dalbey said. "That's the main reason we don't fire you this very day or them days we've kept you on so far. But don't get your hopes up to keep staying around forever, Sergeants. I got my eye on you all the time. Heh, heh."

"Don't keep promising us you'll fire us, Major," J. W. said. "Don't get our hopes all up like that. That'd be called mental cruelty in a divorce proceeding."

"That subject for adjudication you'd know about, all right, J. W.," Major Dalbey said. "But now that you two have figured out where the money in the rectum came from and why it got there, you got to get to the next step. What'll that be, gentlemen?"

"We got to go off somewhere and think," J. W. said. "At least I do. Maybe Sergeant Walker's done figured out what comes next, and he'll tell me. We'll get back to you as soon as we can."

"Where is the rest of that money, the part not yet inserted anally," Tyrone said. "That is the question. Where did that waste money come from before it ended up where it did?"

"Yeah," J. W. said. "Like it or not, we got to start sniffing around."

Lunch for the partners of D'Arcy, Simmons, and Wilde was at the Waverly Grill, a quite decent venue for a business meeting for those wanting to get away from Downtown Memphis in the middle of an ordinary workweek. There was no real view from the Waverly there in Germantown, such as the one of the Mississippi River flowing past Downtown on its way to New Orleans and the Gulf of Mexico, but who needs to look through plate glass in midsummer in the Bluff City? At noon, it was hot, the air was stiflingly still, and the daylight hours were only half gone. Besides that, the three partners had to be back in the firm offices in a couple of hours, at work looking prosperous and intent and unaffected by drink in the middle of day. So it was worth the drive east to the grove of trees in which the Waverly Grill served lunch.

"Two things I think we need to chew over," said Mason Wilde, "apart, of course, from our interview with the gal running that We 2 setup, Monica Moore."

"Before you remind us of the things we need to talk about, Mason," Dallas Simmons said, "can you bring me up to snuff on what this lady wants to hit us with. Not in any detail, of course, but enough that I won't sit here looking like an ignoramus when discussion begins."

"Certainly, Dallas. I momentarily forgot you were out of town when she came to see me and Walker. Sorry to have let that slip my mind. But here's the deal. She runs this thing called We 2, a species of dating service, as I understand it, and she's looking to expand. She needs, she says, what I'd call a sizeable sum to augment expansion of this enterprise. Over a million."

“Sounds like a stone loss to me, up front and right now,” Dallas Simmons said. “How is there money in that business, and haven’t these nationwide hook-up societies already overwhelmed the market for these lonely bastards that can’t hustle up a piece of ass on their own?”

“Your words are so politically correct,” Walker D’Arcy said, taking a sip from his iced tea. “Why don’t you just say what you mean, Dallas?”

All three chuckled at that, and Dallas spoke again. “And hey, Mason, don’t call this professional woman ‘gal’ like you just did. She’ll have you up on charges in a New York minute for that kind of speech offence.”

“Ain’t it the fucking truth?” Walker D’Arcy said. “You have to check every syllable these days before you let words fly. Whatever happened to freedom of speech in this country?”

“That horse has left the paddock, gentlemen,” Mason Wilde said. “And I assure you I’d never call one of the bitches ‘bitch’ to her face. I have been to law school, as I remember. And I’ve learned where I can speak honestly and where I can’t. But all joking aside, this lady, Monica Moore, makes a persuasive argument. And she has the vetted numbers to prove her assertions about the draw this We 2 has already earned. She makes a good case for wanting to borrow enough funds to take it to the next level. She seems on to something, and the two of us think you ought to listen to her pitch, Dallas. See what you think.”

“Behold,” Walker D’Arcy said, “don’t look now, but I see her being directed by one of the flunkies in our direction. Stand up, gents, and act like you were raised right. There she blows.”

“Lord,” said Dallas Simmons, his napkin slipping in his hand far enough for him to have to jerk awkwardly to catch it. “Don’t say anything else about blowing things once she gets here. I sure bet she doesn’t have to pay for dates on We 2.”

After the greetings, the introductions, and the invitation to be seated, all four of the Waverly Grill lunch party looked brightly about, one to the other, remarked upon the seasonably warm weather, spoke to the waiter hovering to approach, and addressed themselves to their iced tea.

“Would you prefer a glass of wine, Miss Moore?” Dallas asked. “The selection here is passable, if you’d like to sample it.”

“No, thank you, Mr. Simmons,” Monica Moore said. “I seldom drink anything stronger than iced tea before the real cocktail hour comes.”

"It doesn't come fast enough at times," Mason Wilde said, and all laughingly agreed.

"I know how much you have upon your plates, and I don't mean lunch," Monica Moore said. "So I'd like to cut to the chase if you don't object."

No one did, and she began speaking, clearly, with wonderful eye contact and group inclusion, and by the time the lunch salads had arrived, Monica Moore had moved from a brief history of the origin of and need for such an enterprise as We 2 to a dissection of the true heart of her song. How much each person paid to use the services of the organization, how revenues had increased, how the market was huge in Memphis and the Mid-South for a serious matching-up sexual service, and how We 2 provided just what was deeply desired and needed and yearning for fulfillment.

"Let's be honest," she said. "Beauty in the female and in the male of this region of America is valued above all other aspects of character, professional and educational and cultural background and makeup of identity. Whatever you want to consider. Now I'm not talking about the East Coast or the Midwest or the West or even California, for God's sake. In all the other regions of our nation, people will argue that beauty is only skin-deep. Now excuse my language, but I say to that one phrase: Bull crap. And if it were after five in the afternoon and I had had my medicinal treat for the day, I'd use even stronger Anglo-Saxon terms.

"Let me put it this way. We are marketing at We 2 to people who find themselves not up to the standards for sexual success prevalent in Memphis and the Mid-South. They want some action, too, and they want it from someone more sexually attractive than they are. And let me tell you, gentlemen, I have shown with We 2 that they will pay good money up front for a chance for connection with a better example of the species than they are themselves. At this point, I require from prospects a starting fee of three thousand American dollars for that chance. And they will and do lay their money down. If they get what they're looking for, they're delighted and they tell all their friends and fellow sufferers from unattractiveness what a great success they've had. If they don't succeed in getting that higher-quality sexual contact they lust for, they'll lie about it and say they did. And they'll try again, and they'll lay more money down. Why?

Because they know their limitations in terms of sexual attractiveness, and they've spent their whole lives not getting the good stuff. And they know there's a damn good reason for it. They live in hope, though. That's the nature of the beast in the southern region of this great country of ours. We refuse to recognize or accept final defeat. We always try again, because we are not a rational people. We do not learn from experience. We do not give up easily, and we will continue to give money to folks who tell us they can help us get well and truly laid."

"So you want a loan," Mason Wilde said. "You have made money and you want to make more."

"I will get a loan, and I will make more money. And I will continue myself to get well-laid, both literally and symbolically. If I don't get the loan I need to expand my enterprise, to grow and develop We 2 from you, I'll get it somewhere else. Not to offend, understand. How do I know I'll continue to succeed? Just look at me and ask yourself that question. You know the answer."

"How much do you need to borrow?" Dallas Simmons said. "And what are you doing tonight?"

All four at the Waverly Grill table laughed at that, and Walker D'Arcy asked for a day to examine the supporting papers Monica Moore had furnished. All three members of the legal and investment firm of D'Arcy, Simmons, and Wilde declared themselves delighted, instructed, and eager to speak further with the CEO of We 2.

"Gentlemen," Monica Moore said. "Thank you for your attention, and to answer Mr. Simmons question, I do have plans for tonight. I'm sure he and all of you have the same aim and will achieve the success a true Southerner desires above all things. To be well and truly satisfied."

After the CEO of We 2 had departed the table and left to make her way outside the Waverly, Dallas Simmons shook his head as though in deep mourning. "Damn, I'd love to make a thorough examination of her assets. From stem to stern."

"You mean a complete opening of Monica Moore's portfolio," Walker D'Arcy said. "A peep into her personal holdings."

After all three had a good lunchtime Memphis chuckle at their wit, not a guffaw since no alcohol had gone down the hatch as fuel, Mason Wilde spoke up. "There's been many a man who wanted to land on that shore that just receded from us. And many a ship's been wrecked on those rocks."

"But what about a life preserver?" Walker D'Arcy said. "Is there no help for a shipwrecked survivor? No way for him to get off his rocks?"

"Fun's fun," Mason Wilde said. "But we got to talk about Fallen Timbers estate now. Stop thinking about theoretical pussy, if you can."

"I'll try," Dallas Simmons said, "but I've never been able to succeed at that yet."

Sonny Johnson had asked for a sit-down with Deangelo Dixon in a daylight hour, and that set off a faint tinkle of an alarm bell in itself. Any time one of the lieutenants wanted to talk outside of the Don't Look Up Bar in South Memphis or maybe from the back seat of one of Deangelo's cars, the boss was ready to give a listen. So Deangelo had okayed the request as soon as it got to him, sending word to Sonny Johnson a.k.a. Jump Steady by way of Stopecia Grubbs and telling her to let Jump Steady know he could come to the general's house right at two in the afternoon.

"I don't like to talk to Jump Steady face to face, General," Stopecia said. "He look real hard and funny at me every time I say anything to him."

"Even if you say it's from the general?" Deangelo said, not able to keep a completely straight face. "What do you think? Is he figuring on cutting in on my dance with my baby?"

"Naw, he never acted like that or said nothing that wasn't nice, you know. But he will let his eyes stay on me longer than I want them to."

"Baby, you have got to realize that no matter if he is talking to the boss's main woman, Jump Steady still got a set of balls on him. And them balls are saying lookie here, lookie here. What a prime cut of meat this is talking at me. But that's just his balls talking. That ain't him. If it ever was, everything would go bad for that lieutenant. Jump Steady knows that."

"I like it when you call me prime meat," Stopecia said. "It make me feel funny inside. Squirmy like."

"Girl, don't get started now," Deangelo said. "I know what you doing. I see what you up to. Lay off now. Just go get me a bottle of Diet Coke instead, so I can cool down. I got work to do."

It never hurt to cheer the troops up, Deangelo had learned over the years of his time as head dog of the Bones Family and cooperator with the Latin Lords, and he considered the hitch he'd thrown in Uncle Sam's army to be the best training he could ever have gotten for his life after serving his time in Afghanistan. He had hated the idea of service and dreaded it before it started up, but looking back he had realized the advantage it had given him in taking over the Bones Family when he came back to Memphis.

He was so grateful to what that time in the military had taught him about organizing a bunch of badass dummies who had no idea how to get things done, much less how to look further ahead than the next snort or dose or injection of feel-good and lie-down and sleep-it-off, so grateful that he called himself the general from that point on, named the ones who worked for him captains and lieutenants and sergeants and privates and grunts. And he got so damn much more done than the rest of the gang families in Memphis through organization and ranking. He could see ahead, and he had learned how to spot when shit was coming down and who was bringing it and who was sound in his troops and who needed killing. Organization, he told himself every night before he dozed off. Organization and the will to take out any and everybody who needs it. Hell, if he had to, he'd told himself and a few trusted officers in the Bones Family, he'd off his own mother if the bitch was trying to fool him. Much less Latin Lords or Beale Street Boppers.

So when Jump Steady showed exactly at two in the afternoon, Deangelo congratulated himself again for the discipline he instilled and inspired in his troops. "Jump," he said, "how's it going, Lieutenant? Welcome to headquarters, and thanks for letting me know you got something on your mind, something I need to be informed about. You do, don't you? You're not here to ask about something you can handle by yourself, are you? Remember the slogan. Be independent when you can, but don't forget the chain of command."

"No sir, General," Jump Steady said. "This is some shit that's strange, and I can't figure it out. I figured you'd want to know about it."

"Cut to the chase. Report, officer."

"Me and a couple of the Bones boys had a little thing with some Lord claimers the other night. That's what it come out of, the thing I can't figure out. I thought I could at first, but I can't. It done got complex on my ass."

"Complex? Where you hear somebody say complex?"

"On TV. You know wherever you go, the white heads on TV talking about complex this and complex that. I know what the word means, but I don't get no good reason to use it, you know. Most of the time."

"Report," Deangelo said. "Get it out to me."

"We found two boxes in that Dodge them claimers run into the curb and messed up. In one of them was a whole stack of Franklins. Brand new, every one of them."

"You already told me about that, just like you supposed to. And you give them hundreds, too. Most of them anyway. I expect y'all kept some out, and I see nothing wrong with that. Shit, y'all worked for it, and you deserved a good hard taste of it. So?"

"That other box in there, not the one with the Franklins, but the other one, it had inside of it something like the real-looking paper for bills, looked just like the paper money is printed on, yo. But it was big sheets of it, not the size of bills, you understand. But it looked like and felt like new bills do when you hold them and rub your finger on it. Like magic. Smooth and full of something other paper ain't got. Them big sheets had them little pieces of what looked like thread through all of them, but there was one thing that wasn't there."

"What?" Deangelo said, sitting up a little straighter in his chair.

"It wasn't no writing on them, and no picture of that old white dude on them. Everything was just white. I mean it was blank, you know. Like computer paper that hadn't been printed on yet."

"You got some with you?"

"Yessir, General," Jump Steady said, reaching into a side pocket. "Here's a piece I tore off of one of them big sheets. It's blank paper for money to go on, you see."

"No such thing as a blank hundred," Deangelo said, studying the torn sheet and rubbing it between his fingers and thumb. "If it ain't processed all the way, it ain't worth shit. Just paper. It ain't real yet, see. Why would they do that?"

"Don't ask me. I don't know nothing about no fake money."

"Where'd they say they taking this shit? Didn't you tell me the claimer said they was supposed to take it to Mississippi? Where? What town? Did he tell you the name of the man they's taking it to? They said it was a white man, didn't you tell me that before?"

"Yessir, I did."

"What was his name? Didn't y'all get the Lords claimer to tell you that much?"

"Well, you know, my driver had got all wound up, you understand, because the claimer had got in his face and said some shit, real disrespectful, so he kindly had to shut him up."

"He did him? Shut him up for good?"

"Yessir, General. I sure do wish he hadn't done that. But he felt like the claimer disrespected him, you understand."

"Goddamn it," Deangelo said. "Some kind of counterfeit deal going on, and we don't know a thing about it, and all that's because a private can't use his fucking head."

"I told him. I said shit. I said goddamn. I said why'd you do that. He couldn't answer me that. Naw, uh-uh."

"Well, we got to think for a while about this. We got to figure it out. It's something big going on with this fake shit that looks just like real money, and we got to get in on it. Let's start looking for some more Lords claimers. I can still reach out to Boom Boom, even if his boy got put down. He owes us. Shit, he owes me. But I don't think this first bunch was flying solo. They're dumb as a raghead in Afghanistan, I know that, but there's got to be somebody else that knows something that'll help us out."

"Yeah, whose money is all that?" said Jump Steady. "What they up to with making this stuff?"

"Don't think too hard about it. You'll hurt yourself."

"It do make my head ache a little bit, all right."

"When you don't use a muscle, the fucker will get weak on you," Deangelo said. "Don't talk to nobody else until I get a chance to counsel with Boom Boom. He going to be all mad and pissed off at first, but I can get him to come around. When he stop thinking about a dead claimer and get his mind all full of big bills, he'll be all right."

"Don't worry, though. Aint nobody of them Lords boys left to talk. It's the other claimer that's dead," Jump Steady said, taking a chance to express an opinion that the general hadn't already put out in front of him. But he knew it was just fine and all right when Deangelo reached out a hand for him to touch and cracked a smile when doing it.

The thing of it was, James Forrest Howell-Reed knew, having learned and tested the accuracy of that knowledge time and time again over the years, his mother might look frail—and she was that, physically, and always had been as long as he'd been conscious of her presence in his life—but May Margaret Howell-Reed of Fallen Timbers Plantation was as tough as a hard night in the drunk tank in Downtown Memphis. Not Midtown, now, where the drunk and/or doped-up youths of privilege, male and female and in-between, would generally find themselves sobering up after a night of carousing in some family home in Central Gardens or a private apartment in a high rise, not there. Instead, in Downtown Memphis, the last refuge of a scoundrel as his father called it before being permanently called away to that realm from which no man returns, Downtown Memphis in the tank with the white and black and yellow and brown trash caught short and locked up tight.

Jesus, James Forrest told himself, don't let your mind wander to one of those memorable nights of captivity, waiting for Lanny Bookwright to show up with a spring in his step, legal writs in his hand, and cash money, untraceable and brand new, on his person. "Jimmy, Jimmy," he would say, "we meet again, in a time of regret and some sorrow, and your father asked me to remember him to you. I hope this time there's no young lady injured in a car crash, is there? Tell me no, please, and I'll kiss you on the lips from where have been so many dreams uttered in darkness only to wither and die in the daylight."

At times, James Forrest had attempted to match wits and boring displays of such with Lanny Bookwright, but he knew he was always at a disadvantage. Number one, he was usually worn out, fucked out, head-poundingly hungover when in the process of being rescued by legal counsel, and number two, why waste time letting Lanny slide into him the subtle blades of a resentful man who'd had to work his own way up in the social jungle of Memphis with nothing but intelligence, average instincts, and good luck at crucial points to allow him to rise? Lanny therefore rose. James Forrest stayed stuck in the same spot.

That in large measure was all behind him now, though, James Forrest knew and swore to keep in his rearview mirror as a reminder, but still there always was Mother. Father had died at a decent age after a fully achieved accumulation of wealth additional to what was already his at birth. Mother had brought her fair portion along with her to the union, not as comfortably and verifiably measured as the Howell money of her husband, but she had all the rest of the requirements for a suitable wife high up the pole in Memphis. She was beautiful, or had been at one point. She had graduated from a Southern women's college when that sign of achievement had meant something. She had never had to work to earn a single dollar in trade or commerce, and she knew how to entertain, attend events, appreciate works of art, talk vapidly to others of her breed, keep her mouth shut and her mind open, and she had produced two children.

There had been the rub, of course. Aha, thought James Forrest to himself as he sat in a chair in his bedroom, a comfortable one positioned by the window so as to allow a splendid view in late spring evenings of woods, water, and plantings well maintained. Aha, indeed. One child was himself, still around, still looking about him at what might be seized, picked up for examination, and cast aside when boredom set in, boredom almost terminal in effect.

The other child was the girl. First born, three years older than James, beautiful of course, long legs and chiseled features, a horse woman, a tennis player who might have excelled nationally had she wished to expend the effort, sought after by men and boys, loved by girls who came to hate her when they became women, and then suddenly one night after a small side party during the spring fling season, gone. Vanished. Evaporated. No more. Where was she? Where did she go? Would she ever return? Had she been kidnapped? If so, why no ransom demands? Had she been abducted, raped, tortured, killed? Had she vanished voluntarily? Had she changed her name, moved north, married a Yankee? Was she living sans wedlock in a dreary tract house, perhaps with a Negro? What could she have found lacking in her life in Memphis and in the circles surrounding Fallen Timbers and its social environs? What else was there to be desired? Had her disappointing younger brother had something to do with the vanishing of Constance Helen Howell-Reed? Hadn't he always been in the shadow of Constance? Didn't he resent her and all she stood for? No answers to any of these questions ever came, and now it had been just under twenty years ago that she had vanished.

So his father was dead, his sister was a part of never-never, and his mother showed no signs of diminishment, except for wrinkles about her eyes, a crepe-like consistency of skin about the backs of her hands, and a relatively new interest in learning bits and pieces about boring facets of nature and humankind, and of pointing these new bits of knowledge out to others, whether they wanted to hear them or not. She would watch documentaries. She would dip lightly into novels supposedly historical. She would take a drink. And another. She would stare into the middle distance as though seeing things no one else could.

May Margaret Howell-Reed had always seemed immune to the ills and accidents that befell people she had partnered with, dined with, endured cocktail parties with, accompanied to spas in the northern states and in Europe, particularly in France and in England in the county of Devon. She had attended fundraisers for worthy causes, attended book club meetings and discussed good books and a few boring ones. None of her people had ever broken laws, dietary or civil. They might cop a feel of some sort now and then, but always quietly. They drove safely and were driven safely, visited children and grandchildren, dabbled in political discussions but only on noncontroversial topics, and they systematically died, one by one by one, and sometimes in clutches, though they all enjoyed good genes and expert medical care. But they died. Decently and reasonably and systematically. They did what they had always done. The expected thing. They ended up dead.

Looking into the depths of his gin and tonic, light on the serious ingredient and heavy on lime, James Forrest spoke softly but firmly to the self inside himself, the only one he could to a degree trust. Mother, he told himself, won't die. She will not. She is as determined as a terrapin to outlive any and every person connected to her by blood. She had found a way to remove her daughter from the scene, as soon as Constance Helen had begun coming into herself, separate not only in youth and vigor and beauty, but also in mind, and his mother had executed the task with dispatch, no real tears or regret or lasting memories after all was said and done. She was as efficient and cold-blooded about the deed as a Gulf shrimper deveining his catch. Wherever Constance was now, it wasn't in Shelby County.

Did James Forrest miss his older sister? Did he cherish memories from childhood of birthdays and happy displays of tumbling and fumbling and playing one game and another? Did he remember looking up as a child at the sister older and wiser than himself while wondering why she always knew more than he did? Did he envy her ease in the world? Did he resent her ability to fool grown-ups about matters large and small and bend them all to her will? Every time he saw her, every time.

But no and no and no to all these reminders of his junior station. What he really resented about Constance Helen was that she had gotten away from Fallen Timbers. She had vanished completely. Was it her own act of will? Or did Mother find a way to remove her? Was her absence accomplished by will, by accident, by death? No matter. She was gone. Little Brother James Forrest was still little brother at home, no matter his age or his acts of defiance or his refusal to be the Howell-Reed he was destined by genes and fate to be. He was yet here. And so was Mother, a bit withered and missing a step or two now and then, physical and mental. But she was here, too, along with her son. She would not decently die on her own, and something had to be done about that. James Russell told himself, sitting by the window in the fading light of sunset, that one of two ways would suffice, but it was best always to go about any task with all guns firing from the first sign of engagement. Make no single choice. Combine, always combine.

Either May Margaret Howell-Reed would cease to be herself by a diminishment and a vanishing of the mind which was at the center of what it took to be her, or she could slip utterly away as a self in the world of eating and drinking and sleeping and voiding waste. But why,

James Forrest asked himself, choose one means of exit over another? Let them be simultaneous. Let the body die, finally and for good. But in the meantime, let the mind wither away while the body knows what is taking place. Both means ended up at the same exit sign, but oh the joys of seeing her realize the inevitable arrival of loss and extinction. Bliss it would be to see it take place. Oh, the sweet diminishment.

"Thank you, gin," James Forrest said aloud. "That will be sufficient for the non." What did non mean, he wondered. No matter. Whatever a thing means, word or deed, so long as it suffices for the need, no understanding of essence is needed. What is essential is what works. It needs no explanation.

The crowd was large enough not to be embarrassing to Willis Sutcliff as he showed Dallas Simmons to the specially reserved seats just at the proper height to be able to see clearly into the octagon and yet close enough to see the sweat pop and the blood fly up from well-placed punches from lightly padded fists. Too close to the octagon and you had to crane your neck to look up at the action. Too far back, and you couldn't get a fair view of the damage being done to eye sockets and throats and lips by well-aimed kicks, punches, and backhands.

"These here seats might look to you at first, Mr. Simmons, like they aren't near enough to the action to see well enough what's going on. I don't know if you ever attended any ordinary boxing or wrestling matches before, but if you did, you'd want a different kind of view from what this mixed martial arts contest is. Things in the old ring style of combat are a lot different from what the octagon provides. See what I'm saying?"

"Yeah, I understand," Dallas Simmons said. "Each sport has its own nature, and requires its peculiar venue for viewing the contest. I get it. It's like the difference in soccer and American football fields."

He hasn't seen anything like this, though, Willis Sutcliff considered as he gestured to a young black man hovering in close attendance to where he and the man with access to serious funding were finding their seats. Dallas Simmons is no doubt expecting scenes of close clenches between two boxers with a referee pulling them apart every thirty seconds and looking into their eyes for concussions, and he's wondering how in the world do me and Tommy Beechum expect to make any real money from just changing the shape of the ring from a square to an octagon and letting two fellows punch at each other with padded gloves. And kick at each other, too. And tackle each other, and hold them and hit while they're down. And choke them until they pass out or tap out.

As the young black man, well-uniformed, polite and attentive, took a drink order from one of the bosses of this new enterprise, Willis Sutcliff sensed a quietness in his companion that made him a tad uncomfortable. He had wanted to have both Dallas Simmons and one other of the three principals of D'Arcy, Simmons, and Wilde come with him to take a look at the venture they were being asked to upfront funds in support of, but the two other big dogs had begged off, saying they were interested, certainly, but that Mr. Simmons was the sports connoisseur. They would ask him for his input and things could, and perhaps would, proceed from there. We'll depend on Dallas's eagle eye, and we'll see, we'll see. Don't think you're the only supplicant working on us. Everybody in Memphis is dying to borrow money. And water it and watch it grow.

When they said that, Willis and Tommy had smiled brightly, said they understood completely, and remarked inwardly to that self that fears and cowers, "Shit, fuck, piss, goddamn it." But here sitting beside Willis Sutcliff was Dallas Simmons of that particular bunch of money men in Memphis, those VCs as they'd be termed on the east and west coasts, and the game was afoot. Venture capitalists, Jesus Christ on crutches. Give me some dollars right now, Mr. VC.

"Now, Mr. Simmons," Willis said, "I've so arranged it that the first match you'll see is between two ladies. Women, really, of course, and these days I'm afraid to call any female a name that might make them uncomfortable or believe I'm seeing them to be of a lesser light than men. Call a woman a lady now and the least thing she might do is sue the living hell out of you."

"I do know what you mean," Dallas Simmons said. "All of us in our group have undergone sensitivity training and have put the entire staff through that. All our people. Several times. I could tell you stories about lawsuits and proceedings and quiet and noisy situations right here in Memphis that have cost small fortunes. And all because some male person, let's don't call him a man since that label's a bit dicey, made a remark in all innocence that set off some woman to thinking she'd been abused or made to feel inferior or uncomfortable or some sort of shit. And she sued, and she settled, and she was granted a ton of money by some overeducated judge. Political correctness is killing our nation."

"Don't tell me, Mr. Simmons," said Willis, feeling a surge of optimism lifting him, "I know exactly what you mean. You can't even tell a woman she looks good any more, much less show interest in her as a female. And meantime she's dressed to the nines with short skirts and tight blouses that you can see her bra straps through, if she's wearing one, and makeup all over her face. Lips all painted up and glossed and pooching out. Eyes highlighted. God a mighty. Just daring you to ask for it."

"So will you be selling alcoholic drinks at these MMA events?" Dallas Simmons asked, moving adroitly away from Sutcliff's comment. Who might overhear? "Were you able to get permission for that? I just wonder, you know, how much alcohol sales can boost revenue."

"Sir, that is in progress, and we expect to be able to sell mixed drinks as well as malt beverages. Right now we can't sell anything this early on. You know the slows of bureaucracy and the long arm of government. But just for today, I've been able to get permission to serve you and me drinks of any description. See, our meeting today is defined as private through a special dispensation. We are not technically part of a public gathering. We are financially interested parties not presently committed to the status of involved participants."

"Good. I don't want more than one or two this time of day, anyway, but how in the world can you attend a sporting event and not take a drink? Is this still America or not?"

"Bingo!" Willis said. "I agree, and I wonder what country we're living in these days. The boy'll be here in a minute with what we ordered. Let me tell you about this first match. Better yet, I'll let you watch it uninstructed, as it were, and then we can dissect what we're trying to do that's a new wrinkle for what we'll call Memphis-style women's Mixed Martial Arts. I am convinced it's a brand-new take on an old tried-and-true method of getting at what ladies can and will do to each other in a combat match-up."

By the time the well-dressed and immaculately trained waiter had delivered the drinks to Mr. Dallas Simmons and Mr. Willis Sutcliff, a low murmur in the crowd had begun to grow, following the start-up of a penetratingly loud burst of music from speakers strategically placed around the hall. "We're going to get those sound effects adjusted, and all the little wrinkles ironed out by the time of the official opening of Memphis MMA," Willis Sutcliff said directly into the ear of Dallas Simmons. "A lot of fine tuning is still yet to be done. In all kinds of ways."

The first song ripping through the banks of speakers was some sort of rap stuff that neither Willis nor Tommy Beechum had had any reason to recognize when they were told it was the real deal early on. But it was torturingly discordant enough to convince it was the real squeal. It was loud enough to burst small blood vessels in the ears of anyone over the age of forty-five. It was a series of shouts, groans as of agony, and imprecations of threats of violence and mayhem coming like a freight train, all squalled with a vengeance. As a crescendo was reached, a spotlight hit a runway stretching back toward a deep side area of the auditorium down from which a clump of women came marching. There was no sign of unity in step or gesture, but clearly attention to a figure in the midst of the tangle was being drawn by a separate white-hot beam. At that, a good portion of the crowd in the old outmoded basketball arena of the departed Memphis Grizzlies erupted in screams, whistles, and foot stomps.

"She's the badass," Willis Sutcliff said to Dallas Simmons, leaning close enough to smell the VC's cologne but not convinced that he could be heard over the crowd din. "That first one coming."

"What's her name?" Simmons said.

"I don't know her real name, but that she's from Arkansas, see, and she wanted to be announced always as Woo, Pig, Sooey. You know, that dumb stuff they holler at football games over there across the river. See, she wanted it to be that, but the people watching her fight have shortened it. Now she's just called Pig Sooey."

"Damn," Dallas Simmons said, chuckling, Willis could tell, though nothing less than a full guffaw could have been heard over the greeting the crowd was making to Pig Sooey. "She answers to that, huh? I bet it took some persuasion to get her to go along with that label."

"We did some opinion testing, all right, to see if that's too strong, but she didn't care what we might come up with. Her real name is Precious Bitty, named by her dumb old mama, I guess, and I forget her surname she goes by. She offered to be called the Destroyer from Hell, but that didn't cut it we finally convinced her. Ain't interesting enough. Lacks zippiness, everybody in the group thought. No imagination in that."

"I bet her last name is something like Cameron or Snopes or Cotton," Dallas Simmons said, his voice almost drowned out completely by the roar of the crowd as Pig Sooey neared the group of referees and judges and inspectors standing by the steps up to the gate opening into the octagon. Willis smiled broadly, white-toothing it, to let the Venture Capitalist know he appreciated the wit of the statement he could barely make out hearing.

Pig Sooey passed near enough to where Willis and Dallas were seated for them to get a good close look at the results of the costuming that had taken place in the locker room before the heavy villainess was deemed ready to show herself to the world. You had to give them credit, Willis considered as he took in what he could see of Pig Sooey's getup and overall look, they have done a hell of a job making this bitch look nasty, mean, pissed-off, ignorant, unbathed, and itching to kick the living shit out of the opponent she'd be facing up on that eight-sided platform enclosed in a ten-foot-high fence of woven and indestructible mesh.

"That octagon in place of the old-fashioned boxing and wrestling ring with the three rope enclosure setup, and that I will argue to any man, is a stroke of genius," Willis said to Dallas Simmons. "Just to look at that pen gives you the shivers, don't you think?"

Dallas didn't answer, staring instead at Pig Sooey like an explorer of the Amazon fascinated by a new tribe of natives heretofore undocumented by civilized man. "Look at all those piercings in her lips and eyebrows and chins," he said. "Couldn't her opponent injure her by grabbing some of that metalwork and jerking it? Damn, that seems dumb, even for a woman named Precious Bitty. That's what you said was her real name, right?"

"Yessir, I did tell what she said her birth name was. But all that metalwork, it's just clip-ons, and the bout inspector will make her pull all that crap off her face before she gets into the cage. She's just showing out how ignorant she's supposed to look. The only thing real she can't get off her body before the bout starts up, that's all those tats she's got all over her."

"God a mighty," Dallas Simmons said. "Pig Sooey does disgust, doesn't she? You got to give her that."

"Thank you, sir, we have worked hard at making her nasty, and she's joined right in, bless her fat old heart. When the costumers and body-shamers got through gussying her up, the crazy thing thanked them. It's probably the first time anybody ever laid a hand on her without meaning to hit her or to try to take advantage of her somehow. Feel of her, you know."

"You suppose she's ever been laid?" Dallas Simmons said, staring hard at the inspector working away at getting Pig Sooey ready to climb up and do battle. The octagon official had about finished, looking into her open mouth to make sure she wasn't carrying a concealed blade or some other instrument of battle therein, and when Pig Sooey spread her jaws wide open, the inspector jumped back as though he'd just seen a venomous reptile, holding his hand to his nose in an exaggerated demonstration of the reek he had been forced to endure. The crowd roared in disgust and delight. Pig Sooey popped her mouth as wide open as it would reach and uttered a high-pitched squall that cut through the din of the crowd like an ax through kindling.

"Oh, I expect there ain't a woman in Memphis that ain't had a sexual experience of some kind," Willis Sutcliff said. "Old and blind, ugly and stinking, armed and dangerous, paralyzed or bedridden, every female in the Bluff City has run upon somebody that was willing to seek sexual congress of some kind with her. Our typical male Memphian will not let any woman go unmounted if he runs upon one he can climb on."

"You are onto something, Willis," Dallas Simmons said. "I will not quarrel with, nor contest those sentiments. What a scene before us."

Willis spoke softly within himself after he'd heard what the Venture Capitalist had just said, saying thank God for Pig Sooey and the costumers who've made her the Memphis woman she appears to be as she waddles her way onto the platform of the octagon. Thank you for the nastiness you've made so evident and so attractive. Praise Jesus for providing the money-making ugliness before me.

"Who's her opponent?" Dallas Simmons was saying. "Another unfortunate female creature from the Delta backwoods?"

"Hear that music cranking up, Mr. Simmons?" Willis Sutcliff said. "I think it will speak volumes and begin to answer your question. We are talking contrast now, you understand, and that's what Memphis Mixed Martial Arts intends to provide in every match we make."

“Let the drama begin,” Dallas Simmons said. “I’m ready to watch these girls rumble. And what is that song that’s playing? It sounds like a melody instead of the shriek of an animal with its foot caught in a trap.”

“That musical contrast is conscious and as necessary to the life we’ve presenting as fresh air is to a man with weak lungs. See if you recognize it.”

“It’s an old one,” Dallas Simmons said. “Real old. Is it a song called ‘Isn’t She Lovely?’”

“If we were at that old TV show Name That Tune, you would have just won yourself a prize, Mr. Simmons,” Willis said. “That’s it, and here she comes, right in behind those two beautiful young blondes scattering rose petals before her. Lookie how regal.”

An excited, though controlled and deep voice came through the arena’s speakers. “Ladies and Gentleman, Memphians and Mississippians, Arkansans and all our visitors from afar, proceeding down the MMA aisle of battle comes Miss Maureen Langlois, tonight’s opponent for Pig Sooey from Delight, Arkansas. Let’s give her a big Memphis welcome, and I know I don’t have to beg you to be polite.”

“Well,” said Dallas Simmons, craning his neck to see past the forest of heads between him and the vision of loveliness coming down the aisle in a drift of rose petals, a musical tribute to beauty, and catcalls and whistles from the gapers of the scene. “She is good looking, all right, from what I can see from here.”

“Good looking?” Willis Sutcliff said. “If she ain’t good looking, I’ll kiss my own daddy full on the mouth. I can swear to that. Now, when Maureen Langlois gets to where the referee checks out the fighters before they get up on the octagon, I want to ask you to listen to what we’ve prepared and have been rehearsing for hours on end.”

“Will this killer blonde make an announcement or something? Will she say a few words to the crowd?”

“No, and like you know from the time you and Mr. Wilde and Mr. D’Arcy met Olga Butina there in your offices, she can’t speak English well enough to convince anybody she’s a Kappa who went to Vanderbilt and turned down being named Miss Tennessee for political reasons. She is from middle Europe, and we have to find ways to keep that a secret. What’s coming up next is the killer scene that sets everything up for the dummies in the audience. After this, they’ll both hate her and love her. And then the combat with Pig Sooey can start up."

"That's true what you just said about beholding a dynamite-looking woman, all right. You do love her and hate her for being that way so far above you. You have just got to tear that bitch down for looking like that."

"You got that right, Mr. Simmons. No doubt about that reading of reality, especially when good-looking women in Memphis are in the picture. Damn if they don't all need snaking down at least two-thirds of the time. Proud? Don't even talk about that to me. I don't need instruction about your typical Memphis bitch."

When the procession reached the stopping point before the steps up to the platform, the two maidens scattering rose petals acted together to pour the remainder of the blossoms at and on the feet of the referee. He jumped back as though surprised, and the crowd roared at the sight of the retired wrestler Dangerous Dan Mayfield of the old days in Memphis suddenly decorated in a floral tribute. He could still act, out of shape as he'd become, and he would ham it up.

"Nice touch," Dallas Simmons said to Willis.

"We think it refocuses the emphasis on beauty battling against ugliness," Willis said, unable to keep a bit of smugness out of his voice. That little bit of show business with the rose petals had been his idea.

"Ladies and Gentlemen, Memphis Mixed Martial Arts fans, Miss Maureen Langlois has asked me to make an announcement," the MC voice boomed over the sound system. "Please listen well, and respect what she wants you to hear. She has taken a vow of silence until decency and harmony among all peoples return to this nation and to our fair city of Memphis in particular. Though she loves to converse with her fellow citizens and to exchange ideas and concerns, she is devoted to silence until appreciable and lasting change takes place. Please understand she will do her speaking not in words but in deeds of kindness and in her battles in the octagon with those who are blind to injustice, fear, and hatred."

"Give me the mic," came a shriek from inside and on the floor of the octagon. It was Pig Sooey, forced to wait, and she was pissed. "I got something to say to Little Miss Priss of Vanderbilt."

A mic immediately placed in her hand, the opponent of Maureen Langlois began to yell words which tumbled over each other in a mishmash of sounds almost impossible to understand until the creature from the wilds of Arkansas began to chant one phrase over and over. That one could have been heard all the way to Union Avenue.

"Kick her ass, kick her ass, I will kick her ass, kick her ass."

Immediately, the lovely Kappa from Vanderbilt shrugged off her tastefully appointed robe, revealing an understated but obviously expensive costume the color of which shifted from one shade to another even as the viewer perceived it. Pin that shade down you could not do. It shifted just like real money always does. Shimmering, winking, fading, and blossoming like the sun. Rather than taking the steps up to the screen opening into the octagon, Maureen Langlois leapt onto the outside of the wall of mesh, scaled it in what seemed like one continuous motion, and dropped to the floor inside immediately in front of Pig Sooey.

Pig Sooey was in the process of ridding herself of the microphone, but by the time she had let it drop, Maureen Langlois had already slapped her face, seized a hank of Pig Sooey's hair and jerked her head down upon her lifted knee. At that, the crowd lost its mind, shrieking as though total war had broken out in Downtown Memphis and the first bombs were in the immediate business of falling, big, destructive, and loud.

"Damn, is that legal?" Dallas Simmons said. "Don't they have introductions first? Isn't the start-up more formal?"

"Yeah, they'll do all that intro stuff. That stunt there's planned to look just extemporaneous," Willis Sutcliff said. "See, Maureen Langlois is just so pissed off she can't restrain herself. But they'll break them up and get things going right in a minute or two."

The referee and handlers of the brawlers and the Memphis Mixed Martial Arts officials sorted things out quickly, but not before Pig Sooey had been knocked down, stepped on, and disrespected by the beautiful spokeswoman for decency and harmony. Introductions then took place, with an accomplished veteran of countless organized fisticuffs and scuffles at the mic, Tom Blagg, and the bell rang for the first official round of combat. Pig Sooey snarled and flung herself forward like she'd been hit with an electric cattle prod.

"What you're going to see now, Mr. Simmons," Willis said, "is a free-form brawl between a representative of beauty and style and the opposite of that in the shape of Pig Sooey."

"No one's going to really be harmed, right? It's like the old TV wrestling shows, all rehearsed and choreographed. Just a show. Fake blood and no broken bones or bruises."

"Well, not exactly. In fact, not at all," Willis said as the two women circled each other, throwing punches which did not yet connect and kicks which missed their target early on. "See, the ugly loser type, our girl Pig Sooey, has been instructed not to do a thing to actively hurt Maureen. Oh, she can land some blows now and then, maybe get to do a takedown and roll on the mat a little bit, grapple some, but that's it."

"I can see the attraction of rolling on the mat with that beauty queen," said Dallas, "all in the name of decency and harmony as our lady of Prague claims she represents, but what's going to keep Pig Sooey from busting her up? That bitch looks mad as hell. And determined to prove it."

"She more than likely is. That's what she represents to the crowd we're playing to. You know, the ones feeling all left out and despised and destitute and made fun of. Full of tattoos and resentment, overweight and undereducated. You know the scene. But you know what psychic disability we're really tapping into by the matchmaking we're doing? And it's really scientific, too, according to the computer modeling and social measuring we hired out to get this Austin, Texas, bunch to handle. You know, IT folks who know how to get dummies to vote right. Here it is, then. Here's the question we posed. Why will these losers come to see their representatives like old Pig Sooey get the crap beat out of them by good-looking folks with money and class? And how can we get the typical Mid-South fans to lay down their money to see the show?"

"That is a thing I've noticed in some business and legal matters I've handled over the years, certainly," Dallas Simmons said. "That self-loathing of the dispossessed and the never been possessed. It can be most useful if you handle it right. But tell me more. Oh, damn, look at that. Maureen just connected with a kick to the fat bitch's side. I bet that smarted."

"The reason why they want to see the good-looking classy folks kick hell out of the ones they're more like, these Pig Sooey types, is that this demographic has been trained to consider themselves losers and misfits condemned to hook up only with sex partners and pals just like themselves. Down deep, see, these researchers have proved that these plug-ugly losers with not two dimes to rub together have accepted the way they're defined by others. Okay, they say, whether they realize or not they're saying it, I am not worth shit, and I'll pay to watch somebody like me get the hell beat out of them by one of the fortunate few. It makes me feel a little less personally born fucked. It's not me getting hammered up there. Pardon my French."

"All that rings true, but what about a few of those plug uglies, I mean the ones that happen to have money and the ability to beautify themselves and improve their lot? Don't they run counter to what you're saying? They have lifted themselves, by hook or by crook, and they're better off now. Is a woman, or a man, doomed to social failure even if they've worked their way into money and position?"

"Mr. Simmons," Willis Sutcliff said, "ugly is not a surface feature. Ugly goes right down to the bone. It cannot be hidden. And we at Memphis Mixed Martial Arts conduct all our business on that premise. Ugly is as ugly does. Poverty possesses nothing, and never did and never will, whether it's of the pocketbook or spirit. Yes, I will admit the question what about Elvis in Memphis, what he did here. Elvis was the great exception. Granted. But this is Memphis, Tennessee, bless its crazy old heart, and we go with that. Beauty is beauty, and ugly is ugly, and poverty is a condition as permanent as death. So be it."

"Pig Sooey has got the beauty queen down now," Dallas Simmons said. "She's just hammering away at her face, it looks like."

"Watch the ref," Willis said. "And notice how Pig Sooey's missing connection with every one of them licks she looks like she's trying to land."

"You're right, Willis," Dallas Simmons said. "I stand corrected and content, and do you suppose we could get that boy to bring us another drink?"

"Look who's standing next to you," Willis said. "Two more, please. Chop chop."

"Yessir, it's coming," the tall young black man said and vanished.

"Knock her out, Maureen," Dallas Simmons said. "Show her who's boss."

"Don't let her up," Willis Sutcliff said. "Keep her down. Whip her ugly ass. Yay, Kappa Kappa Gamma."

13

It couldn't be delayed any longer, J. W. Ragsdale pondered as he sat at his desk a little after 8 a.m., studying the computer screen before him displaying a blank form which blinked over and over in perfect timing its invitation for entry of data. Do it, do it, do it, it seemed to say as always. As soon as he recorded the last bit of summary of last week's tasks completed and this week's recipe for the current docket to come, Major Dalbey would be expecting him to utter words of wisdom about a possible next step in the counterfeit money deal. What are you planning to do now? What about the direction his visit to Lo Lo Tedrick provided? Did that help? If not, what next? Who in Mississippi is of interest? Where in the old home state? Didn't he know that the Secret Service was expecting at least some promise of movement about the fake money in Memphis question? Report, goddamn it, and report good.

Uncle Sam's promise to stand behind the implied promise of payment on every one of his Federal Reserve Notes was being bent somehow by the makers of fake money, and blood had already been lost and shed fatally. But murder was a local crime, right here in Memphis, and that made the duly authorized keepers of the peace in the Bluff City responsible for looking into the whole matter of counterfeit currency.

And that meant the Memphis Police Department, and that narrowed down to the Central Station in whose jurisdiction these related crimes had been and were being committed. And that narrowed even further to Homicide Detectives J. W. Ragsdale and Tyrone Walker. "Stand up, stand up, for Jesus, you soldiers of the Cross," he murmured.

Naturally, he could think quietly inside his own head alone and to himself a whole litany of curse words and imprecations, but a request to God to damn something or someone meant nothing if not spoken aloud. And a simple quiet mouthing of such favors would do no good. "A cuss word not hollered out loud will not do a damn bit of good," J. W. said out loud and in the direction of Lurleen Allen doing something at the desk next to his. "It cannot prosper the man who utters it if he can't yell it out."

"Well, don't go testing that cry for help on me," Lurleen said. "You got to work out your own salvation, Sergeant Ragsdale. Don't burden me with that shit."

"You just proved what I said just then," J. W. said. "When you mentioned excrement. I stand confirmed and proven."

"You talking about standing, you better go stand in Major Dalbey's office. Tyrone's in there, and he told me that as soon as I saw you that they wanted you to come in there with them and to tell you that. So I have. Bye."

"I would cuss out loud right now, if it'd do me any good," J. W. said, rising from his desk and grabbing a tablet of yellow paper. "But nothing avails the just man in these fallen days."

The Major and Tyrone Walker were standing on the same side of a table in the office at which four chairs were kept available for conferences. They were used only lightly, since Major Dalbey liked to stride about the room when he was bothered by some issue under discussion, and that was usually the case when officers were reporting or enduring a harangue from the boss.

"Sergeant Ragsdale," Major Dalbey said, "come look at this, what me and Tyrone have been trying to figure out. Don't sit down first."

A big and bad sign, J. W. knew, for two reasons. The Major was using J. W.'s title as a form of address instead of his name alone, and he was not easing into a talk by an introductory spell of shooting the bull. Oh, Lord. What kind of a load is the boss fixing to shift to the working stiffs?

"Two things I want y'all to ponder on and find out a way to get some stuff put back into the box and took care of. Show J. W. that paper, or whatever you'd call it. A document, I guess."

"That or a threat, or a little psychological warfare," Tyrone said. "One or all of the above, plus some."

"Is it handwriting or print?" J. W. said. "Because I left my glasses out yonder on the desk. Just magnifying specs, now, you understand. I can get along without them. I have not yet had to get a prescription done for my eyesight. It's twenty-twenty, still."

"Yeah, and you ain't lost a step on the gridiron," Tyrone said. "You can still run a hundred yards in less than a minute."

"Go to hell, tailback," J. W. said. "Just don't try to run on my side of the field, unless you want your bell rung."

"Y'all got to get over this competitive sensitivity, gentleman," the Major said. "Face up to the fact that every high school football player in Memphis can outdo you now. Running backwards with his eyes closed."

"Okay, what is that thing you want me to read?" J. W. said, reaching for the sheet of paper the Major was holding. "Let me see."

The sheet of paper was fresh from a sheaf of high-quality bond, but what had been printed on it looked as though it had come from a handwritten source over a century old. The lettering itself reminded J. W. of a couple of old letters written by his great-grandfather during his time in the war between the states, back when Mississippi and the Ragsdales thought they didn't live in the United States. They had been mistaken, and well proven to them had been that fact. Damn good thing, too, J. W. mused as he looked down at the sheet in his hand. It'll be nice when everybody in Memphis and North Mississippi reaches that conclusion and recognizes reality and rejoins the Union in their hearts and minds.

The passage was short, and it began with a salutation to May Margaret Howell-Reed. There followed a few sentences, and then a farewell signing off by two initials and a last name.

"Read it out loud, J. W.," Major Dalbey said. "Show us how good you see."

"May Margaret, my great-great-granddaughter," J. W. began, "I take pen in hand to greet you fondly and to direct you about a matter which is of great concern to all our kin of the Forrest name. You must henceforth forsake Fallen Timbers Plantation, and you must divest yourself of all holdings financial, agricultural, and familial in that place. Discord and rebellion among our people, particularly of the African definition, require such action. I devoted my life on earth to the South when I served our people in Memphis, Shelby County, and the Confederacy. Now in eternity beyond with our Heavenly Father, I continue my service to all to whom I owe allegiance. You must do the same or perish physically and spiritually. Memorials to me as a representative of our family's contribution to Southern civilization are under siege. We must face attack with attack. With a grandfather's love, I remain your devoted kinsman, N. B. Forrest."

"Well, that's all she wrote," J. W. said, "and I read every word of it without glasses. So what's up with this bullshit supposed to be written by a dead man, and what you want me and Tyrone to do about it, Major?"

"I say the old lady wrote it herself, and is thus proved crazy," Major Dalbey said. "And she would have had to be seen to medically, if at all possible. If you know what I mean."

"Well, yeah. And what business is that of the Homicide Division?" J. W. said. "It's time for the nut doctor, isn't it?"

"Yes, and no," Tyrone said. "Should I inform Sergeant Ragsdale of the other complicating circumstances, Major? You're the boss."

"Yeah, you tell him. I don't want to be the one to have all the fun."

"There's a long story and a short story, J. W.," Tyrone said. "And we're going to have to hear both versions and more, over and over again before it's done. Short story is this. We just heard not thirty minutes ago that Miss May Margaret Howell-Reed picked up a historic family heirloom cavalry dragoon pistol about dawn this morning and tried to blow her head off with a large-caliber slug. Luckily, she flinched and missed her target. Just singed her hair a little and grazed her cheek."

"That old firearm worked still, huh?" J. W. said. "You can forever more trust armaments American made back in the day. Where is sonny boy James Forrest right now, by the way? Was he the one that did all the 911 stuff after she pulled trigger?"

"No, it was one of the retainers took on that task," Tyrone said. "And now Miss May Margaret is resting in the Methodist Hospital."

"Her nerves is shot," Major Dalbey said. "If not her brains."

"So what's the deal, then, at this point?" J. W. asked, looking first at Tyrone Walker and then the Major. "That son of hers is trying to drive her crazier than she usually is, of course, and it sounds like he's doing a damned good job of it. It's a matter of money, like always. Where is the little shit?"

"At the bedside of Mama Moneybags, of course," Tyrone said. "James Forrest Howell-Reed knows how to do and when to do it."

"So right now this whole thing is out of our hands at least, right? We ain't involved yet, are we, Major? At least until he tries again."

"J. W. no, you are not directly involved, but Sergeant Walker is, and that is at the order of the mayor of Memphis. See, Miss May Margaret Howell-Reed, as soon as they got her transported and tranquilized and tied down to the bed, she began saying she wanted to consult with the Memphis Police Department and with one officer in particular."

"Not me," J. W. said. "Please, Jesus."

"Hell no, not you. She asked to have that nice colored officer come see her, you know, to get a debriefing and instructions on how to handle written communications and commands from kinfolks that's been dead for over a hundred years. And hold her hand. What to do with the otherworldly is what she's interested in now."

"Colored officer?" J. W. said. "Did she actually say colored, just like that? Doesn't she know better this day and age that there's a new and improved way to refer to folks like Tyrone here?"

"That lady knows full well who she can trust to be caring and responsive and attentive, J. W.," Tyrone said. "But I'm sorry if it bothers you after Miss May Margaret met both of us that she did feel drawn not to a man of her own ethnic background but to a sensitive and thoughtful person whose color does not figure in her estimation."

"Don't get me wrong," J. W. said, after Major Dalbey got through laughing, "I am glad she prefers the way she does and has let me off the hook. Experienced as I am with dealing with crazy folks, I don't know what I'd say to a woman who gets notes from her old dead racist great-great-grand relative like that one I just read."

"Fun's fun, boys," the Major said. "But cut out all the hoorawing now. We have got to keep the mayor from listening any more than he already does to Ovetta Birchard, and if that involves Tyrone going to the hospital to hold hands with that rich old crazy lady and listen to her rave on, that's just wonderful. It is fine. It is a good thing. Don't you forget it."

"Yes, Lord, she couldn't have picked a more qualified man," J. W. said, then turning toward Tyrone, stuck out his hand for a solidarity shake. Tyrone refused to accept that, withdrawing as though J. W. had offered him a water moccasin to pet.

"I'll do it," Tyrone said, "since that kind of weirdness is a large part of what I'm paid to take part in, but the sooner I can find good grounds to arrest that son for trying to drive his old mama nuttier than she already is, the better."

"We can't get him on attempted murder yet," the Major said. "But I got to talk to somebody on the legal side to see how and how far and how fast we can proceed. Why doesn't the little shit do something actionable on the face of it?"

"James Forrest has devoted his life to putting a good spin on crimes and misdemeanors," J. W. said. "He's like that damned fried rat he tried to feed his mama. Something nasty all gussied up to look nice. With sprigs of green salad-looking stuff sprinkled all around the plate."

"All right now, that's the deal with Tyrone, and I don't know how long it's going to take him to get things sorted out," the Major said. "But it's so much money involved we just have to wait it out until we see some way to get a purchase on how to proceed. The mayor is all a-tremble. In the meantime, Sergeant Ragsdale, do you think you have enough information together to know how to take another step or two on this counterfeit money business? Sources and names and gut feelings and shit. Is what you learned from your Bones Family informants something that might help us get off the dime about this fake money thing?"

"I'm glad you asked that, Major. After our little talk with Lo Lo Tedrick and what he said about some big dog connection in North Mississippi, I got to thinking about who I might know in Panola County that most of the time has some sense about what was going on, not only on the low level but at the player level. I need to get down there and talk to some people that might help our thinking about this deal."

"Yeah, hell, do it. At least that'll give me something to say to that Secret Service guy who's all hot about rumblings they been hearing. We don't work for them, but the way they act you'd think we the ones supposed to be putting sugar in the ice tea. Do you know anybody in the Delta that might at least provide me with enough to keep these Washington, DC folks entertained? At least get some of their attention diverted away from Memphis and down toward Mississippi. Give me at least a head fake, J. W."

"I do," J. W. said, stretching the truth as much as he could without snapping it in half right in front of Major Dalbey. "I got connections with white and with black and every other color of folks there who keep an ear to the ground. Any time a shitload of money, real or fake, raises its head in the Delta, people's ears perk right up, and they will talk about it. What you don't have yourself you cannot stop talking about. Let me have one or two conversations with a couple of more Bones claimers here in Memphis first, and see if I can scare up enough information to get me started when I hit Panola County."

"All right, get on that, and let me know when and where and what, so I can say some stuff to that Secret Service bunch and get them off our backs for a while. But, J. W., remember now. What you're supposed to do is learn what you can as fast as you can and then get the hell out of Mississippi. You got to get back to Memphis."

"Major, that has been the story of my life," J. W. said. "Putting Mississippi in my rearview mirror just as soon and long lasting as I can. It's been my dream and my career plan. Good bye, cotton. Hello, crime."

Tyrone Walker cleared his throat at that, and J. W. did not look in the direction of his partner. Long stares and amused looks from Tyrone and J. W. would wait to endure until the two of them were out of the boss's office. Maybe by then, J. W. figured, he could come up with an answer to whatever it was that Tyrone was studying to say. Preparation, planning, and internal rehearsal were essential to enduring a hoorawing from Tyrone. Don't ever take a knife to a gunfight, as J. W. had heard somebody say once. You got to get ready to match wits with Sergeant Tyrone Walker of Homicide. He will not get started on his lunch until he has eaten yours first. Every damn bite of it.

Miss May Margaret Howell-Reed's name was nowhere to be seen on the door of the private room in the Methodist Hospital. The metal slot where the identifier for the current patient was usually printed on a removable label was not only empty, but completely removed. If you don't know the identity of the patient you were attempting to see, Tyrone Walker mused as he waited for the attendant standing beside him to unlock the door to the private room, you have no business being here in the first place. And further, Tyrone predicted, when that door is unlocked and opened, I will discover another person sitting in a straight chair designed to be uncomfortable enough to prevent the occupier from dozing off during his hours on watch. There is no rest for the fully employed. The only man with downtime is the one who doesn't need it.

Ah, the beauty of money when piled high enough. It does make a wonderful insulation against all that foreign matter floating in the atmosphere everywhere you look in Memphis. The only thing it doesn't protect the owner from is other folks with comparable amounts of greenback insulation. Competing insulation will allow stray and dangerous elements to seep right through, particularly if that other owner is part and parcel of what you are yourself. Just ask Miss May Margaret if I'm right about the matter. She'll be able to tell you that now.

"This gentleman here is from the Memphis police," said the woman who'd accompanied Tyrone from the first-floor lobby area of the Methodist Hospital to this upper private floor. "Miss Howell-Reed has sent word she'd like to speak with Sergeant Tyrone Walker, and here he is with the proper credentials to prove it."

She spoke in the professional cheery yet distant tone used by all personnel in a facility designed to deal with people whose mortality has announced itself so strongly they can't ignore the brute fact that all that lives dies. The way she said any and all she said conveyed that message. Look, don't think you're fooling anybody anymore. You have faltered in the race, thrown a shoe, lost a step, fainted and fallen short in some fashion. I haven't done that yet, but you have. So I'm at least one up on you, maybe more. So listen to what I have to say, take my directions and don't question their wisdom or use, and maybe—just maybe—I'll help you find a way to stave off thinking about what we all know is finally coming. Could be later, could be postponed, but it's coming like a freight train, and I am your conductor. Listen up, and act right.

"Miss Howell-Reed," said the guardian of the hospital's top-floor suites, "the gentleman you wished to see is here. Sergeant Tyrone Walker from the Memphis Police."

Miss May Margaret was propped up by pillows on a bed that looked appropriate to the setting, well-positioned between restraining rails, and dressed in garb so white it seemed to glow with a light from within. Her head was swathed in a bandage that covered all of her hair but a white curl which lay precisely in the middle of her forehead. It looked perfectly arranged to Tyrone, as though some consultant had spent time positioning it, moving from place to place in the room to view his work as it might be observed by any and all who encountered it. There, he must have finally said. There. Her hair was perfect. What damage might lay in disarray beneath was lost to view, properly and neatly concealed.

"Sergeant Walker," the lady said, "I'm so glad you were able to come speak to me so soon. It is you in particular I want to be able to consult, and I hope your partner does not feel ignored or passed over for some reason. I don't intend that."

"No ma'am," Tyrone said. "Sergeant Ragsdale is on assignment elsewhere, and I'm pleased to be able to hear directly from you what you can tell us about what's happened to put you here. He sends his regards."

"Please understand and convey to Sergeant Ragsdale my greeting and best wishes. My family does know of the Ragsdales in Panola County, Mississippi. A very sound bunch of fine cotton farmers. Salt of the earth. Yeomen. Hard workers. People like them are what built the Delta into what it was and is."

"I will certainly let Sergeant Ragsdale know what you've said about his family in the Delta," Tyrone said, thinking how he'd enjoy letting J. W. know the people in the big house appreciated the work in the fields that the Ragsdales had done so willingly and so well. I can see him, Tyrone thought, another Ragsdale taking his sweat-stained hat off to show deference and loyalty to the rich folks. I'll put it on thick, Tyrone told himself, see if I can't help J. W. understand better and down to the bone just where he and his Mississippi kind stood. He'll thank me for it.

"You're smiling, Sergeant Walker," Miss May Margaret said. "Would that I had good reason to feel content and secure. Not that I would prefer you to be in any way other than what you are. A fine representative of the Memphis Police Department."

And of my people, Tyrone said to himself, and then aloud, "I smiled just then, I suppose, because I always am gratified to hear good words and commendations for my partner. He is a fine example of many things."

"Yes, he is," Miss May Margaret said, patting gently at her forehead, the hand which she lifted displaying a bandage covering the palm and the first knuckles. "But I know you're here to listen to what I have to say, so when you want me to begin the recitation of the events which put me where I lie in the Methodist Hospital in this condition, please let me know."

"Let's begin, if you will, with your telling me about what led to this, uh, episode to take place. What could have caused you to want to pick up an antique weapon and fire it?"

"You'll remember the visit you made some days ago when I disclosed what's been happening at Fallen Timbers. This current event is part of that situation. Have you seen the communication from our ancestor, General Nathan Forrest? I'm sure you have, the recent letter from him, I mean."

"Not the original, but I have seen a reproduction of what you're talking about. But rather than asking you a lot of questions right now, why don't you just tell me what's put you here in a hospital bed, starting from the beginning."

"Yes, that would be the simplest way to proceed," Miss May Margaret Howell-Reed said, shifting a bit in her bed as she readied herself to tell her story, holding her head back with chin up as though to begin a recitation to a lady's history club about kitchen utensils of old. "Ahem," she said, cleared her throat, and began.

"After the visit from you and your partner to Fallen Timbers in response to my request to the mayor, further strange events took place. Small ones, I admit. Lost jewelry, misplaced small objects, paintings found askew on walls, sounds late at night as of soldiers marching and horses neighing, distant rumbling not as of thunder but of cannon fire, faint singing of old negro hymns as though not by a trained choir but a collection of devout church goers, if you follow me. You must have heard such sounds as you grew up in Memphis, Sergeant Walker."

"Not cannons or soldiers marching, but hymn singing in church, yes indeed," Tyrone answered, thinking to himself that preaching and screeching and falling down and praising of the Lord had figured heavily in all that din, too. But don't encourage this old rich crazy white lady by adding on examples of signs and wonders. She's doing fine all by herself.

"I could bear this, most of it," Miss May Margaret said, "it's amazing what you can become accustomed to, but when I began to receive documentary proof that I could physically touch and hold in my hand, that's when I knew I was in a metaphysical place. That's when I began fearing not only for peace of mind but assurance of physical safety. Do you know what that term means, Sergeant Walker, metaphysical?"

"Yes, I have encountered that word and concept," Tyrone said, thinking I won't let myself be reduced to vocabulary display for this old lady and getting it up to the brag to show her how smart a black man can be. I'll save that for metaphysical discussions with Ragsdale.

"I had an expert at the Chicago Art Institute compare the handwriting on the letters I began receiving from the dead against known verified letters of General Forrest, and the man from Chicago deemed them, and these are his words, strikingly similar. So you see, I did do due diligence. I was sound in my reasoning. And I began, against my will, to believe that from the grave itself came these missives. I was being summoned by otherworldy attention from General Forrest himself, and I told myself I must reconcile and accept and heed what I was being told."

When did the great-great-granddad tell her to blow her brains out, Tyrone considered as Miss May Margaret rambled on about events and sounds and sights and letters all beyond the world of touch and see and taste and smell and hear. Cut to the chase, May Margaret. And you, General Nathan Bedford Forrest, principle founder of the KKK, tell her to put the old blunderbuss to the temple and pull the trigger. Let's get to it. Resolution, please. Less metaphysical stuff and more boom boom.

"And then," Miss May Margaret was saying, "I could hardly eat anything at all, as fearful as I was about what an ordinary serving of some dish might be transformed into. I had seen all these horrors put before me to eat. Salad transfigured into a swarm of worms. English peas become maggots. A set of dentures found at the bottom of a carafe of quite good merlot. A crust of bread suddenly become a mass of carpenter ants. A banana with human lips fixed in a grimace. You cannot imagine the horror of attempting to dine while anticipating a hideously disgusting transformation."

"It would be off-putting," Tyrone said. "Destructive to appetite for any dish."

"The fear of horrid change, of devolution, of a sinking into muck. Witnessing food become garbage before my very eyes. Oh, Sergeant Walker, I knew you'd understand in a way that perhaps your partner would not."

"Sergeant Ragsdale is a rough eater, I must admit," Tyrone said. "A great relisher at the table. But a cleanly one. He will not consume the inedible."

Wait until I tell J. W. that the duchess of Fallen Timbers talked to me about the very nature of his eating habits. He'll be so pleased and gratified by that. I'll wait to tell him that news right before he tears into a side of ribs. It won't stop him from eating, but it'll make him so mad he won't get a full relish from his meal. Maybe a pork rib will turn into something nasty right before his eyes. That won't stop J. W. from eating it, though. As long as it doesn't bite back, he will down it.

Don't laugh at that vision, Tyrone told himself. I don't want this crazy lady to think I'm amused by her eating ordeals.

"What in particular was going on at the time you made the unfortunate decision to pick up that cavalry sidearm, Miss Howell-Reed?" Tyrone said. "Was it something you'd been thinking about beforehand, or was it more spontaneous? You know, a spur-of-the-moment kind of thing."

"Let me think," Miss May Margaret said. "That weapon has always been in family possession. James Forrest had been showing me the sidearm which it's always been reported that the general had carried into battle. The one he'd been firing away at the Northern troops which had him bottled up at that fallen timbers situation. Do I need to explain that setting to you, Sergeant Walker?"

"Oh, no, every school child in Memphis learns of that battle by the time he finishes grammar school," Tyrone lied. He himself had learned the contours of the myth in an American history course at Memphis State and damned if he'd listen to a descendant recite it to him. "So no reason to repeat it. Tell me what happened with you last night, instead, the way you received your injury."

"Of course," Miss May Margaret said, "I had supposed as much. As I said, my son handed me the weapon for closer inspection, and he urged me to point it at some object in the room. He also asked me if I'd like to read the letter of N. B. Forrest, newly discovered by some scholar at Ole Miss, and I did, of course. I took the pistol in hand, and it was quite heavy, so I laid it beside me on a small table, and I began trying to make out what had been written on that sheet of paper so many decades before. And, oh, what it said. It was directed clearly to me personally, and it warned of destruction to come if I did not heed what it said. It told me to lift the pistol, and be prepared to meet a danger coming up from behind me. And when it was written, I could not imagine. Was it prescient of the general, sensing somehow that a descendant would someday in the future need his advice? Or was it created in a spiritual manner during this present moment?"

Good God, Tyrone considered as he watched Miss May Margaret tell her tale, she's good at building suspense, I got to say. But I wonder how the fake letters got manufactured, this one in particular with all that smell of money about it. I wouldn't have thought the dutiful son James Forrest would have been so meticulous in his preparation and study in his plan to have his mother blow her head off with the old slave trader's antique pistol. He never showed that kind of patience and foresight in anything he did back in the day when he was running wild and free all over Shelby County and environs. Age may have slowed him down, but it must have improved him.

"Then," Miss May Margaret said, "I did as I was warned I should by my ancestor, and I pointed the pistol over my shoulder, my left one, since I'm right-handed, and James Forrest put his hand out, concerned about what I was doing. No, I told him, I'm obeying the instructions of the general, and I pulled back from my son's well-intended grasp, and I swear I felt the pistol jump in my hand and someone or something pressed quite hard on my finger. The gun went off, but I didn't hear it, and the next thing I remember is waking in an ambulance fastened to a gurney with straps. And now this hospital stay because of the bullet graze to my head."

"Oh, my, how frightening," Tyrone Walker said. "And luckily you're here in good hands at the Methodist Hospital. Thank you for spending this time with me. And I must leave now for other duties. Is there anything else you'd like to say at this point? We can and will talk later again, of course."

Let her say no, Tyrone said deep within all the recesses of his mind, because if I have to listen to one more crazy word from the great-great-something-granddaughter of N. B. Forrest, I'll pull my own sidearm and take out everybody in the room, including me. If I were J. W.,

I know where I'd be heading as soon as I could get in that sorry old departmental Chevrolet in the parking lot. And I'd be floorboarding it.

"Did you get what you needed from me?" Miss May Margaret asked. "As you know, I wanted to speak particularly to you at this point. I knew you'd be a sympathetic listener with no agenda but my own."

"Ma'am, you are utterly correct in that statement. All I want is to represent clearly to Major Dalbey what I've heard and learned today. As the old folks at home would say, get well."

"Oh, thank you, Sergeant. I have always loved and depended on your people, their loyalty and family feeling."

Goodbyes and blessings uttered, and now out in the hall, Tyrone pondered as he waited for the elevator, I've got to admit I learned some good stuff today for the Major to use and act on, but if it wasn't for all the PR good that does him and Ovetta Birchard and the mayor and the department, I do wish old General N. B. Forrest had been a better shot during today's version of Fallen Timbers than he was.

Safely in the elevator rapidly descending to the lower escape level, Tyrone spoke aloud. "J. W." he said. "Sergeant Ragsdale, where is the bar nearest to the Methodist Hospital located? I know you know, buddy. Channel it to me from wherever you are in darkest Mississippi. I know you can. Come on, now. Be spiritual."

Whenever J. W. Ragsdale left Memphis headed south for his home country of Panola County, he always found himself drawn to thinking about what it meant to be leaving West Tennessee for the deep Delta. One of two lines of thought about sliding south from Memphis was literary, he figured, and it pleased him to consider that fact. Somebody who wrote books had once said something to the effect that the Delta begins in the lobby of the Peabody Hotel in Memphis and ends on Catfish Row in Vicksburg. Thinking that made J. W. feel comforted in the way that no other collection of words ever did. It seemed a lot to him like poetry, but not the kind he'd had to read some of in Batesville High School days.

The Delta was a great chunk of land that meant enough that people talked about it, wrote down words about it, words that other folks in Tennessee and Mississippi and, well hell, everywhere else English was spoken, could read and think about. Knowing that made J. W. feel like he was as real living where he did as anybody in New York, or Chicago, or Saigon, or Paris, or anywhere else in the world could claim to feel. Location, location, location, as his real-estate-selling second wife was always saying. That, among other stuff she said.

Those words about the Delta were a good way to know that what he did or had done every day, whether it was as a kid working cotton in Panola County, Mississippi, or as a cop in Memphis or a grunt in the infantry, was real. He wasn't just functioning in a joke, not just passing time until he finally got tumped into a hole and dirt throwed over him. J. W. had tried to explain that feeling to only one other person, that second wife, during a tender moment, but she had said it didn't make sense, what he was saying. "Sure, you're real," she said. "Don't you eat breakfast in the morning and go to work, and not pay attention to your wife like you ought to? You're talking crazy again."

She was probably right, J. W. admitted to himself, though not to her, and after that second divorce from another woman he had pledged to stay with and take care of forever, he never spoke to another person about the Delta and coming into it down from Tennessee. He did, though, get a book out of the library that was about the Mississippi Delta, where it began and ended and had been, and he read it from start to finish. The part of that reading he liked most was a sentence that said when you came south from Memphis you were leaving the Tennessee Promontory, geologically speaking, and entering the Delta proper. The Delta proper, J.W said to himself one more time as he drove across the state line into Mississippi. When his car was truly and fully and officially into the Delta, he spoke aloud.

"The lobby of the Peabody," he said over the sound of the engine and the air blowing through the vents. "Goodbye, Tennessee Promontory, and hello true Delta. How do you do?" He felt good, like always. He had entered Mississippi in the right state of mind, he was driving his own automobile and getting gas mileage allowance for that, which he wouldn't have if he had taken an official car from the Memphis Police Vehicle Pool, and he'd make money from that deal. And he was truly in the Delta.

"All right," J. W. said aloud. "First stop is Big Daddy's Barbecue where the Sunflower Road crosses Puckett, and then a little informational talk with Paul."

When he pulled his 2007 Chevrolet into Big Daddy's unpaved lot and parked next to a machine that seemed held together with bondo and masking tape, the time was a little short of eleven in the morning, and that meant he had not paid close attention to the demands of the barbecuing of pork. Would Paul have anything ready to eat yet, something that wasn't just left over from a day or two back but had reached the perfection of smoke and heat needful for the best serving up and eating of barbecue ribs just at the perfect time?

After entering the Delta proper, J.W. Ragsdale stopped his car at a ramshackle building, unpainted, just over the Panola County line. J. W. piled out of his car, took a deep breath of the atmosphere into which he'd stepped, and felt encouraged and comforted. All was smelling good. When he had pushed through the screen door and stepped inside, he immediately called out. "Is it anybody in this place doing any cooking this morning? If it ain't, what's all that smoke hanging up in the air for?"

"J. W.," someone called from behind the counter at the far wall of the main room of the house converted into a barbecue joint, "J. W. Ragsdale, what you hollering about? You know it ain't time to eat yet."

"It's time to eat when my belly says it's time to eat. You got to plan around that, Mr. Paul. You can't reason with an empty belly hollering for pulled pork."

"What's this 'mister' business? You ain't drunk already this time of morning, are you? It's too early for a serious eater to get his digestion all messed up with beer and whisky. Meat first, drinking last."

"Paul, no. I haven't touched a drop of alcohol since the last time I did. And I called you Mr. Paul because I'm so used to living in Memphis I done forget how to talk to a man in Panola County. You don't call a man mister in Memphis, he might take offense and he might not. You cannot tell which way he's going to jump. He's cut loose from his roots, see. He's just floating like a balloon about to bust. He has lost his sense of direction, or he wouldn't be in Memphis in the first place."

"You call a man here in the Delta by a strange name, J. W., you liable to be accused of making fun of him, and he'll come up beside your head. You ought to be able to remember that. But I'll overlook that this time, J. W. What you want first? Ribs or pulled."

"Ribs," J. W. said. "Ribs. Get them to me as soon as that lady in the kitchen can dish them up, and we'll see where we go from there."

After J. W. ate a full rack from the woman in the kitchen, a young one J. W. had not seen before in Big Daddy's Rib Shack, much lighter in complexion than Paul, he slowed the consumption of barbecued pork down to a crawl. It did not cease totally, however, and as J. W. and Paul sat talking, J. W. kept picking at what was left on his plate. Each rib bone ought to be shining when the meal was done.

“You back here visiting your folks?” Paul asked. “Catching up on family news? Getting yourself a vacation?”

“I ain’t got no real family left in Panola County, Paul. Some cousins and a real old aunt’s about it. I did have a sister here for the longest time, but she’s moved up to Louisville to be with her husband’s people. So, no, I’m not here for a visit except to see you and your place and maybe some other folks that I’m hoping you’ll tell me to see.”

“Me tell you? What you talking about?”

“Well, it’s got to do with police business, Paul. And not just the Memphis police, neither. We’re talking Feds now.”

“You mean the FBI is getting you to help find somebody for them? Or the IRS? Some kind of federal offense you trying to run down? Is it one of them runaway politicians they need some help catching?”

“Ain’t nobody going to catch a runaway officeholder in Mississippi,” J. W. said. “Those boys down here are too slick for the federal government to get them. If they were easy to catch, they wouldn’t be senators and judges and sheriffs and all that bunch in the first place. No, Paul, what’s got the Memphis police having to fool with Washington, DC, is the business of the Secret Service.”

“Secret Service? Is the president fixing to come to the Delta for some ribs?

“Naw. I know the president would like them ribs of yours, Paul, but it don’t involve him. The Secret Service does more than guard against nuts trying to shoot the president. They handle counterfeiting, too, people making fake money and passing it off as real. So that’s what’s got me down here in my capacity.”

“Capacity,” Paul said. “Capacity, oh my Lord. Big word for a big job.”

“Yeah, we ran across a big bunch of fake hundred- and five-hundred-dollar bills up in Memphis, and these counterfeit bills are connected with some of the gangs in Memphis. Bones Family, Latin Lords, the Beale Street Boppers, maybe some more of them herds of hoodlums.”

“Why you down here in Panola County then? Is it some of that fake money getting passed down here? If it is, I ain’t heard about it.”

“It’s more to it than that, we’re finding out,” J. W. said. “No, I don’t expect anybody’s trying to pass it off as real money here in Panola County. That’s way yonder too low level. See, it’s got to do with the dope cartels down in Mexico and Colombia. Seems like these gangs are funneling counterfeit money through a Mississippi connection.

Why exactly, we don't know. We got word after a killing between some gangbangers in Memphis that the stash of fake money was supposed to be headed for somebody here in Panola County. A middleman to handle that fake shit in its trip south to fool the Mexicans making the dope, you understand."

"What you call somebody from that other place you just mentioned, that Colombia?" Paul asked. "I know what you call a Mexican already."

"I don't know. A Colombian. Asshole? Doper?"

"I see who I'm still dealing with," Paul said. "You never been as curious as I am, J. W. I want to know what things is named and how they work a lot more than you do."

"That's cause you're a cook. It's your nature. Me, I just eat what's cooked. I ain't bothered about how it got on the plate. But speaking about your inquiring mind, Paul, who in Panola County ought I to be thinking about in connection with boxes of counterfeit money? I'm out of touch down here at home, and I been out of touch. Only names I can come up with belong to folks in prison or in the graveyard. My boss come to me about my deep knowledge of all things Panola County, and I had to lie to him and act like I still knew something that might help us."

"Ain't nothing wrong with telling a lie to your boss," Paul said. "That what makes the world go 'round. But it's two people you don't want to lie to and still be able to get along with them."

"The wife is one," J. W. said. "I done lied to two of them, and I got the scars to show it. But what's the other one you don't want to tell nothing but the truth to? Something more serious?"

"Well, it ain't Jesus or the Lord, since they don't believe anything you say anyway. No, not them. I don't know about other counties, but here in Panola, you don't want to lie to Mr. Rayford Rio. You do, and it'll make you have to get up in the middle of the night from a sound sleep."

"Why's that?"

"Your house is on fire, for one, and if you got any livestock, they lying down dead and so full of poison you can't even butcher out and eat any hogs in the bunch."

"I don't know anybody in Panola County named Rayford Rio," J. W. said. "Where's he live and where'd he come from? He sounds nasty."

"He lives over by Drew in that big old chunk of property used to belong to the Aires family. Jackson Aires and them. And after Rayford

Rio moved in here just over a year or so ago, he been buying up everything around him. He likes to joke, see, and he's always saying to folks that he don't want nothing but his own property and then the property touching his. He wants you to laugh when he say that."

"I heard folks tell that old joke lots before," J. W. said. "It ain't been funny for a long time, neither."

"Folks around here's learned to laugh anyway at whatever joke Mr. Rayford Rio decides to tell. And they better act like they ain't never heard it before, too. I've seen them slap their knee and throw their head and just holler 'til tears come to their eyes."

"He sounds to me like he needs somebody to laugh at him instead of what he's saying. Maybe it'd cheer him up a little. But tell me something, Paul. See if I'm guessing right. I bet Rio has a landing strip on that old Aires place. Does he have an airfield on his property? And an airplane or two?"

"He does, and he's got not just a airplane. He's got airplanes, J. W. And he's got a copter, and he's got a bunch of these little old drone things. You'll see them everywhere. Flying over people's places. Over downtown Batesville, the courthouse, the school house, just hovering and taking pictures, they say. He's into everything, Mr. Rayford Rio is. He owns one at least of everything modern and up to date. And he's always looking to get more stuff."

"I think I might have just been told who's who in Panola County. Who happens to be the man most likely to be a friend to some enterprising young folks in Memphis, Paul. You have helped me more than you know."

"Now wait a minute, J. W. I ain't done nothing for you nor no Memphis police, neither. I just fed you some ribs and gossiped about what's new in town since you left for the big time in Tennessee. I ain't said nothing that's not just what everybody knows. I ain't got no opinions. Don't be saying I do, neither."

"You don't got to worry about that, Paul. I know one damn thing you got. And that's the best ribs as far as anybody can see and you got the best eyesight of anybody I know in Panola County, Mississippi. Keep on cooking, and keep on looking. See all you can."

"I can't help but do that, try like I will not to. You going to swing by here again for supper or a snack before you take off back for Memphis, J. W.?"

"Do I have to beg you to let me do that? I will, if I have to. I ain't proud."

"Naw, don't beg. Just be real careful where you poking around, and be sure to save room for ribs on your way back home."

After going back to the kitchen door to say goodbye to the woman who'd brought his plate of ribs to him, J. W. told Paul he'd let him know if and when he'd be back at Big Daddy's before heading back to Memphis again. Paul told him just to text him when he was on the way back, and J. W. had jumped back at that like he'd just seen a water moccasin.

"Texting?" he said. "God almighty, Paul. You got one of them smart phones and you know how to use it? Don't tell me that. I'll get so damn sick at my stomach I'll ruin them ribs I've been eating."

"A man's got to stay up with the times, J.W, especially a man selling barbecue by the side of the road. You mean to tell me you don't text?"

"Oh, I took that workshop they made us go to in the Downtown station, but it didn't take on me. I let Tyrone Walker do all that, and I'd shine his shoes for him if he asked me to do that for payback. As far as you're concerned, Paul, I'll forgive you for texting, long as you don't change how you barbecue that pork."

"That is a perfected deal, J. W., cooking ribs, and there ain't no way to improve it. We got it down to a science. And a art."

"Well, I won't be texting you, but I will call you on a cell phone. I can punch them buttons and do that."

In his Chevrolet and headed toward downtown Batesville, J. W. considered what it might mean that Paul had openly expressed being a little afraid of another man, a man new to North Mississippi. J. W. had never seen Paul express anything other than familiarity with other people, knowledge of what they might or might not do, and a settled sense that he would not mess with them if they didn't mess with him. Paul might be a black man, born and bred and raised in Mississippi with all that that meant, but he had never revealed concern about his living situation in his home country. He would be fair and square in his dealings with other folks no matter their color or history, and he'd do that until they transgressed the unspoken obligations of living with other people. Then all bets would be off.

But Paul seemed leery of this Rayford Rio, and that raised questions that J. W. had never considered in connection to the owner, operator, and cook at Big Daddy's on Sunflower Road. What about this Rayford Rio, this acquirer of all the property that touched his, was making these changes in this part of the Delta?

"Time to meet the man," J. W. said out loud, and then he pulled over to the side of the road so he could call Tyrone Walker and tell him to do what he had to do to ease the mind of Major Dalbey. The boss got nervous when a detective was working away from home, unauthorized in authority outside of the environs of Memphis, even if he had been given orders to do so by the Major himself. He would never completely abandon the officer he had assigned off-location duties, but the Major would carry on and bitch and whine. Better to get him calmed and ready whenever I sense the chance I might be overstepping, J. W. considered as he punched in the numbers.

"Goddamn," he said aloud. "I still miss dialing. I still miss Falstaff beer. Hell, I still miss stuff as close as the 1980s."

The old Aires Saxon place had undergone massive change since last he'd seen it, J. W. Ragsdale observed as he drove toward the entrance of Rio Ranchero. Signs proclaiming identity and border had begun appearing fully a mile before the main gates, and J. W. wondered how the previous owner would have liked to see all the glitz and glamour the new owner had worked and was working to proclaim just what all visitors would behold as they approached.

First of all was a stone plaque growing out of an artfully constructed pile of other stones, intended to suggest a natural fact of landscape somewhere deep in the American West. The pile of stones said this whole thing here was made by forces of nature operating from deep in the earth and casting up evidence of fire, smoke, and particularly water. RIO, the words carved on the plaque high above the natural-appearing collection of stones of many colors, was so designed to suggest the word had grown from water itself. It shimmered, it glowed, it was a great river sweeping all before as it fed the thirsty earth around it. Rio, the river.

"This here is Mississippi, asshole," J. W. had said aloud as he stopped the car to examine closely the stone and water identifier of the property before him. "It ain't drought country. It rains like hell here at any time of the year it decides to. The biggest damn river in the country is running day and night and forever not twenty miles from here. Mr. Rio! What a name. Only thing about water that scares us down here is too much of it.

Get hold of yourself, J. W. thought as he pulled the Chevy back onto the road. You got to do some whitetoothing here in a little while if you expect to learn anything to tell the Major. Get ready to take off your hat and make nice while you try to get some folks to tell you what they ought not to be talking about. And remember, even though you nor nobody else in this whole damn country even wears a real hat anymore, you have got to pretend inside your damned head that you're uncovering before somebody that outranks you. Or at least playing like you are. It's a fine line between being an asshole and pretending to be one. The man you want something from expects you to admit your low rank, or he won't tell you a thing you might want to know. If he thinks you think you outrank him, all he'll want to see is you in hell with your back broke.

So suck up to Mr. Rayford Rio, if you get to see him, and let him know your low opinion of yourself in his presence. He'll like that, if he believes you're playing the game right and obeying all the rules, and he just might let you catch him in that weak moment. If he believes you believe you're the piece of shit he thinks you are, you will be golden.

And your time might come then, the moment when he knows you fooled him and that you never thought he outranked you at all. It'll be kiss-my-ass time then, and it will be sweeter for the fooling you've had to do to get there.

Other signs depicting streams creeping through stone and proclaiming the triumph of water over earth appeared one after the other as J. W. neared the official and ultimate gate at the heart of the holdings of Rayford Rio. Well before then, the outlines of landing areas for aircraft were visible behind the hurricane fences, several hangers of various sizes and capacities were in evidence, and just as J. W. came within sight of the main gate, the deep whisper of a small jet announced the landing of a plane with the single word RIO worked in deep blue on its fuselage. A cresting wave lifted the word, giving the impression it carried the label along like a burden no lighter than a wood chip.

Now why, J. W. Ragsdale asked himself as he studied the artist's creation on the fuselage, does that make me mad enough to want to cuss somebody? No sense in it, at all, but that's the beauty of getting mad. It ain't logical, but it sure does clear the pipes to feel that way once in a while. Damn a picture painted like that, he considered and instantly felt a little lift in the belly. He took a deep breath and felt better for it.

"Here we go," he said out loud, and then considered the best way to approach the massive gate to the holdings of Mr. Rayford Rio. Park the car well short of the gate itself, kill the engine quick, get out, and let your face look as normal as you can make it. No frown, no grin, not even a big smile. Just walk right up there and let that camera show that you come in peace, looking for a consideration of some kind, and being completely unaware you're being recorded visually and audibly. If you had a hat, you'd be taking it off, Boss, and showing how biddable you are. Suck it up. Be nice.

J. W. pressed a large black button located about chest-high on the right side of the steel gate, twisted into the stylized shape of a stream with the name RIO worked gracefully into the design, and in a few seconds a recorded voice came from a speaker near him, matched by the one mounted in the stone work on the other side of the gate arrangement. Stereo, J. W. said to himself, remembering to keep an earnestly pleasant look on his face. Best I can do, he thought, with that. I ain't no professional actor like Tyrone can be when he wants to. Of course, being a black man in Memphis, he had an advantage in the acting arena through practicing how to show himself in the right way for all the years he'd been conscious of himself as being who he was where he was.

Once Tyrone had told J. W., in an unusually candid moment, answering a question put to him by his partner as they had sat in an unmarked car for four hours on a stakeout that yielded nothing, that acting either came naturally to a black man or woman growing up in Memphis or it was learned as soon as events demanded it. "You get well able to show the right face wherever you are, J. W.," Tyrone Walker had said, "or you don't last long outside walking around and doing business. If acting right doesn't come natural to you or you don't put your mind to learning it, you're going to find yourself locked up tight or dead. One or the other. Maybe both. And damn quick."

J. W. hadn't touched that one, figuring it was too hot a topic to try to use as the springboard for a joke. Instead, he had done some acting of his own, not letting a sign of anything show on his face or in his voice as he complained about how tired he got of sitting in the front seat of an unairconditioned car in Memphis in almost any month of the year, waiting for something to happen that might let him hop out and move around a little.

"What is your business with Rio enterprises?" the canned voice coming from the speaker before him said. "And what is your name and professional connection?"

"Uh, I'm just interested in talking with Mr. Rayford Rio about some employment possibilities," J. W. said. "I'm experienced around small and medium aircraft, and I'm not currently connected with any firm or outfit. I just want to know if there's any hiring possibilities, either part or full time or just, you know, maybe just temporary projects. Deals like that, you understand."

A real voice spoke in response, cutting through the canned announcement that had greeted the supplicant at Rio Enterprises, "What is your name, Sir, and how did you choose to visit with Rio today? What led you to us?"

"My name is J. W. Boatwright, and I guess everybody in this part of Mississippi knows about Mr. Rio's business. You know, the good stuff he's doing with his work and all. So I figured I'd ask if there might be some possibility of getting in on some of that. That about says it all for me, I reckon."

"I'll open the small gate on the right for you, Mr. Boatwright, and you can enter. Once you do, you'll see indications of where to go to pick up an application blank. That will be in the small stucco building to your right."

"To the right," J. W. said. "Yessir, I'll do that."

Immediately after he'd been allowed to enter the gate to the Rio Enterprises, J. W. saw a series of signs telling visitors the way, and he followed directions. As he did, the attendant operating the gate mechanism long distance pressed a button which allowed him to record the license plate number of the Chevrolet parked beyond the stone and steel fence.

"Tennessee tag," he said into the mic positioned above his work desk, "I'll run it down and have ID shortly. Will Mr. Rio want to see this one, or should I keep him running as soon as Sheila gives him the employment form?"

Answering what he was told, he said he'd tell Sheila to have this J. W. Boatwright wait in the outer office until Mr. Rayford Rio decided whether he wanted to meet this walk-up would-be applicant from Memphis, Tennessee. "I understand," he said into the mic, "no, he doesn't look to me like he's a mechanic or any kind of aviation veteran. Just somebody poking around, looking for a few weeks of full employment. Let me see what the car tag tells us, though. I'll do the complete follow-up. Won't take long."

J. W. studied the blank form he'd been handed by the good-looking blonde woman who had welcomed him into the white stucco building, noted it called for information which he hoped he could dummy up well enough to at least get a chance to take a look at Mr. Rayford Rio, and sipped at the soft drink fetched him by the lady whose name tag told the world she was Sheila. Always take any refreshment offered during a job interview, J. W. had once been told in a workshop on seeking employment. Saying no to an offer of refreshment might show you're nervous and not social and afraid to relate, the woman running the workshop had said. You have got to show not only trust, but trustworthiness. Look like you can relax. No matter how nervous it makes you.

J. W. had never been interviewed for a job or been offered refreshment in the process after the seminar on employment procedures, but he was ready to suck it up and drink it down if he ever was. And here he was, in Panola County, drinking a free Coke while faking that he was seeking employment. What would he do if Rayford Rio offered to sign him up? Bargain for salary? Ask about health insurance and the leave policy? Maternal leave for the wife? This application stuff might be kind of fun to go through the motions of doing. Hell, maybe he'd say yes to the offer and leave the mean streets of Memphis behind. But there was a drawback to that lure. If he stopped being a cop, he wouldn't legally be able to carry heat and use it when he had to. Oh, well, J. W. was thinking, another dream of sweet release down the drain.

He heard his fake name called, and he looked up to see a man standing next to Sheila's desk, giving him the kind of searching look which J. W.'s father would have called that of "a bull looking at an orphan calf." I know you and I are of the same species, the look said, but damned if that moves me in a positive direction. This is all accidental. So what?

"Mr. Boatwright, if you have a few minutes, Mr. Rio would like to meet you briefly. He's about to leave shortly, but he says to tell you he always enjoys greeting people interested in aviation. Come with me, please."

J. W. did that, having to give up his unfinished Coke to Sheila who kindly reached for it, and in a couple of minutes he was in a different building, much better appointed and cooled and soothed by ambient music of no definition, and shaking hands with Mr. Rayford Rio himself. Rio was dressed like the Howard Hughes figure in the movie of a few years back, and he looked tanned, rested, and ready. Blonde hair, close shave, casual but cool. He's all coiled up, but he's hiding as much as possible of the steel springs that run him.

"Mr. Boatwright," he said. "That's an old Delta surname, I believe. I've heard it around Batesville and Drew and a few other places here in the county."

"I guess so," J. W. said. "My folks are kin to half the county, like a lot of the old collections of relatives around here. So it goes. All these match-ups."

"If you're not kin, you've got to be relative," Rayford Rio said. "If this is a county, how come it looks like a country?"

"What?" J. W. said. "That kind of got by me. But it made sense, I reckon."

"Oh, I like to play with words. Turn them around and inside out. Lift up their skirts, take a look, and see if they holler or back off." At that, the man accompanying Rio laughed as though someone had just held a gun to his head and given him a command to be jolly.

"Tell me, Mr. Boatwright," Rayford Rio said. "Why are you seeking employment in Panola County?"

"It's not the county," J. W. said. "It's your organization I'm interested in knowing more about. I understand that good things are happening here."

If that doesn't hit this word-playing man in the soft spot, J. W. thought, I didn't learn a damn thing in that job-seekers seminar all those years ago. You're supposed to scratch their backs until they roll over and want their bellies rubbed.

"Well, let's just cut to the chase," Rayford Rio said. "And chase to the cut. Why are you down here from the Memphis Police Department, Sergeant J. W. Ragsdale, poking around my organization when you could be on those mean streets being truly mean to all that great supply of criminals you have there in the Bluff City?"

"Oh," J. W. said. "I figured you to be smart, all right, Mr. Rayford Rio, but damn if I know how you got onto me so quick. That's quite a show, I got to admit. Round one to you."

"That's what we do at Rio Enterprises. Discover truth. Run license plates and search names and all that good stuff that makes us human.

Language, Sergeant, it's all a question of communication among thinking mammals. But if you wanted to know about Rio and what we're doing, you didn't need to sneak around. All's aboveboard, and boring as a balance sheet. I'm always glad to talk about what I've done and what I'm doing and what I'm about to do. So just ask, and it shall be given. Seek, and you shall find. I'll be sure you get a brochure. Maybe even a couple of free ballpoints complete with logo."

"Well, my cover's blown, and I'm kind of embarrassed, to tell you the truth. I'm usually better at sneaking around than I am this time. So let me just ask you directly about what's on my mind. Why have you trusted the Bones Family and the Latin Lords and here's the real puzzler, the Beale Street Boppers, to handle any part of this counterfeit money deal? Most of those bangers can't pour piss out of a boot with the instructions printed on the heel. The question is not if but when they are going to fuck things up."

"Well, you are speaking truth to power, and I've got to give you credit for that, Sergeant. But I don't know what you're talking about, and I'm shocked, shocked to think you'd believe I'd be mixed up in such a matter. Counterfeiting? My stars and my bars. My, my. And these bowling teams you mention? Boppers and Bones and stuff? It makes no sense at all."

"Harold," Rayford Rio said then, turning to his assistant. "I think it's time to escort Sergeant J. W. Ragsdale back to his automobile, don't you? I've got a plane to catch here in a little while, and I hear it's lovely this time of year in Colombia."

"Mr. Rio, it's been real," J. W. said, getting up from the chair which held him. "And I know I'll be seeing you later on down the line, like it or not. You'll know that when I show up. And hey, by the way. Your company logo sucks, big-time. It's dumb."

"Now, that hurts, Sergeant Ragsdale. I paid good money to a fine concern in New York City to come up with a tasteful visual emblem of what we do and who we are and how we'll outlast the pyramids, not to mention this shithole of the state of Mississippi. I'm sorry that design doesn't work for you. But tell me something before you leave. Have you really ever flown an aircraft?"

"Not very far. They kept falling out of the sky for me and busting things up. Didn't never stop me from trying, though. I always get up again when I'm knocked down."

Two minutes later outside in the heat of a Delta afternoon, J. W. crawled behind the wheel of his Chevrolet, having to use the heels of his hands to steer, given the ambient heat infesting all surfaces of the vehicle, and spoke out loud. "That little fucker ate my whole fucking lunch. I got to give him credit."

He pondered and knew even as close as it was to his recent consumption of enough barbecued ribs to stun an ordinary eater that he could still worry down a pulled pork sandwich back at Big Daddy's if he put his mind to it. Let's do it, he decided. Man up. Move on.

And what'll I tell Major Dalbey about my little foray into North Mississippi, he wondered. I won't lie to him, as hard as telling the truth is going to be, but I can shade it enough to get by with the boss. That little Rayford Rio all dressed up in his nice duds couldn't resist rubbing it in on me right there at the end, practically bragging about letting me know his next trip was to Colombia. I can't blame him, though, and I will admit to him he won the first round the next time I get in the ring again with the little bastard. Police work is like finishing up your supper. The last bite of barbecue is the sweetest, and being the one to deliver the last lick in a fight makes all that early damage go away. You don't even feel the bruises anymore. When you've won and they hold your hand up in the air, even the blood in your mouth is sweet, sweet, sweet.

"You did put on a show last night, Sweetness," Constance Helen Forrest Howell-Reed said softly, smoothing the hair on Billie Sue Cameron's brow as they lay still entwined and aglow on the king-sized bed in the Peabody Hotel. "I swear when you got me down and began pummeling me on the head, I thought those rednecks were going to go nuts."

"You mean in the third round?" Billie Sue said. "Or in the first when you did the takedown, and I made it look like I had my thumb in your right eye? It's so beautiful, that eye, and the other one, too, sweet girl. I had to stop myself from kissing you when I was supposed to be trying to gouge those baby blues out of your beautiful head."

"You can gouge anything you want to, Baby," Constance Helen said. "Any time of the day or night."

That caused the two of them to do a liplock, which lasted long enough to earn a couple of gasps for air. "Yes, it was in the third, right after Maureen Langlois delivered a left kick to Pig Sooey's liver area," Constance Helen said. "The Pig went down, and Maureen covered her, and then got turned enough to lose leverage, and then it was that Pig Sooey got dirty again."

"Pig Sooey's got it in for Maureen Langlois and her bachelor's degree in art and her reign as homecoming queen every school she was ever in and her fancy gowns and beautiful eyes and long long legs that go all the way up. Pig Sooey resents that more than anything she endured in her growing up and rooting around in the swamps of East Arkansas."

"Oh, and the more you resent, Pig Sooey, the more Maureen's legs just want to spring apart and wrap around you."

"Oh, no, not again. Not right now. I'm just worn out, Sweetheart. I've got to get some rest before I have to crawl back in the octagon tonight and lock assholes with Maggie May, Mid-South Monster. That bitch loses her head at times, as you'll remember, and she gets too damn serious with her kicks. She thinks everything is real, no matter how much you try to reason with the bitch."

"Tell me about it. The last time I went up against her, I believe it was in New Orleans, maybe Birmingham, she kneed me in the jaw so hard I saw stars for the rest of the round. It made me go after her in that last session so hard that I really hurt her. I hurt my own hand, too, even with the gloves on, when I had her down up against the mesh, just hammering away and not even pulling my punches that much."

"I know. I had to hold myself back from crawling over the fence and coming to the rescue, Darling Girl."

"I know, I know. But don't ever do that. You blow the cover once, and it'll cost us money. Maybe even a week's stand somewhere."

"I won't, I won't," Billie Sue said. "It's just that I can't stand to see my baby hurt for real."

"Well, likewise, as you well know. Remember now, I won't be at the arena tonight. I've already told those guys fronting that Memphis money that I won't make it. I have something I want to do, and besides that I don't want to have to see the Mid-South Monster actually get rough with you. I can't be seen by the idiot fans and droolers to be sitting in the audience all concerned about the welfare of Pig Sooey. What would they think?"

"They'd think you love me, and I'd have to show back that I love you, too. And the jig would be up in Memphis. The show must go on, and it's got to look real enough to get those hicks to keep coming and laying their money down."

"Willis and Tommy are still happy, and they claim the money from the big boys in town is about to rain down upon the MMA in the Bluff City, just as long as the fans keep believing."

"Believing," Billie Sue said. "That's a big thing in Memphis, isn't it?"

"That's what Memphis is all about, Honey. Believing in something that can never be proved, and hanging onto lies, front left and center, until death do us part."

"You never have liked your hometown, have you, Sweetness?"

"I always majorly liked it, growing up here with money, and a big house, and most important with a name that everybody recognized and bowed down to. I also hated all that, and that's why Miss Constance Helen Forrest Howell-Reed left town and left her name and all that name possessed and meant. And that's also why she can't forget who she really is, and she can't help but feel torn in two all the time, every day and in every way."

"Don't get yourself all worked up, Darling, and don't cry. Just remember that you can forget all that and get over it. I've forgot most of Arkansas. Not all, I got to admit. That bitch will hang on to you."

"I can't forget it, and I can't get over Memphis, and anybody who's lived here long enough is just the way I am. I hate it, I hate Memphis, and I hated my life here. And I loved it, too, and it was as sweet to me as Tupelo honey, and that's why I'm like everybody in Memphis has to be. Crazy in love with a place that's hateful."

"Why don't you go ahead and see her?" Billie Sue said. "While I'm working tonight, why don't you go see her? Or at least call her up. It might help you remember or forget for good, whatever's the best thing for you. Will you do that, please, Sweetheart, and try to work through some of this thing you're caught in?"

"I'd love to, I'd be willing to, but for one main thing."

"Him?"

"Yes, him. James Forrest Howell-Reed, my little brother. He'll be there. The son of a bitch."

"Don't let him get to you. Just think about me whenever you see him. And really, please think about your mother and how old she is and what might happen any day now. I'll break a leg for you tonight, Love," Pig Sooey said. "There in the octagon."

"Metaphorically only, I hope."

"I'll try to hold it down to that. Now come give me a good kiss before I take my nap."

J. W. had thought through what he'd say as soon as he got back to Memphis and the Midtown station and had to debrief to Major Dalbey. After pondering different scenarios during the ninety miles he had to drive after the final stop at Big Daddy's for the farewell to Panola County pulled pork, he gave up the attempt to dodge the truth. The easiest thing was the hardest, as always in police work, as J. W. had discovered over and over during his time on the job, and he knew he might as well tell the truth as he saw it.

Lies and shading the facts of a thing always required a good memory and recall, so in the end it was less complicated to just tell it like it really had been. You could always leave shit out, J. W. considered as he made his way north out of the Delta proper, but that could cause a problem, too. What if you forgot what you'd left out of a report, slipped up later and mentioned it, and then had to lie some more to hide the fact you'd lied by omission? Too complex and hard on the brain by far. Just tell what happened the best you could remember, and take your medicine and your ass-kicking, and say "sir, yessir" to the commanding officer, or whatever the boss in charge called himself. Make like you're on the football field in the fourth quarter and every damn eye is on you, and you can't hide a thing.

So when J. W. parked the Chevrolet at the back edge of the lot where it was less likely to be banged on by young cops jumping out of their rides in a hurry so as to look eager, he primed himself to go inside at a deliberate pace, ask LaWanda Louvelle if her boss was ready to be talked at, and then go to his desk and sort through the stacks of crap that had been deposited on it in his absence. That would be details of work assignments that should have been handled by somebody lower on the totem pole, now taking advantage of Sergeant Ragdale's absence to try to shift work from them to him, and Lord knows what the damn computer would tell him it had stored up for his perusal.

LaWanda Louvelle was not at her desk when J. W. entered the big room, and that could be either a good thing or a very bad thing, depending on whether she was taking word to the Major about something or taking notes from him as he dictated orders to someone to tackle a job. Right now. Pronto. Get on it. Move. Do what I haven't even told you to do yet. Don't ask. Just do.

"Where's LaWanda?" J. W. said loud enough for anybody in earshot to hear, though no one looked up, officer or clerical staff, and then he spoke further. "Well then, does anybody in this crack outfit know where Tyrone Walker is?"

"In yonder with LaWanda and Major Dalbey," said a young and new secretary, one at the lowest clerical level. "Sergeant Walker said to tell you as soon as you got in that he needed to talk to you."

"Yeah, but he's busy in the Major's office, you just said."

"They want you to come on in there if you got here before five o'clock, and it's a little short of that. So . . ."

"All right, oh hell," J. W. said, and then added, "you're supposed to keep a lookout for me as soon as I get in the door any time that Tyrone Walker wants to see me. You understand that, don't you?"

"I'm sorry," the new clerk said. "I was looking at my screen and didn't see you."

"You ain't never going to see me on a computer screen," J. W. said, thinking to himself that he ought not to be gruff with new young women doing crap work in a police station. But hell, she was the only one around to vent on, so there it is. Be nicer, he told himself. Like both of my former wives told me many a time. Think before you holler.

He knocked on the door to Major Dalbey's office, turned the knob and walked in to find Tyrone and the Major staring at each other as though they were newly met and didn't know exactly the protocol of what to do about it.

"J. W., don't sit down," the Major said. "Save yourself the trouble. I was fixing to send Sergeant Walker to the Family Fare Motel either by himself or with whatever patrolman I could get my hands on out there in the bullpen. But here you are at last, and the two of you can go do this thing."

"All right," J. W. said, thinking there is an upside to all things if you're patient and look for it. I don't have to say a word to the Major right now about what a fool that little fashion model down in Panola made of me when I was trying to be undercover incognito. By the time I do, Dalbey will be cooled off enough to see the humor in it, and he won't chew my ass so hard and immediate and at length. Maybe. "Why are we going to the Family Fare Motel? Is it the one Downtown or that one on McLean?"

"It's the Downtown one. The headquarters station done give it to us, rather than taking it on from out of the big house themselves. Claim they too busy. So y'all get to have all the fun."

"We don't have to hurry too fast, J. W.," Tyrone Walker said. "Everybody there is lying down real still and will be that way until Kingdom Come."

"How many?"

"It's two, a man and a woman, and oh yeah, a dog, too."

"A working girl and her trick?" J. W. said. "That kind of place? Middle of the day and all. Sounds like it. Business as usual."

"We'll see, but it looks a little more interesting than that," Tyrone said. "You ever heard of We 2? The Family Fare's next door to that enterprise."

"Naw, what's that mean? Well, maybe I have. Tell me more."

"Y'all get out of here," Major Dalbey said. "Get it out of my office. GOMER."

J. W. knew to his sorrow that Dalbey had heard that phrase used by a medic some years back to complain about work piling up on him as a result of over-abundant gunshot wounds and penetrations by blades of many descriptions and blunt force injuries from a vast variety of heavy objects. GOMER was the cry used by overworked medicos swamped by the wounded, and it meant Get Out of My

Emergency Room, and the Major had fallen in love with it and the sentiment it expressed.

"We're gone," Tyrone said, and then to J. W. "We 2 is a high dollar dating service, a new one located downtown, office right next door on Main and it's all tangled up with this double down in the Family Fare Motel. We 2 is right down your alley, J. W., and if you cast your mind back, you'll remember that it was a topic of discussion in the Owl not long ago."

"Oh, yeah. Who was it in the Owl that was talking about what wonderful strange snatch was coming out of that outfit?"

"I'll remind you later. Let's go look at the scene and talk to the woman that runs We 2. She is a handful, I'm hearing. A real knockout."

"Reckon she might be looking for some action?" J. W. said. "Needing some business pointers, you know. What's her name, what's she look like, and how old is she?"

"Her name is Monica Moore," Tyrone said. "And she is like most all women. That is to say younger than you, Sergeant Ragsdale. By some years. And a whole lot better set up in every way."

"Yeah, but if I shave real close and hold my head kind of up high enough to smooth out my neck when I'm talking to a woman, it takes a couple of years off. That's what one of them told me, anyway, and she had no reason to lie. She'd done written me off by the time she told me that. She was being nice. Helpful to an old man, you know."

"Women can be kind, J. W. It's built into them not to let you know directly how old and gray you look. They're not like a man looking at a woman and making a judgment. They keep it to themselves."

"Let's don't talk on that topic any more right now," J. W. said. "I've been outpointed in the last couple of days, and I don't need to be reminded about how many steps I've lost over the years. Hell, I might be somebody's grandfather by now, but don't get me wrong. If I am, I don't want to know about it."

"That's called a marker, J. W.," Tyrone said as the two of them got into Tyrone's car. "It's psychology, see. Psychic markers let you know how far along the road to death your mind has reached by a certain point."

"Oh, go to hell, Married Man, and let me tell you about what I learned in my recent tour in Mississippi."

"That I do want to hear," Tyrone said, all business now as they eased into the traffic headed toward the River and Downtown. "Got anything that might help get the Secret Service off our backs? I hope you got something. The Major's been expecting me to come up with anything new he can tell them."

"To get off his back, you mean," J. W. said. "That's why you got ranks in any organization. It's to let that shit get off your plate and roll down to the next man's. But here's what I come up with. I do believe I know who's the focus of this counterfeit money deal. I talked to the man himself who runs it."

"That was fast. How'd you do that so quick. And who is he?"

"Tyrone, you got to know Mississippi and you got to love barbecue ribs coming from the source. Put that together, and you can't go wrong."

"I do not know nor love your home state, Sergeant Ragsdale, but as a member of the race of people who invented barbecue, I do respect what y'all do with expired pigs down yonder. Tell me what you know."

"The man who's the connection to the counterfeit money deal is one Rayford Rio. He owns half the world down yonder, and he's working to get the rest. He looks like one of these pictures of fashion models you see in the magazines in the dentist's office. Slick, dressed up in clothes that women ought to be wearing, and as sure of himself as a Rhodes College fraternity boy drunk and high at a country club dance. He's got the world by the goddamn tail, and he knows it."

"Sounds like he's the kind you'd want to come up beside the head of. What'd you learn from him? Were you able to fool him along all right?"

"Hell, no," J. W. said. "He read me while I was sitting there, hat in hand, saying I was looking for a job. He called me by my name. Mentioned my employment status in Memphis. He did his best to make me want to turn in my badge and retire to an old folks' home in Collierville. He thought so little of me he didn't even try to fool me. He didn't have to. He just played with me."

After finishing his chuckle at J. W.'s description, Tyrone didn't say anything for a space, and then he bounced his fist off the steering wheel. "I understand it now. You let that receiver think you were so slow and weak that he lost all fear of you. So the next snap of the ball, he won't even bother to try to fool you. He'll just juke once and get on by you and take the ball to the house. And you'll be waiting for that, and surprise the shit out of him."

"You could say that, Tyrone, but you'd be telling a lie," J. W. said. "You're saying I was consciously pulling the old pity-fuck move on Mr. Rayford Rio. You know, the kind of thing with a woman you do when you try to make her feel sorry enough for you to give you a pity fuck. But, no, it wasn't that. Rio was not a bit scared of what I might be able to do with what I'd learned about him. He just showed me a move, and that move said this is not even the best I got. I can whip you without even having to give you my best shot. And he was right. But you know what? I have figured out that if I take it like a man we can still put this fashionable-dressed little fucker in a suit that fits real bad and looks like shit in a place where the eats and the clientele are terrible."

"That other thing you just said. A pity fuck. I never got one of them that I know of."

"You never had to, Tyrone," J. W. said, "I expect. But the thing is, see, that trying for a pity fuck and knowing you're doing it is one thing. When you don't even know you got one, that's something else altogether."

"That's pitiful. She doesn't even let on, huh?"

"Tell me about how pitiful it is," J. W. said. "All I know is we got enough info from my little tour of the upper Delta to get the Secret Service off our backs. It'll be their ballgame now. And that's wonderful."

"That won't stop the killings in Memphis, though, J. W."

"Naw, we can count on that keeping us employed and drawing salaries with benefits. God bless the upside of violent crime in the Bluff City."

"Tell me about it. And thanks to crime for keeping me and Marvelle in our house with payments done every month and food in the fridge and kids hollering in the yard."

"Yep," J. W. said, pointing out the window and craning his neck to read the sign on a building. "And lookie here where we've got to. There's the Family Fare Motel, your home away from home. Let's go look at what all we got upstairs somewhere resting all quiet and peaceful."

"I want to see that dog, too," Tyrone said. "Strange it's not a pit bull here in Memphis."

"Probably means the victims are white folks, don't you think? And let me get a gander at this Monica Moore. She's supposed to be a looker, somebody said."

"Your judgment of canines is so superficial, Sergeant Ragsdale,"

Tyrone said. "And women, too. A woman is not just the total sum of her physical appearance."

"Rave on," J. W. said. "Rave on. And let me ask you something before we get into this next one. Do you feel sometimes that everything is happening all at once? Right now in one time and place. I mean, here's one thing and here's another, and before you can straighten one of them out and before you get to the next one, it's another one, whole different from the first ones, and it's popping up, saying look at me, dummy. Here I am, too. Deal with me, too, asshole."

"Sure, it's all happening at once. Tell me a time when at least three things were not jumping up in our face saying feed me, feed me, feed me. Reality does not come in handy little packages, J. W. It comes in clots and dribbles and mostly in full-scale onslaught."

"Don't talk fancy about it anymore right now," J. W. said. "I don't want to hear about that kind of downer right now. Let's go look at that dog. I feel sorry for our canine friend. He wasn't breaking any laws, and he ends up as dead as the people that owned him."

"Dogs can break laws, J. W. And they will. They don't always come when you call them. They will bark and howl and carry on when they get a notion. They'll ignore commands. Now let's go see what we got in the Family Fare Hotel."

Inside and up five flights of the Family Fare Hotel, a uniformed cop was outside of the door of the room where all the action had taken place, and he was talking to a woman who seemed to be medical personnel, given the whites she was wearing, the clipboard in her hand, and the bored look on her face. An ordinary civilian would have been either jabbering non-stop at a crime scene, wired past all reason, or looking as stunned as somebody just hit on the head with a weighty object. This one was cool, all business, and damned good-looking, in J. W.'s estimation.

Tyrone was looking at the uniformed cop rather than the woman, and he was displaying a look which J. W. knew indicated his partner saw something out of place. "Patrolman Reedy," Tyrone said, looking down at the name tag on the cop's chest, "you're at a crime scene. Put your lid on, and report to me and Sergeant Ragsdale what you've learned so far."

"Yessir," Reedy said, replacing his hat on the abundance of curly black hair on his head. "I was just answering a question that this lady had asked me about the crime scene."

Showing off all them damn curly locks to her, more likely, J. W. thought, letting this luscious little dish see what kind of coloration you still got. I wish I had me some hand clippers and we were both in the uniform of our country somewhere in a combat zone. I'd skin that little head until it was nice and shiny and all full of nicks from the clipper.

"Sergeants," said the assistant medical examiner, looking from Tyrone to J. W., "you'll want to look at what's in that room on your own, of course, but I can tell you that it looks in most ways like an ordinary homicide scene involving a male and a female, both African American, but there are some touches I've never seen before. That's your bailiwick, of course, and I'm sure you can make more sense of it than I can."

"You're just interested in the bloody part, right?" J. W. said, and got a chance to get a full-face look at the assistant ME as she focused on him. Completely pale and unblemished in her complexion, he considered, and damn, look at that perfect nose. Something is wrong with me. I got to get over it. I keep looking at young good-looking women as though they might be possibles for somebody in my situation. They ain't that, not any more. But I got to forgive myself for doing that. It's just muscle memory kicking in. It doesn't know any difference between ages or situations. It can't think and make judgments. It's got to depend on the boss to do that, and the boss is no longer trustworthy. A dying set of gonads will lie like a son of a bitch.

"It's my job," she said. "So yes. The bloody part's where I make my living. I don't have to figure out what to do after that's taken care of. You and your partner get to have all that fun. I just talk about where everything's leaked out already."

"Let's go ahead and take a look," Tyrone said. "See where all our fun's located."

The two bodies of the human victims were lying side by side on the king-sized bed of room 527 in the Family Fare Hotel, looking as though they had been placed there neatly after the killings had been done. The dog, its eyes glazed and open and its jaws popped wide, was sprawled at the foot of the bed, with ample evidence of a large gunshot wound to the top of its head. The dead humans were wearing what appeared to be clothes that fit a special pattern, one that J. W. couldn't figure out at first sight. They were so soaked with blood it was hard to tell the exact nature of the costumes, but they looked to J. W. to be high-quality goods.

"What is this stuff they're wearing, Tyrone?" he said. "It looks awful familiar to me, but I can't quite place it."

"The female is wearing what appears to be a nun's habit," Tyrone said. "See there beside the head where the hood has been pulled off. It's hard to tell with all the blood smear, but it used to be mostly white."

"You're right," J. W. said, "and the other one, the man, he's got one of them white collars around his neck. Used to be white, that is."

"A nun and a priest," Tyrone said. "Dressed up like that, at least. I wonder if they really did belong to orders."

"Orders?"

"Yeah, you know, Sergeant Ragsdale. The various categories of separate organizations of clerics and nuns as the Roman Catholic Church defines them."

"Of course," J. W. said, asking himself why he, a man raised as a Southern Baptist, now fallen far away from that, naturally, would be expected to know anything about what the Catholics called themselves and how they divided everything into categories. But again, Tyrone Walker was sure as hell not raised as anything but a church-going black boy being hollered at every Sunday by a series of preachers and listening to all that good singing. But Tyrone seemed always to know about stuff that didn't have a thing to do with him directly. Oh, well, I can always start reading a lot when I'm retired, J. W. told himself. I will, I will.

"Suppose they were really that?" he said. "A nun and a priest all locked up in romance in a hotel room and killed while doing it."

"I doubt it seriously," Tyrone said. "I bet it's some kind of play acting they were doing. And somebody killed them while they were dressed for the performance."

"Some weird shit," J. W. said. "It ain't Mardi Gras in New Orleans in this Family Fare Hotel right now. This here is Memphis down to the bone. Look at all the blood if you doubt what I'm saying."

"Why the dog?" Tyrone said. "If we're talking ritual, what is a canine supposed to mean?"

"Who knows?" J. W. said, and turned to look at one of the other men in the room, one not attached to the medical examiner's bunch. He was a uniformed policeman standing near the door to the bathroom, looking much more professional in J. W.'s opinion than the curly-haired model cop in the hall. J. W. recognized the one in the room from a workshop Major Dalbey had him to conduct on arrest procedures occurring in a large crowd, defined as more than four persons to be detained and that by only one officer. J. W. had gone by the book in his teaching of the workshop, knowing he was being monitored front, left, and center, but he had felt badly constrained in what he was able to tell the young students about the topic under consideration. He hoped afterwards that the anemic instruction he'd been allowed to give hadn't gotten some rookie cop killed or at least shamed and beat all to hell.

He was just about to speak to Officer Antwan Murphy when the loud sounds of a woman's voice came from out in the hall, insisting to the cop stationed there that she had to be allowed to enter the crime scene. "I'm the executive director of We 2," she was saying. "Those victims inside that room are clients of my firm. I've got to be allowed to see what's gone on. We have important issues to address."

"No, ma'am," the cop was saying. "There's no one allowed in there right now but police personnel."

Well, he's learned something, J. W. considered. He's said the right thing. Got to give him that, and now I'll go out there and see what this executive director's up to. "Sergeant Walker," he said. "I'll go tend to all this hollering and carrying on in the hall, unless you want to."

"Do it," Tyrone said. "I'll do some more looking around in here until you get back."

The woman outside was trying to push her way around the cop with the curls, actually putting her hands on his upper arms in the process, and J. W. was disappointed to see that taking place. How in the name of God are rookies being taught these days, he considered as he stepped out into the hall and shut the door to the room behind him. You can't let anybody put hands on you when you're doing business. It's head-busting time, if that happens, even if it is a woman hollering about executive director and clientele and current situation and issues, meanwhile looking like a whole lot of money the way she's acting and presenting herself. She can't do that, regardless, no matter how much she outranks the ordinary Memphian trying to disobey a valid order coming from an officer of the law.

"Ma'am," J. W. said, "please take your hands off that officer. He's being real restrained in the way he's responding to that, and you're lucky you're not a man. Otherwise you'd be nursing a knot on your head by now. Just step back, and tell me what you want, short of getting inside the crime scene. That you're not going to do."

"What is your name, sir?" the woman said. "I'll want that when I speak to the chief about how I've been treated for making a simple request."

J. W. gave her the information she asked for, even spelling his last name for her, and then he asked her the same question about identity she'd posed to him. She was calmer by then, he could tell, and he also recognized she was getting herself controlled and about to attempt a different approach. She's used to trying different ways to go when she has to. She's been negotiating her whole life.

"I've just been so upset," she said. "I'm Monica Moore, executive director of We 2, a social networking service, and one that's aboveboard in every way. For such a thing to happen as what I understand took place in that room is devastating. And I'm just floored by it."

"Do you know those people in there, the homicide victims we're dealing with? Who are they? What do you know about the situation here?"

"I do know them, of course," Monica Moore said. "I can give you their names and addresses. They're clients of We 2, and they were doing some role playing, in a kind of exercise designed to entertain and instruct and strike up familiarity and, you know, just encourage the process of connecting between adults."

"What kind of outfits they wearing in there?" J.W said, telling himself not to let the idea of connecting with an adult go too far in his own personal thinking as he interviewed a party interested in one way or another in a double murder. But Monica Moore did seem to fit the descriptions he had heard of her earlier. Tall, dynamite looking, scary in the eyes. She wore everything well, head to toe. "They seem to have costumes on, but it's kind of hard to tell, you understand. They were wearing these outfits when the violence took place."

"It's part of play," the executive director said. "It's really one of the ice-breaker exercises we offer at We 2. It can and in many cases, as in this one, involve assuming identities well away from the ordinary day-to-day lives of the clients we serve. It can be most freeing, and jolly, and just plain fun. And so effective."

"What do you tell them to do? What kind of exercise you talking about? I mean in this specific situation in that room right there."

"Okay, let me give you a quick and dirty explanation of what I'm talking about. By dirty, I don't mean vulgar or insulting. The exercise is just designed to be barrier-breaking and line-crossing, all in the service of letting possible friendship and human connection become real and vital. Here's how it goes. What we say to the couple seeking We 2 guidance is something like this. Is there a thing, an activity, a notion you have always considered a bit taboo in your thinking and behavior? And yet what you do find a bit alluring about playing in defiance of that prohibition or taboo? What makes you feel more energetic and a wee bit naughty when you think of violating that no-no you've entertained in that deep dark secret place in your mind? Are you following me, Sergeant?"

"Oh, yes ma'am," J. W. said, thinking about a taboo or two he wouldn't mind violating in connection with Monica Moore as she became more and more perked up as she talked. "I think I get what you're saying. It's kind of like saying to yourself that you never jumped out of an airplane tied to a parachute before. What would it feel like to do it?"

"Well, maybe it's sort of like that, but it has to involve more than one person as far as We 2 are concerned. We're talking connection, not just visceral thrill here. We are all over relationship, top to bottom."

"Got you. Go ahead and tell me how that barrier-breaking exercise applies to what's in that room yonder."

"I don't want to violate confidences," Monica Moore said. "We live by that principle at We 2, but I can reveal a bit of this specific couple, I suppose."

"Those people on that bed there are past worrying about getting their confidences violated. They're not worrying about a thing ever again. So you can speak clearly. I bet they'd want you to."

"Oh, of course. Forgive me. In this play situation, or as we call it at We 2, this initial reach-beyond-a-limit, both seekers of connection had been reared since birth as devout Roman Catholics. And both became fascinated by the vows of celibacy that priests and nuns take upon commitment to their new selves. They were also titillated by the notions of what lies beneath the habit and the robe. Where is the body? What is it saying? Is it there? Is it dying to be free? How does it feel?"

"So they dress all up, then," J.W said. "That's why they're wearing what they have on."

"We furnish a variety of cloaks of identity, as we call it, and our patrons who come to us for help in connection and commitment learn not only how to don their new apparel, but how to take it off."

"And how to get it on," J. W. said.

"Yeah, if you want to put it that way. You nailed it, Sergeant."

"You still can't come in there, Miss Moore. It's a crime scene until we get done all we want to get done. When that's done you can go in there, but you probably won't want to then. The bodies won't be there. When a scene is not a crime scene anymore, it's kind of like these encounters you been describing. When all the clothes are off and the business is done, who would want to look at it now? Let me out of here."

"You're a real romantic, aren't you?" Monica Moore said. "A real dreamer."

"I know you don't mean that, but I am turned that way now and then, for sure," J. W. said. "And after all this is over, Miss Moore, can I maybe buy you a drink on down the line somewhere?"

"Yes, sure you can," she said, after a pause in which she looked hard at J. W.'s face. "But be certain you're wearing the right clothes for it."

"I will be, for certain, all my taboos just lined up in my mind. But one more thing about what's in that room wearing all those bloody robes. Who do you think might have wanted to do something like this to this nun and priest?"

"I have no idea. That's not my job, I'm quite certain. It's your gig, Sergeant."

"It is that, for sure, and me and my partner are wearing just the right clothes for it. You take it easy now, Ma'am. And keep on doing what you're doing."

"And what's that?"

"Connecting," J. W. said, "connecting real good and hard."

Thurman Norman Tullos had never thought much about his name until he ended up in Memphis working at one of the Federal Express loading docks, not the main one at the airport facility but one of the little ones in the city itself where folks came carrying cargo that would fit in car trunks and truck beds and even bicycle baskets. At first Thurman Norman Tullos was glad to be anywhere as long as it wasn't in East Arkansas, but after almost a year of picking up packages of all weights and descriptions, not knowing what was in them or where they were going or coming from, he started feeling there was something missing in his day-to-day.

There were plenty of places to go and things to look at in Memphis, bars and cafes and the zoo and Mud Island and baseball games now and then, but taking advantage of things like that by himself got to be pretty old pretty quick for a man who'd spent his first twenty or so years in Marked Tree, Arkansas, in a family big enough to fill up a whole house. Not that Thurman Norman cared that much about being around his sisters and brothers and the old man, drunk most of the time and mean all the time, but they were somebody to talk to who'd notice him whenever he said anything.

That didn't prove to be the case in the Bluff City. The people he worked around in the FedEx facility were most of them married and older than Thurman Norman, and they all took off for home every day when their shift ended like a flock of ducks shot at by somebody trying to kill each and every bird. They didn't look back, and Thurman Norman didn't have anything to say to them anyway. There wasn't anything to talk about. Thurman Norman didn't read the newspaper or anything else, and the TV set he had bought for thirty-five dollars was so old all the color was faded out of the picture, he had no cable connection since it cost so damn much, and there wasn't anything worth watching on what would come in on the screen at any rate. How many times can you look at Happy Days and Andy Griffith and Marshal Dillon do the same things over and over? Old, old, old.

And another thing about Memphis, and it was something Thurman Norman had never thought about even a little before he got to the big city, was the fact that everywhere you looked there'd be niggers. It wasn't that he hadn't been around colored before back in Marked Tree, but the ones in Memphis were a different breed altogether. Uppity? Loud talking and cussing every breath? Making noises and playing that rap shit loud day and night? Not even noticing when a white man walked by one of them or a bunch of them except to say some rude and mean shit if you even looked at them? Showing in every way that they didn't think for one minute that a white man should have more notice and room and respect than they did, even black as the ace of spades as most of them were? And every color in between, and you could smell them coming a block away by the kind of perfume and grease and wax and hair oil they used.

And if you ever showed you were noticing one of them, he would cuss you like you'd cuss a work-mule back in Marked Tree. "What the fuck you looking at?" they'd say. "Honky motherfucker bastard. I'll come up beside your head, you peckerwood piece of shit."

And if you dared to show any comeback to one of them, he would just as soon cut you, or knock hell out of you, or shoot you with one of them sidearms most of them seemed to carry. So all you could do as a white man was just skedaddle, like Mama would say back when you were a kid. So in Memphis as a white man alone you had to take all that grief from the jungle bunnies and act like you deserved it. None of that seemed right.

So one day at a lunch break at the FedEx facility, while Thurman Norman was sitting outside in back eating a peanut butter and jelly sandwich he'd fixed to eat at work, a new man there, who looked to be eight or ten years older than Thurman Norman, sat down beside him and looked inside his own brown paper bag to pull out his lunch.

"Damn," he said, "I get so tired of eating these old cold sandwiches every day that rolls. Don't you? Even with a banana or a Twinkie to follow it up."

"Yeah," Thurman Norman Tullos said, "and I can't afford to pay to eat anything hot that's been cooked. My money just melts away before every payday. Time the eagle shits on Friday, I'm down to pocket change."

"Tell me about it, TNT," the coworker said. "I'm Joe Iserman, if you don't already know my name."

They laid their sandwiches down to shake hands, and that was a thing Thurman Norman hadn't done since leaving Marked Tree. Shake hands with somebody who wasn't a boss telling you where to go and what to do. Just saying hello to another man, and respecting you by shaking your hand when he did. A little thing, but when you never had it now, you missed it.

"You just called me by my initials, TNT," Thurman Norman said. "Why'd you do that? Not that I mind, now. I don't mean that. I knowed it was me you were talking to."

"Them's your initials, and TNT stands for tri-nitro-toluene. And that is an explosive stronger than dynamite. I'd call that a damn good label to be known by. Wouldn't you? TNT!"

"Yeah, that's fine. Just call me TNT. I like that. Never thought about it before."

From then on, his coworker who was over thirty years old, all right, and who was Joe Iserman and had been in the US Army until they busted him out for a set of infractions he didn't want to even give voice to since they were so wrong, called him TNT and he gladly answered to that. Joe had also been in the Tennessee State Penitentiary in Brushy Mountain over in the eastern part of the state for a year, got paroled from a five year stretch for a doped-up charge not any truer than the court-appointed lawyer who'd stipulated Joe's ass off the freedom of the streets and behind bars, and then Joe came back to Memphis to live because by God, it was Memphis with all that that meant. It was still some of what it had been once. A white man's town.

"Niggers and liberals have done all they can to ruin this town," Joe Iserman would tell anybody who'd listen, "but there's still merit left in this great old place yet, if we go ahead and keep up the fight to maintain it. You can't look off. You do, and it'll be gone for good."

TNT noticed that Joe could and would use words like "merit" and "maintain" and other terms which TNT had never had pass from his lips. Joe might be having to work at the same shitty job of lifting up and putting down packages all day as TNT did, but he thought about issues and problems and ways to try to do something to keep good things going and not let sorry ones prosper. "If we don't do it, TNT," he'd ask, "who's going to?"

"Nobody," TNT would say, feeling good he'd been asked. "It's up to us, I reckon, like you say."

One night about three or four months after TNT had met Joe Iserman and started thinking about maintaining the good as Joe helped him understand that, the two of them had gone to the Throw Down Lounge for a beer or two. It was payday, and both of them would be flush for a little bit.

"Listen," Joe said. "I've gotten to know you and where you're coming from, and I want to take things a step or two further along. Think you're ready, TNT, to suit up for the game?"

"Hell, yeah," TNT said, feeling the beer working in him like a blessing. "What you talking about? Put it on me, Hoss."

"All right, here goes. You ever heard of the Klan? The Ku Klux Klan?"

"Yeah, I heard of that. They used to talk about it some back home in Arkansas."

"Klan started right here in Memphis, after the War ended. Nathan Bedford Forrest got it going, the Klan. You've been to Forrest Park, hadn't you? Down by the Methodist Hospital there on Union where his statue is?"

"Nathan whatever you say his name is? Nathan Forrest? I seen a park down there all right."

"Nathan Bedford Forrest. Best general in the whole damn war, and before that, he sold slaves at the market here in Memphis, right downtown. Slave trader, that's what he was. He was taking care of the nigger question then, and he started right in to do it again after the Yankees whipped us in that war. General Forrest made it his life's work to keep the nigger in his place. Hell, that's where he's happy. Either as a slave or as a good biddable worker kept that way by the Klan. Him and his woman and all them kids."

"It is a nigger problem all right," TNT said. "I see it every day everywhere I look in Memphis."

"Tell me about it. Walk out on any street in town and look around you. I'll tell you something. I'm in a Klavern of the Klan right here in Memphis, and TNT you belong in it, too. I been watching you, how you work and how you think, and I believe you would find yourself a true home in the KKK."

TNT had never had the way he thought about anything ever mentioned by anybody before, in Memphis or in Marked Tree, Arkansas. Somebody now smart like Joe Iserman had considered that TNT did think. He had a thought or two. Within a month's time, he was regularly attending meetings of the Memphis Klavern of the Ku Klux Klan, and he had found a set of friends at last. He belonged somewhere with others who belonged there, too. And he was ready to do his part about controlling the nigger question in Memphis, Tennessee, and getting them jungle bunnies straightened out.

He blessed the day he had met Joe Iserman, and he went to work each morning at the FedEx Midtown sub-center ready to see Joe and to learn more about how to solve the problem facing the white race in America. He would do his part in the struggle. He knew he could, and as they told him, it's the white man's burden. We all got to help carry it. Civilization depends on it. I can think about it, and I do. Now I know TNT is thoughtful and has something to say. That's me. I'm TNT. My head works, too, same as anybody else. My brain is strong.

The next big meeting of the Nathan Bedford Forrest Klavern took place in a building way down close to the river landing below the Memphis Bluff. At one time it had been a true building, hooked up to others of its kind. It had had water and lights and glass in the windows. People worked in it at desks and docks and shop areas. Train cars were loaded with cargo and product from the structure built of bricks and stone and steel. It was a consequence. It made money.

Now it wasn't much of a location for a serious gathering to take place, but as Joe Iserman remarked to TNT, you can't make it easy for the fucking liberals and the Memphis police to know where you're getting together to decide how and where to strike a blow for the White Man. Not these days, not like it had been not that long ago in Memphis when you could actually advertise publicly what was going to be a matter of concern to the KKK in West Tennessee.

"Now, I'm not saying that it was ever in my lifetime possible to do things like put up posters and notices about what us KKK men was thinking about doing," said Doug Maysapps, Chief Speaker of the Memphis Klavern to the assembled bunch of members gathered in the ruins of what was once the headquarters of the biggest cotton factory on the Mississippi River. "No, you couldn't act with the freedom they gave white men back then and are giving now to nigger establishments. I'm talking about them church get-togethers today they let hordes of niggers set up right downtown in the Convention Center every year that rolls. Naw, nuh-uh. I'm not talking about that. That's just fine with the establishment."

"Tell it, Son," somebody yelled out. "We can speak truth here. Say it loud right here."

"That's right," Doug Maysapps said. "The Klan's got freedom of speech the same as any American. But, but, I tell you that's true only if you hide somewhere and say it real soft in the dark where nobody but us bunch can hear the message. Oh, yeah. We got freedom of speech. Just ask the media."

"Bullshit," the cry started up, and within a minute or two, everybody was chanting it together. Hearing that and joining his voice with it made a hot spot right in the center of TNT's chest rise up and grow stronger. It was sweet to be with people that believed he had something to say just like other folks. Just like the nigger preachers and the ones on TV jabbering about rights and laws and privileges. "Bullshit," TNT chanted, his voice one of many but one that belonged where it was being heard finally. "Bullshit, bullshit."

It better not be no nigger mess with me tomorrow in the daylight when I'm out on the streets of Memphis walking along minding my business, TNT pledged within. Next one gives me a putdown or a shove or laughs at the way I look or what I'm wearing or makes me leave the sidewalk to get around a bunch of them standing in my way, that sucker's going to pay for it. "I am a man, a white man," the chant began, "and I got rights, too."

"Say it loud," the chief spokesman of the Memphis Klavern shouted into his hand microphone, "say it loud. I am a man, a white man, and I got rights, too."

Tomorrow, TNT promised himself deep inside his own heart and the mind which he had not even known he had, not until he met Joe Iserman and learned of the great work of the KKK, tomorrow I will look for some nigger trying to put me down, and I will show him a surprise like he's never had before. "I am a man, a white man, and I got rights too," he shouted, his voice one among those of his brothers. Rights, rights, rights, the word as an echo, a beating heart in unison within the thoughtful, the proud, the fed-up TNT out of Marked Tree, Arkansas, now in his true home of Memphis, Tennessee. Saying something loud at last.

The next morning, on a day that TNT's shift at FedEx had off, right in the middle of the week, the new member of the Nathan Bedford Forrest Chapter of the KKK found himself out on the streets in Downtown Memphis. I'm just poking around, TNT said to himself, seeing what goes on in the morning on a weekday, not asking for any trouble and not wanting to get into any. But I tell you one thing, Hoss, he said to the self which now lived inside the self of what used to be Thurman Norman Tullos, any nigger that messes with me from now on is going to end up being one surprised spade once I get through with him. Damn, TNT thought in congratulation to himself, I never used to think like that when I'd walk out on the street. Am I worried? Hell, no. Am I going to let anything run over me again? Let me think about it for a spell. Okay, I just did.

Tell you what, Son. Just try it and see. Stick out an evil hand toward TNT, and you going to draw back a bloody nub.

Ahead of him right before the door to the coffee shop where TNT was headed, thinking to treat himself to something other than the instant powdered stuff he ordinarily fixed in the kitchen of his place just off Madison right close to where he worked, he could see walking along and giggling and holding hands a couple he couldn't believe he was beholding. They seemed to be about his age from what he could tell looking at their faces, but they were not like anything he'd ever seen before.

It's a Catholic priest, he told himself, noting the dark suit and the white collar, and he's walking along holding hands with a nun. He could tell that's what the woman was a lot easier than he could make out that the man all snuggled up to her was a priest. You couldn't see but a little bit of her hair sticking out from the white and black rig she had on her head, but her clothes right down to her shoes said NUN like somebody was hollering the word.

But the thing about both of them that was most evident and shocking to TNT was not just the garb the two were wearing, but the fact that they were not white. "Them two Catholics yonder is niggers," TNT whispered to himself, thinking them two ain't supposed to be rubbing all over each other like two dogs in heat. Look at them, just slavering at each other. Feeling each other up. A nun and a priest putting their hands where it's wrong to be. Where it's deadly sin. Right here in the open in Memphis, Tennessee, middle of the morning on a weekday. He discovered himself falling into step behind the two Catholics, matching his gait to theirs so as to be able to watch what was going on and wanting to see where they were going.

TNT didn't have to decide where he was headed and what he would do if the priest and the nun took notice of him, knowing his body would be up to the task of directing where he had to go and what he had to do. Ever since he'd learned he was no longer just Thurman Norman Tullos, but TNT now and a new member of the Forrest Klavern of the KKK, he'd not had to worry about deciding what to do every minute of the day. Before that, in the dead days before KKK, when he was at work at the FedEx facility, he'd not had to worry about what to do when and how, either. The boss showed him that, and he could rest his mind for the whole shift without having to think ahead. That was the good part of the day. The bad part, the sorry hours as he'd thought of them, always came after he was told to leave because his shift was over.

Then he had to go back to the room he rented, unlock that door, look inside where everything was where he'd left it, all just waiting for him to get back with these mute dead things lying there and decide what to move around and what to leave alone. And the TV set was so sorry to watch that he was seldom, if ever, able to lose himself in seeing what it was showing and saying. So he had to keep deciding what to do, if he could be able to come up with something in his head. Every minute he had to think what to do. All he looked at was saying things to him. Look here. Deal with something. Open a can of chili? Drink a coke? Lie down on the sofa where all those springs poked up and hit him in the back every time he moved? Just look out the window of the room, the only window and the only outside light there was, and see that tree limb that hung over it just right in that same place all the time? Maybe a bird would land there, if he watched long enough. But it wouldn't stay if it did, and then there'd be just the same limb as before, nothing different. After the bird left, that limb would just move up and down until it quit and got to be dead like it had been before.

But all that was before he started seeing that Thurman Norman Tullos was really TNT, what the older members of the Klavern called him when they shook hands and slapped him on the back, and when they asked if he was up for the war to come when things would go back to what they had been and had to be again if this country was ever to be what it was supposed to be. A White Man's Nation. A place where the niggers knew their place again and would stay in it and leave their betters alone. Where they'd serve the duties God had intended them for when he let them climb out of the trees to be the White Man's helpers.

Now the priest and the nun ahead of TNT were turning into the coffee shop, the one where he'd intended to get some chocolate-tasting hot drink with sweet foam on the top, and he found himself carried into the shop right behind them by whatever was directing his mission to follow in the steps of the blaspheming couple.

TNT marveled at the fact that a word like blaspheming had come into his head all by itself. That word never had before, but it was happening more and more that new things were coming to him daily, ever since he had become part of something bigger than what he'd been when he'd sat for hours looking out the window as light faded and the tree limb couldn't be seen any longer. Back then, that had once scared him and made him cry real tears even at times as he lay waiting to go to sleep so he could get up in the morning and be told for eight hours what to do by a boss.

I don't need a boss now, TNT said to himself, telling me what to do so I can act right. Now everything I see is easy to face up to. I know I'll follow that nigger priest putting his hands all over that nigger nun, and I'll catch him doing it and her liking it and throwing her head back and letting him stick his tongue in her mouth, and I'll find out what I'm supposed to do. And I'll do it, and I'll be the White Man in this war like I'm supposed to be. We got to win it, and I got to do my part no matter what that voice in my head tells me to do. I'm glad to know I don't have to worry any more. I'm being moved around just the way I been wanting to be. I'm ready for whatever action I'm supposed to take. I'm TNT. I'm dynamite.

J.W. was taking small, short, measured and regular sips from the one bottle of beer he was allowing himself before he met up later with Tyrone Walker. The bottle sat glowing with condensation before him on the table of the Owl Bar, the one table he always preferred to occupy when he visited the favorite late-night retreat of the denizens of the Midtown division of the Memphis Department of Public Safety. That was the name all officers and personnel of the Midtown station were supposed to use now. Don't say police, whatever you do. Don't be waving that old-fashioned word around like a nightstick or a sap or a non-reg sidearm. Say safety. Say public. Say something that doesn't remind folks that we're really talking about things that can get as bloody and busted up as a pole-axed hog at killing time back home in Mississippi. Be nice. Be nonthreatening.

"Be a lying wimp-ass," J. W. said aloud and took his next measured sip of the cheapest beer available for sale in the Owl.

"You talking to me, Sergeant Ragsdale?" asked Ron Spurgeon as he flopped down across from J. W.'s favorite seat, the one that allowed him to see who was sitting at the bar itself and the door opening into the Owl from outside without having to twist around to keep all things important properly observed. "I ain't even said a word to you yet, and here you are calling me a name. I don't mind the lying label but the wimp-ass does sting a little."

"Hey, Ron," J. W. said. "I wasn't thinking about you. Something else that pisses me off instead this time. That's what I was pondering on. But just this time."

"Well, that eases my mind, which makes me want to tell you what I been thinking about. You ain't going to believe this shit, J. W. It's something I been doing you never would have been able to guess."

"What is it? Some more of that strange pussy you been getting from that dating service? Some old crazy lady whose husband is either gone dead-dick on her or dead for sure and is now buried in a hole in the ground? You done told me about that business, and I don't want to have to think about it again. It makes feel desperate enough to switch from beer to hard liquor, and it's not even nine o'clock yet."

"Naw, it's not about We 2 this time, but that's still high on my list of what makes life in Memphis worth living on a cop's salary. But no, not that," Ron Spurgeon said, his eyes dancing as he leaned forward to slap his own longneck bottle on J. W.'s table. "Here's what it is, and I'm going to make you listen to me talk about art whether you like it or not."

"Art?" J. W. said. "Art? What do you know about art? Have you found a Plastic Man funny book in a junk store somewhere to look at? Taking you back to your grade school days?"

"Nah, it's this show at the art museum in Overton Park. You probably never been in there, but I know you've driven by it a million times. See, they've been advertising what kind of a civic show they're putting on. You know, a celebration of life in Memphis low to the ground and close up. If you'd just look around you, you'd learn new things like I do. Stuff to enrich your inner life, you understand. The life of the mind."

"Shit," J. W. said. "The life of the mind. What kind of thing is that to say right here in the Owl Bar talking to a cop still on duty this time of night, not even able to buy enough beer to get in him to feel it?"

"It's a show of local artists they been getting together, see, and the first profession they are celebrating is public safety workers. They announced it and they gave it a name. Police Painting and Cop Art. That's what they're calling it."

"I bet it ain't but one picture to it, that one of the cop sitting by a little boy at a counter, all prettied up. You know he's running off from home or something, and the cop's being nice, instead of just shaking the little fucker real good."

"I know the one you talking about," Ron Spurgeon said. "Painted by somebody famous. It's cute, but no, this is local works of art by real police officers. And you know what? I'll tell you before you say you don't want to hear nothing else about it. I got inspired, see. Something moved me. I took me a piece of newspaper, see, a big page from the *Commercial Appeal*, and I dribbled red paint all over it, like it was blood, you understand. You should see the effect, and then I took a old pair of handcuffs, the ones we ain't even allowed to use no more since they're so nasty looking and hard on the assholes we used to have to cuff with them. Then I dipped them cuffs in the red paint, and I slapped the impression of that in the middle of that bloody-looking sheet, and I named it *To Protect and Serve*."

"Why'd you do that? And how did you think of making up that kind of crap?"

"J. W.," Ron said in a solemn tone. "It just come to me. That's the way art does, see. Nobody can tell where the genius of a work comes from. It's just been brooding like an egg in a hen. It's got to come out. It was in my heart and soul."

"Oh, for Jesus sake," J. W. said. "You been drinking turpentine again, I swear to God you have."

"It gets better. Get ready. My work has won third prize in the category of assembly art. They said it's inspirational and gripping. How do you like them apples?"

"Well, that's just wonderful," J. W. said. "I salute you, Mr. Picasso. Kiss my ass if I don't."

"It's also already got me some pussy, J. W.," Ron said. "I didn't even have to pay for it, neither. Not nearly as much as We 2 does when you count up all the associated expenses."

"Was it high quality?" J. W. asked. "This art lover's piece of ass? I bet it was either real skinny or real overweight, whoever was dispensing it. I bet it wasn't in the same league as the We 2 goods."

"Well, no, it wasn't. But it was cheap. You get what you pay for. And all I had to get in there was to use some old leftover red paint, some outlawed cuffs, and my imagination."

"Well, that's the thing, isn't it? The artist's imagination. That makes all the difference. The genius of creation, huh?"

"What the hell are you two talking about?" somebody said. "Artist's imagination. Didn't I just hear you say that, J. W.? Are you drunk already this time of night, and we still got to make a house call before the patient wakes up and hits the streets of Memphis looking to cause outrage and mischief. Are you getting forgetful?"

"Tyrone," J. W. said. "Damn, I'm glad to see you. My head is just spinning from discussing the pussy-getting power of art with Ron here. He is the artist in question, and he has made a breakthrough which is going to get in all them picture books about, well, you know, about pictures."

"I'll leave you two loudmouths now," Ron said. "But I'll tell you that the Cop Art show is on through the end of the month, and my installation with the winner's ribbon attached to the bottom of it is just to the right of the door as you go in. I will be glad to discuss it with you further after y'all have seen it. I'm sure there'll be comments and questions you'll want answered. Photos are not allowed in the museum, but I'll tell you what. I'll let y'all take a picture of *To Protect and Serve* once I get it home after the show closes."

"What if somebody buys it first?" Tyrone said. "You know, for a gallery or a private collection or to put in a outhouse to scare off rats?"

"Shit, I hadn't thought about that," Ron Spurgeon said. "I got to worry about that now. One thing after another."

"It's part of the price of greatness," Tyrone said. "You got to learn to live with it. You know the artist has got to suffer for his vision. Suffering inspires him."

After Ron Spurgeon had left the table to look for somebody else to inform about his art, head swiveling from side to side to find somebody willing to listen, Tyrone ordered a lemon-lime soft drink and began to huddle with his partner about the night's work ahead.

"I've found out where we're supposed to meet Lo Lo Tedrick tonight, J. W.," he said. "And it's not going to be at his den on Baby Street. Not this time and not any more ever again, he's told me."

"Getting too hot for him with the Bones Family? Not nearly so tight with him anymore, huh?"

"I do believe it's the wages of sin, J. W. Lo Lo claims he's going to be all right with that bunch, as long as he keeps looking clean of connection with folks like you and me. Lo Lo is getting a little nervous, and his sin is not against Jesus but the ones he's been running with ever since he dropped out of the third grade."

"So the Bones Family ain't too comfortable with one of their officers getting a different religion, I reckon. Lo Lo has got to learn the path to the Cross is a tough one. It's all full of briars and stones and pitfalls. Look what it did to Jesus."

"Yeah, but don't start preaching, Sergeant Ragsdale. The way I was raised I'm liable to get worked up and start hollering out loud and praising the Lord. I don't want to do that in this foul den of iniquity called the Owl."

"Okay, got you. No need to worry. I don't praise nothing no more that I can't get in my mouth and savor the sweetness therein up against my tongue. Where're we going to have to meet Lo Lo, and what does he want to tell us about what's what with this killing mixed up with counterfeit money? I done got the Mississippi end of things fixed up clear enough to satisfy the Secret Service boys, I do hope and believe. They now know who to get after. And if we can get the killing at this end all tied up, that'd be one less mess to worry about."

"Lo Lo wants to meet us behind the old Big Boy Diner there just off Madison. You know, close to what used to be Joe's Gins. Now it's Joe's Wines. Classier that way."

"I know all about Joe's Gins and the name change, partner. You don't have to remind me about that, and if you'll just cast your mind back, you'll remember. You can't tell me nothing about liquor stores in Memphis. But the thing about Big Boy Burgers is a little hazy. Is that burger building still standing? I hadn't thought about the Big Boy in a long time, Tyrone. Damn, they used to make a good hamburger."

"You probably stopped seeing it as soon as it stopped meaning something to eat, but yeah the building's still there. And that statue of the Big Boy with his hand out holding a burger is still there. It's shot all to pieces now, pretty much, but the Boy himself is still standing. Still grinning, looking happy and eager to please."

"Boy has still got his big old pompadour in place sticking out?"

"Last time I looked, yeah," Tyrone said. "Anyway, Lo Lo says he's got some good info and the right names for us to follow up on with that killing on Peach Street, and he's ready to divulge."

"How long is Lo Lo going to keep talking to us, Tyrone?" J. W. said, lifting his bottle to his lips for the last swig at the bottom. "He's beginning to sound a little light in the loafers, don't you think? A little unsound?"

"He is about to float on off,"Tyrone said. "He's told me he's so little connected with the Bones Family now he's afraid to see any of them anymore. I expect that's why he wants to talk to us. Get a little ahead of impending events, you understand."

"Damn this religious conversion shit Lo Lo keeps trying to sell," J. W. said. "It does get in the way of harvesting reliable info about illegal doings. Used to be when a young man had gone bad he'd stay that way. You could depend on him to be sorry enough to the core so you could take advantage of that. Not no more with all this mealy-mouth praising of the Lord."

"Yeah,"Tyrone said. "Goddamn a man who's turned soft and now seeks the good. What good is he anymore? Stay evil."

"Let me get this last swig of beer took care of, and I'll be ready to go."

"I was wondering how long you were going to suck on the lip of that bottle,"Tyrone said. "The sides are beginning to cave in, and that reminds me of something I'm supposed to say to you. Something I've been told to relay to you."

"Yeah, what?"

"It's in the romantic area, something a married man don't know a thing about, but a young fellow like you is still in the game of love. Here it is, then."

"I don't need no more heartbreak," J. W. said. "Don't kick a man when he's down. But tell me, damn it."

"That ME girl, the one at the Family Fare killings told me she'd mentioned your name to her colleague, a woman you might remember."

"Oh, shit, don't hurt me now. Please, Tyrone. I know I've done wrong, but don't twist that damn knife."

"No, it's good. Nova Hebert told her to get word to you that she'd like to talk to you on the phone. Or at the morgue the next time you get a chance,"Tyrone said, speaking slowly as though trying to communicate to a person who was not a native speaker of the language. "She sends her greeting to you, Nova does, says the ME lady. Good will is being conveyed."

"Really? Hell, I'll do it. Go ahead and hit me between the eyes with a two-by-four again, I'll tell her. I can take. More than that, I want it. Hit me with your best shot."

“You are sounding too much like a human being,” Tyrone said as though astonished. “My Lord, J. W. Is that you? Seeking connection?”

“Don’t make fun. I can’t take it no more, and I sure ain’t got three thousand dollars to join up with We 2 like Ron Spurgeon’s done. I’m too broke to buy into happiness like he’s done. I’m lonely, but no one can tell.”

“Don’t break into song, Son,” Tyrone said. “You’ll bring me to tears. Let’s go visit the shrine of the Big Boy and see what Lo Lo Tedrick’s got to say.”

20

On the way to the ruined Big Boy restaurant, J. W. and Tyrone talked a little about what tack to take with Lo Lo and wondered why a Bones claimer was looking to say something, and then Tyrone broke off that conversation by saying he had remembered a thing which Major Dalbey had mentioned to him late in the afternoon. It had to do with the Nathan Bedford Forrest statue at the center of the park dedicated to the great cavalry leader of the Confederacy, placed in a large green space cheek by jowl with the medical college of the University of Tennessee on one of the main arteries feeding into Downtown Memphis. The United Daughters of the Confederacy had raised funds for the memorial back in the early twentieth century, determined to keep alive the memory of the slave trader, general, founding father of the Ku Klux Klan, and all-around emblem of resistance, defiance, and admiration. He had been right down the alley of the ladies of the UDC. N. B. Forrest had loomed large in the Bluff City in life, in death, and in memory, and now the central memorial to him was under siege.

"You know what all's been going on with memorials to the Confederacy these days, of course, don't you, J. W.?" Tyrone said. "After all that business with the statue of Robert E. Lee in New Orleans and that bunch of crazies in Charlottesville, it's happening everywhere now. Arguing over statues and language and memorials."

"Yeah, I read the paper, now and then, and see the news, so I know you're talking about these folks wanting to tear down old Forrest's memorial statue. So what's the Major saying about it? Is he smelling trouble again, more than usual?"

"Well, the mayor and the city council and all the big dogs don't want Memphis to be showing up in the media again like it always seems to," Tyrone said. "You know our city's always got dirty britches, the garbage strikes in the sixties, Dr. King being killed here, all that shit that's gone on forever and a day in Memphis. So the administration is planning to take that statue down in the middle of the night soon, well before protesters and defenders of the damn thing get a chance to embarrass us one more time. Beat them to the punch for a change."

"I get you. We got to get there firstest with the mostest," J. W. said. "That's the way you win a battle."

"You are always fooling me, J. W.," Tyrone said. "That's what Forrest was famous for saying about tactics, wasn't it?"

"Sure it was. Don't you know I'm a serious student of history? Hell, I even own two or three books. I ain't saying I read any of them now, but when I was a kid in Mississippi we had to recite the famous words of Confederate generals each night before we went to bed."

"There on the plantation? Where y'all kept the slaves you owned?" Tyrone said. "Singing about Dixie every night? Cutting up and laughing and throwing corn cobs at each other?"

"Yeah, but Tyrone, you realize that not only did the Ragsdales not own slaves back in that time, we didn't own but one pair of shoes in the whole family. We had to pass that pair to the one of us fixing to go to town. But they did pour that propaganda into us, and we still ain't got over it. We been snaked down from our rightful spot, and we know it."

"Tell me about it. I can just look at you and tell that. Anyway, we got to be involved in providing police protection and cover and help in planning about how to tear down General Forrest's likeness without getting folks roughed up and killed, so be thinking about that. We don't need any more negative national news coverage in Memphis than we usually get. I'm just relaying the word of our noble leader, understand. Look, there's the Big Boy with his hand stuck out."

"Oh, hell," J. W. said. "Some asshole has shot his pompadour half off his head."

"The Big Boy's still grinning, though. It's so hard to keep a good man down."

"It was hard to keep his burgers down, too," J. W. said. "Lookie yonder at that Dodge Charger nosed in behind the end of that building. That's got to be Lo Lo Tedrick."

It was, and Lo Lo had obviously been parked in the dark beside the remains of the home of the Big Boy long enough to make him nervous and ready to move. When Tyrone flashed his car lights off and on, Lo Lo did one flashback, popped the door to his Dodge open, and stepped out into the heat of a Memphis night, raising both hands above his head briefly.

"Lo Lo is so well trained that whenever he sees a cop, he just automatically surrenders so he won't get shot at," J. W. said. "You got to admit the boy ain't so dumb he can't learn how to do. Look how nice he throwed them hands up."

"Even amoeba and blowflies respond to light sources," Tyrone said. "All living things shrink from the light. Or fly to it. Don't give our Bones claimer more credit than he deserves. That was not thought. That was automatic. Let's make him sit up here by me, and you get in the back, J. W."

"Make him a little nervous, huh? Make Lo Lo keep having to crane his neck to look around while we're having our nice little conversation."

"Exercise is good for a young man, newly Christian in outlook. It helps him to keep moving in this fallen world, see. Don't get fixed in your ways and hung up in old habits. If you love the Lord, let it show."

"You use your knowledge of psychology in a cruel way," J. W. said. "Where'd you learn them interview tricks? At Memphis State?"

"Naw, from watching you make a whole herd of poor boys squirm and feel loose in the bowels over the years," Tyrone said. "I studied with the master. Maybe you can get out now and usher our little man into the front seat of honor."

Lo Lo was ready to talk, say what he knew, and beg off having to meet with Sergeants Walker and Ragsdale ever again, so he began speaking as soon as he sat down in the passenger's seat. "I can't stay here long, officers," he said. "I'm afraid somebody might see me here talking to y'all. I got to get on back out of here as soon as I can. I got to stay out of trouble."

"Why?" J. W. asked. "Is tonight prayer meeting? It ain't Wednesday, is it?"

"Every night and every day is prayer meeting for me now," Lo Lo said. "Praise Jesus. Lift him up on high."

"Uh-huh," Tyrone Walker said. "Don't get started with that bull now. There's a time and place for each and everything, and right now it is not for talking about Jesus and carrying on with that kind of worship stuff."

"Please, Sergeant Walker," J. W. said. "I've always got time to praise the Lord, and I know that Lo Lo feels the same way. Don't you, son?"

"Yessir, thank you for them words. I lift them up for the Lord to see."

"He will approve," said J. W. "Now tell us what you want to say about the matters we talked about in our last visit with you. That killing on Montgomery where it runs into Peach. You remember that. It ain't been long ago."

"Yessir, officer. I do, and that's one of them things I got to clear my conscience about. It was the Bones Family come down on Two Teeth and Fado Moody there at the end of the street. Latin Lords, both of them was, and the Bones claimers was Jump Steady and Baby Shanks. The other one I don't know."

"We know most of that already," Tyrone said, impatience working through the tone of his voice like blood flowing from a severed artery. Hot, jumping, and costly. "Tell us about the man that fake money was being carried to in Mississippi. Who and where?"

"Them Franklins was counterfeit, and wasn't worth nothing," Lo Lo said. "The things of this world are as dust compared to the Kingdom of God."

"Who's been talking this kind of trash to you?" Tyrone said, turning in the driver's seat to stare directly at Lo Lo. Although J. W. couldn't tell from his place in the rear of the car, he knew Tyrone's eyes would be burning as he stared. Damn, he's good at this shit, J. W. considered. I love being the nice guy when Tyrone really gets into the role of the crazed cop. I can just sit back in wonder.

"Now, now, Sergeant Walker," J. W. said. "This young Christian is new to the Lord and under conviction, and he's doing his best to cleanse his mind of sins of commission he did before he accepted Jesus Christ as his personal savior. He's working through the days of his sinful past, and he's got Glory in his sight."

"Thank you, officer," Lo Lo Tedrick said, a tear in his voice. "You know what I be going through and what I try to be saying. What I tell you is the man the money was going to he has his own airport and airplanes down in a place called Batesville."

"We already know that," Tyrone said. "So what you got to tell us new besides which gangbanger killed which gangbanger? We ain't really worried about what Bones claimer offed what Latin Lord. We wished they was all blowed away. It'd be like cleaning up a dirty commode. What can you tell us?"

"Here is what it is, and next time you see me, I'll be in the same body but with a new soul."

"Yeah, yeah, so?"

"A big new shipment of that fake hundreds and thousands bills of money is going to be coming to the Bones Family a few days from now," Lo Lo said. "It be going to Deangelo Dixon, his place. It going to be the most ever they done got made up. You just heard that from me, and now you'll let me be."

"How come it's coming to the Bones Family? I thought it was the Latin Lords runnin' this scheme."

"I don't know nothin' about that. I don't know what-all connections Deangelo Dixon got. I done forgot it already. It ain't none of me. I don't want no more to do with Bones. I ain't said nothing to nobody."

"What you're saying, Lo Lo, is that you are getting a new soul, a clean one, and you will be about the work of your Heavenly Father from now on out," J. W. said. "Your eyes are turned away from this world and toward the eternal one, instead."

"Yes, Mr. Sergeant. Praise him," said Lo Lo, beginning to weep, "Thank you, Jesus."

"When and where is this transaction going to take place?" Tyrone said. "What else do you know about it? Tell me exactly what you know."

"Then will you leave me to the Lord and Master? Will you not never talk to me again? Please, sir."

"I'll think about it. I won't see you again unless I just have to. What else you got?"

"I'll have more to tell you day after tomorrow," Lo Lo said. "It's a Bones meeting coming by then. They going to talk about it, and I got to be in that sinful place one last time."

"I'll be by to see you, then," Tyrone said. "I don't know if Sergeant Ragsdale can make that next one, but I sure as shit can."

"I hope Mr. Sergeant Ragsdale can," Lo Lo said, easing the car door open "It's easeful to me when he's there, too."

"Love the Lord with all your might," J. W. said after him, leaning forward from the back seat. "Pray to him for all your needs."

After the Dodge Charger pulled away, J. W. looked at Tyrone in the reflected light of the dashboard and shook his head. "I never knew how little you love the Lord, Sergeant Walker," he said. "I'm shocked, to tell you the truth. Shocked and afraid for your soul's salvation. I will keep you in my prayers."

"J. W., the truth is not in you," Tyrone said, beginning to laugh. "If Jesus was taking notes, he'll have a whole indictment ready for your ass as soon as you hit the door of heaven."

"Jesus and me are tight," J. W. said. "Always have been. At least most of the time. He knows when you have to lie. He shaded the truth himself sometimes. What I'd be worried about if I was you is what Dr. Martin Luther King is going to say about your treatment of your black brother. He'll be waiting by Heaven's Door. He will lecture you when you hit them golden gates, and I doubt he will argue too strongly for Saint Peter to let you in."

"Dr. King sinned some, too. It's in the book. All those ladies he wasn't married to."

"Yeah, but he was forgiven. You ain't going to be, Tyrone. Thus sayeth the Lord."

"I'm glad I don't drink, usually," Tyrone said. "But I'm willing to buy you one or two shots if you still got time tonight to stay up for a while longer."

"An old man can't sleep anymore anyway," J. W. said. "And I want top of the line bourbon, not your damned old Rebel Yell whisky. Take me to a fern bar with soft music, Sergeant Walker. You backsliding blasphemer against the light, you."

Oh, Lord, have mercy, Willis Sutcliff said to himself as he sat in one of the prime seats in the coliseum, right next to Dallas Simmons again, if this ain't sweet and gratifying, if things aren't going exactly as planned and hoped, grits ain't groceries, eggs ain't poultry, and Mona Lisa was a man. This was the third meeting of Maureen Langlois and Pig Sooey, the bout that would decide the reigning champion of the Women's Component of Memphis Mixed Martial Arts, Mid-South Division, and it promised to be a bell-ringer. The first match had gone to Maureen Langlois, beauty having beaten the living hell out of nastiness and ignorance in the form of Pig Sooey, doing so with style and vigor and contempt for all ugliness and low behavior, and that match was the one that had fascinated Dallas Simmons, financier and risk-taker.

That money man came the first time to scoff and remained to pray, as the saying goes, Willis considered as he had watched Dallas Simmons suck at the cocktail fetched to him by the impeccably dressed and efficient young black man, hired out as special attendant on loan from one of the best restaurants in New Orleans. High-class money demands high-class service.

In the earliest match, Simmons had been so taken by the sight of Maureen Langlois mounting the tub of lard named Pig Sooey, seizing her by her nasty greasy hair, and pounding her head into the surface of the octagon that Willis Sutcliff fully expected to witness that man with the heavy money bags undergo an unplanned sexual emission. He kept grabbing at his crotch the whole time that Maureen Langlois whanged away at the redneck tub of woman beneath her, at one point even caressing his loins as though to congratulate his organs for showing such signs of life still. Willis felt as though he ought to look away and give the financial backer some privacy, but naturally he didn't. Willis had learned long ago never to avert his gaze from anything human, as revealing of disgusting behavior as it might be. You can always learn something about a man by close attention to whatever he did, consciously or in the low throes of ecstasy. How a man defecates or caresses or ejaculates can speak volumes.

The second bout, just the way it was planned and had to be to satisfy the human need to be threatened and kept in suspense and peril, did not go well for Maureen Langlois. She was prideful, careless, overly confident, assured and contemptuous, and she gave the impression to the crowd that all she had to do was to toy for a spell with the overweight sweating glob of redneck ignorance called Pig Sooey, then tired of the boredom of hammering on her opponent, put an end to her torture of her opponent by a sudden and decisive move to shut the whole event down.

"Put her out of her misery," Dallas Simmons had actually shouted out at one point, three cocktails to the good. "Call in the dogs for the night."

Where had he heard that comment made, Willis Sutcliff wondered. He must have gone on a few coon hunts with the field hands on Daddy Simmons's plantation growing up, all part of the plan to expose the young master to the rougher side of life as he moved toward maturity and the management of the Simmons holdings in the Delta. Looking at the lower depths could be a good learning experience, Willis had heard. See how they live, so as to avoid any romantic notions about the plight of the poor and dispossessed. Learn that they are as nasty as they look.

Whatever caused it in the case of Dallas Simmons, he was wound tight and having fun, right on the edge of psychic orgasm as Maureen Langlois moved in the second meeting with contemptuous ease toward another victory over all that Pig Sooey represented. Then the roof fell in. And the crowd in the coliseum was stilled, stunned, and then galvanized into hoots, cries of anguish and disappointment as Pig Sooey turned the tables on the beautiful woman whaling away at her with fists, elbows, knees, and wonderfully beautiful feet.

Pig Sooey had erupted from her pinned position, turned Maureen Langlois over, around and upside down, and so twisted her arm in a way that caused Maureen to scream and tap out. One, two, three! Down and defeated. Beauty crushed to earth by weight, ugliness, and guile.

"Son of a bitch," Dallas Simmons had cried out. "I can't believe it. That fat bitch beat her. That can't be legal, the way Pig Sooey grabbed her arm and twisted it."

"I'm afraid it is, Mr. Simmons," Willis said. "That tap out means Maureen Langlois gave up to stop her arm from being broke. But don't worry, there'll be a rematch."

"Oh," Dallas Simmons said. "I get it. A teaser."

"No sir, it wasn't no fix in place here, but just look at that crowd behind us. Tell me they ain't going to be here for the next match-up between Beauty and the Beast. And they'll bring their buddies, too, and mama and daddy and all the cousins."

"You have showed me excitement, I must say," Dallas Simmons said. "At least for now, futures seem to be up, investments sound, and money's looking to be made and spent."

So the stage was set, and the house was full, and Dallas Simmons was there beside Willis Sutcliff, and this time Walker D'Arcy was there, too. The rematch that would break the tie, the promise for future endeavors, and the hopes and fears of Willis Sutcliff have so attracted another partner of the investment firm that Willis's had to take a special injection of an outlaw substance into his bloodstream before entering the arena. He turned to Walker D'Arcy, words ready in his head to be uttered in human voice, but all that came out was a low moan as of a beast either in torment or ecstasy.

Walker nodded as though he understood, though, and the roar of the crowd as the music introducing Maureen Langlois began to pour from the battery of speakers put an end to any attempts at language from anybody. I may not can talk right now, Willis said to himself, but I can whistle Dixie like a son of a bitch. Get it on, girls. Make us all a bunch of that money.

The growing light outside the lightly curtained bed chamber James Forrest Howell-Reed customarily used for sleep at Fallen Timbers had become evident enough to allow him to leave his bed. He had never slept well in his entire life, even from childhood, and that defect had served him well when he was young enough to prowl the high and low dives of Memphis in search of a way to speed the passing of time. His goal had always been to lose any sense of what time it happened to be, no matter what the current activity. While others he ran with, or against, or for, began to falter, to beg off and plead obligations elsewhere in time and space, James Forrest had been able to scoff at these signs of weakness and lack of stamina. "Wake up," he relished saying to the short-hitters and weaklings, "would you really rather pass out than to take another hit, hump another gash, see another sunrise over the river, find one more thing to do? Go ahead and lie down, and snore yourself to death. See where it gets you."

That was then. This is now, he considered as he allowed himself to leave the twisted and rumpled sheets of his bed. What I'd like to do now, more than anything else, is to be able to pass out like a dead man, utterly unaware of time and place, and particularly with my mind clear of any dreams. That was the horror. The phantasms in his sleeping head. The situations that crawled up from depths somewhere hidden and festering, yearning to work their way into his mind. "If only," James Forrest said aloud, speaking to no one yet again, but desperate for an understanding audience, "if only I could realize while I was in the grips of the fucking nightmares that I was only dreaming, that would be bearable." That was never the case now, though, as each manifestation of a hidden life bubbled into being as he lay semiconscious in his bed.

Beds. Beds. Beds were designed for comfort and support for the times when the mind demanded surcease from consciousness, the little deaths promised by the fucking poets in their fucking poems, the times when all the muscles of support and movement lost their domination and will. Your body in a state of drop, all rigor lost. You were supposed to be dead to the world, goddamn it, James Forrest considered as he began the tedious tasks of rising from the rack of dreams and preparing to face the conscious world of daylight. In sleep you were supposed to be free of other people, of having to acknowledge other selves outside one's own.

She would be there to be faced yet again, and he would be required by all in him to show toleration and consciousness of her being. Of course, he could leave. Live elsewhere. Escape life as a Howell-Reed in Memphis, Tennessee, heir to a fortune in money and goods and especially to a location in place, a place called Fallen Timbers. That statement of the fact that he could leave was always a thing to admit and to say and to understand as an option. But he had tried that several times. He had left, moved to Los Angeles, tried New York, even spent most of one year in his twenties almost alone on a beach in Mexico. He tried to act like a poor man had to. Live for what's to come, not for what's already there.

If you had nothing, you had an advantage. You had nothing to hold you in place and keep you down and done and obligated. You were free of things. Nothing got in the way.

But the pull of gravity would not allow him to leave the orbit into which he had been born, and which sustained him back in the days when he did not dream. Or if he did, he was not conscious of dreaming. And those times in the nights wherever he slept, wherever he endured and created those visionary plots and people in his head he had been able to know even as the scenes blossomed that they were dreams. That time was past. What was dream and what was real were more and more the same. No separation, therefore no escape.

What James Forrest entertained alone in his unconscious mind was no longer his to understand and categorize. It was real. Each and every vision. And he could neither tell nor label anything separate and apart again.

"I must take real and final action now," he said aloud in the silence of the room where in the night just past he had been tormented by a dream so repulsive and demanding that he had been able to force himself awake. That rousing had been a blessing. But the appearances of such interventions into the world of dream had become fewer and fewer. There was no comfort and no promise of any to come. He could not by will lift himself out of and away from the dream world.

"If I do not increase the pressure upon her, nothing will change," he said aloud again, and then considered silently in his head the fact that the gravitational pull of the Howell-Reed name, and the selfhood of his mother, had proved so powerful over the years of his captivity that it could not be escaped ever in the currency of its form. The gravity of his situation had him in its thrall.

"There must be eclipse," he said aloud, speaking now as he gazed into one of the mirrors on each wall of the room. "It must be total and final. It must be not simply another body coming between me and the sun and moving on its way as gravity demands. There must a total destruction of the known universe. The sun and planets must vanish. Only one meteor may be allowed to survive."

A bell chimed once gently, in tasteful mute, and a recorded voice spoke from the wall in James Forrest's sleep chamber. "Breakfast, as requested, will be served in ten minutes. Please signal agreement or amendment."

James Forrest pressed a button on the control panel, and said quietly to himself words of encouragement and determination. "Accidents will happen today."

After James Forrest had shaved and dressed and finished once again the task of putting on the self he allowed the world to see, the decorations and disguise, the covering and the mask, the boredom yet again of presenting himself to the other, he headed downstairs in the direction of the small dining area where breakfasts and solitary meals were taken at Fallen Timbers. He knew his mother would be there, along with whatever cook was presently on duty, both waiting in silence for him to arrive. Preparations for whatever meal possibilities might arise were waiting, cook-fire heat was rising where it should be, frigid cold was present in its assigned place, table settings were mute, all was in waiting for the last male heir of the Howell-Reed family to arrive for feeding.

There had been a time when James Forrest had studied ways to make dietary demands that could not be met by any ordinary gathering of supplies needful for the first meal of the day. He had even resorted to a thorough study of possible variations of the ways different societies and cultural groupings broke fast at the dawning of a new day. Could he find those which stumped the Howell-Reed cook? Yes, yes he could. But he had become bored with that, and quickly so. How much satisfaction could he count on gaining by stymying the efforts of a black cook to anticipate what he might order for breakfast? It was a question amusing to ask, but not interesting after being put a few times.

It became like the theory of torturing insects by pulling off their wings. Boring, usual, no final possibility for surprise or new expressions of exasperation. So when he walked into the small dining room, James Forrest did not even draw a look from his mother or the cook, one Emerald Bead Longstreet. No one noticed his entrance. Instead both women were considering the telephone Miss May Margaret Howell-Reed had jammed against her head as though it were made of precious metals encrusted with gems.

"What, what are you saying?" James Forrest's mother was shouting into the phone, an outmoded one with a trailing cord coming out of the wall. She would not allow a cell phone in Fallen Timbers proper, of course, only away from the holding itself and in automobiles when driven outside the gates. "Darling girl, is it really you? You're not an imposter, are you?"

Then, turning her head toward Emerald Bead Longstreet, she mouthed silently "I truly believe it's she."

"Praise Jesus," Emerald Bead said.

"Who is she talking about, Emerald?" James Forrest said, breaking the vow he had made to himself coming down the stairs that he would speak to no one in Fallen Timbers mansion for the entire day, ignoring every attempt to draw his attention. But this. This jubilation. What does it mean? My mother looks as though she's about to eat that phone like it were made of French chocolate. Who is talking to her?

"We are here, dearest. We are always here, we will be here waiting to see you again. Oh, my darling, we would wait forever. It seems to me we already have. And, oh, praise be to patience."

No, James Russell said to himself, almost allowing the single syllable to burst from his mouth as though he were spitting out a coal of fire wrongly swallowed. It can't be. But it must be. How, how could it be? Not that!

"Immediately, yes, yes," Miss May Margaret Howell-Reed spoke into the mouthpiece as though she were a black female preacher in Memphis answering a phone call from the Son of God. Eager, ready to jump. On fire for the Lord. "We will be here. No need to wonder about that."

Then handing the phone to Emerald Bead to hang up, the mother of James Russell rose from her chair so abruptly that it tilted, teetered, and fell behind her. A glass followed and shattered. No one noticed.

"Oh, James, she's coming home. She's on her way here now. Home again, at last."

"No," he said, knowing in his very bowels the meaning of what his mother was saying, but pleading to shirk that knowing as though he were a convicted man before a judge about to pronounce upon him a verdict of death by firing squad. As long as it's not said, it can't be true. Don't allow it to be. "No, no. Jesus God, no," he heard himself saying, shocked by his uttering the name of a divinity. How common, how stupid could he be?

"Yes," Miss May Margaret Howell-Reed shouted in triumph, "yes. She's coming home. Your sister is not only still in this world, she has come back home. Constance Helen will be in this very house, at Fallen Timbers, in less than an hour."

"How could she be?" James Forrest said. "She vanished. She insulted all of us and our very name itself, and she left for good. She can't be forgiven for that."

"Of course she can, I know her voice. It's in my heart and my very blood, just as your name is, James. The vanished child is home again. Remember how you called her name when you were barely old enough to speak? Connie, Onnie, you would say, as you ran after her. You loved her so, and now your sister is back."

Oh, God, James Forrest told himself, how can I handle another Howell-Reed woman when the first one's still alive and giving orders? It's too much for one man to do alone. All has turned against me. But I swear I cannot falter, I will not waver, I will never surrender.

"You want some scrambled eggs, Mister James?" Emerald Bead said. "With some of that smoked ham you like? Before Miss Constance Helen gets home?"

"No, no, I'm not hungry," he shouted, stumbling against the chair his mother had knocked over when she rose to scream in welcome to the news of the homecoming of her daughter. "I can't eat. I'm sick. I'm sick."

Then he proved that, all over the floor of the small dining room, the one for casual meals at Fallen Timbers. Emerald Bead Longstreet saw her job and headed for the closet where the cleaning supplies were kept, not making a sign of grumble or surprise.

J. W. Ragsdale was awakened by his trusty and aged radio, set to announce the new day by playing whatever had been lined up by the morning DJ on WRVR. The tune that burst into J. W.'s brain pan after the radio's starting click was the old one by Johnny Cash and June Carter, and the first words heard was the chorus of "We Got Married in a Fever." He began singing some words in Johnny Cash's song, the few he could remember.

Then he performed the act the possibility of which made the old radio an instrument he'd never be able to replace. By slapping a button on top of the set, he was able to turn it off instantly and be blessed by silence in his little rent house on Tutwiler. The RCA product had done its duty, had lapsed into silence, and J. W. was well and truly conscious enough to face the need to rise from his bed.

"In a fever," he sang aloud, no one there to hear him croak the words, and he immediately thought of one of his ex-wives, Wanda Kilmer, the real estate queen of Raleigh. Talk about fever, she had given him that disease enough years back that he seldom thought of her any more. But at the time she had thrown a spell on J. W., and he acknowledged that, but still couldn't understand why he hadn't been able to resist Wanda Kilmer's demand that he marry her. He had tried to reason with her, reminded her that she supported herself much better by skimming all those dollars off the top of every sale of property she made than she ever could expect him to provide. He was a cop. He made no real coin, and all he had to look forward to monetarily was a pension that wouldn't pay for a sick man's supper. And that pension wouldn't kick in for years to come.

He himself had never expected and never tried to make money. He didn't know how, for one thing, and he was too innocent and ignorant to understand how to profit on the side from the kind of work he did. He wasn't on the take from anybody or anything, not because of moral qualms about cheating and lying and feeding off folks like a bloodsucker. No, it was just that he didn't want to have to worry about keeping things straight, like remembering what he might have to hide and lie about and when to cash in and when to back off. You had to keep up all the time to make profits, and that was real work.

I'm too lazy, he had told Wanda during one of the many attempts he had made to hold her off from demands of a permanent change in the status of their relationship. "You could work to get promoted," she would say. "You could get into administration, and stop hitting the streets at all times of the day and night. You could quit having to deal with crooks and robbers and rapists and gangbangers. What does that kind of trash have to offer a man trying to rise in the world? This is Memphis, honey, and you know there will never be any reward for trying to clean up crime in this place. There is not a cent of money in that enterprise. Get with the program. Learn how to run things. Stop dealing with trash and losers."

But J. W. knew deep inside where he wouldn't let Wanda or any other woman see that he liked dealing with trash and losers. It satisfied him down to the bone to run around with working cops, slapping dummies and assholes upside the head for what they'd done, listening to the bullshit stories and lies and excuses they made for their behavior, and putting people who deserved it into cages like bad animals who'd just as soon cut, or shoot, or set on fire folks that didn't deserve that kind of treatment.

"I like being a cop, goddamn it," he'd told Wanda during one of their most savage battles. "I really like it. Just like I used to like running head-on into somebody carrying a ball and trying to get into my territory. It hurt lots of times, but it felt good to me. That's all I know about it. I was doing a real hard job, and I liked it. I still do. I bust their asses and it satisfies me like white gravy on steak."

But within two weeks after that epic argument with Wanda Kilmer, J. W. had stood up with her before a judge he knew and recited the vows of marriage designed to bind a couple together for life. Life for J. W. and Wanda, now man and wife, lasted a little over three years, and that was stretching it way past the expiration date. They divorced, Wanda told him he'd never amount to a hill of beans, and J. W. agreed with her. "Go find somebody that's got a real job with advancement possibilities," he told her. "Marry that sucker, kick him in the balls real hard, and bring him up right."

Wanda Kilmer did that, and she prospered, as far as J. W. knew, and he pledged to himself never to get involved deeply with another woman. Just date them, he'd told himself. Do what Ronnie Yarbrough was always advising anybody who'd listen to him, a beat cop married and divorced three times, at last count. "Just keep hunting for strange pussy," Ronnie would say, drunk or sober. "Don't never let one of them get her claws into you. Find them, fuck them, forget them."

Easier said than done, J. W. knew, though he didn't speak up and announce his plans and failures and need to be around and with a woman, not willing to take the full amount of joshing from fellow cops he'd get if he showed any sign of emotional weakness. Such loss of rigor they called "getting the sweet ass." But he did want and need the company of women, one at the time, and he had pursued possibilities in that area for years now. He had had at least two serious relationships, almost married again, and the last one when it ended did cost him some restless nights and pangs of regret and something he'd never tell anyone. Well, no one except for Tyrone Walker. Now and then when he felt a need to admit to feeling alone and aware of the possibility of a bleak future emotionally just like some of the states of mind he endured off and on these days, he would gingerly speak to his partner about a little of the internal life behind the day-to-day duties of a policeman in Memphis. J. W. would admit to a weakening now and then.

Like, for example, what Tyrone had told him about the ME's message from Nova Hebert to him, indirect though it was, transmitted through two people before it reached him. "Tell J. W. I'd like him to give me a telephone call." That was what the ME at the crime scene of the two dressed-up corpses in the Family Fare Hotel had relayed to Tyrone, and what Tyrone had conveyed to him.

Tyrone meant well, J. W. knew. He didn't rub it in. He didn't dwell on it, and he didn't make it a joke. "Tell J. W. I'd like him to give me a call." That was what Tyrone Walker had communicated. Tyrone was always careful with him when they weren't hoorawing each other about something that didn't matter, and J. W. appreciated that deeply. He wouldn't tell Tyrone that, of course, though. Never whine and say thanks, he reminded himself. Don't show you feel an obligation. Nobody wants to hear that crap.

Looking deep into his first coffee of the day in the kitchen which he had cleaned up the night before, having nothing else to do, J. W. felt a resolution rising in his belly and moving up through his chest. "All right," he said aloud, looking at the coffee maker as though it was waiting to hear what he had on his mind. "I'll do it. I'll call Nova up just like she said she wanted me to do."

His belly eased, he took a deep breath, and he recited the number for Nova's home phone, still stuck somewhere in his head and ready for use if he ever needed it. I do need it, and I'm going to call her just as soon as I finish this first cup, he told himself. I will catch her before she leaves for work.

He did that, hearing the phone ring only three times before it was picked up and Nova's voice came on. "I'm not here. Leave a number."

"Shit," J. W. said before taking the landline phone from his ear and beginning to lower it toward its cradle. Just before he got the instrument turned the right way to replace it, he heard Nova's voice coming out of the earpiece. It sounded alive and unrecorded, so he lifted the phone and spoke.

"Nova, I thought your phone just said you not there. Is this you?"

"It is. I'm home all right, J. W. I see you got my message. I guess you're calling because Tyrone told you to call me up."

"You said on the phone you was gone already. But you're right there. How's that work?"

"Something told me it was you, J. W." Nova said, and then laughed. "Naw, it's voice recognition I've got on this machine. I never answer the phone until it tells me who's calling, if it knows. If it doesn't know, I don't want to talk to whoever it is."

"That sounds like magic to me. My phone's as dumb as I am about the new Memphis we all got to be living in now."

"No, it isn't," Nova said, not laughing this time but sounding friendly anyway. "No instrument of communication is as dumb as you are, J. W. And you know it."

"Well, all right, I'll buy most of that. But let me just ask you what it was that made you tell Tyrone to let me know to call you?"

"I don't want to shuck and jive and play the girly game," Nova said, this time sounding as serious as Major Dalbey telling J. W. to report to a crime scene. "I'm not going to do that. I did it once, and I'll never do it again. Here goes. I'm asking you to call because I just want to see you again, if you're willing to see me. I miss you, you fucking asshole."

"Oh, God," J. W. heard himself saying a name not usually in his working vocabulary, "I miss you, girl, and I want to see you."

"Even though I called you an asshole?"

"Especially because you called me that. I only answer when I'm called the right thing. What time can I come by today?"

"After seven, and we can go get something to eat."

"And drink," J. W. said, feeling better inside than he'd been feeling for a damn long time. He wanted to move, go outside, get into his car and drive somewhere that wasn't here, a destination not yet established. "I'll be by your place then."

"Okay, go on to work. That's where I'm headed. Blood and guts are waiting to tell me what they got to say about who did what to who and when. Somebody else has got to figure out why. Ain't my job. Bye."

Thank you, Lord, J. W. thought as he hung up the phone. I don't know why nor when something's moved outside of me and inside me at the same time, but it sure as hell is doing it now. Long time no see such a feeling for me. "We got married in a fever," he said out loud, croaking Johnny Cash's words.

When J. W. arrived at the Midtown station, he found a note on his desk, that early in the morning, showing a CC to Tyrone and stating he had to see the Major ASAP. "You know what's up?" he said in the direction of LaWanda, who was studiously avoiding acknowledging she had seen him come into the office packed with desks beside which steel handles had been fixed in place for handcuff securing, when and if needed. Comfort collars, some cop had once called them, but the label didn't last.

She nodded her head, looked up finally from her keyboard when she sensed that J. W. was still staring at her and spoke. "Sergeant Walker, he's done in there, and the Major's called me twice to see if you read that note yet. Said to tell you to do it if you hadn't."

"Thanks for your kind aid," J. W. said. "I don't know what I did to piss you off, but I'm just as sorry as I can be."

"That's the truth," she said, laughing a little. "You sure are as sorry as you can be."

A truce between him and LaWanda re-established, J. W. grabbed a yellow pad off his desk and patted his shirt pocket to see if he had something to write with. He did, and he headed for Major Dalbey's office. Neither Tyrone nor the Major looked up when J. W. walked in after knocking once on the pebbled glass as announcement of intent to enter, so he didn't say a word yet, craning his neck instead to see what the two men were studying so intently. It was a detailed map of Downtown Memphis, blown up so close that East Parkway was at the right edge of it.

"Come in and take a look at this here with us, J. W.," Dalbey said, not looking up yet. "Me and Tyrone are figuring out possible escape routes for our general. The time has come."

"General Forrest, huh?" J. W. said, moving in closer to the two officers. "I been reading the *Commercial Appeal* about it. Is it time for this military thing about to happen here at home?"

"Military only in a manner of speaking," Dalby said. "Bring him up to speed, Tyrone, while I get me a cup of coffee and a ballpoint pen."

"We done talked about this thing some, and I got a pen you can use," J. W. said, establishing by that the notion that he'd come prepared for any need, as was his usual habit. He hoped that message got across, subliminal though it was. That habit was one of two things he'd learned at a required departmental workshop for attaining greater efficiency in the workplace, run by a small man with an artificial leg and a booming voice. All personnel had been made to attend this one-day event, one of a random series of such exercises required by the head honcho of the Memphis Police Division, the big dog downtown. The other thing J. W. had learned from the workshop was to sit comfortably in his chair while using the computer. Not to slouch and not to sit in any manner sideways. That would tire you when doing office work.

"Yeah, it is a general," Major Dalbey said, "but it's our general that's been dead must be over a hundred years by now. Right, Tyrone?"

"At least a century," Tyrone said. "But he sure ain't fully dead yet, I can tell you. He's still leading troops. He's not about to quit yet."

"Got your meaning, Officer," Dalbey said. "I got to agree with that. What he means, J. W., is that we have been assigned to help get that damn statue of General Nathan B. Forrest took down without letting things get out of hand. Time has come."

"Let me get this straight," J. W. said. "You do mean that big old statue of Forrest there by the medical school, the one with him sitting on a horse, with the park around him. That one, huh? The one me and Tyrone've been talking about."

"There ain't no other one, I hope to God," Dalbey said. "Yeah, that's it. We don't have to put hands on it, of course. They got monument specialists from Philadelphia brought in to do the heavy lifting and the taking down and hauling off. That might be the easy part. But see, with all these crazies around, some bunch of them might be riled up, one way or another. We got to prevent any kind of violence from taking place. Could even be some of that damned alt-right bunch of nuts coming in from out of town. Might get all mixed in with our homegrown shitheads."

"Us? From Homicide? We got to prevent violence? We just mop up after killings take place, don't we? We not moving into prevention, are we?"

"No, it's not a bunch of us in Homicide have to be there. We'll have a whole division of street police in the area to do that stuff. There ain't going to be any need for officers from Homicide, please God. But you and Tyrone are going to be the face of the enterprise, in charge and official. See, it'll be you, Sergeant J. W. Ragsdale of deep experience in this fair city, and you'll be playing the white officer, of course. And Tyrone, with all his Memphis connections and reputation in football at Central High, and him being black, see, he'll be the coequal of you. It's what Ovetta Birchard and the Mayor and Head Chief of Police Llewellyn have come up with. They asked me to pick out two of my best from Homicide, one white and one black, and give them the job. All of them, the mayor and the council and the rest of them are expecting news coverage, and they want it to be good and positive."

"Shit," J. W. said. "Aw Lord, Major."

"That's exactly the same thing Tyrone said, but he didn't say shit. He said something nicer."

"Well, I don't want to hear what he said, and I don't want to be no token white sergeant from Homicide. That damn Bitchhead. Why can't she ever rest?"

"Well, you're going to be playing the part, like it or not, so buckle up. It's going to be night after next, and it's going to be as quiet and as quick as all of us can make it. If word gets out early, the goddamn KKK bunch will show up and maybe some of the gangbangers and these damn historical-type freaks and I don't know what all. The professional assholes will be there in every description. So let's cut out the foreplay and start planning."

"Where they going to put General Forrest and his horse after they tear them down?" J. W. asked. "Not that I care a damn bit."

"Oh, they'll store him somewhere first and decide later. Set him up in the cemetery maybe? Some museum somewhere? That ain't our worry."

"I wish they'd deposit him gently in the Mississippi River," Tyrone said. "Or melt him down and turn him into tuna fish cans."

"You are so bitter, Tyrone," J. W. said. "Don't you like statuary and art and history?"

"Where'd you learn the word statuary?" Tyrone said. "That's what I want to know."

"In a workshop. I love learning for its own sake."

"Look at this map, you representatives of our noble division of Homicide," Major Dalbey said. "We got to study out these escape routes. We are not going to have a repeat of what went on in Virginia. Not that shit-storm. Not here in Memphis."

"You mean that unpleasantness at Appomattox some time ago or things more recent in Charlottesville?" Tyrone said, but the Major didn't take his eyes off the map of the battlefield that might possibly develop in Memphis. Troop movements and retreats, fields of fire and advances, bayonets and bullets, supply and transport, all took his mind. No time for cute now. J. W. and Tyrone huddled with the boss.

A weeknight at the abandoned warehouse down by the river, a bigger bunch of claimers of the Nathan Bedford Forrest Klavern of the KKK than usual found themselves all attentive and focused on the Memphis Dragon speaking from atop an improvised platform. His perch had originally been a cotton press with a long-ago history of honest service to the need to cram as much fiber in as little a space as possible for shipping purposes, but now it made a convenient platform for a speaker to stand on, lean forward from, walk around on, and rant more effectively to those needing to hear his message.

Doug Maysapps, Chief Speaker Dragon of the local chapter of the Ku Klux Klan of Memphis, Tennessee, looked about him with burning eyes at the larger-than-usual numbers of members of the Nathan Bedford Forrest Klavern of Memphis, and noted that all were finally focused on one person, himself, their preliminary talking and jawing to each other now ceased. Their attention was his now, and he was faced with the most important task that had ever yet loomed before him as Speaker Dragon of that Klavern. He must confront the challenge before him and give direction to men just as General Forrest had done so many times in his service in defense of the Confederacy in that War for Southern Independence long ago. Forrest had never faltered, never quailed, never showed the white feather, no matter what faced him. If surrounded by overwhelming numbers of Yankee troops, he did not quit. He attacked in all directions at once, fearless, noble, and determined to draw blood from the enemy. "Get there firstest with the mostest," he was credited with saying. Take no prisoners. That was his creed.

"Brothers of the Forrest Klavern of the KKK, I speak to you tonight about a matter of such weight and threat as we have never faced before. And I stand on a ruined cotton compressor, once of great use to the people of Memphis and the South. Do you know who fed to this compressor the beautiful white bolls of the cotton plant which enriched our great land until the thieving Yankee traders and soldiers took it from us? Do you know who it was that used and operated this machine which contributed so much to the richness of our people at one time?"

"Slaves?" came the answer from several voices at once. "Wasn't it slaves?"

"It was. It was, but that was in a time when the black knew his place, worked biddably for his white masters and owners. And he knew peace then, and prosperity, and direction. But the Yankees ruined that happy and satisfied society. Where is the nigger now? What is he doing? What is his future?"

"He's full of dope," some shouted.

"He's making bastard babies by the thousands," someone shouted.

"He's figuring ways to kill white folks," another said.

"He's raping pure white ladies, and he's rutting and laughing like an ape."

Others joined the chorus, shouting their scenes imagined, until Doug Maysapps lifted his hand to quiet them. "All you say is true, but before us now ain't those problems the nigger is giving the white folks of our country, but it's something right before us here in Memphis. It's something we can touch, and we can see ways to battle. It's this, oh brothers."

"What, what?"

"This is what we're facing. For one thing, they are going to be pulling down the statue of President Jefferson Davis, the one downtown in Confederate Park on Main Street. That's bad enough to move us, I know. And cause us great sorrow. But worse than that is what I'm telling you now."

"What, Dragon, what is it?" Thurman Norman Tullos, a.k.a. TNT, heard himself shouting amid the voices of the others around him. That surprised and made him feel a great heat rising in his body, working its way up from his belly and into his throat and head. He felt a life working in him stronger than anything he'd ever experienced before. It was hot, a blaze rising from fire within. "What is it, Dragon?" He screamed it louder this time.

"They are going to take down the sacred statue of General Nathan Bedford Forrest, that's what they're planning to do tomorrow night."

"The sons of bitches," voices rang out together. "No, not the general."

"Our patron," Doug Maysapps, "our spiritual leader. Our blood brother all the way from Fallen Timbers and Chickamauga and all them places of brave battle up to now right here in Memphis. That's the sin they plan to commit."

"Is it niggers doing it?" a brother of the Klavern called out.

"Not just them. No, they're the ones running it, I do believe, but it's the mayor and the police and the liberals and the college professors and the Satan-bound preachers. That's who is leading the charge. It's the white race turning on itself again, biting its own sides with poison, and running to mate with that crowd lower than dirt. It's a system of self-destruction. That's who it is."

"Let's stop them," voices yelled out. "We can't let it happen."

"No, we can't," said the Dragon of the Memphis Klavern. "But brothers, it will draw blood from many of us. It will test us. It will demand will and courage and blood sacrifice."

"We'll draw more blood from them nappy heads than they will from us," TNT heard himself yelling. And hearing himself say that, he was proud and happy to learn what kind of man he was now. He'd earned a new name and a new life, and it bubbled inside him like boiling lead. He yelled, he hollered, he screamed, and each sound he made played like music in his head and in his guts and balls. He'd proved himself as a white man already, and he'd do it again.

That ought to about do it, Doug Maysapps told himself. Stop talking about that part and get some other folks to plan how to resist and get ready to put themselves in harm's way. I have got to save myself for the great war to come, not get caught up and maybe harmed in a skirmish like this one. The general stays behind the lines and directs forces. He don't stick his own personal neck out. He delegates and stands aside to observe his orders being carried out. He is the precious brain directing the muscles of others.

"Brothers," he called out right before jumping down from the cotton compressor, "let's get organized and do some real planning. We got to think like General Forrest now, and strike a blow they'll never forget. We got to get ready. We got to get there first."

"With the mostest," came the scream back, echoing in the ruined cotton warehouse empty and dark and close to the bank of the big river.

The reunion and return of Constance Helen Howell-Reed to Fallen Timbers had begun in tears of joy and jubilation, the errant and lost daughter in the arms of her mother again and at last and finally. Her companion, her friend, and her lover as Constance had declared to her mother as soon as she'd entered the main house, stood apart at first, eyes down and hands clasped and an expression of approval for the scene of prodigal return pasted on her face. That separation lasted no longer, however, after Constance Helen had declared to her mother her love for the woman the MMA crowd called Pig Sooey. "Welcome to our family," Miss May Margaret Howell-Reed had said, "and as the love of my dear daughter you are now as much one of us as any member of our illustrious line, past and present. When you've met your new brother, James Forrest, he will welcome you as one of us. I know we'll all come to know each other in joy and celebration, as we live together in this blessed place, this wonderful seat of Fallen Timbers."

"Where is Jamie?" Constance Helen asked, reaching toward her lover so as to draw her into the ongoing embrace of mother and daughter now so well established. Billie Sue Cameron joined the hug. "Is he at home today or out on the roam somewhere?"

"Oh, no, he's not elsewhere. James Forrest is here in his room, recovering from a sudden stomach attack of some sort. Emerald Bead told me that he had a real sinking spell soon after he rose this morning."

"Does he know I'm here again?" Constance Helen said, giving both mother and lover a little squeeze preliminary to drawing back a bit. Hugs are nice, hugs are vital, but they do have a life span, she knew. The self must retreat to self periodically.

"Yes, right after Emerald Bead told him the wonderful news he endured what she called a kind of swoon. I don't know where she learned that word, but she's very proud of it. He actually sank to the floor in a faint."

"I'm not surprised by that," Constance Helen said. "James Forrest has always been subject to swooning at the announcement of upsetting events."

"Upsetting? He's not upset in any negative sense," May Margaret said. "To the contrary, I'd wager he was overcome with emotion at the thought of his dear sister's return after all this time."

"I'm sure he is," Constance Helen said. "He must be aghast and atwitter at the news. Is my brother the same old James Forrest as always? Out late and home only at times he needs sleep or additional funding for some enterprise?"

"She's making a clever little joke," May Margaret said to Billie Sue, a.k.a. Pig Sooey. "My girl has always been one to jest and come up with the most amusing commentary on events."

"She's that way still," Billie Sue said. "Just full of fun and clever comment."

"Where are you from, dear?" May Margaret asked. "I do detect a hint of the South in your speech. Thanks to God for that."

All three women chuckled in obligation for that comment, and Billie Sue admitted that indeed she was from the Southern part of the United States. Arkansas, in fact, in a location in the eastern part of the state.

"Where in particular?" May Margaret said. "I do know the rice-growing area of Arkansas rather well. The family had holdings in rice farms at one point, but when we got out of agriculture rather completely, I lost any real connection to that part of the world."

"Mother, before we get too far off the subject of James Forrest, what can you tell me about him these days? Still the man about town? Still one cute lady friend after another? Still a frequent flyer with officials downtown in government facilities? Still seeing his old friends on a regular, and irregular basis? Still not bound to the ordinary day-to-day life of employment?"

"He has matured and changed so much, dear," May Margaret said, and then turning toward Billie Sue, "James Forrest was quite the gallant for more years than usual. It was a pattern expected but quite awkward for us all at times. But he's done what all young men of substance finally do. He's settled down, still loves fun, but has become serious about family affairs, financially and socially. I'm quite pleased and proud of him, just as I am of Constance Helen. You'll find him charming, Billie Sue."

"I'm sure that's true. How could anyone related to my love Constance

Helen not be charming. Her mother included."

"How gracious and how lovely. Thank you," May Margaret said. "Is your full name Roberta with Billie Sue a familiar form of address? A diminutive for use by one's people?"

Before Billie Sue Cameron could respond, a voice called from the door into the room. "Who are these strangers? Do we have a visiting minstrel show at Fallen Timbers? Where is the music?"

"Oh, you joker," Constance Helen said. "My brother, the wit. Please meet the love of my life, James Forrest. She is Billie Sue, and age cannot wither, nor custom stale, her infinite variety."

"John Keats?" James Forrest said, advancing into the room.

"Shakespeare," his sister said. "You never were much for literature, were you, Jamie?"

"No, but I've always been strong in praise of women. Is this one of that breed?"

"Judge for yourself," Constance Helen said. "You'll be getting to know Billie Sue, I do believe, and you'll discover as I have just how much of a woman she truly is."

"I can already see the resemblance she has to that gender. Does she speak up for herself, or do you have to translate? And more important, is she as witty and will-o'-the-wisp as my dear sister?"

"She will surprise you, brother of mine, and I hope you'll feel free to discover that for yourself," Constance Helen said. "Unlike some people, she's a great deal more than what meets the eye."

"There's a lot to meet the eye, I do declare. Oh, I'm all aquiver," James Forrest said. "If I poke her, does she bite?"

"Try that and see. I dare you."

"Now, daughter and son, please," May Margaret Howell-Reed said. "You sound like you did when you were only children. I know you're just joshing and attempting to get your mother all wound up a bit, but remember. We have a guest in our midst."

"Oh, but mother," Constance Helen said. "This guest has come to stay. She's part of the family now."

"Oh, joy," James Forrest said, directing his attention toward Billie Sue. "Oh, wonderful news. Now tell me, O Silent One, will you join me in having a cup of coffee?"

"Now, you're talking, Buster," Billie Sue said. "Lead me to it and get out of the way."

Deangelo Dixon was deep into a planning session with key members of the Bones Family, though he wouldn't have called the topic under consideration any business of anybody but himself. Nobody was saying a word, but for him, and not a pair of eyes in the big front room of D's house were trained in his direction. He would tell whoever he wanted to speak or to engage directly with him in any fashion just when to do that. When a name was called and a direct question was asked or a recognition of a need to respond was evident, then and only then would a voice other than Deangelo Dixon's be heard. Speak when you're spoken to, motherfucker.

"Shadorm," Deangelo said after having spoken some directions for a full minute at a pace more rapid than usual, "you get what I'm saying about this fake money deal down in Mississippi? You following me, Dog?"

Encouraged by being called "dog" by the head of the Bones Family claimers, a label used for the most part as a sign, if not of approval but at least of acknowledgment of the existence of the recipient as a creature worth noting, Shadorm Washington ventured to say one word. "Yeah," he uttered and when Deangelo said nothing in return, Shadorm dared to put a question forward.

"You want me to say something about that, what you just told us?"

"Duh, yeah, unh-huh, yes. We talking the same language, ain't we? You need to hear any more than that?"

"No sir, I don't. You ask me if I'm following and I say I be doing that. I am. Yeah."

"Talk then, Dog. Tell me."

"That man down there in Batesville in Mississippi, I can't call his name right now, but I know who I'm talking about. The man with all them airplanes, he want us to get the rest of that bad paper to him by two days from now. He want it right then, he say. Not before, not after. He be sending it down in one of them planes to the bunch in Mexico so's to trade and get the dope back here where it's headed."

"It ain't Mexico it's going to, it's Colombia, Shadorm. Didn't you learn nothing in school about where anything in the world is? Is all you know Baby Street and Jackson Avenue?"

"I didn't go to no school past that first grade or so. That's when I learned I didn't have to do that shit no more. So I ain't never learned much about Mexico. They talk funny, I know that. Jabber like in a restaurant, them folks do."

"Okay, forget about how dumb you grew up to be. What I want is, I want to know do we be ready. Tell me what I want to hear," Deangelo said, thinking to himself how badly public education in Memphis had failed most Bones Family claimers he had to deal with. He himself had gone all the way through the eighth grade, leaving school only when his mother died and so had stopped making him go to the school building most of the time. He had fought her on that, but now he was grateful she had made him a learned man. She had been strong, a lot stouter than any man Deangelo had known growing up. Deangelo knew his level of education had done more for him in taking over the Bones Family than any and all instruments of physical force had ever done. Most of the fools who could depend only on fire power ended up dead or in prison by the time they were fifteen or sixteen, and only the scholarly kind survived long enough to take over the business. Thank you, Mama, for making me smart.

"We be ready, Boss," Shadorm was saying. "All that bad paper money is here and ready to be took down to Mississippi, but one thing only seem to be getting in the way."

"I know it ain't the Memphis cops," Deangelo said. "They too busy taking care of car robbers and break-ins and bar shootings to look up from studying all the blood in the streets. So I know what you talking about. It's the fucking feds, right?"

"They be called the Secret Service. That's what I be hearing. That ain't the FBI is it, D?"

"Use the full name or title, son, when you talking to me," Deangelo said. "But yeah it's the government all right. The feds. They got all the equipment in the world. Guns, cars, vests, communication devices, all that shit. Money and lots of it. Only thing we got going for us is just one thing. The fucking Secret Service don't know Memphis. And we do. And you got to know Memphis if you going to operate here. So we still ahead at the halftime. But you know what?"

"No sir, Boss. What?" Shadorm said, looking around him at the three other Bones claimers in Deangelo's big room in the house. They had not spoken yet, having not been recognized to do so, and they stayed silent. They did look back at Shadorm, though, since he wasn't Deangelo.

"They's another whole half of the game to go. We ahead now, but we can't let down. Can we, Bones boys?"

"Naw sir," the other claimers in the room said together, sounding mournful but determined to hold that line and rush that quarterback in the next half.

"Right, dogs," Deangelo said. "One more thing. I done got word they's going to be a bunch of redneck assholes and cops and them college kids all together in Forrest Park a couple of days from now. The mayor of Memphis and them other ones that think they run this place, they going to be taking down a statue in the park. I don't want no Bones Family boys over there then. It'll be enough folks there as it is."

"Boss," one of the silent three ventured to ask, thinking Deangelo seemed to be a little mellowed out by now. "What that statue is? Is it the soldier on that old iron horse? Bird shit all over him?"

"Yeah, and it means something to these white assholes, so they liable to start fighting over it. It ain't nothing to the brothers, whatever it is. So put the word out. No niggers in that Forrest Park when all them dummies get to hollering at each other. Pushing and shoving. Carrying on. Let them fuckers worry about it."

"Got you, Boss," one of the claimers said. "I be resting that night. Sitting at home watching the TV on the wall."

Everybody laughed at that, after they saw that Deangelo was amused by what had just been said, so they began falling about the room and trading Bones signs with each other until the Boss chased them out of his house.

J. W. Ragsdale lay damp with sweat among wrinkled sheets, even the fitted bottom one that had been worked loose from the mattress in Nova Hebert's bedroom in her little house just off Goodlett Street south of Cooper. He had one hand lifted to cover his eyes and the other extended to touch Nova's back, turned to him. She might have been asleep, he didn't know, and he didn't want to wake her if she was. It was well after midnight, J. W. proud of himself for being able to do blazingly what a man ought to be able to do but fully aware that such moments were rare and certain to decrease in number and intensity as time took its toll, and so he ought to savor the moment while he could. Don't think it to death.

All this took place after, not before, a full meal at a new Mexican place where Nova had met him around seven, and after, again not before, margaritas not counted in the restaurant and g and t's in a new fern bar on Mud Island, one with real oak fittings and what looked like silver flourishes all over the place. Quiet, soft music. No loud mouths. They hadn't talked much, having exhausted months ago before the breakup all the chit-chat needful in new relationships. Instead, they had eaten a meal that tasted good, drunk good-label liquor, told each other they were both sick of playing the dating game, yet were not looking for permanent certification of relationship, and still liked each other and missed being with and seeing each other. And particularly, they each declared in words what they felt when they touched each other, whether accidentally or on purpose.

"Shit, goddamn it," J. W. had said to Nova early on the evening even before they had left the Mexican place and headed toward the location where serious imbibing could take place, "I miss the hell out of you, and I'm sick as a dog trying not to show it, and not able to just tell myself to shape my ass up."

"Oh, what gentle poetic words of love, J. W.," Nova had said. "You really know how to sweet talk a girl and make her all giggly. Tell the truth now. Did you write that speech out before delivering it so eloquently and then practice over and over saying it in the lovely way you just did?"

"That's one of the things I like about you," J. W. had said. "You appreciate a man who thinks before he talks."

"When I find one, I'll let you know," she had said. "I'll also keep digging in the backyard of my house, looking for pirate treasure. It's there, I just know it is."

All that which had gone before J. W. and Nova had tumbled into bed and disarranged the sheets and pillows had been enough talk and done enough good to satisfy. And now J. W. touched the skin of the back turned to him as Nova slept, and marveled again at how smooth and soft it felt to him. Was that natural, he wondered, that finely textured feel of flesh so different from his own. All women were softer than men, he knew, in flesh and in other ways not easily measured, but damn if Nova's skin didn't feel like that of another species altogether. Am I getting nutty in my advancing age? J. W. asked himself. Am I thinking about stuff I ought to just leave alone? What if Tyrone knew I had crazy questions like that running around in my head? Would he give me that look he uses when I pop off something?

Worse than that, what if some other cop in the division was to learn how soft I'm getting in the head? There's not a one, other than Tyrone, who will always cut me slack, who wouldn't ride me about it until I'd have to come up beside his head with a blunt instrument. Don't worry about it anymore, J. W. told himself. Just touch this woman, relish what it does for you, and try to get up the nerve to let her know about it.

Would being with her all the time or at least as long as she'd let me hang around, would that ruin it? You get so used to somebody or something and you forget about what it does for you, just being around her. I don't want that to happen with me and Nova, he told himself. I won't let it get away. What's that saying I heard in some movie about a love affair? Familiarity breeds contempt. Damn if I'll let it do it this time.

"Nova," he said softly. "Little girl. Sweetheart." She couldn't hear him in her sleep, he hoped, so he went ahead and said it. "I love you."

Damn, he told himself. Shit. I've done it now.

It had taken every bit of will James Forrest Howell-Reed could muster to get up from the floor after Emerald Bead had told him his sister was back at Fallen Timbers. Not only back, returned as though from the dead dragging her chains, but in jubilant conversation with their mother. And when he had ordered Emerald Bead to leave his room, assuring her he was not ill nor had he fainted, he had found in his chambers not a single unit of any chemical aid to which he could resort. What good were sleep aids and pain killers and not even the smidgen of cocaine he located in a plastic sleeve hidden in a shoe in one of the closets, what good was any substance available in propping him up well enough to face the two of the women together?

No way to avoid scurrying to where they were, though, not if he was to maintain status enough to begin doing what had to be done. He had to face them calmly, unafraid, and competent to handle this terrific jolt to his plans, short and long range. They must believe he was unfazed, surprised, of course, but ready and able to meet this new and hideous challenge. Jolts to the system might come, plans might have to be altered in terms of timing and fulfillment, but ultimate goals would be reached. He was not to be considered vulnerable, he was not to be dismissed as inconsequential, he was to be recognized as a force inevitable and destined for victory, and he was to be seen as implacable as the old bastards themselves. His father, dead these years past, and the progenitor himself. General Nathan Bedford Forrest, the original master of mayhem to all enemies.

"The bitches," James Forrest said aloud. "I'll show them an iron will. I'll attack in all directions at once. I'll get there firstest with the mostest."

Having been fortified by saying that, he talked a bit to himself, silently but at least internally, and after sitting stiffly in the overstuffed chair facing the bank of windows to the south, he made some promises to himself. "Man up," he said aloud, his gaze fixed on the distant tree line beyond what at one point had been fields for crops, and he made himself rise to make ready to face the cadre of women he could not continue to avoid. He'd do that. And he'd make one last attempt to drive his mother into a state of mind all medical doctors would agree merited removal to a facility more suitable for a demented old lady of great wealth than Fallen Timbers itself. Maybe she could be shelved, mentally and physically.

That meant he had to move more quickly in his campaign to drive his mother into a state of mental instability than he had planned. The rat business had been fun to plan and execute. She had been taken off her feed by that to a wonderful degree. Her loss of weight was becoming obvious. Changes provoked by the strange noises and gibbering voices he'd introduced electronically into her sleeping had just begun, and they had real promise. Now with Constance Helen home again, that campaign had to be shortened and maybe even abandoned.

"Our illustrious ancestor must now visit May Margaret Howell-Reed," James Forrest whispered to himself. "The hour's here. His time to rise from the grave has come, and he must appear in mother's sleeping chamber two nights from now. He's restless and eager to issue commands. When the city fathers of Memphis dare to take down that statue of homage to his will and contribution to the city and Tennessee and the South, N. B. Forrest must move against the enemy's works. He's been disturbed and he will act. And where is more appropriate to appear in the flesh once more than Fallen Timbers Plantation?"

James Forrest arose, attired himself, and left his chamber to greet Constance Helen, his dear sister returned at last to grab up all that remained in the Howell-Reed coffers. We'll see about that, James Forrest declared within, me and the old general himself. It's time to start the skirmish. And I am not afraid, and I'm ready. Let's get right up in those women's faces. As my old fraternity brother from Corinth, Mississippi, would always say, you fuck with the bull, and you'll get a horn up your ass.

Let's be Forrest, boys. Ride to the sound of the guns.

"What's all this jollity, J. W.?" Tyrone said from the passenger seat of the three-year-old Chevrolet just checked out of the Midtown police fleet. It was one which every detective avoided having to drive whenever possible, some even getting close to a scuffle to avoid being assigned that particular car. It ran all right, for the most part, and it hadn't suffered too many bumps and scrapes and scratches, but it did stand out among the rest of the vehicles available for duty for one glaring reason. It stunk. It reeked. And the stink was not only strong and long lasting but also contagious. Any cop, man or woman, riding around in it even for just a couple of hours announced that fact pungently whenever he or she entered an enclosed space. "Goddamn it," someone would announce, "you been driving the shit wagon, haven't you? Get away from me. You stink."

The car had been washed many times, fumigated, driven at high speed on the interstate with all windows open, and sprayed with a variety of patented odor fighters. Nothing had finally worked, though, and now J. W. and Tyrone had drawn the short straw for the piece of transportation that would take them to Nathan Bedford Forrest Park to preside over the de-honoring of the best Confederate cavalry leader in the western theater of the War Between the States all those decades ago.

"Oh, no reason. I'm just feeling perky tonight," J. W. answered Tyrone. "Up tempo, you understand."

"No, I don't understand," Tyrone said. "Riding here in the stink wagon, going to Forrest Park to preside as the white and black team captains of the homecoming game between the redneck assholes and the racially sensitive liberals, not even to mention any brothers that might show up, and you say you're feeling perky? Perky? That cute talk's not in your vocabulary, J. W. You haven't already been fortifying yourself tonight with C2H5OH, have you?"

"What's that?"

"Alcohol, Sergeant Ragsdale. And if you have, that's a new low for you while on duty."

"I never take a drink while I'm working, Tyrone, and you know it, partner."

"Well, yeah, I know, and I'm just poking at you to see what's up. Have you got it in for General Forrest? And like I said I've never heard you use that word before."

"What?"

"Perky, that's what. It sounds real funny coming from you. Sounds like something a woman of a higher class than you would say. That's all. Besides, if we talk while we're riding along to the site of this possible bloodbath, I don't think as much about how bad it stinks in the shit wagon."

"Do you think it might be some bloodshed tonight?" J. W. said, changing the subject from the way he felt after seeing Nova again, not wanting to let word out yet about the change in his love life. Tyrone wouldn't give him much grief about it, but he might let something slip to some lower-minded cop, some evil-headed bastard, and then there'd be all that hoorawing to put up with. J. W. knew he could handle such as that and give it back in kind. But it took energy and thought, and J. W. felt like he just wanted to bask for a while. Don't use that word "bask" to Tyrone, he told himself. More to explain and evade if he did.

"Lots of lights up there past that UT medical school," he said. "I thought they were going to try to make everything look as normal as they could."

"My Mississippi friend," Tyrone said. "There ain't a damn thing in the world normal about a racist old KKK general stuck up horseback in a statue on a pedestal. So we better get ready for fourteen kinds of weird crap to come down."

"All right, yeah. But they're saying by doing this thing fast and at night and not letting on that anything's in the works probably the count of crazies will be a lot lower than it could be."

"Let's hope so," Tyrone said. "I sure don't want to have to get into any physical contact while they're deboning the old bastard."

"Physical contact," J. W. said, slowing down to make the turn off Union onto the side street running by Forrest Park. "I don't expect you're talking about shaking hands, now are you? You don't mean engaging in physical force, do you?"

"You been reading manuals again, haven't you?" Tyrone said. "You're talking like a book again. Look up there at the uniform cop waving us to the side. I don't think he understands what an important pair of dudes he's signaling."

"I imagine he's noticing the shade of your skin color, Sergeant Walker. He's shaking in his boots, I bet you. Thinks you're some kind of a doped-up brother come to do some bloodletting."

J. W. pulled off to the side as directed, and stuck his head halfway out the window and flashed ID at the patrolman. "Yessir, they told us downtown that y'all from Homicide would be showing up early to show official presence," the young cop said, stepping back from the car. "Up yonder's where you can park your vehicle, just past them trucks lined up next to the green space."

"You mean the grass and bushes and stuff?" J. W. said, "all them nice plantings the general's been enjoying? That's what you mean by green space?"

"That's part of the approved nomenclature they had learned us downtown, yessir," the cop said, looking earnest and groomed as he fell into a pretty good approximation of the present-arms position.

"I sure am glad I get to operate way out there in the Midtown boondocks," Tyrone said to J. W. "I don't believe I could measure up to Downtown standards. I know I couldn't, and just think about me away from Midtown. They'd have to put me on the watering-the-prisoners in the drunk-tank lockup downtown to get any good out of a cop colored like me."

"You'd spill half of that water before you got to the first drunk fraternity boy in for the night after a dance in the country club," J. W. said. "They'd have to give you remedial training to handle that kind of spat. Let's get on out of this stink mobile and see how far things have got by now. It's a pretty good crowd already, looks like to me."

J. W. was right. The crowd was big enough to make an ordinary cop nervous, and it was quiet enough to raise neck hairs on anybody charged with keeping order. J. W. and Tyrone had learned over their years on the force in Memphis that a crowd hooting and hollering and jabbering among themselves was not nearly as prone to letting loose physically as one quiet and brooding. The loud drunk trying for attention was directing most of his energy toward getting a fair share of notice, while the shut-mouth brooder was likely to demonstrate his presence by swinging something heavy up against somebody's head, or shoving a blade into a soft body part or, push come to shove, letting off some rounds of lead in the direction of others.

The collection of folks there in the green space to witness the humiliation of General Nathan Bedford Forrest, and all he stood for and meant one way or another according to the psychic needs of the various segments of the onlookers, was paying close enough attention to what was going on to give J. W. and Tyrone and the other peacekeepers a crawling sense of dread.

"Damn it," J. W. said to his partner, nodding toward a cadre of men clumped together like a blood clot newly formed, "look at that bunch yonder. They look like they just got off work at the chicken-killing plant. They ain't drunk, and they don't see a drink coming in their near future."

"More likely the last shift at the plywood factory, on that final day before it closed down for good in Tupelo," Tyrone said. "That last paycheck is cashed and gone, and there won't be any more in the foreseeable future. No beer, no corn meal, no cable TV, just the old lady bitching."

"It ain't no future left. It's just now what there is going to be all the time, every day, every day, every day," J. W. said, and then went on. "Let's tell a few of the uniforms to work their way a little closer to where those old boys are using that blowtorch."

"You mean where they're cutting off the bolts holding the statue up?" Tyrone said.

"Yeah, them busting things loose is taking longer than makes me comfortable. Every noise it makes is throwing the jitters into these rednecks."

"Not even to mention that bunch with the tiki torches, just waiting to fire them up. Looks like a World War Two documentary on the History Channel."

"If they get those babies going, they're going to think it's Charlottesville time, and then it could get tight and nasty around here."

"Well, more and more cars keep coming in off Union," Tyrone said. "I don't know why they haven't got it better blocked off. I'm going to ease over there and ask that captain a question or two. Things need to go faster."

"Be nice when you do all them questions," J. W. said. "Don't be rude."

"Why do you think I'm doing it rather than asking you to?" Tyrone said, and laughed for the first time since they'd left the car.

J. W. walked a short distance away from where he'd been watching the work crew burning away at the steel supports of the general on horseback, turning to look behind him at a different bunch of spectators, this one generally younger and dressed in clothes that looked as if they hadn't been worn to go to work that day. He noted a few neatly gotten-together graybeards and the female equivalents to the older men, the women with their hair pulled back into buns and ponytails, some with scarves or hats covering their hairdos and all looking eager and satisfied. This would be the liberal intellectuals, J. W. told himself. The right-minded folks. College educated or want-to-be's, folks that go to churches where the congregations didn't get too excited or noisy and who simply love the humanity in folks, not their tortured souls or a God up in the clouds. If they even believed in souls or God, he considered as he observed this segment of Memphians jabbering among themselves and seeming as satisfied as a bunch that had paid money to listen to a concert of music, not a bit of which had been given squalling birth in the River City. No singing, no tune, nothing to dance to. That's the tunes that speak to their kind. Dead and flat. Oh, well, these folks were harmless at an event like the deflowering of a Confederate general, unless they started singing together some modern hymn. Then everybody in hearing distance would want to take a swing at them. But they wouldn't sing, probably. Just moan around some and sway back and forth as best they could.

Not many black folks in evidence, J. W. noted, wondering a bit at first about the reason for that, but after putting his mind to it for a minute or two, coming up with an answer that he considered might not be right, but one that would let him stop thinking about that possible segment of witnesses to General Forrest's farewell. Why would the brothers, the gang claimers at least, why would they take any satisfaction in this event in Memphis history?

First of all, they didn't know shit about what happened only just yesterday in Memphis, not to mention what took place when real horses did all the pulling and carrying around town. They hadn't been taught shit, wouldn't have listened if they had been, and couldn't give a flying fuck about a statue of an old white man wearing funny looking clothes while perched up on a steel horse in a park. The Latin Lords and the Bones Family and the Beale Street Boppers and the rest of the gang claimers of any and all persuasions were not about to hang around to watch something pulled down and hauled off on a big truck wrapped up in plastic you couldn't see through. That ain't no fun.

No, J. W. considered as he watched the sparks fly up from the cutting torches working to bust loose and take down what a bunch of nice old ladies had paid for a hundred years ago, there shouldn't be any reason to worry about the claimers taking any real interest in coming up beside a selected or random assortment of heads. Might be some freelancing going on, but that would be disorganized and contained, and enough uniformed cops were milling around to put a quick stop to that kind of action before it got out of hand.

It'll be white folks, various combinations of trash and high-minded liberals who might bear close attention. And the Nazi-looking assholes with the tiki torches could be a consideration, too. The thing of it was, J. W. had learned to his sorrow on the job, it had all to do with the damn television. Crazies could watch every move of what other crazies did all over the country, all over the world, and they could and would get eat up with performance envy. Why can't we do that here in Memphis? If they can pull off wild crazy shit in a place like Charlottesville, Virginia, we can sure match and outdo that here in Memphis. We got balls as big as grapefruit compared to the wimps back east. This is the River City, goddamn it! Get out of the way. I'm fixing to come up beside your head. Bitch!

Not a hundred feet across the way from where Sergeant J. W. Ragsdale stood pondering matters cultural, mythic, and violence-inspiring in the America of today, TNT waited in silence with the squad detailed by the Nathan Bedford Forrest Klavern of the Ku Klux Klan, a cadre assigned a task of observance and honor at the scene of desecration in the heart of the very city where the founder had come into the selfhood of his well-earned place in the history of racial strife in America. They were a fit audience, though few, the Speaker Dragon had told them, and they were not to engage in actual combat with those defilers of the tribute to General Forrest. They were outnumbered, of course. Heavily armed police in uniform and others in civilian garb were in great evidence. No reason to tip their hand now. Come a better chance and good odds, though, and watch what punishment we can deal out.

Any attempt to stop the taking down of the statue of General Forrest was not to be made, though. "Your task is to bear witness," the Dragon had said. "Consider your presence to be akin to the loading of a firearm. It will be fired in due time when its effects can be successful. That is not now. Now, as you see this assault on our founder and our ideals, you are loading the weapons of the future. Their time will come. You are being baptized into the holy body of the Klan."

When TNT heard those words, he felt them enter his ears, work their way down through his entire body, touching the liver and lights of his system, warming the blood of his heart to a state of boil, and settling in the testicles drawn up into hard knots at his groin.

"I feel my balls burning," TNT had shouted aloud, not choosing to utter those words, but hearing them burst forth as though vomited from deep within every fiber of his body. "My nuts is on fire. They got to get relief."

"They will, warrior, they will," the Dragon had said. "In due time, the load they bear will burst forth in flame."

Now TNT uttered to himself the words of caution he had heard in the abandoned warehouse on the bank of the Mississippi River, struggling against the impulse to break ranks and charge the devils burning away at the hooves of Forrest's steel mount at the heart of Memphis. But he could not break his vows of allegiance to the Klavern. This he knew. But he could shout out words of resistance against the horror he saw before him. He could sound a battle cry, he could announce his claim of defiance. He felt his lips parting, his mouth opening, and words forming on their own, gathering themselves to launch forth in this dark night of insult to the founder of the Klan.

"I done killed a nun for you, General Forrest," TNT heard himself shout. "She wasn't a real one. She was a lying nigger woman in a hotel. I killed her priest, too. He was just like she was. A liar. A fornicator. He was a Catholic priest fornicating on a lying nun. They hated Jesus. They was not regular. Not regular. Not right."

A couple of the brothers of the Forrest Klavern of the KKK standing beside TNT in rank and solidarity took up the last few words he had offered in homage to the general, yelling raggedly at first but then joined by others of the cadre of homage, "Not regular. Not right. Not regular. Not right."

J. W. Ragsdale had been startled by what the redneck screamer had yelled at first, but by the time Tyrone Walker had reached him, he was grinning from ear to ear. "Partner," he said. "You know what? I never would have thought I'd be allowed to identify a prime suspect for a homicide so easy, just by showing up to watch folks cut down a hundred-year-old statue."

"That crazy-looking little bastard might not be telling the truth," Tyrone said. "But I do expect his claim is going to lead to where we want to go."

"It's a gift," J. W. said. "And I think we ought to thank the general for it."

"The general?"

"Sure, he inspired the whole confession, Tyrone. And folks will still claim N. B. Forrest never did nothing but sell slaves and burn bridges and kill Yankees and start up the KKK. He just gave us this little nut for two homicides. Bless him."

"You're saying bless Forrest?"

"Even a blind hog can find an acorn now and then, Tyrone. You want to go over there and tell that little runt pig he's got to go downtown where he can talk better?"

"I'd love to," Tyrone said. "Here we go. We'll detain him for questioning in the matter of two homicides. I'll get one of the uniforms to take him down. I do want him to see me, though. I expect it'll tickle the little runt to see what color I am."

"It'll confirm all his prejudices, I do believe. He knows y'all got it in for him. Always have hated the white man, haven't you?"

J. W. stayed where he was, pleased to be able to see Tyrone and the uniformed cop in action as they singled out the squeezed-up little runt who'd been announcing his deeds to everybody in earshot. By the time the uniformed cop had hustled his good arrest off, the attention of the crowd had shifted to the drama at the center of the event, the actual lifting of the metal Forrest on horseback up and away from the stone platform where it had rested peacefully, centrally, and generally unnoticed through Memphis rain, snow, and burning Delta sunshine for all those years.

Cheers came from the professional right-minded people, the graybeards and grayhaired, the PhDs and the humanists, the retired ministers and their families from liberal congregations; applause broke out in accompaniment to the whine of the gears of the lift, and a cadre of off-beat and off-tempo singers of the Battle Hymn of the Republic lifted their voices. Competing singers, though few in number but loud in squall, began singing Dixie. A couple of children began to weep loudly as they observed their parents acting stone weird.

A great groan arose from the cadre of unannounced members of the Forrest Klavern of the KKK, coming from deep within the hollows of their guts, livers, and lights, answered almost immediately by the many more voices of younger people unaffiliated with any organized segments of Memphis society. It was the sound of the chant from the one-hit wonder singing group called Steam Heat, and it swelled so loudly and so immediately that no other sounds could successfully compete. It was the jubilant crow of winners at athletic competitions of every description, at all announcements of those who'd come out on top at any public event, and it rang through all of the park established for and dedicated to the memory of Nathan Bedford Forrest. "Na, na, na, na, na, na, na, na, hey, hey, goodbye." The repeated chant lasted long enough to annoy, to exasperate, and to disgust, but it had the effect of a purgative, as well. Not a soul hearing it wanted to do anything but get the hell out.

As the truck carrying the toppled tribute worked its way across the green space toward hard cement and asphalt, J. W. watched the crowd begin to disperse in bit and pieces and rips and tatters, headed for cars and sidewalks and bars and eventually beds. Too bad for that Nazi bunch with the tiki torches they laid down their hard money for, J. W. considered as he strolled through the bunch of people all headed for somewhere else right now. That mob didn't even get to fire up what they'd paid for, much less get to march around saying the Jews would not replace them.

I wonder if Nova's gone to bed yet, he considered. Maybe I ought to give her a call on my cell phone and see if I can come over and say howdy. That is, if I can get the damned thing to work right.

26

At the time the deflowering of the tribute to General Nathan Bedford Forrest was taking place in greater Memphis, James Forrest Howell-Reed, a distant descendant of the scourge of the Western Theatre of the War of Northern Aggression, alone now in his bedchamber, was reading about castor plants. He was not doing so online, knowing that IT freaks were able to resurrect each and every click ever made on any topic visited electronically on any and all computers. Damn such advances in technology. True privacy was a thing of the past for any and every man these days. And such a violation of individual rights even extended to library books borrowed, to books purchased, and movies rented and attended. But if one were to steal a copy of a book on household plantings and garden design and maintenance and if the one doing the stealing was unobserved, at least there was one last way left to do research in the privacy of one's own home.

These facts and suppositions and hopes had led James Forrest to do just that, having heard randomly from somewhere a statement that the castor bean properly processed would yield a poison so powerful and secret that any one ingesting the ricin it produced would surely die and do it quickly. So he had visited one of the last large bookstores still operating in Memphis, it itself a vanishing breed, since everything was fucking online now, and he had slipped a volume on household and ornamental plants into an inside coat pocket. The book was paperback, small and light, and easily concealed, and James Forrest had left the bookstore undetected in his theft. He hoped. No hidden cameras, he prayed.

It's a sorry state of affairs in America today that a man who has the financial wherewithal to buy a goddamn bookstore itself has to lower himself to stealing a paperback book that might help him kill three women. There was a time when surveillance of a man's affairs had not been so wide-ranging and pervasive that he couldn't buy the tools he needed to do the job he had to do. Not anymore. You have to sneak around like a damn pauper to be able to take out a trio of bitches standing in the way of your enjoyment of what was rightfully yours. Maybe not all of them at once, James Forrest told himself. Just the old bitch first, the one currently holding the purse strings. It might look too damn suspicious even for Memphis cops if all three of them dropped at the same time. Age has its priority, even in forming a line for getting offed.

Oh, well, he considered, as he began to seek the written answer to the question before him, look at it as a science assignment in a chemistry course back at Washington and Lee. What kind of horseshit questions did that nutty professor of chemistry say? What is the aim, what are the steps needful to achieve the result desired, what are the hard facts of material reality that impede, what are the scientifically necessary precautions and procedures pertinent to what is possible to obtain success?

James Forrest had never liked messing around in lab work in courses in prep school at Memphis University School and in college at Washington and Lee, and he had never been able to pass any science requirement on his own. Money always made academic success possible, though, since there was never a lack of nerds for sale everywhere one went in those days. But this experiment at hand was his and his alone, James Forrest recognized. He was the lonely scholar. The sole operator of his enterprise. Money in no amount would help him now. Time to hit the books, he told himself. Put on the fucking eyeshade. Get mad at science, and make it serve you for a change.

Once again opening his stolen book, he began to pore over the descriptions of and warnings about castor plants and the mighty power they contained. The extensive back garden at Fallen Timbers was full of the little devils, he knew, having read a whole litany of praise of the beauty of ornamentals such as the castor plant. The colors and shapes of the oversized leaves were wonderful framers for smaller succulents. Book in hand, he had wandered the ornamental gardens of Fallen Timbers, doing his best to match up what he saw there with the color shots in his manual.

Didn't Miss May Margaret Howell-Reed allow her beautiful plantings to be viewed as part of the Spring festival of Shelby County each and every year? Hadn't hundreds of ladies in hats and gloves and colorful frocks come in waves and surges to sneak looks at how the truly wealthy lived? Didn't scores of them suck up to the mistress of the manor by praising her ornamentals, chief among them the castor? Hadn't she therefore stacked up a debt of gratitude to the plant which harbored the wondrous chemical compound called ricin?

If that ain't irony, James Forrest considered as he turned all the attention he could muster to the handbook of death which lay before him, you can kiss my well-endowed ass. And I ain't street talking about what I sit down on, he chortled to himself. I'm talking about what will come to me as my rightful due when the beautiful castor plant does its job. Damn, this is fun, he told himself. I haven't ever enjoyed reading something more than I am right now. Literature is a healer of what ails you, and it's a killer of what's holding you back.

Major Dalbey had left word with LaWanda to send Sergeants Ragsdale and Walker into his office as soon as they hit the door on the morning after the takedown of the N. B. Forrest statue the night before. So as soon as J. W. slipped quietly through the door to the room everybody called the bullpen, LaWanda was waiting to hail him. "Sergeant Ragsdale," she called. "Now you're here, too, and I can stop worrying about you getting by me without me knowing you snuck in the building."

"What you mean, LaWanda?" J. W. said. "I always say howdy to you soon as I hit the door. I come in here every day wanting to see you. Wondering how you been and how you're feeling. Hoping there ain't nothing or nobody been bothering you. Hoping I'd see your smiling face so I could begin my day happy and satisfied and ready to whip the world."

"You already been drinking in the morning even before the sun's got good and up?" LaWanda said. "You talking out of your head. You got a alcohol consumption problem."

"Naw, I meant what I said. You know me. There ain't a bit of deception in my very nature. I say what I mean, and I mean what I say."

"Talk about mean. You are nutty this morning. Have mercy. I ain't got time to listen to you raving on. Sergeant Walker's already in there with the Major, and they waiting for you. So get on in there, like what the Major said."

J. W. did that, stopping first to get coffee and to grab a notepad, knowing the Major was always pleased to see a police officer ready to record his executive utterances. Dalbey didn't allow himself to believe the notetakers ever referred back to what they'd written, but he knew it was the thought and not the action that mattered in office work. That was just the opposite from what was true for cops out in the field, of course. Action usually had to come before there was much time for thought to kick things off, but that was the name of the game anywhere cops roamed, especially in Memphis. Do it first, and then tell what it was supposed to be. Lie like a bastard when and if you had to.

"J. W., sit down and take a load off. I see you already got you some coffee. Is it fresh enough? I'll get LaWanda to bring in some hotter for you, if you need it."

J. W. looked at Tyrone Walker sitting across the room facing the Major behind his desk, but Tyrone wouldn't meet his gaze. Had Dalbey gone nuts? J. W. wondered. What's all this concern for the quality of J. W.'s coffee mean? There had been times, too many to count, when the Major had told J. W. and Tyrone and anybody else present to quit sucking at their coffee and pay attention, even occasionally telling them to pour that crap out. Look at me, not the rim of that damn cup.

"No, Major, this coffee's fine. It's just a habit. I don't really need it that much. Lord knows I'm awake."

"Tyrone," the Major said, "tell Sergeant Ragsdale here what I just told you."

"All right," Tyrone said, but before he could launch into saying anything else, the Major began talking.

"Here it is, then. I want to tell it, Tyrone. The Secret Service has informed us that they did a raid based on what you have discovered down in Panola County, and Batesville, Mississippi, J. W., and they have seized several million dollars printed up of counterfeit money, some bales of dope, and not only that, they got what they think is the core of an operation working with cartels in Colombia. Ain't that something?"

"Well, hell," J. W. said. "I knew something was wrong, but I knew them folks in Batesville had me figured out for sure as a Memphis cop poking around where he shouldn't be. I hadn't even said a word, and that little Rio fucker was chewing my ass as soon as I hit the door. I'd already been researched. Just so you know. But what you telling me now is prime. Do I think it's something? Uh, yeah."

"This Rio bunch figured your being down there was so dumb a move that they didn't have a damn thing to worry about. So they didn't try to hide a single thing, didn't hurry up nothing, and the Secret Service just scooped them up. And the Secret Service thought that us here in Memphis Police was planning every bit of that and playing dumb on purpose."

"Now you're talking," J. W. said. "Playing dumb, that came easy to me. That ain't no stretch."

"Preach it, Sergeant Ragsdale," Tyrone said. "I know that all you had to do was act naturally."

"Y'all love to hooraw each other, don't you?" Major Dalbey said, a touch of fatherly fondness in his tone.

"Well, but the fact of the matter is," said Tyrone, "is that J. W. preached the gospel to Lo Lo Tedrick over on Baby Street like they were in a revival meeting. Lo Lo gave up Bones Family stuff that led directly to what the Secret Service was able to do. In fact, Lo Lo said so much, it's liable to get him killed. J. W. was so good at talking about Jesus and at preaching the evils of money and greed that it brought tears to my eyes. Time he was through, I was rethinking how far I've fallen away from the true faith."

"All I know is it worked, and I want to buy you boys a drink one of these days," the Major said. "Even though I quit that shit myself years ago."

"I did the same thing yesterday morning," J. W. said. "Coming off from consuming too much the night before. And I vowed not to touch another drop."

"Until you get thirsty," Tyrone said.

"Well, yeah," J. W. said, and everybody got a chance to chuckle.

"One last thing," Major Dalbey said. "That statue of Forrest bullshit last night came off real good, and I wasn't expecting that to work so damn well. And the bonus is we got that nut job from the KKK saying he was the one killed that couple in the hotel all dressed up in

Catholic robes and shit. He's resting easy now and jabbering like a son of a bitch."

"You know what?" Tyrone Walker said. "Given all this great news, I do believe we got crime whipped and stopped in Memphis for good."

All three men laughed at that until LaWanda opened the door to Dalbey's office and asked to be let in on the joke.

27

Lunch hour again in one of the smaller and more intimate dining areas of the University Club in Midtown Memphis, and the principals of D'Arcy, Summers, and Wilde Investments sat alone at the prime table, the one next to the window opening on the garden directly east of the main building of the club. The air was cooler than ordinary in Memphis, and the sunlight touched all beneath it a bit less harshly than usual. When Mason Wilde reserved the location for the lunch gathering, he had not had to identify what he wanted by name. He had simply informed August that he and his partners planned to discuss some topics away from the general dining area, and nothing further was mentioned after August had whispered the words "Of course, sir."

All three men arrived at the same time, Mason a few seconds ahead of the other two, and when all three were seated and had ordered drinks—a good stout cab instead of their customary stronger choice of bourbon—Walker spoke first.

"Which one do we begin with?" he said, his voice tight. "Do we tackle two or all three?"

"Let's do them all, get it over with. Three, you say? Every one of them is pending," Mason said. "This is no time to linger."

"All right. I agree," Dallas Summers said. "Let's think about We 2 first, and that chunk of credit we advanced to Miss Monica Moore. You'll remember I never felt strongly about that in the first place."

"She did a great presentation," Mason Wilde said. "You got to give her that. She did fill the eye. But I agree, and I confess I did too much thinking from below the belt when I jumped all over what she had to propose."

"We all did. The little head talked, and the big head listened. Let's admit it. Cut our losses, and move on," Walter D'Arcy said. "As soon as I heard about the killings in the hotel, and read all that slavering goo the *Commercial Appeal* heaved up about We 2 clients playacting as priests and nuns fucking, for God's sake, I knew we had to hit the silks."

"The silks?" Mason said.

"That's a metaphor, you know. It means jumping out of a burning plane with a parachute."

"Cute," Mason said. "Not funny, though."

"Let's don't snipe at each other," Dallas said. "Let's move on. So now that our stellar police have picked up a KKK member for putting the knife to those sex freaks, we have to cut all ties with We 2, financial and otherwise."

"Quit talking about cutting this, that, and the other thing. It makes me queasy. I can't eat my fucking salad for thinking about knife blades," Mason Wilde said. "Can we agree to say no and unh-unh to Miss Moore? Call in the dogs. Demand a recount. Get our investment back?"

"As much as we can, yes," Dallas said. "The contract allows for some drawback. We weren't complete fools when she made pretty and hot to trot. Next?"

"Memphis Mixed Martial Arts," Walker said. "A medium-sized problem which leads to the huge one. Now it gets nasty, and it gets complex."

"What did she say when she called you this morning?" Dallas asked. "And how much did she explain? And what insane mood did she display in the midst of all this new development?"

"Let me lay out for you the bare bones. I'll leave off lingering over the flesh until later. Here goes. Miss May Margaret called me at dawn in the most manic mood I'd ever witnessed in her or in anybody else.

Wait, take that back. I did see my four-year-old back in the day act much in the same way May Margaret Howell-Reed did when I gave him a pony."

"Ha ha," said Dallas. "Cut to the fucking chase. No cute stories, please."

"She said Constance Helen was back, along with her same-sex partner—her husband, May Margaret called the woman. She went on to say that Maureen Langlois of the Memphis Mixed Martial Arts was indeed Constance Helen and that her husband is Billie Sue Something from Dumbshit, Arkansas, or some place with a name like that. She said that Billie Sue has been going by the stage name of Pig Sooey. She said all is well at Fallen Timbers now, and that family life will go on in the most delightful way. All is forgiven. All is love."

"Bullshit," Mason shouted, loud enough to cause the waiter at a distance to spin around to see if a fight was breaking out in the University Club with the time being only lunch and not the cocktail hour on a Friday. "No, it can't be. I saw Maureen Langlois fight that ugly bitch in the octagon. Half of the rednecks in Memphis did. They put on a great show. It was incredible."

"There was money being made," Dallas said. "You got to admit. It was paying off like a busted slot machine in St. Louis."

"Not in future," Walker said. "The end for all that has come, gentlemen. The milk train doesn't stop here anymore. But it gets worse. Miss May Margaret had more to say."

"What did the crazy old bitch say? What about the Fallen Timber holdings? What about the estate, for Christ's sake? What about James Forrest, the little drunk doped-up loser? What will he do now? Talk about a loose cannon. Talk about dirty drawers."

"We're talking about the possibility of a huge financial disaster pending," Walker said. "Our losses in investments would be huge. They could be killing."

"Pending, my ass," Mason yelled. "It ain't pending. It's here. What about all the investment of time and money and planning and placating and predicting what has to be done when? What's going to happen to all we thought we had in place after working every angle possible? We had everything covered, even James Forrest, the goddamn nut."

"Who knows?" Walker said. "We are in a shitstorm, and it's only going to get worse."

"How could it?" Mason said. "What else can happen? All could be lost, couldn't it? Or be on the verge of being lost. Isn't this the worst?"

"Let me answer that. Think about these words, fellow principals of D'Arcy, Simmons, and Wilde. Think about what they might mean as having come from Miss May Margaret Howell-Reed of Fallen Timbers Estate and Associated Holdings this morning. And backed to the hilt by the return to Fallen Timbers of the princess of the family. Think of these two phrases as descriptions of possible ends for the estate, as announced by the controlling holder of that property and all connected legally to it. The first phrase is bird sanctuary. The second is free school for the underprivileged children of Shelby County, Tennessee."

"Motherfucker," Mason yelled. "Cocksucking motherfucker."

"Precisely," Walker said. "Hold your voice down, Mason. People might notice."

Ordinarily the server's costume the ash blonde was wearing would have drawn at least close notice from Willis Sutcliff, if not also inspiring him to speak the best comment he could come up with at the moment. Something like, "Honey, ain't you got something on the back of your dress?" And she, being wise to all give-and-take in the lobby bar of the Peabody, would have done her best to color prettily, smile as though she understood perfectly what was going on and what she must say to keep in the game and up that tip at the end of the hour session of Willis and his running buddy Tommy Beechum, and then respond.

"Now, you fooled me once saying that, and I'm not going to let you do it again. You're being a bad boy now. I'll just take your drink orders and be just as nice as I can be."

Then Willis would have acted like he didn't know what she was talking about, and they would have joshed back and forth until the blonde server turned around, stuck out her cute little butt for him to brush off the invisible foreign matter he had claimed to see, and everybody would have laughed loud and long and ordered up. And she would have flounced off, pretending to pout.

Instead, when she walked up to the table where Willis and Tommy were sitting, all they did was ask the name of the bar bourbon being served in the Peabody Lobby bar these days. She had told them, they had nodded at her, said not a word until she left to fill the order, and both men looked at each other in silence. Willis finally spoke up.

"I'm afraid to even ask you to even tell me more. And if what you've said so far is right, not only will I not be ordering Maker's Mark in the Peabody anymore, I won't be able to even feel steady enough financially to move my taste on down to Heaven Hill."

"It's true, though, and don't tell me you didn't see some of it coming," Tommy Beechum said. "I ain't been feeling right about Memphis Mixed Martial Arts since I first heard this part of the story. Had to be a lie, I figured. It's just some asshole in the Boxing Commission raising the same damn questions they always ask. Licensable, they holler. How certain are financial prospects and current resources? How mixed up in it is the mayor's office? Is the damn legislature making noises about regulations? Where can we stick our runny noses in the feedbag before the oats are all eat up? That's the kind of crap I was worried about."

"That ain't nothing compared to this," Willis said. "And you damn well know it. The way it felt at first, it was too good to be true. And to have the damn heart cut out of it by two dykes like that. Goddamn, it hurts. I feel betrayed is what it is, mainly. Not even talking about money now. I mean character."

"Fuck being betrayed. I been fooled and lied to and money has been took out of my pocket, and all the money I've already put in expecting some return. Not only is nothing going to come in again, all we put in the damn thing is gone, too. I was betting on money to come."

"Remember how it felt when that crowd went nuts the first time Maureen Langlois beat the living hell out of that fat-assed Pig Sooey? Remember how they spent money the next week after that first bunch of bouts with them two as the highlight match-up?"

"Yeah, don't talk about it. I'm too sick even to bear it."

"Think about this, then, if you can stand it. Just imagine them two in bed with nobody watching, not like when it was the Kappa Kappa Gamma sweetheart beating the piss out of Pig Sooey, but instead it's Constance Helen Howell-Reed just getting rooted around in by that big old ugly sow."

"It makes me want to puke," Tommy Beechum said. "Where's that damn girl with that Heaven Hill shit?"

"Look, she's coming yonder, but think about this. Now that Howell-Reed little bitch is back home with mama, and she's give up show business and took us down right along with the MMA. And that family's got a monster share of all the money in Shelby County. And I ain't just worried about the money. I'm scared about what them other fuckers might do to me," Willis said, taking the glass from the blonde server's tray before she could lift it herself, not saying a word to her in the exchange. In fact, he didn't act like he even knew she was there. She had leaned forward really far to let him look down the neck of her maroon dress, too. He hadn't even done that or made any kind of a joke about it.

"You ain't talking about Summers and D'Arcy and Wilde are you?" Tommy said. "They don't use muscle. Hell, they're up about high as you can get in Memphis finance. They're respectable and all that shit, ain't they? Deep pockets, like everybody says. It's also just profit and loss with them."

"Sure, they ain't about to do anything personally in Memphis that'd make them look bad, but they'll farm stuff out to folks in New Orleans that make a living settling up busted deals gone wrong."

"Oh, shit," Tommy said. "It's not just money we got to worry about then."

"Any time it's Memphis money getting siphoned off in a bad deal, it's time to worry big, and not just about financing gone wrong, Bubba. I can tell you I'm feeling all hot and flustered just thinking about the kinds of heavy-duty people I'm talking about. Anything we got left, we got to find ways to hide, and I'm already thinking about casino life in Mississippi. Maybe there's a little something there. But that's going bad, too, they tell me. They about wrung all the money out of that part of the country that ever was there."

"You figure then that the Memphis Mixed Martial Arts is on the ropes?" Tommy said. "That's what you coming up with?"

"The MMA in the Bluff City, son, is as dead as pro football is in Memphis," Willis said. "That I know. It's gone as bad as the fucking pyramid on the river did."

"All the money is getting burned to hell, then," Tommy Beechum said. "It's gone. Lost. Our share of it is over and done with. We are fucking broke as the ten commandments."

"Memphis money will do that," Willis said. "It will go the way cotton did, and it will go the way of that damn river out there. Just rolling along full of crap and garbage between them banks all the way to New

Orleans and then out to the Gulf where it gets to be just part of all that dirty salty water that nobody can drink."

"I want some more Heaven Hill," Tommy said. "And I want it now."

"I want out of here," Willis said. "And I want to stop thinking about them women rolling around on each other. Hugging and kissing. Moaning and carrying on. What a waste of money-making talent. Godamighty, I got to get out of the Bluff City with what little I got left."

28

The book on castor and related plants which James Forrest had lifted from the bookstore was helpful, he had to admit. Like all problems he'd had to face in study at MUS and W and L, it didn't yield up quick answers the way he imagined a cookbook should do. There would be steps you could follow one, two, and three, in a cookbook, he thought, though admitting he'd never really had to cook or prepare any dish in his life and was only making an educated guess, but it did make sense.

In a cookbook, directions for any recipe would tell you what you needed to have at hand, every ingredient, and it would start at a beginning point, move through the stages necessary to make the dish, and when you did that, you'd have the cake or the soufflé or the crab salad or whatever the hell it was you were creating. Isn't that what family servants did every day? It couldn't be hard to follow a recipe if they could do it.

But in every course he could remember sitting through at MUS and W and L, there was never any straightforward set of instructions laid out to follow. No, not that, naturally. It'd be too easy, and the salaries that teachers and professors drew, though too small as they always whined, had to be justified somehow. So they never just laid matters out, provided the right answers you needed to do whatever it took to pass the damn course and advance to the next one. No, they wanted you to think for yourself much too often, and they'd proudly tell you about that intention, some so much you wanted to find a way to make them suffer for not doing the full job for which you or the old man or the trust fund was paying.

Why tantalize and tease, and why smirk and smile like they knew the answers already and were not going to tell you what they knew until you sweated and suffered over having to solve problems that had already been solved, write essays and answers to questions that had already been discussed and decided years ago? It made no sense. That slow unnecessary torture had gone on, though, until they finally broke your will and made you sweat over questions and problems already taken care of years ago. And it was hard at times to find some nerd to hire to do that needless work for you, and the teachers and professors were always finding ways to make it harder to jump over all the obstacles they put in the way of advancing to the point where you were free of the chains they had on you.

You would think, James Forrest considered as he pored over the text on castor bean plants and the ricin that could be extracted from them, that if all you wanted was to be told how to do what you had to do to get the vegetable matter that would solve your particular problem, and you weren't trying to pass some fucking course of study, that the instructions would be clear and to the point. All I'm trying to do is to poison three women, for Christ's sake, three women standing in my way to the rightful enjoyment of what my dead father and all the others before him have created and need no more. I'm simply asserting my right to control what's mine by inheritance and name. And I don't care a gnat's asshole about the beauties of the castor plant as an ornamental and ways to handle it safely, so as not to set loose its power to kill quickly, well, and completely.

How do you pay attention to reading stuff that's not interesting, not to the point, not relevant to your need to be instructed? Talk about the scholar's lamp as old four-eyed Professor Christesen called it in that W and L class in philosophy. I understand what he meant now, and I hate like hell having to learn what he kept saying. "Be patient, be diligent, be humble," the old fool would tell us in that damn required course in Western philosophy. "Be content with partial understanding, but never give up in despair."

I'm trying, old fool, I'm trying. I won't quit until I figure out a foolproof way to get ricin extracted, get it introduced into the gullets of my mother, my sister, and my sister's fat dyke lover from the swamps of Arkansas, and reap the benefits of all of them laid out stone cold.

Looking deep into the page before him, James Forrest wondered if Arkansas had swamps. If it didn't, it ought to, and I'll be goddamned if I hunt for it in a book somewhere. One book to worry about is enough, and let me find a shortcut to where I want to go. I'd like to just cram some leaves from a castor plant into their salads, but that won't work according to this book. Ricin has to be extracted to get strong enough to do the job. And now I've got to find the way to do that, and that means I've got to keep rooting around and thinking about the same thing for longer than I want to. I've got to get some relief, and I know right where I keep the magic powder that lets me relax, go to sleep, and have wonderful dreams that I never remember. That's what I want, and I'll give myself that just as soon as I figure out this book. Patient, diligent, and humble. Here I come, Professor Christesen.

Look at it this way, James Forrest considered. You've worked hard to convince Mother May Margaret she's going crazy, you've used electronic means to create light and sound horror shows, you've employed sleight of hand to feed her braised rats and snake pasta, you've dressed in a costume of the old granddaddy Nathan B. Forrest and popped up in the strangest places, you've written a letter from the grave of the battling old bastard to her using authentic paper and ink from the nineteenth century, and all that's accomplished is to have her call in the Memphis police. I'm not afraid of cops as cops, but the two that visited last seem to be the type that believe nothing, want nothing, and give away nothing. That big black one seems as settled in his mind as a stone in deep water, and the white redneck type one looked at me like he was seeing into my soul. His eyes were as blue and cold as my old ancestor's heart, and I expect Nathan Bedford Forrest wouldn't trust him to do a thing without thinking about it first. Both of those Memphis cops seemed unimpressed by anything, not even Fallen Timbers. They walked around like they owned it.

What I've got to do is be so careful and so removed from the scene when I finally get this ricin thing figured out and done that those two won't be here to sniff around again. How to do that, I don't know yet. First things first, though. Poison these bitches and worry about fallout later. Right now I've got to take some medicine and lie down for a healing session. I'll awake a new man and a scholar. W and L, I'll owe it to you.

Deangelo Dixon sat brooding in the great room of his three-story house situated just at the edge of the territory where brothers typically didn't reside in Memphis. Finding the right spot for where he'd live had been crucial for him. The question almost always about most placement planning is where is the prime location for events to be centered, he had always considered, and the current problem he was having to face seemed more demanding than most. Events determined where things did and should or should not take place. Location, location, location, as the real estate woman had told him during his search for the right place to call his own for headquarters.

The agent was a white woman, of course, Deangelo knowing he didn't want to deal with a soul sister who'd have baggage working in her head, whether she knew it or not. That was another one of the advantages white folks with money had over black folks with just as much resources. What they also had hanging around somewhere in the back part of their minds was a load the white folks didn't have. A black man or woman, well fixed financially and in terms of rank with their own people, still had to worry with all that crap fixed somewhere deep inside. Something was always festering and making things harder to handle, even when spending lots of money, and most brothers and sisters didn't even know that load was always there just waiting to do damage.

So Deangelo Dixon had fought his way up and succeeded in beating back all opposition not because of superior firepower or aid from others, but because he knew and admitted the limitations of being black and poor in Memphis, Tennessee, right from the onset of his life. Yeah, he had learned to tell himself at times needful, I'm at a disadvantage from the get-go, but the fact that I understand and accept that means I can have my way with everybody else who doesn't get the story. I know why I'm fucked up, and that's two-thirds of the battle. They don't, the dumb ones all truly crippled in the head, and I do.

So in the house where he lived, right on the edge of what some folks called the ghetto, Deangelo Dixon stayed and operated and prospered. Now he had yet one more thing to deal with, a situation that could end him up in jail or the grave, and he had to find a quick way to handle it. If he didn't, he'd have that pair of Memphis cops who seemed to know him better than anybody else except for one of his daughters, Avalene, the one who left home and went to college and moved to Baltimore and got a job with the federal government, and never looked back. She would send a card now and then, but she made it clear she was as gone as yesterday's breakfast.

Who was leaning and looking in? Two of them, the same ones again. Tyrone Walker, that was the name of the brother, the one who'd played the white man's game in Memphis better than most anybody else, whether it was football or college or police force, and Deangelo was afraid that brother knew him up one side and down the other. The other one, that cold-eyed white cop who liked nothing better than making a brother feel nervous about what was going on, his name was J. W. Ragsdale. He didn't seem to think he ever needed to take notice of a damn thing around him, but he was always there when shit was going down. And he made it land hard.

Counterfeit money, Deangelo said to himself. That's what's put me in the pinch right now. Fucking bad money. I knew it was crazy and too dangerous to deal with, and that too many people from every side would be mixed up in it, some of them in Memphis, some in St. Louis, some in DC, and some in South America in that country called Colombia. Good damn product did come from down there, it was true, but to have fake money sent back and forth, money the Secret Service would be after, money that the fucking cartels would come after you for as soon as they found out they'd been paid for their dope by loads of bills worth nothing, then everything in Memphis could turn to shit in a heartbeat. And it was doing that, like a load of lumber not tied down to the bed of a truck, flying down the interstate, two-by-fours and plywood taking to the air. Nothing holding things together.

Tuck Bunny was the key, the only one really on the inside far enough to get his boss set up for a target. "I got too hungry," Deangelo said out loud, causing his pair of pit bulls, Before and After, to rouse up and look at him. "I should have been satisfied with one plateful, not tried to hog the whole goddamn pot of beans. I knew better. I wasn't that hungry, but I made myself want every damn bite of it."

Tuck Bunny was unsound, prone to brag and strut around, tell stories he starred in, and look for attention wherever he could get it. He would heave his guts and not even know he was doing it. He had to be taken out, then, after all these years going back to when they were nappy-headed kids together, scuffling around to swipe orange drinks and dumdums and cigarettes from the 7-11, growing up side by side in the Bones Family and learning how to do and how to make it. Too bad. What a shame. I won't enjoy taking him out, but I got it to do. And really, I got to say I will get a kick out of seeing his eyes bug out when he sees what I'm fixing to do.

"Come here, Before and After," Deangelo Dixon said to his killer dogs, both dozing. "Give Daddy some sugar. And I might give you a hunk of meat."

29

Patrolman Juan Simon, new to the Memphis Police Force and eager to do a good job no matter where they put him at first, had been assigned for the early morning shift on the riverfront, where nothing usually happened except for barges going up or down the Mississippi with their loads of cargo. Hardly a soul was even around, except for street people sleeping off last night's medicine, if they had been lucky and got fixed, and staring into the rising sun as they scratched itches that never eased. Another day, another scramble.

A few black kids were picking their way around the edge of the big water, calling out to each other if they found something they could brag about and claim was worth having, and Patrolman Simon asked himself if he should warn them not to step into the water of the Mississippi no matter how peaceful it looked close to shore. It was powerful beneath that foam and trash and bits of leaves and bark and plastic and paper on the surface, and Patrolman Simon had grown up fearing moving water. There was always something going on beneath what you could see. Something that would suck you down.

So when one of the black kids came trotting toward him, Patrolman Juan Simon prepared to give him a brief lecture on water safety before the boy wandered off. He realized his job was not to be a lifeguard, but he was a public servant, as he'd been told many times during training for his new job as Memphis cop, and it wouldn't hurt to say a few words to the black kid about what could happen in moving water.

"You a policeman, right?" the kid said. "You want to know when peoples is dead or messed up or cut or shot, don't you?"

"Yes, son," Juan Simon said, "all us police want to take care of people in Memphis. You thinking about being a policeman when you get grown?"

"Naw, I don't want to be no cop," the kid said. "I be going to play basketball in the NBA so I can make some real money and buy all kinds of stuff. But that ain't what I'm talking about. See yonder? That old building by the river, where all them docks is fell into the water?"

"I do see it. You been playing in there? You got to be careful in old buildings like that. You might step on a nail and get lockjaw. Fall and hurt yourself. Slip into a crack or something."

"I ain't stepping on nothing. I watch all the time where I put my feets. That's why I can play ball so good, see. But I can tell you what's in that building. It's a dead man. We seen him this morning, me and Lister. Lister he didn't want to tell you about it. Might get in trouble he said. But I said that's your business, dead folks. Ain't it?"

"You say you did see a dead man in that old warehouse? Maybe he was sleeping, you know. Not dead, but dead drunk more likely," Juan Simon said, thinking this is a chance to connect with a black kid, show him police were his friends, not somebody to be scared of and lie to.

"I know what a drunk man look like. This one ain't drunk. He been shot in the back of the head with probably a .44 caliber. It left a big old hole, and you could see all the way inside his brain if it wouldn't for all that blood and stuff in the way. I know he's dead just from looking at him. Lister he poked him, too. He ain't moving. Ain't never going to move again."

"Uh, let's go see," Patrolman Juan Simon said, thinking if the kid was right he'd be witnessing his first murdered body in Memphis. Don't call it in until you're sure, he told himself. If you're wrong, they'll hooraw you for a rookie until you're worn out with it.

The kid was right, though, and the black man sprawled face down on a still intact part of the ruined cotton warehouse still looked as though he'd not been dead long. Blood was congealed, brain matter was evident, but not many flies were swarming yet, so Patrolman Juan Simon had his chance to call in his first murder scene he'd discovered in Memphis. The thing he wondered about as he gave report, though, was how did that kid not over eight or nine years old know about the size of the wound a .44 caliber round would leave in the rear of a skull. Better get ready, he told himself, to get surprised in all kinds of ways in the Bluff City. People know weird shit here.

"Sergeant Ragsdale," Tyrone Walker said as soon as J. W. hit the door a little after nine in the morning, "I've got some hot news for you. Official."

"Look, Tyrone, if it has to do with the Major saying he always wants to see me in the building before this time of day, I don't want to hear about it. And I know when you call me by the title which limits the amount of money I make—I'm talking the label of sergeant now—you got to have some news which is going to bother me and bring my ass down."

"This will surprise and maybe even delight you, Sergeant Ragsdale," Tyrone said. "A rookie cop on Downtown early patrol found a dead man shot in the back of the head in one of those old wore-out and falling-down cotton warehouses on the river, and can you guess who it was?"

"There's lots of people I'd want it to be, but I ain't got time to list all of them. Who was it?"

"Ja'Neal Washington, a.k.a. Tuck Bunny. That's who."

"No shit? Tuck Bunny. Damn. I'm not surprised, but you say he was shot in the back of the head. That sounds plumb planned to me. It's almost as nice a killing as you'd get in a picture show about Chicago in the old days. An execution, hey? Why would somebody off Tuck Bunny? Won't Deangelo and the Bones claimers be pissed off? Time for war maybe, huh?"

"Yeah, but keep thinking. You are about to string together some motives and some names, I do believe. If you'll just let your mind wander, you'll come up with my conclusion or a reasonable alternative."

"Reasonable my ass," J. W. said. "Let me see. I bet it's got to do with that counterfeit money deal and the Panola County Mississippi connection, and it's got Bones Family all over it. Money, money, money. The real deal cash and the fake shit, too."

"Who in the Bones Family would have the means, the planning, and the nerve to blow Tuck Bunny's brains out all over a warehouse downtown?" Tyrone said. "And be able to do it so quick after the Secret Service got that counterfeit mess cleaned up and people indicted?"

"You know as well as I do," J. W. said. "Somebody's had to take the blame, and somebody else has had to point that out by blowing that first somebody's lights out. Tell the Major he's got to make Downtown let that killing alone and let us have it. They don't know shit down there about what's going on, and they'll just fuck it up."

"Now just think, J. W., about what you have to tell me to do, the directions you got to give me. Cast your mind back. What do you suppose I've been telling Major Dalbey this morning while you were still fighting your way out of them sweaty old bed sheets?"

"I know, I know. You're already ahead of me, and you wouldn't have called me Sergeant Ragsdale if you hadn't been. You're already in the enjoyment phase of crowing over your opponent. When we going downtown?"

"Just as soon as you wipe the sleep out of your eyes. And another thing, I have already reserved for us a relatively new sedan in the fleet. We'll be riding in style this morning."

"Woo hoo," J. W. said. "What you saying? No stink wagon today?"

"No, it's gonna smell like Memphis early on a spring morning in the fleet car we'll be driving."

"Let that spring morning be in a nice part of Memphis, Lord God, please," J. W. said. "Let's go."

30

The descriptive paragraphs on the beauties of castor plantings in ornamental gardens in the book James Forrest had stolen from the bookstore out on Poplar Avenue were not necessary, he considered as he soldiered through all the author had to say about the heavy burden of his subject. Who could care about just where a particular species needed to be in the overall garden in a terrain open to full sunlight most of the day? Women reading this crap, James Forrest told himself, that's who. They'd care, and you had to give the writer his due after all. He wanted to focus on the castor plant as a feature of utility in the pursuit of beauty. Dennis J. Ryan, PhD, of the department of horticulture of the University of Tennessee was not really interested in growing the castor plant successfully so as to be able to poison his mother, his sister, and some fat bitch from Arkansas. No, he was thinking ornamental, and I'm the one thinking fatal.

I am that person Dr. Ryan fears, James Forrest Howell-Reed told himself as he read yet again all the admonitions about care and safety in handling the castor plant so as to avoid terrible consequences if sound advice goes unheeded. Dr. Ryan doesn't know me, but he understands people who will not pay attention. He's afraid I won't pay proper attention. He thinks I'm too dumb to listen. I want to get past all these hedges Ryan drones on about having to observe in handling the castor plant, and I on the other hand want to make every mistake possible that some fool might commit. Let me get my order of business written out in plain English sentences that make up a series of procedures that will lead to the desired end. Damn, I didn't think I could say a sentence like that so well, James Forrest went on to tell himself. It proves that I might not have been listening much to that bunch of old fools in prep school and college jabbering up in front of all those classrooms, but I picked up the idea of how to tackle a problem in a logical way. Worth every cent of the tuition the trust fund paid, I have to admit.

Those guys in the cheap suits in the front of the lecture halls wouldn't have approved of what I'm doing with what I picked up from them without even trying, but who could care what those fools would judge? All their money from every one of them put together over all the years of their lives wouldn't amount to a fart in a high wind when compared to what I'm about to come into complete control of. But I do tip my eyeshade, if I was wearing one, to each and all. You taught me enough, old dummies, to get this job done right, whether you'd approve or not.

All right, here we go, he told himself, looking back again at his notes and the steps for the procedure laid out in them, let's go over them one more time. And once I check and double check, I'll have to go out to one of the gardens to do a little harvesting well after midnight, bring in my crop, process it, prepare it, and get ready to put it into the nice family meal we'll all have tomorrow. Together again, the Howell-Reed inheritors and the hanger-on whore from Arkansas. Around the festive table, we'll settle down to our repast. It'll be me, mother, sister, fat ugly sister-in-law, or would that Arkansas sow actually be a brother-in-law? What do they call these weird relationships these days? Oh, I do hope I won't be politically incorrect, James Forrest told himself in a voice he heard within as that of a college senior of contemporary age and situation, trying his best not to offend any social group. I'll do my best to refer to each and all persons by their chosen pronoun, whatever it may be. He, she, it, they, something. I will not offend. I promise.

Finding himself laughing out loud as he stared into his notes, James Forrest wondered yet again at his ability to be amused in whatever circumstance he found himself. That is a gift and a blessing, he thought, if I believed in blessings. I don't. We make our own history, our own way, and it's our sole and best possession. It might be lonely, but better your own company than that of other people reaching in on you, trying to get your stuff.

All right, here we go. It is the castor seed which when correctly processed will create ricin. The leaves of the castor contain no poison, no danger. The coverings of the pods are themselves not poisonous. It is only the seed pod within its covering, properly stripped and properly ground and heat-dried that will yield ricin. The ricin itself, in and of itself, is deadly and undetectable after it has had its fatal course of entry and operation into the victim.

Ricin is tasteless, finely ground, and fatal in the tiniest of doses, James Forrest read from his notes, this particular point having been underlined and scored several times on his worksheet. This whole series of steps and statements I've gleaned and recorded from Dr. Ryan's book looks like what a hired nerd might create in a biology class at W and L, James Forrest noted. He felt proud about the resemblance, and he felt almost nerd-like in his glowing sense of accomplishment and his careful recording of steps to that successful conclusion.

"I could have done all that academic bullshit by myself those years ago," he said aloud. "See, if I'd wanted to. I'm smart, I'm able, and I'm about to be just about the wealthiest single individual in all of Shelby County, Tennessee. Go it, James Forrest Howell-Reed. Go it, ricin! Get some!"

He turned his attention back to his notes, pausing only to reach out to the tools he'd be using in the night to come: the shears, the pharmacist's tools and containers, the Bunsen burner, the small drying oven, the book by Dr. Dennis Ryan itself. He patted each object belonging to his project, caressing each and every element of his venture in turn. "Soon," he said, "Soon, my lovelies." That made him chuckle and say one last thing before reaching for his separate container off to one side, tried and true and filled with cocaine of high quality. "I'm starring in my own horror movie," James Forrest declared aloud. "If the Academy Award fix wasn't already in, I'd get the Oscar for script writing if not for best actor." If this isn't fun, he asked himself, if this isn't total fulfillment, what the fuck is? I understand chemistry for the first time, and it's great!

The crime scene in the abandoned cotton warehouse was fairly close to what had been reported to the Midtown station, J. W. and Tyrone discovered when they reached the edge of the river where the Downtown cops had already put up barriers, some real sawhorses strung together by boards and some symbolic orange tape marking off prohibited access. The rookie patrol cop who'd reported the body was there, eager to meet the sergeants from Midtown he had already heard stories about from a few older officers.

"You say these two guys, Ragsdale and Walker, have spent their whole time in Memphis out at the Midtown station?" Juan Simon had said to the cop who seemed to know both sergeants fairly well. "I can see starting out in Midtown, but wouldn't you want to be closer to the action in the center of Downtown somewhere along the way? I know I would."

"These two officers have always been out there, as far as I know. More gang stuff centered there, and Ragsdale and Walker want more geography to work in than I do. They like it, and hell they spent half their time roaming all over the place in Memphis and Shelby County anyway."

"Isn't the county outside of Memphis not in police jurisdiction?" Juan Simon had said. "Territoriality and all that. Isn't that sheriff country like they told us during training?"

"Well, yeah, but not in hot pursuit, though. Walker and Ragsdale got a real loose definition of hot pursuit, too," the older Downtown cop had said, beginning to chuckle a little. "Ragsdale even gets down into Mississippi as much as he can. That's home country for him. All around us is part of Metro Memphis, the way he sees it. Anything he can drive to in less than a day."

"Yeah, you could say that," another cop listening in said. "That pair got their own definition for a lot of things."

So when Juan Simon saw the two veteran sergeants from Midtown come out of the Chevrolet and begin to pick their way along the cobblestones of the river marge, he reminded himself to stay cool and not let on how excited he'd been to find his first homicide victim in Memphis. Not too much rookie acting, he told himself. Don't start jabbering. Let them ask the questions and all you do is respond without saying anything not to the point. Be cool.

"Hey," the white sergeant said, "you the one found the deceased here this morning?"

"Yessir, a kid playing around in the warehouse put me onto it. It looked like a pretty recent homicide."

"Yeah, last night sometime late. Before the sun got good and up," Sergeant Ragsdale said. "That's when it woulda gone down."

"Who ID'd him? Some officer that knew him, I suppose," said Tyrone Walker. "He did get around town, Tuck Bunny did. Already made a good name for himself in the greater Memphis area. Active young citizen."

The other Midtown officer laughed a little at that, and said he knew Tuck Bunny would be proud to be remembered in that way. Then all three of them walked into the opening to the cotton warehouse, a gap left where there had been sliding doors at one time, hauled off long ago to serve some other purpose. The crime scene processors were there in the warehouse, white suited and waiting to be told they could start their work as soon as the officers took their look at the body, locations, and whatever else they took to be pertinent before turning the corpse over to the team.

"The kid that found the body said he thought it was a .44 that did the deed, I understand," Tyrone Walker said. "That right?"

"Yes, the kid said the wound was from a .44, and I wondered how he would know that," Juan Simon said. "He's not over ten or twelve years old, I'd say."

"Loose kids that age in Memphis do know their ordnance, wouldn't you say, Sergeant Walker?" Ragsdale said. "Real students of firearms. And blades."

"They could give me lessons in most things in the streets of Memphis," Walker said.

"And do," J. W. Ragsdale said. "Do you need to see anything else, Tyrone?"

"Naw, it's clear what went down. He made Tuck Bunny turn his back after he'd made him come in here. Put the .44 up to his head but didn't touch it to him, and let her go."

"Didn't need to waste another load on him, neither."

"No, but he did stomp on that little finger. See how it's all bloody and busted up? It's a twin to the pinky on the other hand. That's to let all interested parties know if anybody is watching that the Bones

Family giveth and it taketh away,"Tyrone said. "Thus sayeth the Lord. In case anybody was wondering. Say, listen. Don't you think, J. W., nothing ought to be said about the Bones Family affiliation, and that the name of the victim we give out ought not to be the street label?"

"There you go, thinking again," J. W. said. "Yep, let's don't advertise all we know before we go making visits to interested parties."

"You took the words right out of my mouth," Tyrone said. "And I'll make sure to give them Tuck Bunny's name his mama slapped on him at birth to use. I know it, and I know you do, too."

"I do know it, but I don't like it near as much as the label Tuck Bunny. That was a cute name, a sweet one, don't you believe?"

"Yeah, for a murdering little shitass it was awful nice," Tyrone said, and then turning to the crime scene crew, "Gentlemen and ladies, it's all yours. Have fun."

"Just for curiosity's sake," J. W. said to the boss lady of the crew, "will what's her name, Nova Hebert, will she be involved in this one? Just wondering. Worked with her before some."

"She's the senior ME," the boss lady said, "she don't go out on the scene of little old street killings like this one. She'll look over what we report, maybe take a look at the body if she got a question or something. You know, stuff like that."

"Just wondering," J. W. said. "Tell her hello for me and Sergeant Walker."

After the two officers left the scene and got back into the clean-smelling car from the Midtown fleet, Tyrone Walker began to chuckle, while J. W. did his best to play innocent and ignore him. "You did it, didn't you?" Tyrone said. "You broke down, I can tell."

"What?" J. W. said. "You think we ought to go straight to where Deangelo Dixon dens up, or should we stop at the station first?"

"You answered her call, and picked up the phone, and next thing you knew, you were asking folks who work for her to say her name out loud. And that way, you could say it yourself, and you were dying to do that. Just to hear it said."

"You sound like some kind of a relationship adviser like that woman on Channel 17 every morning," J. W. said. "I'm surprised a man like you would watch stuff like that, educated and cool like you are."

"J. W., it doesn't take a trained psychologist to figure you out. You are back in love again, just dying even to hear Nova's name said out loud by a stranger. And you know what?"

"No, what? Damn it. Don't pick at me while I'm driving east on Union. I'll run into something."

"You have already run into something, and I'm glad you have. Do I have your permission to tell Marvelle that we'll be double-dating with y'all again soon?"

"People don't date any more, Tyrone," J. W. said. "They just hook up, see?"

"I do believe you're a man that stays right on top of the changing habits of the times and does keep up," Tyrone said. "I don't doubt that you've become a man of the twenty-first century. But I bet you won't tell Nova that what y'all are doing is hooking up."

"Have your damn fun, married man," J. W. said. "Let's tell the Major we want to go make a call on the head man of the Bones Family. Got to let the Bones boss know one of his brothers has got himself offed."

"It'll break the boss's heart, and I think we ought to get on over there. Hell, let's don't even stop to buy a sympathy card for Tuck Bunny."

"Double dating," J. W. said, steering around a slow-moving pickup loaded with bed springs and mattresses headed up Union. "Huh."

"Hooking up," Tyrone said, beginning to laugh. "Double huh. Let's go see Deangelo Dixon. But first, I want to talk to Lo Lo Tedrick."

"You're right," J. W. said, glad to have the subject changed but gratified by the exchange with Tyrone about Nova. "He might be able to cough something up that'll give us an advantage for when we pay our little visit to Deangelo."

"You think we'll find Lo Lo at home on Baby Street this time of day?"

"The boy does not keep regular hours, practicing Christian though he is. He might well be home still laying up in bed. Let's go see."

31

"Your brother doesn't like me," Billie Sue said. "And that's putting it mildly. Is there anything I can do to improve the atmosphere in this big old monster house?"

"James Forrest has never liked anything about anybody connected to me," Constance Helen said, "so don't think about it, and don't let it worry you."

The two women were not yet out of bed, and they were not in a hurry to be, though some matters of business were pending and had to be addressed downtown in the offices of D'Arcy, Simmons, and Wilde in the early afternoon. It was all preliminary with no need for hasty announcements, arrangements, and discussion, but it was needful. As Walker D'Arcy liked to say, an ocean voyage begins not at full steam ahead but with a long series of untyings, unravelings, loadings, and securings, and gentle nudges toward the commencement of moving to a new location.

Billie Sue had already been party to three meetings with one or other of the principals of the firm charged with handling the financial affairs of the estate and holdings of Miss May Margaret Howell-Reed of Fallen Timbers, sitting quietly beside her love Constance Helen as matters of weight and moment were considered, and after the first ten minutes of the first of these encounters she had been so bored and benumbed she had to keep pinching her forearm to stay awake.

"What has happened to your sweet little wrist?" Constance Helen had asked her afterwards. "Did you get scratched by thorns in one of our gardens? Is it a rash? Does it hurt?"

"Nothing hurts when I'm near you," Billie Sue had said. "All I ever feel around you is peace and calm and brooding passion."

"I love it when you talk all hot like that to me," her wife-to-be had said. "Stop it or I'll jump on you right now."

"Will you put me in a full arm bar? Or do a takedown right in front of everybody?"

Sweet talk among lovers, Billie Sue told herself, as she felt the need to rouse up and leave the bed finally, late as it was in the morning, a strong pang of hunger deep in the belly as much a factor as anything else. "Do you suppose we can find anything left for breakfast, Love?" she said.

"Don't worry about anything being left. The cook won't start anything until we let her know it's time. Are you ready to take breakfast?"

"I could eat, yeah."

"Can you? I don't doubt that for a minute. You eat all things so well. Let's go on down. I expect Mother will have waited to join us."

"What about your brother? Will he be eating the same time as us?"

"I seriously doubt that," Constance Helen said. "And if he chooses to do so, it'll be because he's up to something. His little world is rocking right now, and change drives him nuttier than usual. He'll have thought up something to annoy."

"Well, I won't do anything to upset him, if I can help it. But finally I just don't give a shit."

"Now you're talking, Love of My Life. Let's go eat."

32

When J. W. turned the car into Baby Street, he could see immediately that two sedans and a utility vehicle were parked on the street close to Lo Lo Tedrick's den and that pulled up into the driveway was a black Dodge Charger, dull in finish with nothing shiny showing anywhere on its surfaces.

"That ain't just some kind of first-coat stuff on that Charger, is it?" he said. "Don't tell me Lo Lo is just driving a car still in the process of beautification, is he?"

"I do wish you'd keep up with the times and the fashions, J. W.," Tyrone said. "If you want to run with the big dogs you got to wear the right collar and get off the porch. That there, the dull undercoat look on a black Charger, that is the way to go now. It understates and therefore highlights the serious nature of that vehicle. It's not just gussied up to look pretty. Naw, uh-uh. It says I know what I am and you do too, fool. Don't expect me to try to impress with flash and filigree. I am dangerous, and I am as serious as a heart attack."

"I got you," J. W. said. "I wonder where that one was stolen from."

"I would not know, and I don't worry about petty theft these days. It is not in my current job description."

"Tell you what, Sergeant Walker. When we go in there and rouse Lo Lo from his bed, I recommend you continue to play the part of a man who knows what's going on in this day and time. Me, I'm going to be what I was the last time Lo Lo and me got the chance to talk about theological matters. I will sympathize and understand, and you be just as ignorant about matters of the spirit as you truly are. See how that goes for us."

"I stand instructed, J. W.," Tyrone said. "That worked before, and let's see if you can work the boy again this time by taking that road. Pull in behind that stud Charger, and let's get going and say howdy."

"I won't be working alone, you unbeliever. I'll have Jesus and his old man helping me, and if they are with thee, thou need not be of little faith. Their rod and their staff will comfort me."

"Preach it, son," Tyrone said. "I will stand aside and shake the tambourine when it's offering time. Let's go knock on Lo Lo's door."

"Knock and it shall be given. Seek and you shall find. Let's see what's shaking."

Only one or two knocks were necessary for sounds to begin coming from within Lo Lo Tedrick's nest on Baby Street, and when the door opened it was the man himself, wide awake and fully dressed, as early in the day as it was. "Hello, officers," Lo Lo said. "I ain't that surprised to see y'all today." He stood aside to let them through the door.

"Lo Lo," J. W. said. "I got to tell you this. The last time I saw you and we had that chance to talk about the new path the Lord has put your feet upon, that has stayed with me. It made a great impression, it knocked me over, and you can ask Sergeant Walker if I've been talking to him or not about that."

"You don't have to ask, Lo Lo," Tyrone said. "I'm here to tell you that Sergeant Ragsdale has mentioned and gone into long discussions about what you and him talked about that last time we were here. I don't know the true words to use to describe it right, but I think probably the sergeant does. Am I right, Sergeant Ragsdale?"

"What you're looking for is this word here, Sergeant Walker. Conviction. The word is conviction and it ain't got a thing to do with the law or imprisonment or this dirty world we have to live in day by day. It ain't a legal term. No, what conviction means when I think of it in connection with Lo Lo Tedrick is the burden of truth that the Lord God Jehovah has laid upon this man. Conviction. What is true, what is holy, what proves to be the righteous path for the man who loves God to follow. That's conviction."

"I ain't thinking about that very word," Lo Lo said. "I guess because I didn't know what it meant until you just told me about it. And I thank you for that. But what you say it means is what I been feeling. It's like a burden, hard to lift and hard to carry but you got to pick it up."

"Brother," J. W. said, opening his arms toward Lo Lo, "will you let me just hug you as a fellow creature in Jesus Christ?"

"Yes sir," Lo Lo said, falling into J. W.'s embrace and beginning to weep as he did so. "I got such a burden on me, officer."

"Let it out, Lo Lo," J. W. said, looking over the weeping man's shoulder at Tyrone. His partner shook his head and gave a thumbs-up, twisting his expression into one of praise and impending laughter, enough so that J. W. had to look away to keep a straight face. "Tell us what that burden is, and let the Lord take it off your shoulders and put it on his. We are weak, and he is strong."

"Jesus gonna have to carry it for me," Lo Lo said tearfully. "I can't do it by myself. I'm a sinner."

"We're all sinners, equal in the eyes of God," J. W. said, loosening his grip on Lo Lo and easing back a bit. "What is that burden? Jesus wants you to tell it, confess it, and give it to him to carry. He got the divine shoulders for it."

"What it is that I just did what Deangelo told me to. I got Tuck Bunny to meet me at the old Daughdrill warehouse on the river. That one about to all fall into the water. Told Tuck Bunny I had come into more coke than I could handle and would give it to him to sell. Told him it was over two Ks. And he showed up to get it."

"What happened then?" J. W. said. "Tell the Lord all of it. Don't hold it back. He wants to lighten that load you been carrying all by yourself."

"It wasn't me who capped him," Lo Lo said. "It wasn't me did that to Tuck Bunny. I didn't have to do that, and maybe I couldn't have done it even if Deangelo told me to. But no, I didn't have to. D, he did it. He wanted to be the one, he said. It was a Bones Family debt he had to pay. Time to settle the account, D said. He come in behind Tuck Bunny and put the round in his head. I seen him fall down, oh Lord, and his eyes stayed open the whole time. Then the light in them, it went out like when you blow out the candles on a birthday cake."

"Well, I think you've told Jesus all you need to, and he's told the Lord already what happened. It passed from son of God to God himself like lightning just as soon as you told Jesus. The father and son, they will sure sort it out for you, the two of them together, and now all you got to do to make it a done deal and a sin fully forgiven is to come with me and Sergeant Walker down to Midtown and say again what you just shared with Jesus."

"I can't go down to the station. It's a girl working in there will let Deangelo Dixon know I been there. He'll come after me. She talk to him all the time, see?"

"I understand, Lo Lo. You don't have to go to the station. Let's just go over to my house there on Tutwiler Street, and you can talk into my tape machine I keep over yonder. You know, you just tell it what you just settled up with Jesus, and oh, one other thing. You can tell us who that girl is, the one working in the Midtown station that tells Deangelo who's been visiting the police."

"All right, I'll do it," Lo Lo said. "Then can I get back home pretty quick after that? And that girl she's called by Teenie."

"Why, sure, you can get back home quick," J. W. said, then looked at Tyrone. "Don't you agree with me on that, Sergeant Walker? And you got the name of that nice young woman in Midtown, right?"

"Sure, certainly," Tyrone said. "Sure. Everything's going to be fine for Lo Lo once all this business part of things gets done. And for Teenie, too."

"I know one thing for certain as true as the blood on the Cross," J. W. said. "Lo Lo Tedrick is now got right with the Lord. All is settled in Heaven."

"Praise him," Tyrone said. "Let's go out to the car, get everything all took care of."

"Can we pray a little bit together, me and Sergeant Ragsdale before we get in y'all's car?" Lo Lo said.

"We'll pray all the way over to Midtown," J. W. said. "It'll be like a revival, you and me together talking to the Lord."

"Yeah, you two can just sit in the backseat while I drive us to Tutwiler," Tyrone said. "I'll get us to the right place really quick."

"I think I might have already done that, Sergeant Walker," J. W. said. "What you think?"

"I wouldn't ever quarrel with you nor Lo Lo Tedrick, neither," Tyrone said. "Followers of the Cross like you are."

"Let's ride," J. W. said. "Us two sinners in the backseat feel a prayer coming on us real strong."

33

Now, be calm, James Forrest said to himself as he prepared to enter the kitchen area near the breakfast room in the Fallen Timbers mansion. Don't make a big production to the cook Emerald about this unusual participation by you in the preparation of food for others to consume. Others, he thought, tossing the word around in his head a bit. I don't even ever prepare any kind of meal or snack for myself, much less others, not when there's some servant on salary assigned that duty. I'll have to make a bit of a fuss about this sudden change in habit so that she won't have any suspicions to report to anyone who might come calling, asking questions and making assumptions once all is accomplished.

Why do I say someone might come calling? They'll be here all right after the deal goes down. It'll be instantaneous. Anytime real money is in the process of changing hands, interested parties of every description will show up, hoping some portion might float their way. Those bastards in mother's favorite cash-fondling firm, D'Arcy, Simmons, and Wilde, will be here slavering and shaking, afraid they're losing and elated about the possibilities of getting their snouts deeper into the trough. Police? Will they show? Duh. Yeah. So it'll be a prolonged poking about by all sorts of entities, interested and vindictive, greedy and afraid, suspicious and convinced, drooling and smacking, with every one of them trying to find ways to fuck me out of my money.

So here's the deal, to put it simply. Here's what I'll tell cook. And here she is in the small kitchen, back turned to me rattling some sort of utensils around and about. It's show time. Let's do it.

"Emerald! Good morning to you and what a wonderful morning it is for me and mother, don't you think?" James Forrest boomed out as he stepped into the small kitchen devoted to preparation of meals on those solo family occasions with few if any guests involved.

"Yessir, Mr. James," she said. "Looks like everybody is home now here at Fallen Timbers. Together again where they all started out. All the little chicks has come home."

She was speaking carefully, giving nothing away, and James Forrest appreciated and admired that fact. She had worked all her life for people who needed and demanded circumspection, and she had learned how to project that quality somewhere along the way. You have to give these black servants credit, he mused, as he began his pitch to her to explain why he was about to do what he was about to do. Typically, the women were more careful than the males of their race, more attuned to unspoken expectations and demands from employers than the men they lived with, had children by, and supported much too often as compared to the white women who employed them to make things run right. But there was a downside to intelligence, too, he knew. They could figure out motives, they could sense hidden hostilities, they knew underground war when they saw it. And they remembered everything. James Forrest knew he had to be doubly careful with the cook now standing before him with a spatula in her hand. She was listening, and listening hard.

"Here's the deal, Emerald. I want to surprise Mother and Sister and her friend in an unusual way this morning. I was so knocked over by Constance Helen's sudden return after her being gone for so long that I didn't know how to respond at first. I handled it badly, I must say. When I think how I acted when she surprised us so, I'm a little embarrassed. I'm afraid I didn't show how happy I was. Just the opposite, I think, was the way it appeared I felt. So I want to make up for that and show how happy I am by helping with cooking breakfast this morning."

"Well, I always like help in the kitchen," the cook said, laughing in the approved way of a black female servant with a white male employer.

"So I'll be glad to put you to work. What do you want to do? Crack open some eggs? Toast some English muffins?"

They both laughed at that, and then James Forrest said that was not his highest priority. "What about if I squeeze some oranges or fix Bloody Marys or do something with tangerines or grapefruit. Something along those lines."

"That sounds real good. Do you want to ask them ladies what kind of drink they want along with their coffee or tea? They already in the little dining room sitting and talking."

"Why don't you take their orders, Emerald," James Forrest said, "and I'll be making myself a breakfast drink while you do that? Tell them I'll be serving a breakfast drink they won't forget."

"All right, I'll do that and be right back," she said, wiping her hands on a towel and straightening the front of her uniform.

"Good. I'll start doing my tomato juice business. First things first, you know," he said, and both of them laughed. "Cook gets the first choice always."

"You got that right, Mr. James," the cook said, putting a servile but jolly lilt in her voice.

The ground castor seeds, well peeled and macerated, had been fairly white in color, but after James Forrest had roasted the mass of vegetable matter in the portable oven, careful to follow the directions of Dr. Dennis Ryan as found in that scholar's study of the plant and its killer product, the color of what was produced was a pale tan. That had nothing to do with the lethal power of ricin, James Forrest read, but it stopped him for a space in his plan for how to administer the doses to his mother, sister, and that fat slug from Arkansas. If it were added to any food stuff which would allow the tan color to stand out, it could interfere with the diner's assessment of what she was about to eat. It had to be less obvious. No opportunity for rejection could be allowed.

It couldn't be sprinkled on an egg dish, nor mixed with artificial sweetener, nor spooned into jelly or jam, certainly not made part of honey or shaken on rolls or breadstuff. What then, he had asked himself. How do you get your victim not to pause in consuming it? Then an answer came to him. Put a killer dose in a drink. Mix it up before serving. It would never be seen, and it would go down the gullets undetected, just aching to do its work.

What, though, he'd asked himself, if one or more of the bitches would not drink their portion of the wonderful beverage he'd prepared? He could imagine someone saying she didn't like this juice or that one. I only want coffee and water, he could hear one of them saying. No juice for me, thank you.

A plea, he thought. I'll make an emotionally placating plea. I'll go against the grain, I'll make a statement, an admission of fault in my response to my sister's return with that Arkansas sow. I'll say I've gone through a dark night of the soul, searching for redemption and forgiveness and vowing a new attitude and a new life with my family. I've made this special breakfast drink to commemorate and celebrate the wonderful return and the transformation in my soul, and I ask you to join me in sipping this libation in acknowledgment of this new day in the clan of the Howell-Reeds. Let us break bread together in celebration. In a manner of speaking. If that doesn't get them, I never attended the Cotton Carnival in Memphis, Tennessee.

James Forrest patted the vial in the right-hand pocket of his trousers. It felt like touching a magic charm, even a bit tingly to his nudge. Talk to me, baby, come on, say something sexy and get me hard.

On the way back to the Midtown station, the second time they'd made the trip home since the visit to Lo Lo Tedrick on Baby Street, J. W. and Tyrone began to talk in more detail about what the next step should be. What should they do about Deangelo Dixon and when and what would or could be the outcome of nailing him on a murder rap coming from the killing of Tuck Bunny? J. W. was finding himself for the first time not being in full agreement with his partner about a next step to be taken springing from a homicide investigation.

"Here's the way I see it," he said to Tyrone. "Deangelo put a round from a .44 into the head of a man, rendering said victim as dead as last week's newspaper ads, and he did it in the presence of an eyewitness who's already sworn a statement. We got him dead to rights. We have run the head of the Bones Family up into a corner of a pen where he can't get out. He is cornered, and it's time for the Major to talk to the DA's office about all the heavy-duty goods we got on the murdering bastard."

"Yeah, all that's true and makes sense," Tyrone said from behind the wheel, "and it sure would be a load off my mind to put Deangelo Dixon in a box locked up for life. It'd be simple and clean and over with. But let's think a little bit further about what other road we could take and where it might lead us."

"What other road? What are you talking about? We got our foot on his neck. Let's push it on down harder and see if something won't fracture. It'd be a sweet sound, all them bones breaking."

"All right, just for argument's sake, think about this. Who'd take over heading up the Bones Family with D gone? Where would this new one go and where will he take things? What would we know about him and where and when and what we ought to start making plans for?"

"We don't know anything about what might happen or who might pop up to take over Bones," J. W. said. "No way to tell. But I tell you one thing. It's plenty of the murdering fuckers trying to break in line, get to the front, and get some."

"Is it better to handle the devil you know or to have to figure out a new devil? That's what I'm asking. We know how Deangelo works, and with the goods we got on him now, we'd be a whole lot more able to point the boy in the right directions, know where he's going, and how to keep him damped down."

"Damped down? What does that mean? Do you think he'd be letting us lean in on him? Deangelo? Shit, Tyrone. He's as crooked as a barrel of snakes. You can't believe a thing he says. He speaks with forked tongue, white man."

"Watch those color references, son. But yeah, we know those snakes he handles, up and down, and now we'd be even better able to look inside that barrel and see which snake's working and which one's not."

"It sounds like it'd take a lot of thinking about things all the time. If we pull the trigger on Deangelo and the Bones Family now, it'd clear things up, at least in that part of gang-run crime in Memphis for a while. Maybe a good long while. Longer than two weeks, maybe."

"Let me put it this way, J. W.," Tyrone said. "Do you think there's any chance of civic peace and quiet beginning to blossom in the Bluff City? Will house break-ins, and holdups, and carjackings and the drug business and all that the shit that goes along with that, will any of that slow down now? Will putting Deangelo Dixon behind bars until he's eighty years old make it any easier for police to keep order and stomp down whatever hell pops up every day?"

"Why, no. Hell, no. Of course not. It ain't never going to get any better in Memphis. You know that and the mayor knows that and every cop does, too. But that don't stop us from trying, does it?"

"No, it doesn't,"Tyrone said. "Maybe we should try something new."

About then, Tyrone began to pull the sedan into the Midtown station parking lot, and J. W. slapped at his shirt pocket. No pack of Pall Malls again, and there hadn't been for years, but Lord didn't he want to light one up right now if it'd been there.

"Well, Tyrone. What are we going to do? Dalbey is happy as a king we got the chance to take down the head of the Bones Family, and he's itching to say to Birchard and the mayor that a load of good info can now be shared with all news outlets, like he's always begging us to give him something good to say. And this is it. A damn nice piece of police work with a happy ending for a change. Deangelo Dixon, chief asshole of the Bones Family, arrested for the murder of one of his own boys. Now put that in your pipe, Memphis, and smoke it."

"Oh, I know it, J. W.,"Tyrone said. "I know what you and me have to do. I was just dreaming of a better end for this one, if we could figure out how to do it."

"Don't you go talking administrative on me, now. I don't like the way that sounds. I ain't about to let you out of having to ride along with me looking for blood and guts and brains on the sidewalk. You know you like it, you know you do. You love the splatter."

"All right, all right. Let's go tell the Major we're ready for the next step in the dance, and then he'll turn us loose to put on our show."

"It's a dance all right," J. W. said. "And you know all the steps. Let's tell Dalbey what we're going to do, and then see if we can't pay a house call on Deangelo Dixon. Take that man's temperature, see what kind of medicine he needs. He doesn't even know he's sick yet, and we're just the ones to tell what he's got to take."

"And just how big a dose,"Tyrone said. "But I can dream, can't I?"

"Not as good as you can dance, not near as good."

34

LaWanda began talking as soon as J. W. entered the staff room of the Midtown station of the Memphis Department of Police and Public Safety, followed closely behind by Tyrone. "Y'all finally got here," she said, "and I'm sure glad of it. Major Dalbey's been buzzing me every two minutes to see if you in the office yet. Now it's off my hands and I can get some work done. Let me buzz him back, and y'all don't bother to sit down until he tells you to hit his door."

"The Major could've called on Tyrone's cell phone," J. W. said. "We ain't been out of touch. We been doing business, girlfriend, and we always ready to respond. We are wired electronically."

"Uh-huh, yeah, you sure always ready to talk about being ready, J. W.," LaWanda said. "I done buzzed him, and he says come on in his office right now. He wants y'all face to face."

Tyrone and J. W. did that, and as soon as they entered the boss's office, Major Dalbey had already started his first statement. "I just got a call from Miss May Margaret Howell-Reed," he said, "this time of morning already, and she wants the two of you to come out to Fallen Timbers and see to what's got her about out of her mind. She is a crazy woman for sure now."

"Is it another ghost?" J. W. said. "Or a dead rat casserole or something else to eat along those lines?"

"No, this is real this time. And Miss May Margaret said particularly that she wants that nice African American officer to be sure to be one of the ones coming out to that big old place. She mentioned you, too, J. W., but I expect she could get along without you by the way she was talking about Tyrone. He is the essential man."

"Story of my life," J. W. said. "It stopped hurting a long time ago when a woman said she didn't care whether I showed up or not, just as long as the real man got there. I done got used to it. I can take it, Major. Just give it to us straight and don't pull no punches."

"It's the manner of the way I pay attention to what a woman says when she's making her case to me," Tyrone said. "That's the difference. You got to look like you're interested in what they're saying and you're hanging on every word. They eat that up."

"Well, you are the master teacher all right. I'm always ready to learn."

"Let me get a word in here edgewise," Major Dalbey said. "What's happened is that sorry-assed son of hers has keeled over at breakfast, and it looks like he's now dead as Kelsey's nuts. Miss May Margaret's done called the EMTs, and they on their way, but she wants to make sure as soon as she can that what took the boy off is nothing but natural causes. And she wants that nice officer name of Tyrone Walker to be there to see what's gone down and why. She wants somebody she trusts."

"Maybe James Forrest Howell-Reed got offed by one of them ghosts that's been bedeviling his old mama," J. W. said. "Or more likely, her one and only son took himself a bigger dose of coke than he could stand."

"Could be just natural causes," Tyrone said, "no reason to jump to conclusions. We'll sure go out to Fallen Timbers and try to calm the waters, Major, if that's what you want us to do."

"That's exactly what I want you to do, and I want J. W. there, too, so I can let the Mayor and Bitchhead and the damn cabinet and the *Commercial Appeal* and everybody's brother know we're on top of this thing. Thing is that when one of the folks that own half of the damn county of Shelby, State of Tennessee, kicks off in an unnatural manner of departure, we got to be sure to step up and reassure. Sudden disaster ain't supposed to happen to rich folks."

"We got to let everybody know the Memphis police are on top of it, right?" said J. W. "Eyes on the prize and feet on the ground and all the right questions asked and answered."

“You better be serious when you say stuff like that, Officer Ragsdale,” Dalby said.

“I’m serious as a heart attack. I flat tell you that. I ain’t shucking and I ain’t jiving.”

“It could be just a heart attack that’s killed one of the biggest money men in Memphis,” Tyrone said. “People die all the time, I’ve noticed. The EMTs can tell what the facts of the matter are, and that ought to quiet everything down. People get used to it, but you got to give them time.”

“Son,” Dalbey said. “You know as well as I do that when the big money is turned loose by some shit happening like this, somebody dying by fair means or foul, all kind of stuff flies up in the air. They don’t just kick the dust. They kick the bank accounts. We got to be sure that all of it we got to deal with looks like we done the job we been hired to do. After we’re off the hook, I don’t give a damn what happens. But right now, we got to make Miss May Margaret Howell-Reed satisfied that we done the job we supposed to be doing. Get that, gentlemen?”

“Sir, yes sir,” J. W. barked just as he been told in basic training to say to respond to an order by a superior officer. He got away with saying that as far as Major Dalbey was concerned, judging by the look on his face, but Tyrone shot him a glance that J. W. was glad to see. Bull’s eye, he told himself. You got to always hold back a little when the boss is talking. He’s the boss all right, but he ain’t got every edge on you.

With Emerald gone from the small breakfast room kitchen, James Forrest had reckoned he had at least one or two minutes to get his specially prepared vial of ricin entered into what he intended to be an orange juice-based celebration cocktail before the cook returned to her preparations for the three women of Fallen Timbers Plantation. First meal of that day and inaugural repast for the many more to come for the lady of the manor, her daughter home at last with the redneck tub from Arkansas in tow, the hour of ending what was and what would now be had come. The chemical hour is upon us.

Four glasses, all good but not exceptional crystal, cubes of ice small enough to be delicate but of a size to cool the liquid and disguise any taste other than that of juice and good vodka, and finally a dose administered directly into the pitcher from which pouring would come. But for one, James Forrest told himself, but for one. That one being his own, his celebration drink, pure lovely orange juice with that good Russian vodka embraced therein. And each small tumbler of crystal blessed with a sprig of mint, save for one, as well. That one, the bartender's own, would be adorned not with mint but with a common weed from the border of one of the many walkways of Fallen Timbers. He had picked it just at dawn, the sun only a dim promise in the sky.

A thought of using for his identifying glass not an approved plant, the mint, but a weed, maybe Johnson grass, maybe sorrel—who could tell its true name and pedigree?—but a gesture perfect for its chooser, that thought came to him full-blown. I'm a weed in the Forrest Howell-Reed garden, and it's fitting and proper for a weed to warn me against the fatal drink others would quaff. Let them drink from the approved and proper chalice. I'll take mine straight from a fruit jar with a weed to show its true self. I ain't particular, as folks in Arkansas say. Chug a lug.

But they were all talking in the small dining room, Mother laughing a bit and Constance Helen trilling that voice he remembered so well from the countless times in the past when she'd charm the old folks and he'd be left trying to break into notice amidst all the loving hilarity of the beautiful girl child, so James Forrest thought that now's moment would furnish the needful time to make his presence and his plans for the celebratory breakfast to be announced. Gird your loins, he told himself. Go in there and lay out a scenario they'll have to accept and won't be able to say no to taking part in. Especially the toasting part.

"Ladies," he called out in his most exuberant tone, "get ready for a morning call. Let me tell you how it's going to go."

That seemed to have quieted the happy sounds of three women, rich and happy and on the cusp of a new day, and when he entered the small dining room, James Forrest was smiling ear to ear and jabbering like a child at Christmas.

"That glass is chipped," Emerald back in the kitchen said out loud. "He has done knocked against something with all that messing he's been doing, and there ain't no telling where them chips he busted off has got to."

What I'll do, she said to herself, silently now, is change them drinks to four other glasses that look just like that one James Forrest has messed up. I'll pour out all what he's put in there, and go to that other big jug of orange juice in the ice box, and leave the glass he done put aside for him to drink out of. I'll leave that weed looking sprig he got in there, too. I'll pour out what's in that one, and just put what's in one of them other ones in his so he won't get all in a uproar if he sees what I've done. Miss May Margaret got the eyes of a eagle if something's chipped, and I'll be damned if I'm going to take the blame for the messing he's done done this morning.

It took Emerald less than a minute or two to change the messed-up glasses to another set of crystal ware, listening all the while to James Forrest jabbering away to his mother and sister and that big old hard-featured white girl Constance Helen kept calling her husband, and when the son of the Howell-Reeds returned to the kitchen, all looked unchanged enough to fool any man. A woman, if she was to look close, would spot the difference in design between two sets of crystal, but most men wouldn't have noticed a thing. Now, James Forrest did ask, though, if all was in place as he had left it, and Emerald told him yessir, it sure is. See yonder.

It was, too, for all practical purposes, his old mess for the women poured out except for what he put in that weed-decorated tumbler, juice and ice in beautiful serving glasses, a bottle of vodka showing some still left in it but enough gone so anybody looking would know the drinks were ready for the celebration James Forrest had kept talking to the women about in the small dining room.

"That glass there," James Forrest said, pointing to the one he'd set aside for his consumption—probably got more and better vodka in it, Emerald supposed—was right where the original one had been. That little sprig of weed was right there, too. "Still where I put it, right?"

"You can see it sitting there, can't you, Mister James?" Emerald said, putting on the gruff voice white folks liked to point out and be amused about when discussing the way the help worked in the kitchen. They loved to say stuff like "She is the queen of the kitchen. Don't get in her way when she's making dinner. She is all business, bless her heart," and then they'd laugh and everybody listening would do the same and tell their stories about how their help bullied them. That ate that crap up, like Newgene would say to her when they talked about the way rich white folks in Memphis carried on around colored help.

"I do, I do see it, Emerald," James Forrest said. "Thanks for all you've done to help me this morning of celebration at Fallen Timbers. The family's all together again, just like I've been telling the ladies. And you know what, Emerald? You're a big part of it, that's what."

Then he took a big drink from his glass, poured some vodka in it to bring the level back up to where it'd been, and took another big drink. He set it down then, as Emerald was to say to the policeman who'd come over from Midtown Memphis after Miss May Margaret had called in to say her one and only son had collapsed in the little dining room while making a toast.

"I heard him say all the last words he had to let out in this world," Emerald had told the soul brother policeman, Sergeant Tyrone Walker his name was, and he was so good looking and so much a man that Emerald had to look off when she talked to him or she'd forget what she was fixing to say next, "and here's what I heard him say, Mr. Sergeant. Mr. James Forrest, he put both his hands up to his throat like this." She showed that on her own throat. "And then he said a bad word and then he said his last words in this world."

"Tell us exactly what he said," the other police said, the white man that looked like he'd stayed out in the sun too long for a person with skin that pale. He had blue eyes, real pale, eyes that would make you nervous looking at them. "All the words you can remember."

"Mr. James Forrest, he said this, best I can remember. Jus these words right here, and he said them. I didn't myself. Here's what come from his mouth. Motherfucker, you got the wrong goddamn glass. But it had the fucking weed. It burns, oh God, it burns. That's what he said, Mister James Forrest did. All them words I just told out. That ain't the way I talk, you understand."

"We both understand," the colored brother police, Sergeant Walker, said. "You're just reporting what happened. That's not you talking."

"You got that right. Then Mr. James Forrest, he just keeled over like a big pine tree being cut down out in the woods. He hit the table, busted it down, leg flew off and hit against the wall, everything fell, Miss May Margaret, she started hollering and did that for a long time. Miss Constance Helen, she said he's more than drunk, but it's not just a heart attack. That other lady, the one Miss Constance Helen says is her husband, she said something like mouth to mouth is called for, but not in this situation. I don't know what she meant by that."

"I think we'll find out soon enough what it was James Forrest Howell-Reed took a wrong drink of," the white sergeant said. "The ME will determine why he said what he said when he drank from the wrong glass."

"It wasn't that active glass he started out with," Emerald said. "See they got all mixed up, them glasses. I do believe Mr. James Forrest never meant to use that very glass he did use. He was being real particular about that. He kept asking me in the kitchen if it was the one he'd set down there. I told him it was because it was."

"I ain't surprised he got things switched up," Sergeant Ragsdale said, looking over at the other police. "Are you?"

"Nothing surprises me much anymore in Memphis," Sergeant Walker said. "I'm just waiting for the ME to get here and clear it all up for us. I know you're just dying to see the ME get here, J. W., more than anybody else."

"Don't pick at an old man who's off his feed," the white sergeant said, puzzling Emerald by saying that.

"Thank you, Miss Emerald," Sergeant Walker said. "I know you'd like to clean that whole ruined room up as soon as you can, but don't be doing a thing to anything until the ME releases the scene. Don't touch a thing in there."

He needn't have worried about that, Emerald thought as she left the big room where they'd been asking her questions. All I want to do is go lie down and talk to the Lord about all this dying business. I'm through making breakfast, cleaning up the little kitchen, and watching a crazy white man choking and dying on the floor in front of me. I need me some relief. The Lord'll listen to me even better than them Memphis police sergeants do.

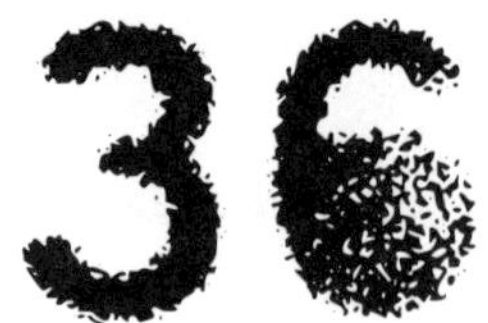

Back at Nova Hebert's apartment later that night, full of a chicken-fried steak dinner from Tucker's Eat Shop plus a few drinks before and after, J. W. began asking again just what it was that had killed James Forrest Howell-Reed in such a wonderfully efficient manner. "Some kind of poison, right? Something he didn't mean to take a dose of himself. It was a present meant for mom and sis and sis's husband, or whatever that big old girl keeps getting called by Constance Helen Howell-Reed. That's the outline of the case, right? Poison. Toe-turner-upper."

"Yes, J. W. you've nailed it all right, just like you did the first time you said that to me. It was something immediate and deadly with not an antidote possible. The last surviving male of the Forrest line has now joined the great majority."

"That's a nice way to put it," J. W. said. "Real civilized sounding. The great majority. My old daddy would have said that James Forrest has joined the bird gang. He said that when somebody would die."

"What does that mean? Joined the bird gang. It doesn't make sense. Some kind of a folk thing, I suppose, coming straight from your Scottish forebears."

"Forebears, I like that, too. That label," J. W. said. "We'd just call it in Panola County, Mississippi, something else. Old folks, maybe?

Grand Pa or something. Forebears is a lot better sounding than trash. Anyway, what poison was it? Antifreeze, maybe?"

"No, it was organically based, it was quick, and we'll figure it out soon. I expect it was ricin. Has all the characteristics."

"Don't tell me any more about it," J. W. said, his mouth up close to Nova's ear as they lay across her bed. "I want to have something to dream about, not just to know up and down and all the way to the ground. Besides, I got to get my mind right for what Tyrone and I got to do just about daylight. We got a pressing appointment we got to make."

"At daylight? What could that be? Isn't everybody with any sense still asleep at daylight? Or if not still asleep, asleep at last, anyway."

"You said it right, Nova. Anybody with any sense would be sleeping the sleep of the righteous at that time of day. But the party me and Tyrone are going to be calling on, he don't observe civilized hours."

"Oh," Nova said, moving her head to a more comfortable spot on the pillow. "You're lying on some of my hair. Who's this sorry no-count you two will be seeing?"

"We are calling on him at that hour because we've learned from our wonderful police informants that the individual we're wanting to see will be at home and available for unannounced visits at that time of day. Just about, oh, I'd say three hours from now. And he is the main man for a killing that took place down on the river a couple of days ago."

"You mean the .44 slug in what you in your amateur ignorance would call the back of the victim's skull, I suppose. I looked at that one myself. It was my baby."

"Honey," J. W. said, "if I'd known you were going to be the one to take a look-see and announce all them findings you come up with, I would have pinned a Valentine heart on the back of the victim's head. Sealed it with a kiss, maybe, even. Made a little love note to you."

"You are such a romantic, J. W." Nova Hebert said. "You make a medical examiner get all giggly and girlish."

"Well, that's just my nature. But the deal is me and Tyrone will be calling on Deangelo Dixon, catching him asleep or passed out or comatose, and we'll bring that chief executive of the Bones Family in for questioning about that very Valentine he left down by the river."

"Shouldn't there be more than just the two of you doing that? That's bad odds, isn't it? Won't he be heavily armed?"

"Naw, we want Deangelo to feel real diminished by how few police it takes to bring him before the bar of justice. That ain't no problem for a stepper like me and Tyrone. We going to show him that."

"So when a man's down . . ." Nova said.

"Kick him," J. W. finished her thought for her and then added his own. "And when a woman's down . . .

"Kiss her," Nova said.

Just under three hours later, J. W. sat in the passenger's seat of one of the newer cars from the Midtown police fleet, discussing with Tyrone Walker the best way to go with the pick-up job before them. Major Dalbey had wanted to send a squad-sized contingent of officers to confront and arrest Deangelo Dixon, arguing the wisdom of overwhelming force and latent fire power for the job. "Why even give the man even any hope of resisting? Make him throw up his hands and come crawling out of his hidey hole, all caved in and creeping and asking what's going on."

"That sounds good, all right," Tyrone had said. "From one perspective. A man with any sense would hold out both wrists and beg for cuffs to be attached, but we're talking about the head man of the Bones Family of Memphis, Tennessee, you understand. Deangelo Dixon has got a whole ethos to defend and support. You come at him too strong, and he's going to do his damnedest to take out as many cops as he can. He's a tough bastard with a reputation to defend. He's fighting for his country, Major, not just himself."

"His country? You make him sound like General Patton back in the big one, Tyrone. Dixon is just a little old pissant gangbanger in Memphis."

"That's the way J. W. and I want to treat him. Hell, he thinks he is George Patton, if he knew who Patton was, and he doesn't. He might have seen that old movie. Maybe. But he's got a high opinion of himself, and so do all the little bastards he heads up. We want to show him what he really is, and that won't take more men than me and Sergeant J. W. Ragsdale."

"Okay," Major Dalbey had said. "You know these little fuckers better than I do, I reckon."

"Amen to that," J. W. said. "One thing you got to admit about Tyrone Walker. He knows a shithead when he spots one."

So the two Midtown officers sat in a cleaned-up unmarked car watching a line of growing light in the eastern sky, deciding what each one would do when another couple of minutes passed.

"Tell you what," Tyrone said. "Let me go up to the door, get into my best ghetto voice, and tell the boss I just got to see him."

"You think he'd answer to that? Would anybody come to him asleep in his own bed this time of day, banging around and waking him up? Wouldn't they just do his cell phone?"

"They might, and they might not. I expect even the head boss of the Bones Family would want to know what in the hell's going on this time of day. He won't be thinking right this early in the day, all woke up and one of his boys all excited and crazy at his door. Deangelo would at least be mad enough to want to see who it is so he can give a piece of his mind."

"Don't go saying things like a piece of his mind to Deangelo Dixon today, now, Tyrone. He'll think he's dreaming in a game show on TV with talk like that going on."

"You just listen, J. W., to how a master of disguises handles a situation like this one. And don't never forget that growing up and living in Memphis has made me an expert in playing all kind of different parts. Hell, I could do Hamlet if I had to."

"I know what you're talking about, Tyrone," J. W. said. "Don't think we didn't learn about Shakespeare and all kinds of famous shit in the public schools of Panola County."

"I'll buy just a part of what you're saying," Tyrone said, opening the car door and exiting without making much of a sound at all. "But I just heard my cue. Get ready for the first soliloquy."

J. W. followed Tyrone down the street and up the walkway to the front door of the house where Deangelo Dixon, head of the Bones Family, stayed. Nobody in the circles in which Deangelo moved ever claimed to reside or live anywhere. They stayed, and staying was claimed always as only temporary and subject to immediate change at any point. Nobody was fastened anywhere, nor did they ever expect or want to be that. I be staying. That was the way to tell it in Memphis. Here's where I be staying just now.

By the time J. W. got halfway up the stone walk to the house, his firearm touched and patted for luck and assurance so it would be ready if some shit went down, Tyrone was beginning to hammer on the door and yell a short version of Deangelo Dixon's name.

"Dee, Dee," he was saying, his voice at a high pitch, its tone and tenor nothing like what Tyrone Walker displayed in his ordinary speech. He is putting on a show for sure, J. W. thought, sounding like something bad has done gone wrong here in the world of the Bones Family and the Latin Lords and the Beale Street Boppers and all that collection of less-known and less-profitable gangs running just below the surface of the muddy waters of Memphis. If I didn't know that was my partner, Sergeant Tyrone Walker, bachelor of arts from Memphis University, I'd be fumbling at my armpit getting close and personal with my ordnance piece. If what he's doing up there at that door doesn't roust Deangelo Dixon out of bed, no matter how hard he's sleeping, Dee's got to be deaf or dead, one or the other.

"I got to tell you this thing, Dee," Tyrone was yelling. "You got to hear it. I can't wait no more."

A low-pitched voice came from behind the door, cursing a little but not a lot, that outburst not really the burden of the message Deangelo was trying to deliver, and a rattle and scrape of chains, an electronic buzzing, and a sucking sound as the door began to swing inward announced the coming reveal of what was inside. J. W. patted at his armpit, loosened the piece there, and stepped to the right side of the walk, out of the direct line of approach that Tyrone was setting as he slipped to the left side of the doorway.

No full light came from within the opening the door allowed as it swung inward, but the outline of a man's head and shoulders was apparent just as he began to say something.

"That you, T Bird? What the fuck you want from me?"

"I want you, boss man," Tyrone said, still in the voice he'd identified earlier as ghetto, and then he was grasping the right forearm of Deangelo, pulling it toward him and simultaneously twisting his upper body to the left. The result looked to J. W. still ten or so feet away as though Deangelo was a large dark cork being popped out of a bottle of high-dollar champagne. The man Tyrone had turned into a simple object of weight overpowered by superior movement came stumbling out the door, tripped over the leg Tyrone had planted for that particular job, and tumbled off the elevated step to the stone walk leading to it. By the time Deangelo was able to turn his head to get a better view of who had just done what to him at the entrance to his house, J. W. was on him, planting his right knee in the man's chest and pulling his left arm out straight to receive the cuff waiting to be snapped on it.

"What the fuck you doing to me?" Deangelo Dixon said. "Who you?"

"Giving you a wake-up call," Tyrone said in his usual educated-black-professional voice, "and showing you a new kind of exercise movement that comes in handy when rising in the morning before the sun is good and up."

"That was for sure some pretty moves you put on this sleepy gentleman," J. W. said, fastening the other cuff on Deangelo's right wrist. "I got to admit. But you do owe me for being here with you, Tyrone. Hadn't have been for the lightning-like speed I put these cuffs on with, you'd have to tussle with him some. Got your clothes dirty, maybe even tore the knees of your britches or something."

"Now, don't get me wrong, J. W.," Tyrone said. "I appreciate your effort, but I had all and everything well in hand. That was nothing for a stepper."

"Motherfuckers," Deangelo Dixon said. "Midtown cops. Walker and Ragsdale."

"Thanks for that recognition," Tyrone said. "We treasure being known by a man like you. You don't know what it means to us. I feel plumb uplifted."

"Why you doing this?" Deangelo said. "I ought to be able to talk to y'all, not just get throwed around in front of my own house."

"I agree," J. W. said. "And I bet Tuck Bunny would, too."

"You know Tuck? Where is he? I ain't seen him in a week or so."

"Yeah, yeah, yeah," Tyrone said. "Sure. But let's don't talk right now. Let's just take a ride all the way downtown. I bet we can beat most of the morning traffic if we get on out of here quick."

"You right, Sergeant Walker," J. W. said. "Memphis is sure pretty early in the morning before the sun gets too high and starts frying things. Let's do it."

"Can't I lock that door behind me?" Deangelo Dixon said. "You leave a house open around here, and you just asking for trouble. They'll take everything ain't red-hot or nailed down."

"Crime is a problem in the Bluff City," J. W. said. "I swear it is. You have sure touched on a truth, Mr. Dixon."

"Amen," said Tyrone Walker. "Let's go on Poplar Street and see how we can address some of that ongoing problem in our beloved hometown."

37

Two nights later, Deangelo Dixon well confined and waiting for arraignment in the main holding facility close to the Mississippi River tirelessly carrying its load of water, wreck, and ruin south, J. W. and Tyrone were sitting at a table in one of the high-dollar restaurants currently in vogue on Mud Island, there along with Marvelle Walker and Nova Hebert. Both men were two drinks ahead of the game, and the women were sipping at fluted glasses of sauvignon blanc. J. W. was explaining the strategy he'd developed over the years when dining at a destination the main attraction of which was not barbecued pork.

"See, all you need to do in a place like Big Daddy's or Stephens's or Mama's down in the Delta is order the cheapest beer they got on hand, and get ready for the paper plates and the ribs to come when they're good and ready to be eat. No need to be trying to decide anything. It's inevitable what's going to come and what's going to happen to it, and the only thing yet to be decided is how many ribs you going to tackle. You can rest easy and not worry about how and what to order. It will come when it comes."

"You continue to surprise me, J. W.," Tyrone Walker said. "I swear I would not have predicted to any man, or woman, that you'd know the word inevitable, much less use it in a conversation about the etiquettes of barbecue consumption."

"Y'all have had enough time by now to pick at each other and try to get the last laugh," Marvelle Walker said. "Now you got to tell us something interesting. Am I right or not, Nova?"

"As usual, yes, you are," Nova said. "I was getting so bored by hearing these guys talk like they hadn't seen each other in a month that I was already tuning them out so I could make up my shopping list for the weekend when I get a chance to go somewhere besides work."

"Why aren't they tired of each other? That's the question, but I don't want either one of you to try to answer it. Here's what I want to know, and it's got nothing to do with people killing each other in Memphis. Ready, boys? Are you listening?"

"Both us were born ready," J. W. said. "Dead game. Right, Tyrone?"

"Yep, shoot, beautiful wife of mine. What's worrying you?"

"Tell us what Miss May Margaret Howell-Reed said to you when you showed up after her son dropped dead. She asked for you in particular, and I wonder why. Did she know what was really going on with that son and had been going on for a good long while?"

"She did, but you got to understand something about money folks, Marvelle," Tyrone said. "They don't have to recognize what's real and what's not real. They can make things be what they want them to be, and if stuff doesn't fit together like it ought to, they can spend enough money to make it fit anyway."

"Yeah, but Miss May Margaret's son is now dead, poisoned in some weird way, and how can she fix that?

"My partner will now testify," Tyrone said. "You may begin, sir."

"Let me try to tell you how, Marvelle," J. W. said. "And where is that waiter? I'm about to dry up. But here's my answer to you. She will handle what's happened in her family by money, of course. What's she's going to do about her departed offspring is to turn Fallen Timbers, that great big old mansion with all that land, she's going to make it into a fancy home and school for the poor and deprived children of Memphis and Shelby County. At least some of them anyway."

"What?" Nova Hebert said. "How do you know that? That's not been announced publicly, has it?"

"No, but it will be in the *Commercial Appeal* this Sunday. You wait and see. And how I know it is I got friends in the news business that'll tell me anything I want to know. Hell, they'll even make up things for me. They owe me big for favors done and deeds forgot."

"Sergeant Ragsdale is right," Tyrone said. "He's got himself a little book just chock-full of notes and debts owed, right J.W?"

"Well, it ain't a actual book. It's just in my head. I don't write a thing down."

"Have you got anything on me?" Nova said. "You better not have."

"Not as much as you got on me, Sugar," J. W. said.

"Stop all this billing and cooing and tell Nova and Marvelle the best part about the new charity being set up at Fallen Timbers, J. W.," Tyrone said.

"All right. Just like Tyrone said, it's going to happen and you'll never guess what the name of it's going to be. Get ready. Imagine this on signs and legal documents out the wazoo everywhere. Welcome to the James Forrest Howell-Reed Memorial Center for the Development of Healthy Children in Shelby County, Tennessee. There, I said all that in one breath."

"No, you got to be kidding," Marvelle said. "Named for him? Her son? The one everybody knows tried to drive his mother crazy and kill her and his sister and his sister's partner?"

"That situation there is what my newspaper friends call irony," J. W. said. "See it's got a double meaning. And besides nothing's been proved against James Forrest and never will be because he's dead. And the only evidence against him is a bunch of theories from the minds of scientists."

"Science will bite you in the ass, J. W.," Nova said. "You can't fool it like you can some dummy with a gun or a knife."

"Do you promise me that now, Honey?" J. W. said. "About the biting part?"

"You two stop all this love talk when we're trying to eat in public," Tyrone said. "It's stomach turning."

"Not as much as processed castor beans," Nova said.

And then for a space of time, all four diners turned their attention to the dishes they'd been served in the fancy restaurant on Mud Island in the Mississippi River just offshore from Memphis, Tennessee.

Later, after feeding and drinking and laughing and telling stories, true and false, the two partners in Homicide and their ladies walked across the bridge to the city of Memphis proper, and as they left the connecting causeway, a young boy carrying a shoeshine box accosted J. W.

“Say, mister,” he said, speaking in a rhythmic patter of words as he danced back and forth. “I bet I know where you got them shoes. I can tell you. I bet you two dollars. Two dollars I bet.”

“Oh, yeah,” J. W. said. “I bet you don’t know where I got these shoes. Tell me.”

“You got your shoes on your feet, you got your feet on the street in Memphis, Tennessee. Give me that money.”

“Here’s your two dollars, son,” J.W said, reaching for his wallet, “but that bit is an old New Orleans original. Did you know that?”

“This money I won, though, it ain’t no old New Orleans,” the kid said. “It spends real good. It’s Memphis money.”

“You got me,” J. W. Ragsdale said. “Now, let me tell you something. You keep going after that Memphis money hard and fast and all the way. Work it, son, work it.”

“Mister, I will,” the kid said. “I love this Memphis money.”

GERALD DUFF won an award for the best book of fiction about Texas, *Blue Sabine*, from the Philosophical Society of Texas; the Cohen Prize for Fiction from *Ploughshares* magazine; the silver medal for a novel from the Independent Publishers Association; and a finalist designation for the 2015 Spur Award. He is a member of the Texas Institute of Letters and the Texas Literary Hall of Fame.